B.J. Daniels is a *New York Times* and *USA TODAY* bestselling author. She wrote her first book after a career as an award-winning newspaper journalist and author of thirty-seven published short stories. She lives in Montana with her husband, Parker, and three springer spaniels. When not writing, she quilts, boats and plays tennis. Contact her at www.bjdaniels.com, on Facebook or on Twitter, @bjdanielsauthor.

Julie Anne Lindsey is a multi-genre author who writes the stories that keep her up at night. She's a self-proclaimed nerd with a penchant for words and proclivity for fun. Julie lives in rural Ohio with her husband and three small children. Today, she hopes to make someone smile. One day she plans to change the world. Julie is a member of the International Thriller Writers (ITW) and Sisters in Crime (SinC). Learn more about Julie Anne Lindsey at www.julieannelindsey.com.

Also by B.J. Daniels

Cowboy's Redemption
Dark Horse
Dead Ringer
Rough Rider
Renegade's Pride
Outlaw's Honor
Hero's Return

Also by Julie Anne Lindsey

Federal Agent Under Fire
The Sheriff's Secret

Discover more at millsandboon.co.uk

COWBOY'S REDEMPTION

B.J. DANIELS

THE SHERIFF'S SECRET

JULIE ANNE LINDSEY

MILLS & BOON

First Published in Great Britain 2018
by Mills & Boon, an imprint of HarperCollins*Publishers*
1 London Bridge Street, London, SE1 9GF

Cowboy's Redemption © 2018 Barbara Heinlein
The Sheriff's Secret © 2018 Julie Anne Lindsey

ISBN: 978-0-263-26571-2

39-0518

MIX
Paper from
responsible sources
FSC® C007454

FSC
www.fsc.org

This book is produced from independently certified FSC™ paper to ensure responsible forest management.

For more information visit: www.harpercollins.co.uk/green

Printed and bound in Spain
by CPI, Barcelona

COWBOY'S REDEMPTION

B.J. DANIELS

This one is for Stelly, who even at four loves stories where the heroine gets to help save herself.

Chapter One

Running blindly through the darkness, Lola didn't see the tree limb until it struck her in the face. It clawed at her cheek, digging into a spot under her right eye as she flung it away with her arm. She had to stifle the cry of pain that rose in her throat for fear she would be heard. As she ran, she felt warm blood run down to the corner of her lips. The taste of it mingled with the salt of her tears, but she didn't slow, couldn't. She could hear them behind her.

She pushed harder, knowing that, being men, they had the advantage, especially the way she was dressed. Her long skirt caught on something. She heard the fabric rend, not for the first time. She felt as if it was her heart being ripped out with it.

Her only choice was to escape. But at what price? She'd been forced to leave behind the one person who mattered most. Her thundering heart ached at the thought, but she knew that this was the only way. If she could get help…

"She's over here!" came a cry from behind her. "This way!"

She wiped away the warm blood as she crashed through the brush and trees. Her legs ached and she didn't know how much longer she could keep going. Fatigue was draining her. If they caught her this time…

She tripped on a tree root, stumbled and almost plunged headlong down the mountainside. Her shoulder slammed into a tree trunk. She veered off it like a pinball, but she kept pushing herself forward because the alternative was worse than death.

They were closer now. She could feel one of them breathing down her neck. She didn't dare look back. To look back would be to admit defeat. If she could just reach the road before they caught up to her…

Suddenly the trees opened up. She burst out of the darkness of the pines onto the blacktop of a narrow two-lane highway. The glare of headlights blinded her an instant before the shriek of rubber on the dark pavement filled the night air.

Chapter Two

Major Colt McCloud felt the big bird shake as he brought the helicopter low over the bleak landscape. He was back in Afghanistan behind the controls of a UH-60 Black Hawk. The throb of the rotating blades was drowned out by the sound of mortar fire. It grew louder and louder, taking on a consistent pounding that warned him something was very wrong.

He dragged himself awake, but the dream followed him. Blinking in the darkness, he didn't know where he was for a moment. Everything looked alien and surreal. As the dream began to fade, he recognized his bedroom at the ranch.

He'd left behind the sound of the chopper and the mortar fire, but the pounding had intensified. With a start, he realized what he was hearing.

Someone was at the door.

He glanced at the clock on his bedside table. It was after three in the morning. Throwing his legs over the side of the bed, he grabbed his jeans, pulling them on as he fought to put the dream behind him and hurry to the door.

A half dozen possibilities flashed in his mind as he moved quickly through the house. It still felt strange to be back here after years of traveling the world as an Army helicopter pilot. After his fiancée dumped him, he'd planned to make a career out of the military, but then his father had died, leaving him a working ranch that either had to be run or sold.

He'd taken a hundred-and-twenty-day leave in between assignments so he could come home to take care of the ranch. His father had been the one who'd loved ranching, not Colt. That's why there was a for-sale sign out on the road into the ranch.

Colt reached the front door and, frowning at the incessant knocking at this hour of the morning, threw it open.

He blinked at the disheveled woman standing there before she turned to motion to the driver of the car idling nearby. The engine roared and a car full of what appeared to be partying teenagers took off in a cloud of dust.

Colt flipped on the porch light as the woman turned back to him and he got his first good look at her and her scratched, blood-streaked face. For a moment he didn't recognize her, and then it all came back in a rush. Standing there was a woman he'd never thought he'd see again.

"Lola?" He couldn't even be sure that was her real name. But somehow it fit her, so maybe at least that part of her story had been true. "What happened to you?"

"I had nowhere else to go." Her words came out in a

rush. "I was so worried that you wouldn't be here." She burst into tears and slumped as if physically exhausted.

He caught her, swung her up into his arms and carried her into the house, kicking the door closed behind him. His mind raced as he tried to imagine what could have happened to bring her to his door in Gilt Edge, Montana, in the middle of the night and in this condition.

"Sit here," he said as he carried her in and set her down in a kitchen chair before going for the first-aid kit. When he returned, he was momentarily taken aback by the memory of this woman the first time he'd met her. She wasn't beautiful in the classic sense. But she was striking, from her wide violet eyes fringed with pale lashes to the silk of her long blond hair. She had looked like an angel, especially in the long white dress she'd been wearing that night.

That was over a year ago and he hadn't seen her since. Nor had he expected to since they'd met initially several hundred miles from the ranch. But whatever had struck him about her hadn't faded. There was something flawless about her—even as scraped up and bruised as she was. It made him furious at whoever was responsible for this.

"Can you tell me what happened?" he asked as he began to clean the cuts.

"I... I..." Her throat seemed to close on a sob.

"It's okay, don't try to talk." He felt her trembling and could see that she was fighting tears. "This cut under your eye is deep."

She said nothing, looking as if it was all she could do to keep her eyes open. He took in her torn and filthy dress. It was long, like the white one he'd first seen her in, but faded. It reminded him of something his grandmother might have worn to do housework in. She was also thinner than he remembered.

As he gently cleaned her wounds, he could see dark circles under her eyes, and her long braided hair was in disarray with bits of twigs and leaves stuck in it.

The night he'd met her, her plaited hair had been pinned up at the nape of her neck—until he'd released it, the blond silk dropping to the center of her back.

He finished his doctoring, put away the first-aid kit, and wondered how far she'd come to find him and what she had been through to get here. When he returned to the kitchen, he found her standing at the back window, staring out. As she turned, he saw the fear in her eyes—and the exhaustion.

Colt desperately wanted to know what had happened to her and how she'd ended up on his doorstep. He hadn't even thought that she'd known his name. "Have you had anything to eat?"

"Not in the past forty-eight hours or so," she said, squinting at the clock on the wall as if not sure what day it was. "And not all that much before that."

He'd been meaning to get into Gilt Edge and buy some groceries. "Sit and I'll see what I can scare up," he said as he opened the refrigerator. Seeing only one egg left, he said, "How do you feel about pancakes? I have chokecherry syrup."

She nodded and attempted a smile. She looked skittish as a newborn calf. Worse, he sensed that she was having second thoughts about coming here.

She licked her cracked lips. "I have to tell you. I have to explain—"

"It's okay. You're safe here." But safe from what, he wondered? "There's no hurry. Let's get you taken care of first." He'd feed her and get her settled down.

He motioned her into a chair at the kitchen table. He could tell that she must hurt all over by the way she moved. As much as he wanted to know what had happened, he thought she needed food more than anything else at this moment.

"While I make the pancakes, would you like a hot shower? The guest room is down the hall to the left. I can find you some clothes. They'll be too large for you, but maybe they will be more comfortable."

Tears welled in her eyes. He saw her swallow before she nodded. As she started to get to her feet, he noticed her grimace in pain.

"Wait."

She froze.

"I don't know how to say this delicately, but if someone assaulted you—"

"I wasn't raped."

He nodded, hoping that was true, because a shower would destroy important evidence. "Okay, so the injuries were…"

"From running for my life." With that she limped out of the kitchen.

He had the pancake batter made and the griddle heating when he heard the shower come on. He stopped to listen to the running water, remembering this woman in a hotel shower with him months ago.

That night he'd bumped into her coming out of the hotel bar. He'd seen that she was upset. She'd told him that she needed his help, that there was someone after her. She'd given him the impression she was running from an old boyfriend. He'd been happy to help. Now he wondered if that was still the case. She said she was running for her life—just as she had the first time they'd met.

But that had been in Billings. This was Gilt Edge, Montana, hundreds of miles away. Didn't seem likely she would still be running from the same boyfriend. But whoever was chasing her, she'd come to him for help.

He couldn't turn her away any more than he'd been able to in that hotel hallway in Billings last year.

LOLA PULLED OUT her braid, discarding the debris stuck in it, then climbed into the steaming shower. She stood under the hot spray, leaned against the smooth, cool tile wall of the shower and closed her eyes. She felt weak from hunger, lack of sleep and constant fear. She couldn't remember the last time she'd slept through the night.

Exhaustion pulled at her. It took all of her energy to wash herself. Her body felt alien to her, her skin chafed from the rough fabric of the long dresses she'd been wearing for months. Stumbling from the shower, she wrapped her hair in one of the guest towels. It felt good to free her hair from the braid that had been wound at the nape of her neck.

As she pulled down another clean towel from the bathroom rack, she put it to her face and sniffed its freshness. Tears burned her eyes. It had been so long since she'd had even the smallest creature comforts like good soap, shampoo and clean towels that smelled like this, let alone unlimited hot water.

When she opened the bathroom door, she saw that Colt had left her a sweatshirt and sweatpants on the guest-room bed. She dried and tugged them on, pulling the drawstring tight around her waist. He was right, the clothes were too big, but they felt heavenly.

She took the towels back to the bathroom to hang them and considered her dirty clothing on the floor. The hem of the worn ankle-length coarse cotton dress was torn and filthy with dirt and grime. The long sleeves were just as bad except they were soiled with her blood. The black utilitarian shoes were scuffed, the heels worn unevenly since she'd inherited them well used.

She wadded up the dress and shoved it into the bathroom wastebasket before putting the shoes on top of it, all the time feeling as if she was committing a sin. Then again, she'd already done that, hadn't she.

Downstairs, she stepped into the kitchen to see Colt slip three more pancakes onto the stack he already had on the plate.

He turned as if sensing her in the doorway and she was reminded of the first time she'd seen him. All she'd noticed that night was his Army uniform—before he'd turned and she'd seen his face.

That he was handsome hadn't even registered. What she'd seen was a kind face. She'd been desperate and Colt McCloud had suddenly appeared as if it had been meant to be. Just as he'd been here tonight, she thought.

"Last time I saw you, you were on leave and talking

about staying in the military," she said as he pulled out a kitchen chair for her and she sat down. "I was afraid that you had and that—" her voice broke as she met his gaze "—you wouldn't be here."

"I'm on leave now. My father died."

"I'm sorry."

He set down the plate of pancakes. "Dig in."

Always the gentleman, she thought as he joined her at the table. "I made a bunch. There's fresh sweet butter. If you don't like chokecherry syrup—"

"I love it." She slid several of the lightly browned cakes onto her plate. The aroma that rose from them made her stomach growl loudly. She slathered them with butter and covered them with syrup. The first bite was so delicious that she actually moaned, making him smile.

"I was going to ask how they are," he said with a laugh, "but I guess I don't have to."

She devoured the pancakes before helping herself to more. They ate in a companionable silence that didn't surprise her any more than Colt making her pancakes in the middle of the night or opening his door to her, no questions asked. It was as if it was something he did all the time. Maybe it was, she thought, remembering the first night they'd met.

He hadn't hesitated when she'd told him she needed his help. She'd looked into his blue eyes and known she could trust him. He'd been so sweet and caring that she'd almost told him the truth. But she'd stopped herself. Because she didn't think he would believe her? Or because she didn't want to involve him? Or because, at that point, she thought she could still handle things on her own?

Unfortunately, she no longer had the option of keeping the truth from him.

"I'm sure you have a lot of questions," she said, after swallowing her last bite of pancake and wiping her mouth with her napkin. The food had helped, but her body ached all over and fatigue had weakened her. "You had to be surprised to see me again, especially with me showing up at your door in the middle of the night looking like I do."

"I didn't even know you knew my last name."

"After that night in Billings... Before I left your hotel room, while you were still sleeping, I looked in your wallet."

"You planned to take my money?" He'd had over four hundred dollars in there. He'd been headed home to his fiancée, he'd told her. But the fiancée, who was supposed to pick him up at the airport, had called instead with crushing news. Not only was she not picking him up, she was in love with one of his best friends, someone he'd known since grade school.

He'd been thinking he just might rent a car and drive home to confront the two of them, he'd told Lola later. But, ultimately, he'd booked a flight for the next morning to where he was stationed and, with time to kill, had taken a taxi to a hotel, paid for a room and headed for the hotel bar. Two drinks later, he'd run into Lola as he'd headed from the bar to the men's room. Lola had saved him from getting stinking drunk that night.

Also from driving to Gilt Edge to confront his ex-fiancée and his ex-friend.

"I hate to admit that I thought about taking your money," she said. "I could have used it."

"You should have taken it then."

She smiled at him and shook her head. "You were so kind to me, so tender…" Her cheeks heated as she held his gaze and remembered being naked in his arms. "I'm sure I gave you the wrong impression of me that night. It wasn't like me to…with a complete stranger." She bit her lower lip and felt tears well in her eyes again.

"There is nothing wrong with the impression you left with me. As a matter of fact, I've thought of you often." He smiled. It was a great smile. "Every time I heard one of those songs that we'd danced to in my hotel room that night—" his gaze warmed to a Caribbean blue "—I thought of you."

She looked away to swallow the lump that had formed in her throat before she could speak again. "It wasn't an old boyfriend I was running from that night. I let you believe that because I doubted you'd have believed the truth. I did need your help, though, because right before I collided with you in that hallway, I'd seen one of them in the hotel. I knew it was just a matter of time before they found me and took me back."

"Took you back?"

"I wasn't a fugitive from the law or some mental institution," she said quickly. "It's worse than that."

He narrowed his gaze with concern. "What could be worse than that?"

"The Society of Lasting Serenity."

Chapter Three

"The fringe religious cult that relocated to the mountains about five years ago?" Colt asked, unable to keep the shock from his voice.

She nodded.

He couldn't have been more stunned if she'd said she had escaped from prison. "When did you join that?"

"I didn't. My parents were some of the founding members when the group began in California. I was in Europe at university when they joined. I'd heard from my father that SLS had relocated to Montana. A few years after that, I received word that the leader, Jonas Emanuel, needed to see me. My mother was ill." Her voice broke. "Before I could get back here, my mother and father both died, within hours of each other, and had been buried on the compound. According to Jonas, they had one dying wish." Her laugh could have cut glass. "They wanted to see me married. Once I was on the SLS compound, I learned that, according to Jonas, they had promised me to him."

"That's crazy." He still couldn't get his head around this. "Jonas is delusional but also dangerous."

"So you were running from him that night I met you?"

She nodded. "But, unfortunately, when I left the hotel the next morning, two of the 'sisters' were waiting for me and forced me to go back to the compound."

"And tonight?" he asked as he pushed his plate away.

Lola met his gaze. "I escaped. I'd been locked up there since I last saw you within miles of here at the Montana SLS compound."

Colt let out a curse. "You've been held there all this time against your will? Why didn't you—"

"Escape sooner?" She sounded near tears as she held his gaze.

He saw something in those beautiful eyes that made his stomach drop.

Her voice caught as she said, "I had originally gone there to get my parents' remains because I don't believe they died of natural causes. I'd gotten a letter from my father right before I heard from Jonas. He wanted out of SLS, but my mother refused. My father said he feared the hold Jonas had on her and needed my help because she wasn't well."

"What are you saying?"

"I think they were murdered, but I can't prove it without their bodies, and Jonas has refused to release them. Legally, there isn't much I can do since my parents had signed over everything to him—even their daughter."

Murder? He'd heard about the fifty-two-year-old charismatic leader of the cult living in the mountains outside of town, but he couldn't imagine the things Lola was telling him. "He can't expect you to marry him."

"Jonas was convinced that I would fall for him if I spent enough time at the compound, so he kept me there. At first, he told me it would take time to have my parents' remains exhumed and moved. Later I realized there was no way he was letting their remains go anywhere even if he could convince me to marry him, which was never going to happen."

Maybe it was the late hour, but he was having trouble making sense of this. "So after you met me..."

"I was more determined to free both my parents and myself from Jonas forever. I wasn't back at the compound long though, when I realized I was pregnant. Jonas realized it, too. I became a prisoner of SLS until the birth. Then Jonas had the baby taken away and had me locked up. I had to escape to get help for my daughter."

"Your daughter?"

She met his gaze. "That's why I'm here... She's *our* daughter," she said, her voice suddenly choked with tears. "Jonas took the baby girl that you and I made the first night we met."

COLT STARED AT HER, too shocked to speak for a moment. *What the hell?* "Are you trying to tell me—"

"I had your child but I couldn't contact you. Jonas kept me under guard, locked away. I had no way to get a message out. If any of the sisters tried to help me, they were severely punished."

He couldn't believe what he was hearing. "Wait. You had the baby at the compound?"

She nodded. "One of the members is a midwife. She delivered a healthy girl, but then Jonas had the child taken away almost at once. I got to hold her only for a few moments and only because Sister Amelia let me. She was harshly reprimanded for it. I got to look into her precious face. She has this adorable tiny heart-shaped birthmark on her left thigh and my blond hair. Just fuzz really." Tears filled her eyes again.

Colt ran a hand over his face before he looked at her again. "I'm having a hard time believing any of this."

"I know. If Jonas had let me leave with my daughter, I wouldn't have ever troubled you with any of this," she said.

"You would never have told me about the baby?" He hadn't meant to make it sound like an accusation. He'd expected her to be offended.

Instead, when she spoke, he saw only sympathy in her gaze. "When I met you, you were on leave and going back the next day. You were talking about staying in the Army. Your fiancée had just broken up with you."

"You don't have to remind me."

"What you and I shared that night…" She met his gaze. "I'll never forget it, but I wasn't fool enough to think that it might lead to anything. The only reason I'm here now is that I need help to get our daughter away from that…man."

"Don't I have a right to know if I have a child?"

"Of course. But I wouldn't be asking anything of

you—if Jonas hadn't taken our daughter. I'm more than capable of taking care of her and myself."

"What I don't understand is why Jonas wants to keep a baby that isn't his."

She didn't seem surprised by his skepticism, but when he looked into her eyes, he saw pain darken all that beautiful blue. "I can understand why you wouldn't believe she's yours."

"I didn't say that."

"You didn't have to." She got to her feet, grabbing the table to steady herself. "I shouldn't have come here, but I didn't know where else to go."

"Hold on," he said, pushing back his chair and coming around the table to take her shoulders in his hands. She felt small, fragile, and yet he saw a strength in her that belied her slim frame. "You have to admit this is quite the story."

"That's why I didn't tell you the night we met about the cult or the problems I was having getting my parents' remains out. I still thought I could handle it myself. Also I doubt you would have believed it." Her smile hurt him soul deep. "I wouldn't have believed it and I've lived through all of this."

He was doing his best to keep an open mind. He wasn't a man who jumped to quick conclusions. He took his time to make decisions based on the knowledge he was able to acquire. It had kept him alive all these years as an Army helicopter pilot.

"So what you're telling me is that the leader of SLS has taken your baby to force you to marry him? If he's so dangerous, why wouldn't he have just—"

"Forced me? He tried to…join with me, as he put it. He's still limping from the attempt. And equally determined that I will come to him. Now that I've shamed him…he will never let me have my baby unless I completely surrender to him in front of the whole congregation."

"Don't you mean *our* baby?"

Lola gave him an impatient look. Tears filled her eyes as she swayed a little as if having trouble staying upright after everything she'd been through.

He felt a stab of guilt. He'd been putting her through an interrogation when clearly she was exhausted. It was bad enough that she was scraped, cut and bruised, but he could see that her real injuries were more than skin deep.

"You're dead on your feet," he said. "There isn't anything we can do tonight. Get some rest. Tomorrow…"

A tear broke loose and cascaded down her cheek. He caught it with his thumb and gently wiped it away before he let him lead her to the guest bedroom where she'd showered earlier. His mind was racing. If any of this was true…

"Don't worry. We'll figure this out," Colt said as he pulled back the covers. "Just get some sleep." He knew he wouldn't be able to sleep a wink.

Could he really have a daughter? A daughter now being held by a crackpot cult leader? A man who, according to Lola, was much more dangerous than anyone knew?

Lola climbed into the bed, still wearing his too-large

sweats. He tucked her in, seeing that she could barely keep her eyes open.

"Dayton." At his puzzled look, she added, "That's my last name." They'd shared only first names the night they met. But that night neither of them had been themselves. She'd been running scared, and he'd been wallowing in self-pity over losing the woman he'd thought he was going to marry and live with the rest of his life.

"Lola Dayton," he repeated, and smiled down at her. "Pretty name."

He moved to the door and switched off the light.

"I named our daughter Grace," she said from out of the darkness. "Do you remember telling me that you always loved that name?"

He turned in the doorway to look back at her, too choked up to speak for a moment. "It was my grandmother's name."

LOLA THOUGHT SHE wouldn't be able to sleep. Her body felt leaden as she'd sunk under the covers. She could still feel the rough skin of Colt's thumb pad against her cheek and reached up to touch the spot. She hadn't been wrong about him. Not that first night. Not tonight.

She closed her eyes and felt herself careening off that mountain, running for her life, running for Grace's life. She was safe, she reminded herself. But Grace...

The sisters were taking good care of Grace, she told herself. Jonas wouldn't let anything happen to the baby. At least she prayed that he wouldn't hurt Grace to punish her even more.

The thought had her heart pounding until she realized the only power Jonas had over her was the baby. He wouldn't hurt Grace. He needed that child if he ever hoped to get what he wanted. And what he wanted was Lola. She'd seen it in his eyes. A voracious need that he thought only she could fill.

If he ever got his hands on her again... Well, she knew there would be no saving herself from him.

COLT KICKED OFF his boots and lay down on the bed fully dressed. Sleep was out of the question. If half of what Lola had told him was true... Was it possible they'd made a baby that night? They hadn't used protection. He hadn't had anything. Nor had she. It wasn't like him to take a chance like that.

But there was something so wholesome, so innocent, so guileless...

Rolling to his side, he closed his eyes. The memory was almost painful. The sweet scent of her body as she lay with her back to him naked on the bed. The warmth of his palm as he slowly ran it from her side down into the saddle of her slim waist to the rise of her hip and her perfectly rounded buttocks. The catch of her breath as he pulled her into him and cupped one full breast. The tender moan from her lips as he rolled her over to look into those violet eyes.

Groaning, Colt shifted to his back again to stare up at the dark ceiling. That night he'd lost himself in that delectable woman. He'd buried all feelings for his former fiancée into her. He'd found salvation in her body, in her arms, in her tentative touch, in her soft, sweet kisses.

He closed his eyes, again remembering the feel of

her in his arms as they'd danced in his hotel room. The slow sway, their bodies joined, their movements more sensuous than even the act of love. He'd given her a little piece of his heart that night and had not even realized it.

Swinging his legs over the bed, he knew he'd never get any rest until he checked on her. Earlier, he'd gotten the feeling that she wanted to run—rather than tell him what had brought her to his door. She hadn't wanted to involve him, wouldn't have if Jonas didn't have her baby.

That much he believed. But why hadn't she told him what she was running from the night they'd first met? Maybe he could have helped her.

He moved quietly down the hallway, half-afraid he would open the bedroom door only to find her gone and all of this like his dream about being back in Afghanistan.

After easing open the door, he waited for his eyes to adjust to the blackness in the room. Her blond hair lay like a fan across her pillow. Her peaceful face made her appear angelic. He found himself smiling as he stared down at the sleeping Lola. He couldn't help wondering about their daughter. She would be three months old now. Did she resemble her mother? He hoped so.

The thought shook him because he realized how much he wanted to believe her. A daughter. He really could have a daughter? A baby with Lola? He shook his head. What were the chances that their union would bring a child into this world? And yet he and Lola had done more than make love that night. They'd connected in a way he and Julia never had.

The thought of Julia, though, made him recoil. Look how wrong he'd been about her. How wrong he'd been about his own mother. Could he trust his judgment when it came to women? Doubtful.

He stepped out of the room, closing the door softly behind him. Tomorrow, he told himself, he would know the truth. He'd get the sheriff to go with them up to the compound and settle this once and for all.

Colt walked out onto the porch to stare up at the starry sky. The air was crisp and cold, snow still capping the highest peaks around town. He knew this all could be true. Normally, he would never have had intercourse with a woman he didn't know without protection. But that night, he and Lola hadn't just had sex. They'd made love, two lost souls who'd given each other comfort in a world that had hurt them.

He'd been heartbroken over Julia and his friend Wyatt. Being in Lola's arms had saved him. If their lovemaking had resulted in a baby…a little girl…

Yes, what was he going to do? Besides go up to that compound and get the baby for Lola? He tried to imagine himself as a father to an infant. What a joke. He couldn't have been in a worse place in his life to take on a wife and a child.

He looked across the ranch. All his life he'd felt tied down to this land. That his father had tried to chain him to it still infuriated him—and at the same time made him feel guilty. His father had had such a connection to the land, one that Colt had never felt. He'd loved being a cowboy, but ranching was more about trying to make a living off the land. He'd watched his father struggle for years. Why would the old man think he would want this? Why hadn't his father sold the place, done something fun with the money before he'd died?

Instead, he'd left it all to Colt—lock, stock and barrel, making the place feel like a noose around his neck.

"It's yours," the probate attorney had said. "Do whatever you want with the ranch."

"You mean I can sell it?"

"After three months. That's all your father stipulated. That you live on the ranch for three months full-time, and then if you still don't want to ranch, you can liquidate all of your father's holdings."

Colt took a deep breath and let it out. "Sorry, Dad. If you think even three *years* on this land is going to change anything, you are dead wrong." He'd put in his three months and more waiting for an offer on the place.

When his leave was up, he was heading back to the Army and his real job. At least that had been the plan before he'd found Lola standing on his doorstep. Now he didn't know what to think. All he knew was that he had to fly. He didn't want to ranch. Once the place sold, there would be nothing holding him here.

He thought about Lola asleep back in the house. If this baby was his, he'd take responsibility, but he couldn't make any promises—not when he didn't even know where he would be living when he came home on leave.

Up by the road, he could see the for-sale sign by the gate into the ranch. With luck, the ranch would sell soon. In the meantime, he had to get Lola's baby back for her. His baby.

He pushed open the door and headed for his bedroom. Everything was going to work out. Once Lola understood what he needed to do, what he had to do...

He lay down on the bed fully clothed again and closed his eyes, knowing there was no chance of sleep. But hours later, he woke with a start, surprised to find sunlight streaming in through the window. As he rose, still dressed, he worried that he would find Lola gone, just as she had been that morning in Billings.

The thought had his heart pounding as he padded down to the guest room. The door was partially ajar. What if none of it had been true? What if she'd realized he would see through all of it and had taken off?

He pressed his fingertips against the warm wood and pushed gently until he could see into the dim light of the room. She lay wrapped in one of his mother's quilts, her long blond hair splayed across the pillow. He eased the door closed, surprised how relieved he was. Maybe he wasn't a good judge of character when it came in women—Julia a case in point—but he wanted to believe Lola was different. It surprised him how *much* he wanted to believe it.

LOLA WOKE TO the smell of frying bacon. Her stomach growled. She sat up with a start, momentarily confused as to where she was. Not on the hard cot at the compound. Not locked in the claustrophobia-inducing tiny cabin with little heat. And certainly not waking to the wonderful scent of frying bacon at that awful prison.

Her memory of the events came back to her in a rush. What surprised her the most was that she'd slept.

It had been so long that she hadn't been allowed to sleep through the night without being awakened as part of the brainwashing treatment. Or when the sisters had come to take her breast milk for the baby. She knew the only reason, other than exhaustion, she'd slept last night was knowing that she was safe. If Colt hadn't been there, though...

She refused to think about that as she got up. Her escape had cost her. She hurt all over. The scratches on her face and the sore muscles were painful. But far worse was the ache in her heart. She'd had to leave Grace behind.

Still dressed in the sweatshirt and sweatpants and barefoot, she followed the smell of frying bacon to the kitchen. Colt had music playing and was singing softly to a country music song. She had to smile, remembering how much he'd liked to dance.

That memory brought a rush of heat to her cheeks. She'd told herself that she hadn't been in her right mind that night, but seeing Colt again, she knew that was a lie. He'd liberated that woman from the darkness she'd been living in. He'd brought out a part of her she hadn't known existed.

He seemed to sense her in the doorway and turned, instantly smiling. "I hope you don't mind pancakes again. There was batter left over. I haven't been to the store. But I did find some bacon in the freezer."

"It's making my stomach growl. Is there anything I can do to help?"

"Nope, just bring your appetite." He motioned for

her to take a seat. "I made a lot. I don't know about you, but I'm hungry."

She sat down at the table and watched him expertly flip pancakes and load up a plate with bacon.

As he set everything on the table and took a chair, he met her gaze. "How are you feeling?"

"Better. I slept well." For that he couldn't imagine how thankful she was. "On the compound, they would wake me every few hours to chant over me."

"Sounds like brainwashing," Colt said, his jaw tightening.

"Jonas calls it rehabilitation."

He pushed the bacon and pancakes toward her. "Eat while it's hot. We'll deal with everything else once we've eaten."

She looked into his handsome face, remembered being in his arms and felt a flood of guilt. If there was any other way of saving Grace, she wouldn't have involved him in this. But he had been involved since that night in Billings when she'd asked for his help and he hadn't hesitated. He just hadn't known then that what he was getting involved in was more than dangerous.

Once Jonas knew that Colt was the father of her baby... She shuddered at the thought of what she was about to do to this wonderful man.

Chapter Four

Colt picked at his food. He'd lied about being hungry. Just the smell of it turned his stomach. But he watched Lola wolf down hers as if she hadn't eaten in months. He suspected she hadn't eaten much. She was definitely thinner than she'd been that night in Billings a year ago.

But if anything, she was even more striking, with her pale skin and those incredible eyes. He was glad to see her hair down. It fell in a waterfall of gold down her back. He was reminded again how she'd looked the first time he'd seen her—and when he'd opened the door last night.

"I've been thinking about what we should do first," Colt said as he moved his food around the plate. "We need to start by getting you some clothing that fits," he said as if all they had to worry about was a shopping trip. "Then I think we should go by the sheriff's office."

"There is somewhere we have to go first," she said, looking up from cutting off a bite of pancake dripping with the red syrup. "I know you don't trust me. It's all right. I wouldn't trust me, either. But don't worry, you will." She smiled. She had a slight gap between her two front teeth that made her smile adorable. That and the innocence in her lightly freckled face had sucked him in from the first.

He'd been vulnerable that night. He'd been a broken man and Lola had been more than a temptation. The fact that she'd sworn he was saving her that night hadn't hurt, either.

He thought about the way she'd looked last night when he'd found her on his doorstep. She still had a scratch across one cheek and a cut under her right eye. It made her look like a tomboy.

"You have to admit, the story you told me last night was a little hard to believe."

"I know. That's why you have to let me prove it to you."

He eyed her suspiciously. "And how do you plan to do that?"

"Do you know a doctor in town who can examine me?"

His pulse jumped. "I thought you said—"

"Not for that. Or for my mental proficiency." Her gaze locked with his. "I need you to know that I had a baby three months ago. A doctor should be able to tell." He started to argue, but she stopped him. "This is where we need to start before we go to the sheriff."

He wanted to argue that this wasn't necessary, but they both knew it was. If a doctor said she'd never given birth and none of this was real, then it would be over. No harm done. Except the idea of him and Lola having a baby together would always linger, he realized.

"I used to go to a family doctor here in town. If he's still practicing…"

DR. HUBERT GRAY was a large man with a drooping gray mustache and matching bushy eyebrows over piercing blue eyes.

Colt explained what they wanted.

Dr. Gray narrowed his gaze for a moment, taking them both in. "Well, then, why don't you step into the examination room with my nurse, Sara. She'll get you ready while I visit with Colt here."

The moment Lola and Sara left the room, the doctor leaned back in his office chair. "Let me get this straight. You aren't even sure there is a child?"

"Lola says there is. Unfortunately, the baby isn't here."

The doctor nodded. "You realize this won't prove that the child is yours—just that she has given birth before."

Colt nodded. "I know this is unusual."

"Nothing surprises me. By the way, I was sorry to hear about your father. Damn cancer. Only thing that could stop him from ranching."

"Yes, he loved it."

"Tell me about flying helicopters. You know I have my pilot's license, but I've never flown a chopper."

Colt told him what he loved about it. "There is nothing like being able to hover in the air, being able to put it down in places—" he shook his head "—that seem impossible."

"I can tell that you love what you do, but did I hear you're ranching again?"

"Temporarily."

A buzz sounded and Dr. Gray rose. "This shouldn't take long. Sit tight."

True to his word, the doctor returned minutes later. Colt looked up expectantly. "Well?" he asked as Dr. Gray took his seat again behind his desk. Colt realized that his emotions were all over the place. He didn't know what he was hoping to hear.

Did he really want to believe that Lola had given birth to their child to have it stolen by some crazy cult leader? Wouldn't it be better if Lola had lied for whatever reason after becoming obsessed with him following their one-night stand?

"You wanted to know if she has recently given birth?" the doctor asked.

"Has she?" He held his breath, telling himself even if she had, it didn't mean that any of the rest of it was true.

"Since she gave me permission to provide you with this information, I'd say she gave birth in the past three months."

Just as she'd said. He glanced at the floor, not sure if he was relieved or not. He felt like a heel for having even a glimmer of doubt. But Lola was right. He'd had to know before he went any further with this. It wasn't like he really knew this woman. He'd simply shared one night of intimacy all those months ago.

There was a tap at the door. The nurse stuck her head in to say that the doctor had another patient waiting. Behind the nurse, he saw Lola in the hallway. She looked as if she'd been crying. He quickly rose. "Thank you, Doc," he said over his shoulder as he hurried to Lola, taking both of her hands in his. "I'm sorry. I'm so sorry. You didn't have to do this."

Her smile was sad but sweet as she shook her head.

"I just got upset because Dr. Gray is so kind. I wish he'd delivered Grace instead of..." She shook her head. "Not that any of that matters now."

"It's time we went to the sheriff," he said as he led her out of the building. She seemed to hesitate, though, as they reached his pickup. "What?"

"Just that the sheriff isn't going to be able to do anything—and that's if he believes you."

"He'll believe me. I know him," he said as he opened the pickup door for her. "I went to school with his sister Lillie and her twin brother, Darby. Darby's a good friend. Both Lillie and Darby are new parents. As for the sheriff—Flint Cahill is as down-to-earth as anyone I know and I'm sure he's familiar with The Society of Lasting Serenity. Sheriff Cahill is also the only way we can get on church property—and off—without any trouble."

She still looked worried. "You don't know Jonas. He'll be furious that I went to the law. He'll also deny everything."

"We'll see about that." He went around the truck and slid behind the wheel. As he started the engine, he looked over at her and saw how anxious she was. "Lola, the man has taken our daughter, right?" She nodded. "Then I don't give a damn how furious he is, okay?"

"You don't know how he is."

"No, but I'm going to find out. Don't worry. I'm going to get to the bottom of this, one way or the other."

She looked scared, but said, "I trust you with my life. And Grace's."

Grace. Their child. He still couldn't imagine them

having a baby together—let alone that some cult leader had her and refused to give her up to her own mother.

Common sense told him there had to be more to the story—and that's what worried him as he drove to the sheriff's department. Sheriff Cahill would sort it out, he told himself. As he'd said, he liked and trusted Flint. Going up to the compound with the levelheaded sheriff made the most sense.

Because if what Lola was telling him was true, they weren't leaving there without Grace.

SHERIFF FLINT CAHILL was a nice-looking man with thick dark hair and gray eyes. He ushered them right into his office, offered them a chair and something to drink. They took chairs, but declined a beverage.

"So what is this about?" the sheriff asked after they were all seated, the office door closed behind them.

Colt could see that Lola liked the sheriff from the moment she met him. There was something about him that exuded confidence, as well as honesty and integrity. She told him everything she had Colt. When she finished, though, Colt couldn't tell from Flint's expression what he was thinking.

The sheriff looked at him, his gray eyes narrowing. "I'm assuming you wouldn't have brought Ms. Dayton here if you didn't believe her story."

"I know this is unusual." He glanced over at her. Her scrapes and scratches were healing, and she looked good in the clothes they'd bought her. Still, he saw that she kept rubbing her hand on her thighs as if not believing she was back in denim.

At the store, he'd wanted to buy her more clothing, but she'd insisted she didn't need more than a couple pairs of jeans, two shirts, several undergarments and hiking shoes and socks. She'd promised to pay him back once she could get to her own money. Jonas had taken her purse with her cash and credit cards. Her money was in a California bank account. Once she had Grace, she said she would see about getting money wired up to her so she could pay him back.

Colt wasn't about to take her money, but he hadn't argued. The one thing he'd learned quickly about Lola was that she didn't expect or want anything from him—except help getting her baby from Jonas. That, she'd said, would be more than enough since it could get them both killed.

At the time, he'd thought she was exaggerating. Now he wasn't so sure.

"I believe her," Colt told the sheriff. "What do you know about The Society of Lasting Serenity?"

"Just that they were California based but moved up here about five years ago. They keep to themselves. I believe their numbers have dropped some. Probably our Montana winters."

"You're having trouble believing that Jonas Emanuel would steal Lola's child," Colt said.

Flint sighed. "No offense but, yes, I am." He turned to Lola. "You say your only connection to the group was through your parents before their deaths and your return to the States?"

"Yes, they became involved after I left for college. I

thought it was a passing phase, a sign of them not being able to accept their only child had left the nest."

"You never visited them at the California compound?" the sheriff asked.

"No, I got a teaching job right out of college in the Virgin Islands."

Flint frowned. "You didn't visit your parents before you left?"

Lola looked away. "By then we were…estranged. I didn't agree with some of the things they were being taught in what I felt was a fringe cult."

"So why would your parents promise you to Jonas Emanuel?" the sheriff asked.

She let out a bitter laugh. "To *save* me. My mother believed that I needed Jonas's teaching. Otherwise, I was doomed to live a wasted life chasing foolish dreams and, of course, ending up with the wrong man."

"They wanted you to marry Jonas." Flint frowned. "Isn't he a little old for you?"

"He's fifty-two. I'm thirty-two. So it's not unheard-of."

The sheriff looked over at Colt, who was going to be thirty-three soon. Young for a major in the Army, he knew.

"I doubt my parents took age into consideration," Lola said. "One of the teachings at the SLS is that everyone is ageless. My parents, like the other members, were brainwashed."

"So you went to the compound after you were notified that your parents had died," the sheriff said.

"I questioned them both dying especially since

earlier I'd received a letter from my father saying he wanted out but was having a hard time convincing my mother to leave SLS," she said. "Also I wanted to have them buried together in California, next to my older sister, who was stillborn. My parents were both in their forties when they had me. By then, they didn't believe they would ever conceive again."

"So you had their bodies—"

"Jonas refused to release them. He said they would be buried as they had wished—on the side of the mountain at the compound. I went up there determined to find out how it was that they had died within hours of each other. I also wanted to make him understand that I would get a lawyer if I had to—or go to the authorities."

"That's when you learned that you'd been promised to him?" the sheriff asked.

"Yes, as ridiculous as it sounds. When I refused, I was held there against my will until I managed to get away. I'd stolen aboard a van driven by two of the sisters, as they call them. That's when I met Colt."

"Why didn't you go to the police then?" Flint asked.

"I planned to the next morning. I'd gone into the back of the hotel when I saw one of the sisters coming in the front. I ducked down a hallway and literally collided with Colt. I asked for his help and he sneaked me up to his room."

The sheriff looked at Colt. "And the two of you hit it off. She didn't tell you what she was running from?"

"No, but it was clear she was scared. I thought it was an old boyfriend."

Flint nodded and looked to Lola again. "You didn't trust him enough to ask for his help the next morning?"

"I didn't want to involve him. By then I knew what Jonas was capable of. This flock does whatever he tells them. The few who disobey are punished. One woman brought me extra food. I heard her being beaten the next morning by her own so-called sisters. When I had my daughter, they took her away almost at once. I could hear her crying, but I didn't get to see her again. The women would come in and take my breast milk, but they said she was now Jonas's child. He called her his angel. I knew I had only one choice. Escape and try to find Colt. I couldn't fight Jonas and his followers alone. And Jonas made it clear. The only way I could see my baby and be with her was if I married him and gave my life to The Society of Lasting Serenity."

Flint pushed back his chair and rose to his feet. "I think it's time I visited the compound and met this Jonas Emanuel."

Chapter Five

Colt followed the sheriff's SUV out of town toward the Judith Mountains. The mountains began just east of town and rose to the northeast for twenty miles. In most places they were only about ten miles wide with low peaks broken by stream drainages. But there were a number of peaks including the highest one, Judith Peak, at more than six thousand feet.

It was rugged country. Back in the 1950s the US Air Force had operated a radar station on top of the peak. The SLS had bought state land on an adjacent mountaintop in an isolated area with few roads in or out. Because it was considered a church, the SLS had rights that even the sheriff couldn't do anything about.

So Colt was nervous enough, but nothing compared to Lola. In the pickup seat next to him, he could feel her getting more agitated the closer they got to the SLS compound. He reached over to take her hand. It was ice-cold.

"It's going to be all right," he tried to assure her—and himself. If what she'd told him was true, then Jonas would have to hand over the baby. "Jonas will cooperate with a lawman."

She didn't look any more convinced than he felt. He'd dealt with religious fanatics for a while now and knew that nothing could stop them if they thought they were in the right.

"Jonas seems so nice, so truthful, so caring," she said. "He's fooled so many people. My parents weren't stupid. He caught them in his web with his talk of a better world." She shook her head. "But he is pure evil. I hate to even think what he might have done to my parents."

"You really think he killed them."

"Or convinced my mother to kill herself and my father."

Colt knew that wouldn't be a first when it came to cult mania.

"Clearly the sheriff wasn't called when they died. Jonas runs SLS like it's his own private country. He told me that his religious philosophy requires the bodies to be untouched and put into the ground quickly. Apparently in Montana, a religious group can bury a body on their property without embalming if it is done within so many hours."

The road climbed higher up the mountain. Ahead, the sheriff slowed. Colt could see that an iron gate blocked them from going any farther. Flint stopped, put down his window and pushed a button on what appeared to be an intercom next to the gate. Colt whirred down his window. He heard a tinny-sounding voice tell him that someone would be right down to let them in.

A few minutes later, an older man drove up in a Jeep. He spoke for a few moments with the sheriff before opening the gate. As Colt drove through, he felt the man's steely gaze on him. Clearly the SLS didn't like visitors. The man who'd opened the gate was wearing a gun under his jacket. Colt had caught sight of the butt end of it when the man got out of his rig to open the gate.

As they passed, he noticed something else interesting. The man recognized Lola. Just the sight of her made the man nervous.

LOLA FELT HER BODY begin to vibrate inside. She thought she might throw up. The memories of being imprisoned here for so long made her itch. She fought the need to claw her skin, remembering the horrible feel of the cheap cloth dresses she was forced to wear, the taste of the tea the sisters forced down her throat, the horrible chanting that nearly drove her insane. That wasn't all they'd forced on her once they'd quit coming for her breast milk. There'd been the pills that Sister Rebecca had forced down her throat.

She felt a shiver and hugged herself against the memories, telling herself she was safe with Colt and the sheriff. But the closer they got to the compound, the more plagued she was with fear. She doubted either Colt or the sheriff knew who they were dealing with. Jonas had gotten this far in life by fooling people. He was an expert at it. At the thought of what lies he would tell, her blood ran cold even though the pickup cab felt unbearably hot.

"Are you all right?" Colt asked, sounding worried as he glanced over at her.

She nodded and felt a bead of perspiration run down between her shoulder blades. She wanted to scratch her arm, feeling as if something was crawling across it, but feared once she started she wouldn't be able to stop.

Just driving up here brought everything back, as if all the crazy they'd been feeding her might finally sink in and she'd be a zombie like the other "sisters." Isn't that what Jonas had hoped? Wasn't that why he was just waiting for her return? He knew she'd be back for Grace. She couldn't bear to think what he had planned for her.

By the time they reached the headquarters and main building of the SLS, there was a welcome group waiting for them. Lola recognized Sister Rebecca, the woman Jonas got to do most of his dirty work. Sister Amelia was there, as well, but she kept her head down as if unable to look at her.

Lola felt bad that she'd gotten the woman in trouble. She could still hear Amelia's cries from the beating she'd received for giving her extra food. She could well imagine what had happened to the guards after she'd escaped. Jonas would know that she hadn't been taking her pills with the tea. Sister Amelia would be blamed, but there had been nothing Lola could do about that.

Flint parked his patrol SUV in front of the main building. Colt parked next to him. Lola felt her body refuse to move as Colt opened his door. She stared at the two women standing like sentinels in front of them and fought to take her next breath.

"Would you feel better staying out here in the truck?" Colt asked.

She wiped perspiration from her lip with the back of her hand. How could she possibly explain what it was like being back here, knowing what they had done to her, what they might do again if Colt didn't believe her and help her?

Terrified of facing Jonas again, she thought of her baby girl and reached for her door handle.

COLT WONDERED IF bringing Lola back here wasn't a mistake. She looked terrified one moment and like a sleepwalker the next. What had they done to her? He couldn't even imagine, given what she'd told him about her treatment. They'd taken her baby, kept her locked up, hadn't let her sleep. He worried that was just the tip of the iceberg, though.

One of the two women, who were dressed in long simple white sheaths with their hair in braided buns, stepped forward to greet them.

"I'm Sister Rebecca. How may we help you?" Appearing to be the older of the two, the woman's face had a blankness to it that some might have taken for serenity. But there was something else in the eyes. A wariness. A hardness.

"We're here to see Jonas Emanuel," the sheriff said.

"Let me see if he's available," she said, and turned to go back inside.

Colt started to say something about Jonas making himself available, but Flint stopped him. "Let's keep this as civilized as we can—at least to start."

The second woman stood at the foot of the porch steps, her fingers entwined and her face down, clearly standing guard.

A few moments later, Sister Rebecca came out again. "Brother Emanuel will see you now." She motioned them up the porch steps as the other woman drifted off toward a building in the pines where some women were washing clothes and hanging them on a string of clotheslines.

"Seems awfully cold to be hanging wash outside this time of year," Colt commented. Spring in Montana often meant the temperature never rose over forty in the mountains.

Sister Rebecca smiled as if amused. "We believe in hard work. It toughens a person up so a little cold weather doesn't bother us."

He thought about saying something about how she wasn't the one hanging clothes today in the cool weather on the mountaintop, but he followed the sheriff's lead and kept his mouth shut.

As Sister Rebecca led them toward the back of the huge building, Colt noticed the layout. In this communal living part of the structure, straight-backed wooden chairs were lined up like soldiers at long wooden tables. Behind the dining area, he could hear kitchen workers and the banging of pots and pans. An aroma arose that reminded him of school cafeterias.

What struck him was the lack of conversation coming from the kitchen, let alone any music. There was a utilitarian feeling about the building and everything in it—the workers included. They could have been robots for the lack of liveliness in the place.

Sister Rebecca tapped at a large wooden door. A cheerful voice on the other side said, "Come in." She opened the door and stood back to let them enter a room that was warm and cozy compared to the other part of the building.

A sandy-haired man, who Colt knew was fifty-two, had been sitting behind a large oak desk. But now he pushed back his office chair and rose, surprising Colt by not just his size, but how fit he was. He had boyish good looks, lively pale blue eyes and a wide, straight-toothed smile. He looked much younger than his age.

The leader came around his desk to shake hands with the sheriff and Colt. "Jonas Emanuel," he said. "Welcome." His gaze slid to Lola. When he spoke her name it was with obvious affection. "Lola," Jonas said, looking pained to see her scratched face before returning his gaze to Colt and the sheriff.

"We need to ask you a few questions," Sheriff Cahill said, introducing himself and Colt. "You already know Ms. Dayton."

"Please have a seat," Jonas said graciously, offering them one of the chairs circled around the warm blaze going in the rock fireplace to one side of the office area. Colt thought again of the women hanging wet clothes outside. "Can I get you anything to drink?"

They all declined. Jonas took a chair so he was facing them and crossed his legs to hold one knee in his hands. Colt noticed that he was limping before he sat down.

"How long have you known Ms. Dayton?" Flint asked.

"Her parents were founding members. Lola's been a member for the past couple of years," Jonas said.

"That's not true," she cried. "You know I'm not a member, would never be a member."

Colt could see that she was even more agitated than she'd been in the truck on the way up. She sat on the edge of her chair and looked ready to run again. "Just give me my baby," she said, her voice breaking. "I want to see my baby." She turned in her chair. Sister Rebecca stood at the door, fingers entwined, head down, standing sentry. "My baby. Tell her to get my baby."

Colt reached over and took her hand. Jonas noticed but said nothing.

"As you can see, Ms. Dayton is quite upset. She claims that you are holding her child here on the property," the sheriff said.

Jonas nodded without looking at Lola. "Perhaps we should speak in private. Lola? Why don't you go with Sister Rebecca? She can make you some tea."

"I don't want any of your so-called tea," Lola snapped. "I want my child."

"It's all right," Flint said. "Go ahead and leave with her. We need to talk to Jonas. We won't be long."

Lola looked as if she might argue, but when her gaze fell on Colt, he nodded, indicating that she should leave. "I'll be right here if you need me." Again he could feel Jonas's gaze on him.

After Sister Rebecca left with Lola, the leader sighed deeply. "I'm afraid Lola is a very troubled woman. I'm not sure what she's told you—"

"That you're keeping her baby from her," Colt said.

He nodded sadly. "Lola came to us after her parents died. She'd lost her teaching job, been fired. That loss and the loss of her parents... We tried to help her since she had no one else. I'm sure she's told you that her parents were important members of our community here. On her mother's death bed, she made me promise that I would look after Lola."

"She didn't promise Lola to you as your wife?" Colt asked, and got a disapproving look from the sheriff.

"Of course not." Jonas looked shocked by the accusation. "I had hoped Lola would stay with us. Her parents took so much peace in living among us, but Lola left."

"I understand she ran away some months ago," Flint said.

"A year ago," Colt added.

Again Jonas looked surprised. "Is that what she told you?" He shook his head. "I foolishly suggested that maybe time away from the compound would be good for her. Several of the sisters were making a trip to Billings for supplies. I talked Lola into going along. Once there, though, she apparently became turned around while shopping and got lost. In her state of mind, that was very traumatic. Fortunately, the sisters found her, but not until the next morning. She was confused and hysterical. They brought her back here where we nursed her back to health and discovered that while she'd been lost in Billings, she'd been assaulted."

Colt started to object, but the sheriff cut him off. "She was pregnant? Did she say who the father was?"

Jonas shook his head. "She didn't seem to know."

The man looked right at Colt, his blue eyes giving nothing away.

"Where is the baby now?" Flint asked.

"I'm afraid the infant was stillborn. A little boy. Which made it all the more traumatic and heartbreaking for her since we all knew that she had her heart set on having a baby girl. I'm not sure if you know this, but her mother had a daughter before Lola who was stillborn. I'm sure that could have played a part in what happened. When Lola was told that her own child had been stillborn, she had a complete breakdown and became convinced that we had stolen her daughter."

"Then you won't mind if we have a look around," the sheriff said.

"Not at all." He rose to his feet, and the sheriff and Colt followed. "I'm so glad Lola's been found. We've been taking care of her since her breakdown. Unfortunately, the other night she overpowered one of her sisters and, hysterical again, took off running into the woods. We looked for her for hours. I was going to call your office if we didn't hear from her by this afternoon. When she left, she forgot her pills. I was afraid she'd have another psychotic event with no one there to help her."

"Don't you mean when Lola *escaped* here?" Colt asked.

Jonas shook his head as if trying to be patient. "Escaped?" He chuckled. "Do you see razor wire fences around the compound? Why would she need to escape? We believe in free will here at Serenity. Lola can come and go as she pleases. She knows that. But when she's in one of her states…"

"What kind of medication is she on?" the sheriff asked.

"I have it right here," Jonas reached into his pocket. "I had Sister Rebecca bring it to me when I heard that you were at the gate. I was so glad that she had come back for it. I believe Dr. Reese said it's what they give patients with schizophrenia. I suppose she didn't mention to you that she'd been taking the medication. It helps with the anxiety attacks, as well as the hallucinations."

"Dr. Reese?" Flint asked.

"Ben Reese. He's our local physician, one of the best in the country and one of our members," Jonas said.

"I'd like to see where the baby was buried," Colt said.

"Of course. But let's start with the tour the sheriff requested."

Colt memorized the layout of the buildings as Jonas led them from building to building. Everywhere they went, there were people working, both men and women, but definitely there were more women on the compound than men. He saw no women with babies as most of the women were older.

"Our cemetery is just down here," Jonas said. Colt followed Jonas and the sheriff down a narrow dirt path that wound through the trees to open in a meadow. Wooden crosses marked the few graves, the names of the deceased printed on metal plaques.

He spotted a relatively fresh grave and felt his heart drop. It was a small plot of dark earth. What if Jonas was telling the truth? What if Lola had had a son? *His* son? And the infant was buried under that cold ground?

"It is always so difficult to lose a child," Jonas was saying. "We buried him next to Lola's parents. We thought that would give her comfort. If not now, later when she's…better. We're waiting for her to name him before we put up the cross."

"I think I've seen enough," Sheriff Cahill said, and looked at Colt.

Colt didn't know what to think. On the surface, it all seemed so…reasonable.

"Sister Rebecca took Lola to the kitchen," Jonas said. "Lunch will be ready soon. I believe we're having a nice vegetable soup today. You're welcome to join us. Some of the sisters are better cooks than others. I can attest that the ones cooking today are our best."

"Thank you, but I need to get back to Gilt Edge," Flint said. "What about you, Colt?"

He knew the sheriff wasn't asking just about lunch or returning to town. "I'll see what Lola wants to do," he said, after taking a last look at the small unmarked grave before heading back toward the main building.

"If Lola is determined not to stay with us, I just hope she'll get the help she needs," Colt heard Jonas tell the sheriff. "I'm worried about her, especially after your visit. Clearly she isn't herself."

LOLA SHOVED AWAY the cup of tea Sister Rebecca had tried to get her to drink. She'd seen Colt and the sheriff go out to search the complex with Jonas. "I know you hid her the moment the sheriff punched the intercom at the gate. Please…" Her voice broke. "I just want to see her so I know she's all right."

Sister Rebecca reached over to pat her hand—and shove the tea closer with her other hand.

Lola jerked her hand back. "You can't keep her. She's mine." Tears burned her eyes. "Keeping a baby from her mother…"

"You aren't taking your medication, are you? It makes you like this. You really should take it so you're more calm."

"Brain-dead, you mean. Half-comatose, so I'm easy to manipulate. If you keep me drugged up, I won't cause any trouble, right?"

"You wouldn't have left here if you'd been taking your medication." Sister Rebecca shook her head. "You know we were only trying to help you. I should have been the one giving you your medication instead of Sister Amelia. She let you get away with not taking it and look what's happened to you, you poor dear."

Lola scoffed. "As if you care. And Sister Amelia didn't know anything about what I was doing," she said quickly, fearing that the next beating Amelia got could kill her. "I was hiding them under my tongue until she turned away."

The woman nodded. "Well, should you end up staying here, we won't let that happen again, will we."

"I'm not staying here."

Sister Rebecca said nothing as the front door opened and Colt came in. Through the open doorway, Lola could see Jonas and the sheriff standing out by the patrol SUV. She could tell that Jonas had convinced the sheriff that she was crazy.

Standing up too quickly, Lola knocked over her chair. It clattered to the floor. Dizzy, she had to hang on to the table for a moment. When the light-headedness passed and she could let go, she started for the door. But not before she realized Colt had seen her having trouble standing.

She swept past him, determined not to let the sheriff leave. Her baby was hidden somewhere in the complex. Jonas had had one of his followers hide her. The sheriff had to find her. Lola had to convince him—

At the sound of a baby crying, she stumbled to an abrupt stop. "Do you hear that?" she called down to the sheriff from the top of the porch steps. "It's my baby crying." He looked up in surprise. So did Jonas. Both seemed to stop to listen.

For a moment, Lola thought that she had imagined it. Fear curdled her stomach. She felt Colt's hand on her shoulder as he reached for her. She could see that they believed Jonas. Her eyes filled with tears of frustration and pain.

And then she heard it again. A baby began to squall loudly. The sound was coming from the laundry. She shrugged off Colt's hand and ran down the steps. Jonas reached for her, but she managed to sweep past him. Grace. It was her baby crying for her. She knew that cry. She'd heard it in the middle of the night when the sisters had come for her breast milk. Somehow Grace had known she was here.

"Lola, don't," Jonas called after her. "Sister Rebecca, help Lola. She's going to hurt herself."

She could hear running footsteps behind her, but she was almost to the laundry-room door. Sister Rebecca had set off an alarm. As Lola burst into the room, a half dozen women were already looking in her direction. Lola paid them no mind. She ran toward the woman holding the baby.

Inside this room with the washers and dryers going, though she could barely hear the baby crying, all Lola could think about was getting to the woman before they hid Grace away again. Reaching the woman, she heard the infant let out a fresh squall as if the mother had pinched the poor thing.

Lola grabbed for the baby, but the woman swung around so all she got was a handful of dress cloth from the woman's shoulder.

"Lola, stop." It was the sheriff's voice as he stepped between her and the woman with the child. "May I see your baby," he said to the woman.

Chapter Six

Colt watched the woman with the infant look at Jonas standing in the doorway. The leader nodded that she should let the sheriff look. Colt held his breath as the woman turned so they could see the baby she held. The infant had stopped crying and now looked at them with big blue eyes fringed with tear-jeweled lashes.

"Grace?" Lola whispered as she tried to see the baby.

"May I?" the sheriff asked, and held out his arms.

After getting Jonas's permission, the woman released the baby to Flint. He carefully pulled back the knitted blanket the infant was wrapped in. Colt found himself holding his breath.

The sheriff peeked under the gown the baby wore. Colt knew he was looking for the small heart-shaped birthmark that Lola had told him about. He checked under the baby's diaper. His shoulders fell a little as he looked up at Lola and shook his head. "It's a little boy."

"No," Lola cried. "I heard my baby. This isn't the baby I heard crying. It can't be. Sister Rebecca pulled the alarm. She warned them to hide my baby." She looked from the sheriff to Colt and back again before bursting into tears.

Colt stepped to her and pulled her into his arms. She cried against his chest as he looked past her to the sheriff. He'd watched the whole thing play out, holding his breath. The baby the sheriff had taken from the woman was adorable and about the right age. Was it possible Lola was wrong about the sex of the infant she'd given birth to? Maybe the baby hadn't died.

But Lola had been so sure it was a little girl. She'd convinced him. And there was the tiny heart birthmark that Lola had seen on their daughter. But what if she was wrong and Jonas was telling the truth about all of it?

Now he felt sick. He thought of the small grave next to Lola's parents'. He felt such a sense of loss that it made him ache inside. He pulled Lola tighter to him, feeling her heart breaking along with his own.

As the sheriff spoke again with Jonas, Colt led Lola out of the laundry and down the path toward his pickup.

"I heard her," she said between sobs. "The first baby I heard. It was Grace. I know her cry. A mother knows her baby's cry. Sister Rebecca pulled the alarm to warn them so they could hide her again." She began to cry again as he led her to the truck and opened the passenger-side door for her. "Please, Colt, we can't leave without our baby."

He tried to think of what to say, but his throat had closed with all the emotions he was feeling, an incredible sense of loss and regret. It broke his heart to see Lola like this.

Lola met his gaze with a look that felt like an arrow

to his chest before she climbed into the pickup. As he closed the passenger-side door, the sheriff walked over. "You all right?" Flint asked.

All Colt could do was nod. He wasn't sure he would ever be all right.

"I think we're done here," the sheriff said. "If you want to take it further…"

He shook his head. "Thanks for your help," he managed to get out before walking around to the driver's side of his pickup. As he slid behind the wheel, he saw that Lola had dried her tears and was now sitting ramrod straight in her seat with that same look of surrender that tore at him.

He started the engine, unable to look at her.

"You don't believe me. You believe…" She stopped and he looked over at her. She was staring straight ahead. He followed her gaze to where Jonas was standing on the porch of the main building. There was both sympathy and pity in the man's gaze. "He's lying." But Lola said it with little conviction as Colt started the pickup and headed off the compound.

LOLA CLOSED HER EYES and leaned back against the pickup as they headed down the mountain road. What had she expected? That Jonas would just hand over Grace? She'd been such a fool. Worse, she feared that they'd made things worse for Grace—not to mention the way Colt had looked at her. Leaving them alone with Jonas had been the wrong thing to do. She knew what that man was like. Of course the sheriff would believe anything the leader told him. But Colt?

"What did Jonas tell you?" She had to ask as she squeezed her eyes shut tighter, unable to look at him. "That I'm crazy?"

"He said your baby died. That it was a little boy. He showed me the grave."

She let out a muffled cry and opened her eyes. Staring straight ahead at the narrow dirt road that wound down the mountain, she said, "Is that what convinced you I was lying?"

"Why didn't you tell me you were on prescription medication?" Colt asked.

She let out a bark of a laugh. "Of course, my *medication*. What did he tell you it was for?"

"He hinted it was for schizophrenia and that after your breakdown—"

"Right—my breakdown. What else?"

He glanced over at her. "He said you were fired from your teaching job."

Tears blurred her eyes. She bit her lower lip and drew blood. "That at least is true. I resisted the advances of the school principal. When some materials in my classroom went missing, I was fired. Three days later, I heard that my parents had died. Perfect timing," she said sarcastically. "I'm not a thief. I wouldn't give in, so she did what she said she would, she fired me, claiming I stole the materials. It was my word against hers—even though it wasn't the first time something like that had happened involving her. I had planned to fight it once I took care of getting my parents remains returned to the California cemetery. So what else did Jonas tell you about me?"

"That you're a troubled young woman."

"I am that," she agreed. "Given everything that has been done to me, I think that is understandable." Ahead she could see Brother Elmer waiting at the gate for them. Elmer was her father's age. When she'd first arrived at the compound, she'd asked him what had happened to her parents and Elmer had been too terrified to talk to her. She'd only had that one opportunity. Since then Elmer had kept his distance—just like the rest of them.

"Stop up here, please," Lola said, even though the gate was standing open.

Colt said nothing and did as she asked.

She put down the truck window as Colt pulled alongside the man. Elmer met her gaze for a moment before he dropped his head and stared at his feet. "Elmer, you know I'm not crazy. Help me, please," she pleaded. "You were my father's friend. Tell this man the truth about what really goes on back there in the compound."

Elmer continued to focus on the ground.

"Okay, just tell me this," she said, her voice cracking with emotion. "Is Grace all right? Are they taking good care of her?" She didn't expect an answer. She knew the cost of going against Jonas. Everyone did. If she was right and Jonas had had her parents killed…

Elmer raised his head slowly. As he did, he grabbed hold of the side of the truck, curling his fingers over the open window frame. His fingers brushed her arm. His gaze rose to meet hers. He gave one quick nod and removed his hands.

"You should move on now so I can close this gate, Sister Lola."

COLT BLINKED, TELLING HIMSELF he hadn't just seen that. His heart beat like a war drum. He swore under his breath. He'd seen the man's short, quick nod. He'd seen the compassion in Elmer's eyes.

Jonas Emanuel was a liar.

Colt wasn't sure who he was more angry with, Jonas or himself. He'd bought into the man's bull. He'd *believed* him. But the man had been damned convincing. The grave. The pills. The crying baby that wasn't Grace.

Shifting the pickup into gear, he felt as if he'd been punched in the gut numerous times. He kept seeing that tiny grave, kept imagining his son, their son, lying in a homemade coffin under it—just as he kept seeing Lola sobbing hysterically in his arms after hearing what she thought was her baby crying.

"Lola."

"Please, just leave me alone," she said as she closed her window and tucked herself into the corner of the pickup seat as he pulled away, the gate closing behind him. When he looked over at her a few miles down the road, he saw that anger and frustration had given way to emotional exhaustion. With the sun streaming in the window, she'd fallen asleep.

Colt was thankful for the time alone. He replayed everything Lola had said, along with what Jonas had told him. He hadn't known what to believe because the man was that persuasive. Jonas had convinced the sheriff— and Flint Cahill was a shrewd lawman.

But as he looked over at the woman sleeping in his pickup, he felt his heart ache in ways he'd never experienced before. He would slay dragons for this woman. He wanted to turn around and go back and…

He couldn't let his emotions get the best of him. He never had before. But this woman had drawn him from the moment he'd met her. He thought about the fear he'd seen in her eyes that first night. There'd been no confusion, though. If anything, they'd both wanted to escape from the world that night and lose themselves in each other. And they had. He remembered her naked in his arms and felt a pull stronger than gravity.

Would he have believed her if she'd told him on that first night what was going on? Probably not. Look how easily he'd let Jonas fool him. Colt was still furious with himself. He would never again question anything she told him.

Glancing in the rearview mirror, he wasn't surprised to see that they were being followed. Everything she'd told him had been true.

So where was the child he and Lola had conceived? He couldn't bear the thought of Grace being in Jonas's hands. But he also knew that they couldn't go back there until they had a plan.

As he slowed on the outskirts of Gilt Edge, Lola stirred. She shot him a glance as she sat up.

"Before we go back to the ranch, I thought we'd get something to eat," he said, keeping his eye on the large dark SUV a couple of car lengths behind them.

"There is no reason to take me back to the ranch. You can just pull over anywhere and let me out."

"I'm not going to do that."

"I can understand why you don't want to help me, but I'm not leaving town until—"

"You get Grace back."

She stared at him. "Are you mocking me?"

"Not at all," he said, and looked over at her. "I'm sorry. I should have believed you. But I do now."

Tears welled in her eyes and spilled down her cheeks. "You believe me about Grace?"

"I do. I saw that armed guard who let us through the gate. I saw him nod when you asked him about Grace."

She wiped at her tears. "Is that what changed your mind?"

"That and a lot of other things, once I had time to think about it. That first night, you were scared and running from something, but you weren't confused. Nor do I think you were confused the next morning. You checked my wallet to see who I was. You considered taking the four hundred dollars in it, but decided not to. Those were not the actions of a troubled, mentally unstable woman. Also, we're being followed."

Lola glanced in her side mirror. "How long has that vehicle been back there?"

"Since we left the compound."

She seemed to consider that. "Why follow us? If they wanted to know where you lived…"

"I think they are more interested in you than me, but I guess we'll find out soon enough. That's the other thing that made me believe you once I was away from Jonas's hocus-pocus disappearing-baby act. I saw guards armed with concealed weapons around the perimeter of the compound. While there might not be any razor wire and a high fence, that place is secure as Fort Knox."

"So how are we going to find Grace and get her out of there?"

"I don't know. I haven't worked that out yet."

She looked at him as if afraid of this change in his attitude. "The sheriff believes Jonas."

"I don't blame Flint. Jonas is quite convincing. He certainly had me going."

Lola let out a bitter laugh. "How do you think he got so many people to follow him to Montana? To give him all their money, to convince them that to find peace, they needed to give up everything—especially their minds and free will."

"Why wasn't he able to brainwash you?" he asked as he glanced in the rearview mirror. Their tail was still back there.

"I don't know. The meditation, the chanting, the affirmations on the path to peace and happiness? I blocked them out, thinking about anything else. Also, I didn't buy into any of it. I was surprised my father did. It's one reason I didn't see them for so many years. My father wrote me and I spoke with my mother some on the phone, but there was no way I was going to visit them on the compound and they never left except to move to Montana with SLS."

"How was it your father was one of the founding members if it wasn't like him to buy into Jonas's propaganda?"

"My father would have done anything to make my mother happy. That's why he didn't leave after he quit believing in Jonas. He wouldn't have left her there alone. I'm sure he finally saw what my mother couldn't. That Jonas was a fraud. I feel terrible for those lost years."

"The man at the gate…"

"Elmer? He and my father were friends. It's possible that, like my father, he has doubts about SLS and Jonas. Also, not everyone is easily brainwashed into believing everything Jonas says. They might believe he has a right to my child because he says so. But that doesn't mean some aren't sympathetic to a mother losing her baby, our baby, to Jonas."

"I still don't understand how Jonas thinks he can get away with this."

"Because he has."

He glanced over at her, seeing that she was right. Jonas did rule that compound like it was his own country, and because his society was considered a church, he was protected.

"He has Grace," she said. "He knows I can't live without her. Except he's wrong if he thinks I'll let him keep my child, let alone that I would ever be his wife."

Colt glanced over at her. "So he knows we'll be back."

Chapter Seven

Lola looked out the side window as the road skirted Gilt Edge. Her heart beat so loudly that she thought for sure Colt would be able to hear it. Tears stung her eyes, but this time they were tears of relief.

Colt believed her.

The liberation made her weak. She'd seen his face earlier in the laundry when the baby had turned out not to be hers. She'd seen the heart-wrenching sympathy in his gaze, as well as the pain. He'd been so sure at the moment that she was everything Jonas had told him. A mentally unstable woman who couldn't accept the death of the baby she'd carried for nine months. *His* baby.

But Colt had seen the truth. He'd seen Elmer's slight nod, and when he looked at everything, he knew she was telling the truth.

She wiped at her tears, determined not to give in to the need to cry her heart out. They still didn't have Grace. Her stomach ached with a need to hold her baby. Jonas had Grace and that alone terrified her. Would he hurt the baby to get back at her?

No. He'd fooled the sheriff. He would feel safe and

superior. He would simply wait, knowing, as Colt said, that they'd be back. Or at least she would. Jonas thought he'd fooled Colt, too.

She tried to assure herself that Jonas wouldn't hurt Grace just to spite her. The baby was his only hope of getting Lola back to the compound. She'd looked into Jonas's eyes as they'd left. He hadn't given up on her being his wife. He would need Grace if he had any hope of making that happen.

At least that must be his thinking, she told herself. It would be a cold day in hell before she would ever succumb to the man. And only then so she could get close enough to kill him.

"Do you think Jonas knows I'm Grace's father?" Colt asked, dragging her out of her dark thoughts. "He looked me right in the eye and told me that you swore you didn't know who the father was."

"I did. I was afraid he'd come after you. Or send some of his men to hurt you—if not kill you. He was quite upset to realize I was pregnant. I told him I didn't know your name. You were just someone who'd helped me."

"Helped himself to you. Isn't that what Jonas thought?"

She shrugged. "He was so angry with me. I'm not sure when he decided he wanted my baby. Our baby."

"Well, he can't have her."

"We will get her back, won't we?"

He reached over and took her hand.

"I mean, if you dig up the grave and prove that—"

"Lola, that would take time and be very iffy. First off, that is probably what Jonas is expecting us to do.

Second, even if we had proof that your baby didn't die, I'm not sure we could get a judge to send up an army to search the place for Grace."

"Then what do we do?" She felt close to tears again.

"The problem is that it is hard for the authorities to get involved in these types of pseudo-religious groups, especially when, according to Jonas, you're a member—and so were your parents. It's your word against Jonas's. So I'm afraid we're on our own. But that's not a bad thing." He smiled at her. "I'll do everything in my power and then some to bring Grace home to you."

She smiled and squeezed his hand, knowing that she could depend on Colt.

COLT PULLED UP in front of the Stagecoach Saloon on the outskirts of Gilt Edge. The large dark SUV that had been following them drove on past. He tried to see the driver, but the windows were tinted too dark. The license plate was covered with mud, no accident either, he figured.

But it didn't matter. He knew exactly where it had come from.

"The sheriff's brother and sister own this place," Colt said as he parked and turned off the engine. "They serve some of the best food in the area. I thought we'd have something to eat and talk. It shouldn't be that busy this time of the day."

Lola's stomach growled in answer, making him smile. "I thought I would never eat after Grace was taken from me. But soon I realized that I needed my strength if I had any hope of getting her back. Not that I was given much food on the compound."

They got out, Lola slowing to admire the place. "I love this stone building."

"It was one of the original stagecoach stops along here. Lillie Cahill bought it with her brother Darby, to preserve it." He pushed open the door and Lola stepped in.

"Something smells wonderful," she whispered to Colt as they made their way to an out-of-the way table by the window. All this time eating nothing but the swill that had come out of the compound kitchen had left her ravenous.

There were a few regulars at the bar but other than that, the place was empty. A man who resembled the sheriff came over to take their orders. He had Flint's dark hair and gray eyes and was equally good-looking. "Major McCloud," the young man said, grinning at Colt.

"Just Colt, thank you."

"I heard you were back. Welcome home. Again, so sorry about your father."

"Thanks, Darby." All of the Cahills had been at the funeral. Colt's father would have liked that. He'd always respected their father, Ely Cahill, even though a lot of people in this town considered him a nut. "This is my friend Lola."

Darby turned to Lola and said, "Nice to meet you."

"Congrats on the marriage and fatherhood. How's your family?" Colt asked, since that's what small-town people did. Everyone knew everyone else. He was sure

Darby had heard about Julia and Wyatt since they'd all gone to school together.

"Fine. Lillie's married and now has a son, TC. She married Trask Beaumont. If you're sticking around for a while, you'll have to meet Mariah and my son, Daniel. Don't know if Flint mentioned it, but his wife, Maggie... Yep. Expecting."

Colt laughed. "Must be somethin' in the water. Which reminds me. Ely still kickin'?"

Darby laughed. "Hasn't changed a bit. Still spends most of his time up in the mountains when he's not hanging around the missile silo." He sighed. "So what can I get you?"

"What's cooking today? Something smells delicious."

"Our cook, Billie Dee, whipped up one of her down-home Texas recipes. Today it's shrimp gumbo. Gotta warn ya, she's determined to add some spice in our lives and convert us Montanans."

"I'll have that," Lola and Colt said in unison, making Darby chuckle.

"Two coming up. What can I get you to drink?"

Colt looked at Lola. "Two colas?" She nodded and Darby went off to place their order.

"What was that about... Ely?"

"The Cahill patriarch. Famous in these parts because back in 1967, he swore he was abducted by aliens next to the missile silo on their ranch." Colt explained how the government had asked for two-acre plots around the area for defense back in the 1950s. "You might have seen that metal fence out in one of my pastures? There might be a live missile in it. No one but the government knows for sure."

"The missile silos on your property would be scary enough, but aliens?"

He laughed and nodded. "What makes Ely's story interesting to me is that night in 1967 the Air Force detected a flying-saucer type aircraft in the area. Lots of people saw it, including my father."

"So it's possible Ely is telling he truth as he knows it," she said, wide-eyed.

He shrugged. "I guess we'll never know for certain, but Ely swears it's true."

Darby brought their colas, and they sat in companionable silence for a few minutes.

"It feels so strange to be in a place like this," Lola said. "It's so…normal. I haven't had normal in way too long."

"How long had you been held at the compound before I met you in Billings?"

"Almost a month. The first week or so I was trying to get my parents' remains released to a mortuary in Gilt Edge. Jonas had been kind enough to offer me a place to stay until I could make arrangements. I didn't realize that he was lying to me until I tried to leave and realized there were armed guards keeping me there. At least I wasn't locked up in a cabin that time. I had the run of the place, or I would never have gotten away in the back of the van when the sisters drove to Billings."

And Colt would never have met her. They would never have made love and conceived Grace, Colt thought. Funny how things worked out.

Darby put some background music on the jukebox. The sun coming in the window gave the place a golden glow. Colt had been here a few times when he was home on leave. He was happy for Lillie and Darby for making a go of the place.

"How did you manage to get away this last time?" he asked.

"I'd been hiding my pills under my tongue until Sister Amelia left my cabin. I would spit them out and poke them into a hole I'd found in the cabin wall. The night I escaped, I pretended to be sick and managed to distract Sister Rebecca. When she wasn't looking, I hid the fork that was on my tray. She didn't notice that it was missing when she took my tray and left. I used the fork to pick the lock on the window and went out that way."

Darby returned a few moments later, accompanied by a large woman with a Southern accent carrying two steaming bowls of shrimp gumbo.

"Billie Dee, meet Colt McCloud," Darby said as he joined them. "Colt and I go way back. He's an Army helicopter pilot who's finally returned home—at least for a while, and this is his friend Lola."

"Pleased to meet you," the woman with the Texas accent said. "Hope you like my gumbo."

"I know we will," Colt said, and took a bite.

"Not too spicy for you?" the cook asked with a laugh.

"As long as it doesn't melt the spoon, it's not too spicy for me," Colt said, and looked to Lola.

She had tasted the gumbo and was smiling. "It's perfect."

Billie Dee looked pleased. "Enjoy."

Darby refilled their colas and gave them pieces of Billie Dee's Texas chocolate sheet cake to convey both "welcome home" and "glad to meet you."

Left alone again, Colt asked, "How are you doing?"

Lola realized that she felt better than she had in a long time. Just having food in her stomach made her feel stronger and more able to hold off the fear and frustration. She needed her baby.

But Colt believed her, and that made all the difference in the world. That felt like a huge hurdle given how convincing Jonas could be. Even more so, she was glad that she hadn't been wrong about Colt. They'd only been together that one night, but she hadn't forgotten his kindness, his tenderness, his protectiveness. Just having someone she could depend on... Her heart swelled as she looked over at him. "We're going to get Grace back, aren't we?"

JONAS STOOD AT the window of his cabin. He'd had his cabin built on the side of the mountain so he could look down on the compound. For a man who'd started with nothing, he'd done all right. He often wished his father was still alive to see it.

"Look, you sanctimonious old son of a bitch. You, who so lacked faith that I would accomplish anything in my life. You, who died so poor that your congregation had to scrape up money to have you buried behind the church you'd served all those years. You, who always managed to cut me down as if you couldn't stand it that I might do better than you. Well, I did!"

Thinking about his father made his pulse rise dangerously. He had to be careful not to get upset. Stress made his condition worse. So much worse that some of his followers had started to notice.

He stepped over to the small table where he kept his medication. He swallowed a pill and waited for it to work. He tried not to think about the father who had kicked him out at sixteen. But it wasn't his old man who was causing the problem this time. It was Lola.

"Lola." Just saying her name churned up a warring mix of emotions that had been raging inside him for some time. Over the years, a variety of willing women had come to his bed in the night. He'd turned none of them away, but nor had he wanted any of them to keep for himself. Until Lola.

Her mother had shown him a photograph of her daughter back when Maxine and her husband, Ted, had joined SLS. The Society was just getting on its feet in those days. The Daytons' money had gone a long way to start things rolling.

Jonas had especially liked Maxine, since he knew she was the one calling the shots. Ted would do anything for his wife. And had. All Jonas had to do was steer Maxine in whatever direction he wanted her to go and Ted would come along as a willing participant. If only they were all that easy to manage, he thought now with a sigh.

The photo of Lola had caught him off guard. There was a sweetness, a purity in that young face, but it was what he saw in her eyes. A fire. A passion banked in those mesmerizing violet eyes that had made him want to be the one to release it.

He'd done everything he could to get the Daytons to bring Lola to the California ranch. But the foolish girl had taken off right after high school to attend a college abroad. She'd wanted to become a teacher. Jonas had groaned when Maxine told him, and he'd conveyed his thoughts.

I think she could be anything she wants to be with my help. I really want to help her meet her potential. Lola is destined to do so much more than teach. She and I could lead the world to a better place. She might be the one person who could bring peace to the world.

Maxine had loved it, but Lola hadn't been having any of it. Right after college she'd headed for the Virgin Islands to teach sixth-grade geography at a private school down there. What a waste, he'd thought, not just for Lola but for himself. He had imagined what he could do with a woman like that warming his bed at night. They could run SLS together. Lola would bring in the men. He'd bring in the women. They could build an empire and live like royalty.

He'd known that Ted wasn't happy after the move to Montana. Jonas had heard him trying to get Maxine to leave. That was the first time that Jonas had realized that Ted had held out on him. Ted hadn't bought into SLS either mentally or financially. He hadn't turned over all his money. He'd set some aside for Lola, and no small amount, either.

Ted's dissatisfaction and attempts to get Maxine to leave hadn't fitted into Jonas's plan. He suddenly realized there was only one way to get Lola to come to him. Maxine and Ted would have to die—and soon.

Getting Maxine to sign a paper of her intentions to persuade Lola to marry him had taken only one private session with her. Maxine had bought into SLS hook, line and sinker. If she wanted to save her daughter... He'd promised to give Lola the kind of life her mother had only dreamed of. Then he'd had Ted and Maxine disposed of and, just as he'd planned, Lola flew to Montana, bringing all that fire inside her.

But he'd underestimated her. She was nothing like her mother. He'd thought that his charm, his wit, his sincerity would work on the daughter the way it had on her mother. That was where he'd made his first mistake, he thought now as he watched dusk settle over the compound.

There'd been a series of other mistakes that had led to her getting pregnant by another man. That was a blow he still reeled from. But it hadn't changed his determination to have Lola, one way or another. Not even some Army pilot/rancher could stop him. No, he had the one thing that Lola wanted more than life.

She would be back. And this time, she wouldn't be leaving here again.

Chapter Eight

After shrimp gumbo at the Stagecoach Saloon, Colt took them to the grocery store. He and Lola grabbed a cart and began to fill it with food. He loved her enthusiasm. After being locked up and nearly starved for so long, she was like a kid in a candy store.

"Do you like this?" she would ask as she picked up one item after another.

"Get whatever sounds good to you."

She scampered around, quickly filling the cart with food she obviously hadn't had for a while as he grabbed the basics: milk, bread, eggs, butter, bacon and syrup.

"I suspect you can live on pancakes," she said, eyeing what he'd added to the cart.

He'd only grinned, realizing that he'd never enjoyed grocery shopping as much as he had with her today. They felt almost like an old married couple as they left the store. He found himself smiling at Lola as she tore into a bag of potato chips before they even reached the pickup. He unloaded their haul and had started to replace the cart in the rack when he heard someone call his name.

"Colt?"

He froze at the sound of Julia's voice. Somehow he'd managed not to cross paths with her since he'd been back in town, but only because he'd shopped either very early or very late. He'd picked a bad day to run out of groceries, he thought now with a grimace.

"Colt?"

Lola set her potato chip bag in the back of the pickup bed and walked over to join him. He could feel her looking from him to Julia, wondering why he wasn't responding. With a silent curse, he turned to face the woman he'd been ready to marry a year ago.

Julia looked exactly the same. Her dark hair was shorter, making her brown eyes seem even darker. She looked good, slim and perfect in a dress and heels. Julia always liked to dress up—even to go to the grocery store. Gold glittered at her ears, her neck and, of course, on her ring finger, along with the sizable diamond resting there. The one he'd bought hadn't been nearly as large.

He swore under his breath. As many times as he'd imagined what it would be like running into her again, he'd never imaged this. Lola was watching the two of them as if enjoying a tennis match.

Colt had hoped that he wouldn't feel anything, given what Julia had done to him. But he'd believed in this woman, believed they would share the rest of their lives; otherwise, he would never have asked her to marry him. It had taken him almost three years to pop the question. He'd wanted to be sure. What a fool he'd been.

"I heard you were back," Julia said, and glanced from

him to Lola beside him. "I was so sorry to hear about your father. I was at the funeral…"

He'd seen her and managed to avoid her.

"How are you?" she asked, sounding as if she cared.

As if sensing who this woman was and what she'd meant to him, Lola reached over and took his hand, squeezing it gently.

"I'm good," he said, squeezing back. "And you?"

"Fine." She looked again at his companion, her gaze going to their clasped hands.

"I heard you've put the ranch up for sale." Julia hesitated. She brushed a lock of her hair back from her forehead, looking not quite as confident. "Does this mean you're going back into the military?" His joining the Army's flight program had been a bone of contention between them.

He shook his head, as if what he planned to do was any of her business.

"I was just wondering," she said, no doubt seeing him clenching his teeth. "I was hoping that if you were staying around Gilt Edge we could…" Again she hesitated. "Maybe we could have a cup of coffee sometime and just talk."

Just talk the way they had before she'd had an affair with Wyatt? Or talk the way they had when she hadn't shown up at the airport to give him a ride home?

"Our last conversation…" Julia looked again at Lola for a moment. "It went so badly. I'd left you messages. I had no way of knowing you hadn't gotten them or the letter I sent."

"You were clear enough on the phone the last time

we talked," he said, wishing she would just say whatever it was she needed to say so he didn't have to keep standing there. He could tell that she was waiting for him to introduce her to Lola, but his heart was beating too hard. Julia and Wyatt had hurt him badly. Her and one of his friends? Equal amounts of anger and regret had him shaking inside.

But he didn't want to get into an argument here in the grocery store parking lot in front of Lola. He didn't want Julia to know just how much she and Wyatt had hurt him. And he feared that if he started in on her, he wouldn't be able to stop until all of his grief and rage and hurt came pouring out.

"I'm glad you're home." Julia looked from him to Lola again and forced a weak smile. "It was good to see you. If you change your mind about that cup of coffee…" She stood for a moment, looking awkward and unsure, something new for Julia, he thought. And he realized that she needed him to tell her it was okay, what she'd done. That he forgave her. That he wanted her and Wyatt to be happy. Julia was struggling with the guilt.

That alone should have made him feel better, he thought as she turned and left them standing there. Instead, he felt as if he'd been ambushed by a speeding freight train.

"I'm sorry," Lola said as she let go of his hand.

He couldn't speak so merely nodded as he took the cart to the rack and quickly returned to the pickup. Lola grabbed her potato chips out of the back and joined him in the cab. He'd expected her to be full of questions.

Instead, she buckled up, holding the bag of potato

chips as if she'd lost her appetite, and quietly let him process what had just happened. He was thankful to her for that. And for taking his hand back there.

"Thanks," he said, after he got the truck going and drove out of the parking lot.

"It was the first time you've seen her since…since the breakup." It wasn't a question, but he answered it anyway.

"I've managed to avoid her. Just my luck…" He shook his head.

"I can see how painful it is."

"I'm more angry than hurt."

Lola looked out the side window. "Betrayal is always painful." She hugged herself.

He glanced over at her, thinking what a strong, determined woman she was. Not the kind who would give up when things got a little tough.

"Julia turned out not to be the woman I thought she was," he said. "I'm better off without her."

Lola said nothing, no doubt sensing that no matter what he said, he wasn't completely over his former fiancée or what she had put him through.

It made him angry that his heart hadn't let go of the hurt. The anger he didn't mind living with for a while.

WHAT WOULD LOLA do now? That was the question Jonas knew he should be asking himself as he stepped back inside his warm, elegantly furnished cabin.

She must think him a complete fool. Her great escape. He let out a bark of a laugh. Did she really think she could have gotten away unless he'd let her? Sure, he'd had his men chase her with instructions to make sure that she got away.

He'd known she would run straight to the father of her baby. As if he hadn't known she was lying about not knowing who she'd lain with. He scoffed at the idea. Sister Rebecca had seen her with a man near the hotel bar that night. Unfortunately, Lola and the man had disappeared on the elevator too quickly.

But Rebecca had managed to get the information. Major Colt McCloud. An Army helicopter pilot. Jonas would ask what she could see in a man like that, but he wasn't that stupid. The man was good-looking, part cowboy, part flight jockey. He had just inherited a large ranch.

Not that Jonas had been certain Colt McCloud was the man who'd knocked Lola up. No, he hadn't known that until today when the man had shown up with Lola and the sheriff.

Lola was too bound up from her conservative upbringing to go to bed with just anyone. So she'd seen something beyond Colt McCloud's good looks. Jonas swore under his breath as he moved to the fireplace to throw on another log. Just the thought of the cowboy pilot made his blood boil. How dare the man come up here making demands.

Jonas thought he might have convinced Colt that Lola was unstable and not to be believed. She'd certainly played into his plan perfectly when she'd lost it in the laundry room. But he couldn't be sure about Colt. The man was probably smitten with Lola and would want to believe her.

At least the sheriff wouldn't be returning. He'd been sufficiently convinced. Law enforcement always backed off when it came to churches. Just like the government did. He smiled at the thought of how he'd been able to build The Society of Lasting Serenity without anyone looking over his shoulder.

Until now.

"You could return the baby," Sister Rebecca had dared to say to him before the dust had even settled earlier today. "You know she'll be back if you don't."

"Mind your place," he'd snapped. He'd seen how jealous the older woman was of Lola. He suspected she'd been mean to her, cutting her rations, possibly even being physically abusive to her. He hadn't stopped it, wanting Sister Rebecca's loyalty.

But now he wondered how much longer he might be able to count on Rebecca. Once Lola was back—and she would be back—Sister Rebecca might have to be taken down a notch or two. Then again, maybe it was time to retire her. Not that she would ever be allowed to leave. She knew too much.

Strange how a valuable asset could so quickly become a liability.

As soon as he had Lola… Yes, he would dispose of Sister Rebecca. It would be almost like a wedding gift for his new wife. Not that he would tell Lola what had really happened to the older woman. Let her believe he'd given Rebecca a golden parachute and sent her off to some island to bask in the sun for the rest of her days.

He stared into the flames as the log he'd added began to crackle and spark. If he was Colt McCloud, what would he do? Jonas smiled to himself, then picked up the phone. "We're going to need more guards tonight, especially around the cemetery."

AFTER RUNNING INTO JULIA, Colt had known it was just a matter of time before he and Wyatt crossed paths. He'd promised himself that when it happened, when he finally did see his traitorous, former good friend, he would keep his cool. He wasn't going to lose his temper. If Wyatt wanted Julia, a woman who would betray her fiancé while he was fighting a war oceans away, then she was all his.

He'd visualized seeing both of them, but even in his imagination, he hadn't known what he would do. He'd told himself that he would tell them both off, make them feel even more guilty, if possible, hurt them the way they had hurt him.

But look what had happened when he'd seen Julia. He'd been boiling inside, his heart pounding, anger and hurt a potent mixture. And he'd said none of what he'd planned. Instead, he hadn't wanted them to know how much they'd hurt him. Or even how angry he still was.

After seeing Julia, it made him wonder when it could happen with Wyatt. How would Wyatt react? He just hoped Lola wouldn't have to witness it again. Colt thought that Wyatt must be dreading the day when they would come face-to-face again as much as he was. Colt hoped he'd given Wyatt a few sleepless nights worrying about it. Because, in a town the size of Gilt Edge, a meeting had to happen.

But Colt was sorry that it had to happen at this moment as he stopped to get gas on the way out of town. Lola had gone inside the convenience mart to use the ladies' room.

As he stood filling the pickup with gas, Wyatt drove up, pulling to a pump two away from him.

Colt froze, his heart in this throat, as he watched Wyatt get out of his pickup and step to the fuel pump. He thought about staying where he was, pretending he never saw him. But that was way too cowardly. Anyway, he wanted to get this over with.

He finished fueling his truck and walked down the line of gas pumps. Wyatt looked up and saw him and seemed to freeze. They'd grown up together, hung out with many of the same friends since grade school. It was only after college that Colt, needing to do something more with his life, had enlisted in the Army helicopter program.

Wyatt had tried to talk him out of it. "Why do you need to go so far away? You're going to get yourself killed and for what?"

Colt hadn't been able to explain it to him. So he'd left to fly and fight while Wyatt had stayed on his family ranch and stolen Julia.

He took a step toward the man he'd thought he'd known better than himself. As he did, he wondered what he would come out of his mouth or if he would be able to speak. His pulse thundered in his ears as he advanced on his former friend.

"Colt." Wyatt was a big, strong cowboy. He put up both hands in surrender but held his ground. "Colt, whatever you're thinking—"

Colt hit him hard enough to drive him back a couple of steps. Wyatt banged into the side of his pickup.

"I don't want to fight you," Wyatt said as one large hand went to his bleeding nose.

"That's good," Colt said. "Since you'd probably take me." He knew that might be true since Wyatt had a few inches on him and a good twenty pounds, but as angry as he was, he'd fight like hell.

His hands were balled into fists, but he didn't hit him again. Wyatt's bleeding nose looked broken. Colt was reminded of the time Wyatt had taken on the school bully, a kid twice his size back then. His former friend was tough and had never backed down from a fight in all the time Colt had known him.

He took a step back, hating that he was remembering the years of their friendship. His eyes burned with tears, but damned if he was going to cry. Looking at Wyatt, he realized that losing Julia had hurt; losing someone he'd considered a close friend, though, had ripped out his heart.

He turned on his heel and walked back to his pickup before he made a complete fool of himself. His knuckles hurt, but nothing like his heart as he listened to Wyatt get into his truck and drive away.

LOLA HAD SEEN everything from the front window of the convenience store when she'd come back from the restroom. The "fight" had ended quickly enough.

She didn't have to ask who the man had been.

Wyatt Enderlin. When she'd asked Colt about him, he'd said they'd been friends. "It's a small town. We make friends for life here." She could imagine how much Wyatt's betrayal hurt Colt.

She pushed open the door and walked out to Colt's truck, climbing in without a word. Out of the corner of her eye, Lola saw him rub his skinned and swollen knuckles before he climbed behind the wheel.

It wasn't until they were in the pickup headed toward the ranch that Colt said, "You saw?"

She hesitated, forcing him to look over at her. "I wanted you to hit him again."

He smiled sadly at that. "I hadn't planned to even hit him once."

"Do you feel better or worse?"

Chuckling, he said, "Better and worse."

"Well, you got that out of the way."

"Right, I got to see them both on the same day. Lucky me." He drove in silence for a few minutes. "Wyatt and I were like brothers at one point growing up. I'd always wanted a brother..." He shook his head.

"He was your friend."

"*Was* being the key word here. My other friends like Darby Cahill never would have done that."

"Which hurts worse?" she finally asked.

Colt shot her a glance before turning back to his driving. "Wyatt."

"Maybe one day—"

"I don't think so. Being in the military you learn which men you can trust in battle. Those are the men you want watching your back. Wyatt, as it turned out, isn't one of them."

"I'm sorry." She let the words hang in the air for a moment. "Do you believe in fate?"

They were almost at the turnoff to the ranch. Ahead she could see the for-sale sign. They hadn't talked about it. She doubted they would because she already knew from the first time they'd met how Colt felt about flying the big birds in the military.

"Fate?" he asked, glancing at her for a moment before he slowed for the turn.

"Maybe it was fate that has brought us all to this point in our lives."

FATE? LOLA COULDN'T be serious. If his fate was having his fiancée hook up with his good friend behind his back, then he'd say he was one unlucky bastard. He said as much to Lola.

"I was thinking more about the way we met."

Instantly he hated having rained on her parade like that.

"If Julia hadn't broken up with you and had met you at the airport like she was supposed to, then you wouldn't have been in that hotel that night and I wouldn't have…"

Would some other man have saved her? Or taken advantage of a young woman who was obviously inexperienced and desperate? The thought made him sick to his stomach, but he wouldn't have known because he would never have laid eyes on Lola Dayton.

Nor would he be worrying about how to get their baby away from a madman at an armed and dangerous cult compound at the top of a mountain, he thought as he parked in front of the house at the ranch and shut off the engine.

But as he looked over at Lola, the anger he'd been feeling ebbed away. "You're right," he said, softening his tone as he reached over and squeezed her hand. "It definitely was fate that brought us together." Damn fickle fate, he thought, realizing with growing concern how much Lola was getting to him.

He put Julia, Wyatt and the past out of his mind and concentrated on what to do next. He knew what he was going to have to do. It went against his military training. A man didn't go in alone with no backup. Nor did he take matters into his own hands. He went through proper channels.

But there was no way the sheriff was going to be able to get a warrant to have whatever was buried on the church grounds exhumed—even if Colt could talk Flint into doing it. Jonas would fight it and drag out the process. Meanwhile, that madman had their baby. Baby Grace, the daughter he had yet to lay eyes on.

After helping put the groceries away, he went into the ranch office. The maps were in a file—right where his father had kept them. He found the one he needed and spread it out on the desk.

"We need proof that Jonas is lying," Lola said from the open doorway.

"Proof won't do us any good. We need to find Grace and get her out of there."

"But that grave. If you dig it up—"

Colt shuddered at the thought. "That's exactly what Jonas will expect me to do." He recalled a shortage of manpower on the compound. But a woman could be just as deadly with a gun, he reminded himself. "While they're busy guarding the cemetery, I'll find Grace."

"I'm going with you," she said, stepping into the small office.

He shook his head, hating how intimate it felt with her in here. "It's going to be hard enough for me to get onto the grounds—and away again—without being caught."

"Exactly. They will expect you and will have doubled the guards. You're going to need me."

He started to argue, but she cut him off. "I have lived there all this time. I know the weakest spots along the perimeter. I also know the guards. And, maybe more important, I know where to look for Grace."

Admittedly, she made a good argument. "Lola, if we are both caught, no one will know we're up there. If Jonas is as dangerous as you think he is, we'll end up in the cemetery."

"If one of us is caught, then the other can distract them while whoever has Grace gets away."

He hated that her argument made sense, more sense than him trying to find Grace on his own. "Can you draw a map of the place?"

She nodded.

"Good. We leave at midnight."

LOLA HADN'T DARED HOPE, but as she watched Colt studying the web of old logging roads around the mountain compound on the map, she let herself believe they could succeed. They would get in, find Grace and slip back out with her. Once she had Grace in her arms, no way would she let anyone rip her out again. Especially Jonas.

"I'll need paper and a pen," she said as she leaned over the desk. Their gazes met for a moment, his gaze deepening. She felt goose bumps ripple over her skin. Heat rushed to her center. Then he quickly looked away and began searching for what she needed.

She drew a map of the compound buildings, marking those that were used for housing. "I know you got a tour, but I thought this would help. As you can see there are two women's dorms, one for the women with babies. There is only the one men's dorm on the opposite side the main building."

"What's this?" Colt asked as he moved to her side to point at a large cabin away from the others and at the top of her diagram.

"Jonas's. He likes to look down on his followers."

"And this one at the bottom right?" His fingers brushed hers.

A shiver ran the length of her spine. She felt her nipples harden to pebbles under her top. "That's the storage room, shop and health center." Her voice cracked with emotion.

"And this one bottom left?" There was no doubt. He'd purposely brushed against her as he pointed to the only other structure. The bare skin of his arm was warm. His touch sent more shivers rippling through her. Her nipples ached inside her bra.

"Laundry." She turned enough to meet his eyes. What she saw made her molten inside. His gaze was dark with desire as his fingers trailed up her arm to brush against the side of her breast.

WHAT THE HELL are you doing? As if he could stop himself. He looked into Lola's beautiful violet gaze and knew he was lost. He wanted her. Needed her. Thought he would die if he didn't have her right now. This had been building inside him all day, he realized. Maybe since the first time he'd met her.

"Colt?" she breathed, and shuddered as his fingers brushed over the hard tip of her nipple. She moaned softly, her head going back to expose her slim silken neck.

He bent to kiss her throat, nipping at the pale skin, and felt her shiver before trailing kisses down into the hollow between her breasts. "Yes, Lola?" he asked, his muffled voice as filled with emotion as hers had been.

When she didn't answer, he raised his head to look into her eyes. He held her gaze, seeing the answer in all that lovely blue.

Cupping her other breast, he backed her up against the office wall and dropped his mouth to hers. Her lips parted and he took the invitation to let his tongue explore her as his free hand found the waistband of her jeans and slipped inside.

She let out a gasp as he found the sweet cleft between her legs. "Colt." This time it was a plea. She was wet. He began to stroke her, drawing back to look into her eyes. Her head was back and her mouth open. Tiny sounds escaped her lips as he slowly stroked, until he could feel her quiver against his fingers and finally cry out.

Withdrawing his hand, he swung her up into his arms and strode to his bedroom. He didn't want to think about later tonight when they would go up the mountain. Nor did he want to think about the future or even why he was doing this right now.

All he knew was that he wanted her more than his next breath. The only thing on his mind was making love to this woman who had captivated him from the first time he'd laid eyes on her.

Chapter Nine

Just before midnight, Lola and Colt loaded into his
pickup and headed toward the SLS encampment. Colt
had programmed his phone with the latest GPS information and had mapped out their best route up the mountain.

They'd both dressed in dark clothing. Lola had borrowed one of his black T-shirts. Her blond hair was
pulled up under one of his black caps.

Earlier, after making love several times, they'd showered together, then sat down again with the map. His
plan was to approach this like a battle.

Lola had showed him on her diagram what she
thought was the best way in—and out again. The layout
of the compound was star shaped, with the large main
building at its center. It was where everyone ate, met for
church and meetings, and where Jonas had his office.

From it, the other buildings formed the points of a
star. At the top was Jonas's cabin, on the left center
were the women's two dorms and on the right, the men's
dorm. At the bottom was the laundry to the left and the
health center, shop and storage building to the right.

"Once we grab Grace, someone will sound the alarm. Everyone will get a weapon and go to the edge of the property."

"The SLS is sounding less and less like a church by the moment," Colt had said.

"If the intruder or escapee is caught, a second signal will sound announcing the all clear," she'd said.

Colt had studied her for a moment. He couldn't help thinking of her earlier, naked in his arms. He wondered if he could ever get enough of this woman. "You're sure about this?"

She'd smiled, nodding. She really did have an amazing smile. "Whichever one of us has Grace gets out if the alarm goes off. Whoever doesn't have her distracts the guards to give them a chance to escape."

"Who will have Grace?" he'd asked.

"I guess it will depend on who finds her first. Once we approach the housing part, someone is bound to see us."

Colt would have preferred a more comprehensive plan. "You must have some idea where they are keeping Grace."

"Normally, she would be in the second women's dorm where the other babies are kept," she'd said. "But Jonas will know that I haven't given up. He might have ordered that Grace be kept in the other women's dorm."

"Where were they keeping you before you escaped?"

She'd drawn in a tiny box. "That's the cabin. It serves as the jail."

"And you could hear Grace crying when they came to pump your breast milk?" She'd nodded. "You're thinking they had our baby in this dorm, the farthest one to the west and closest to the cabin where you were being kept. I'll take that one, then head east to the second women's dorm if I don't see you. They won't expect us to come in from different directions."

"We'll meet up there. Or if the alarm goes off, just try to meet back at the pickup"

Now, as the road climbed up the mountain, he looked over at Lola. She appeared calm. Her expression was one of determination. She was going after her baby. *Their* baby. Her last thought was her own safety.

His heart ached at the thought of their lovemaking. He couldn't let anything happen to this woman. Grace needed her. He needed her, he thought and pushed the thought away. What he needed was to get himself, Lola and their baby out of that compound alive tonight. Later he'd think about what he needed, what he wanted, what the hell he was going to do once Lola and Grace were safe.

The night was thankfully dark. Low clouds hunkered just over the tops of the tall ebony pines. No stars, let alone the moon, shone through. Colt thought they couldn't have picked a better night.

Still, he was anxious. So much was riding on this and he felt they were going in blind. What he did know had him both worried and scared. If Jonas or any of his followers caught them...

He couldn't let himself go down that trail of thought. If they wanted to get Grace out of there, they had no choice but to sneak in like thieves, find her and take her. Isn't that what Jonas had done?

LOLA HAD BEEN lost in thought when Colt pulled the pickup over, cut the engine and doused the lights. She'd been thinking about the ocean and the time she'd almost drowned.

Her father had saved her, plucking her from the depths and carrying her to the beach. She remembered lying on the warm sand staring up at the sky and gasping for breath as her father wept in relief over her.

She had no idea why that particular memory had surfaced now. Anything to keep her mind off what was about to happen once they reached the compound. She'd learned to let her mind wander during Jonas's attempts to brainwash her. She would think of anything but what was happening—just like now.

With the headlights off, they were pitched into blackness. She listened to the tick, tick, tick of the cooling engine, her heart a hammer in her chest.

"You ready?" he asked, his voice low and soft.

She nodded and locked gazes with him. Colt looked as if there was something he wanted to say. She'd seen that same look earlier after they'd made love.

Earlier, she'd put a finger to his lips. She hadn't wanted him to say the words that he thought he needed to say. Colt was an honorable man, but she couldn't let him say things that he'd later regret. Nor had she been able to bear the thought of him pouring his soul out to her at that moment. Just as now.

There was too much riding on what they were about to do. Emotions were high and had been since she'd appeared at his door in the middle of the night. There was no need to say anything then or now, though she understood his need. She too wanted to open her heart to him because both of them knew how dangerous this mission was. Neither of them might get out of this alive.

Just as he started to speak, she opened her door and stepped into the darkness. She gulped the cold spring-night air and fought her fear for Colt and their daughter, a gut-wrenching fear that made her eyes burn with tears.

COLT SAT FOR a moment alone in the cab of the dark pickup. What had he been about to say? He shook his head. Lola had cut him off—just as she had earlier.

He sighed, wondering at this woman.

Then he got out, and the two of them headed through the dark pines for the hike to the compound.

They moved as silently as they could once their eyes adjusted to the darkness under the towering pines. A breeze stirred the boughs high above them, making the pines sigh.

Colt led the way until they were almost to the SLS property. The whole time, he'd been acutely aware of Lola behind him.

Now he stopped and motioned her forward. They stood inches apart for a long moment, listening.

Lola had suggested entering the property on the opposite side of the cemetery and the farthest away from any main road up to the mountaintop.

The main road was gated, so Jonas wouldn't be expecting them to come that way. That was also the most visible, so they'd opted for this approach.

But now it was time to separate. Colt could feel the tension in the air, as well as the tension between them.

Lola had made it clear that she didn't want any words of undying love. But, after everything they'd shared, he felt the need to say something, do something.

He drew her close, looked into her violet eyes and kissed her.

"What was that?" she demanded in a whisper. "It felt like a goodbye kiss."

He shook his head and leaned close to whisper, "A promise to see you soon." As he drew back, he saw her smile. "Good luck," he whispered, and turned and headed in the opposite direction, his heart in his throat. If things didn't go well, he didn't want his last memory to be of her standing in the darkness, looking up at him with those big blue eyes and him not doing a damned thing.

Now he thought of her slightly gap-toothed smile and held it close to his heart for luck. Ahead he saw the no-trespassing sign and knew a guard wasn't far away.

LOLA TOUCHED HER TONGUE to her lower lip as she made her way through the pines. Just the thought of Colt's kiss made her heart beat a little faster. If she'd been falling for him before that moment, well, she'd just fallen a little further. She warned herself that this wasn't any way to go into a relationship.

Her mother would have called it "going in the back door." Maxine would not have approved of Lola having a baby out of wedlock when she could have married Jonas and given Grace a father.

But Grace did have a father. A fine father. Lola just didn't see them becoming a family. She shook the thought from her head and tried to concentrate. Getting Grace back, that was all that mattered.

She hadn't gone far when she saw a faint light bobbing through the trees ahead of her.

Ducking down, she watched as Elmer made his way along the edge of the property. She waited until he was well past her before she rose and sneaked onto the compound. The only lights were the ones outside the buildings that illuminated parts of the grounds.

Lola edged along the pines until she reached the edge of the men's dorm. Only one light shone at the front. She moved cautiously along the back, keeping to the dark shadows next to the building and being careful not to step on anything that might make a sound.

She had no desire to wake anyone, though she thought the men's dorm was probably fairly empty. All of the men would be on guard duty tonight and maybe even some of the women.

Elmer would be turning back soon on his guard circuit. If she hurried, she should be able to reach the closest women's dorm and slip inside the nursery before he started back this way.

Before the first time she'd escaped, she'd had the run of the place, including the one women's dorm, where she'd stayed with the sisters. She'd even helped with the babies a few times. Because of that, she knew where to find the main nursery.

"If I find her first, how will I know her?" Colt had asked.

She'd smiled and said, "You'll know her and she'll know you."

"No, seriously."

"There were two babies born in the past six months that I know of. The boy we saw in the laundry and Grace."

At the end of the men's dorm, Lola stopped to listen. She heard nothing on the breeze. The distance between her and the women's dorms was a good dozen yards— all of them in the glow of the men's dorm light.

She looked for any movement in the darkness beyond. Seeing none, she sprinted the distance and dropped back into the shadows. Her heart pounded as she waited to see if she'd been spotted by one of the guards. The only one she'd seen was Elmer, but she knew there were others stationed around the compound, more than usual, just as she'd told Colt.

As she caught her breath, she thought of Colt and wondered where he was. Saying a silent prayer for his safety, she crept along the edge of the building to the door to the main nursery and grasping the knob, turned it.

COLT RECOGNIZED THE guard as one he'd seen here yesterday. The man looked tired and bored as he moved along the edge of the property and fiddled with the handgun holstered at his hip.

The guard had only gone a few feet when he stepped into the shadows and suddenly drew his weapon like an Old West gunfighter. He took the stance for a moment, pointing the gun into the darkness ahead of him and then holstered his weapon again as he moved on to practice his fast draw a few yards later.

Colt had been startled for a moment when the guard

had suddenly drawn his weapon. He'd been more than a little relieved to see that the man's gun was pointing only at some imaginary person in the dark.

He slipped behind the man, closing the distance from the dense pines to the edge of the closest women's dorm. Stopping to listen, he heard a sound that froze him in place.

A low growl followed by another. This part of the country had its share of bear from black bear to grizzly. But the low growling sound he'd just heard wasn't coming from the darkness, he realized. Instead, it floated out of the open window on the back side of the women's dorm. Someone was snoring loudly.

It gave him good cover as he moved cautiously along the dark side of the building. Only a dim light shone inside. Staying as far back as possible, he peered in. The large room was filled with bunk beds like a military barrack. He recognized the woman in the closest lower bunk. Sister Alexa, a woman Colt had met in passing the day Jonas gave him the tour.

She let out a snort and stirred. He saw her eyes flicker and he froze. She blinked for a moment before her eyes fluttered shut and her snoring resumed.

Colt ducked away from the window and made his way down to the end that Lola said could house a second nursery. The outside light high over the front door of the main building cast a circle of golden light.

He watched from the dark shadows at the edge of the light. He'd only seen two guards so far, one on the way in and another crossing the complex, before he'd made his way to the far end of the building where he would find the nursery.

From where he stood, he could see toward the cemetery where Lola's parents were buried. He wondered about the small mound of fresh dirt next to them. Was something buried under there?

Jonas seemed like a man who didn't take chances. At the very least, he would have buried a small wooden casket. Colt remembered seeing the shop on his tour of the complex. Followers made wooden crosses in the shop that they sold when they went into town to raise money for the poor, Lola had told him. She said she doubted the poor ever saw a dime of it.

"I think it's Jonas's way of keeping them busy and making a little extra cash. The crosses are crude, but I think people feel sorry for the followers and give them money."

He thought now about the small casket he'd seen in one corner of the shop during his tour and swallowed hard. What if Jonas had filled the casket under that mound of dirt since their visit?

The thought made his stomach roil. He pressed his back against the side of the women's dorm and waited for the guard he'd seen earlier to cross again.

From inside the women's dorm, he heard a baby begin to cry. His heart lodged in his throat. Grace?

LOLA TURNED THE knob slowly. The door creaked open an inch, then another. A small night-light shone from one corner of the room, illuminating four small cribs. In one of the cribs, a baby whimpered.

She looked toward the doorway into the sleeping room with its bunk beds. She could hear someone snoring softly, heard the rustle of covers and then silence.

Her heart pounded as she slipped through the door and into the nursery. The first two cribs were empty. She moved to the third one. The baby in it was small. A newborn. Sister Caroline's baby, she realized. Caroline had been due when Lola had run away from the compound that night.

She stepped to the last crib, looked down at the sleeping baby and felt her heart begin to pound.

COLT STOOD AGAINST the wall in the darkness outside the nursery. Inside, he heard the sound of footfalls as someone awakened in the dorm and headed for the nursery.

A few moments later, he heard a woman talking soothingly. The baby quit crying. He could hear the woman humming a tune to the child, but he didn't recognize the song.

Then again, he knew no children's songs. He tried to imagine himself getting up in the middle of the night to calm his crying infant and couldn't. It was so far from what he'd been doing for the last eleven years.

What kind of father would he make when he didn't even know a song he could sing a child? Or could even imagine himself doing something like that? In all his years he'd never held a baby. He'd be afraid he would drop it with his big clumsy hands.

He could see the woman's shadow as she'd come into the room and now watched her swaying with the infant in her arms, singing softly, willing the baby back to sleep. Was the baby Grace?

He waited, staying to the dark shadow of the building as, in the distance, he saw the guard come back from making his rounds. The man was headed for the men's dorm. Change of shift? He hadn't anticipated that and realized he should have.

Where he was standing, the man would have to pass right by him. Colt had no chance of going undetected. Nor could he move away from the building without being seen.

Inside the nursery, he saw the shadow of the woman move. The singing continued as she seemed to lay the infant back into its crib. The man was getting closer now. His head was down. He looked tired, bored, ready to call it a night.

Where was his replacement? For all Colt knew, there could be another guard headed from the opposite direction.

He realized the music had stopped inside the nursery. Reaching over, he tried the door. The knob turned in his hand.

He had no choice. He could stay where he was and be seen by the guard, or he could chance slipping into the nursery and coming face-to-face with the woman tending the baby.

He slipped into the nursery to find it empty except for four cribs lined up against one wall. As the door closed behind him, he heard voices outside. Two men. And then silence.

Colt waited a few more seconds before he approached the cribs and saw that all but one of the cribs was empty.

He moved quietly to the crib being used and looked down at the sleeping baby. The infant lay on its back, eyes closed. He carefully reached in and pulled up the homemade shift the baby wore.

FOR A MOMENT, Lola couldn't move or breathe. Her heart swelled to bursting as she looked down at the precious sleeping baby. She would have recognized her baby anywhere, but still, with trembling fingers, she lifted the hem of the infant's gown.

There on Grace's chubby little left thigh was the tiny heart-shaped birthmark. A sob rose in her throat. She desperately wanted to lift her daughter from the crib. For so long she'd yearned to hold her baby in her arms.

She tried to get control of her emotions, knowing that once she picked up Grace, she would have to move fast. With luck, Grace wouldn't cry. But being startled out of sleep she might, and it would set off an alarm that would awaken the women in the dorm, if not the whole complex.

Lola wiped at the warm tears on her cheeks as she stared at her daughter. Grace was beautiful, from her tiny bow-shaped mouth to her chubby cheeks. As if sensing her standing over the crib, Grace's eyes fluttered and she kicked with both legs.

Lola grabbed two of the baby blankets stacked next to the cribs. Reaching down, she hurriedly lifted her daughter. Grace started, her eyes coming wide-open in alarm.

Quickly wrapping her infant in the blankets, Lola turned toward the door and felt a hand drop to her shoulder.

Chapter Ten

Lola had been in midstep when the hand dropped to her shoulder. The fingers tightened, forcing her to stop. She turned, terrified of who she would find standing behind her.

Sister Amelia put a finger to her lips before Lola could speak. Their gazes locked for what seemed an eternity. Neither looked away until Grace stirred in Lola's arms.

"Go," Amelia whispered, and pushed her toward the door. From back in the dorm came the sound of footfalls. "Go!"

Lola stumbled out the door, Grace wrapped in a blanket and clutched to her chest. Behind her, she heard Sister Amelia say something to the woman who'd awakened. Then the door closed behind her and she was standing out in the dark of the building.

Run! The thought rippled through her, igniting her fight-or-flight impulse. She had Grace. If she could get her off the compound...

From the dark, she heard a sound. A whisper of movement. A dark shadow emerged and she saw it was one of the guards. She recognized him by the arrogant way he moved. Brother Zack. She'd seen the way the former military man looked at her when he thought no one was watching. She'd heard that he'd been drummed out of the service but could only guess for what. He'd struck fear in her the nights when she knew he was the guard working outside the cabin where she was being held.

If Sister Rebecca hadn't been in charge of her "re-habilitation" and had sisters coming every hour or so to chant over her, Lola feared what Brother Zack might have done.

Now she watched him move through the darkness, her heart in her throat. Had he seen her? He appeared to be headed right for her. From inside the baby blankets, Grace whimpered.

COLT CHECKED THE BABY. No heart-shaped birthmark on either chubby leg. The moment he lifted the thin gown, the baby began to kick. Its eyes came open. Colt froze, afraid to breathe. The baby's gaze became more unfocused. Its eyes slowly closed.

He took a breath and let it out slowly. Grace wasn't here. He stepped toward the door. The floor creaked under his boot. He froze again, listening. With a glance over his shoulder, he stepped to the door, pushed it open a few inches and slipped outside.

The dark night felt like a shroud over the complex. Only circles of golden light from the outside lamps illuminated a few spots around the complex. He waited for his eyes to adjust, keeping himself tucked back against the shadow of the building. Nothing seemed to move but the pine boughs in the breeze.

Off in the distance, an owl hooted, then the night fell silent again. He had no idea how long he'd been inside the nursery or where the guards might be now.

On the way in, he'd thought they'd been changing shifts. That meant the new ones might be more alert, having just started. He thought of Lola. She'd gone to the other women's dorm. Had she found Grace?

His fear was that Jonas would want the baby closer to him, knowing Lola wouldn't give up. But wouldn't he want one of the sisters watching over her? Jonas didn't seem like a hands-on father figure. Colt wondered if he, himself, was. He could only hope that Lola had already found Grace.

He looked around, but saw no one. It appeared that most of the guards were out by the cemetery. Jonas had thought Lola would try to get evidence to take to the sheriff. He had thought no one believed her—not even Colt. Maybe especially Colt.

He spotted one of the guards moving slowly through the pines out on the perimeter. He wanted desperately to go look for Lola, but they'd agreed that the best plan would be for them to meet at the pickup. That way if one of them was caught, the other could go for help rather than walk into a trap that would snare them both.

As soon as the guard was out of sight, Colt crossed between the buildings and worked his way along the dark side of the second women's dorm.

He reached the end of the building and looked to the

expanse of open land he would have to cross to reach the dark safety of the pines.

As he started to take a step, he heard a sound behind him and spun around to come face-to-face with Lola. One glance at her expression told him that the bundle in her arms was Grace.

She took a step toward him, smiling, tears in her eyes, and suddenly the night came alive with the shrill scream of an alarm.

LOLA FELT GRACE start at the horrible sound. From inside the blankets, the baby began to cry. Lola tore the blankets from the crying baby and thrust Grace's wriggling small body at Colt. "Take her and go!" she cried. "Go! I'll distract them." She could see that he wanted to argue. "Please."

He grabbed the now-screaming baby and, turning toward the pines, ran.

Lola felt a fist close on her heart as she looked down at the empty blanket in her hand. She didn't have time for regrets. She'd gotten to see her daughter, hold her for a few priceless minutes, but now she had to move, and she knew the best way to make the alarm stop.

Grabbing up several large stones lying along the side of the building's foundation, she quickly wrapped them in the baby blankets, then hugged the bundle against her chest. It wouldn't fool anyone who got too close, but it might work long enough to get her where she needed to go.

Turning, she hurried back toward the center of the

compound. She desperately needed to distract the guards and give Colt a chance to escape with Grace.

SLS members poured out of the dorms in their nightwear. She half ran toward Jonas's cabin, screaming at the top of her lungs. Guards came running from all directions.

Zack saw her and charged her. He would have taken her down, but Jonas had come out of his cabin. Seeing what was happening, he shut off the alarm with his cell phone.

"Leave her alone, Brother Zack!" he yelled down. "Don't hurt the baby."

Zack stopped just inches from her. She could see his disappointment. He hadn't cared if he hurt the baby. He had been looking forward to getting his hands on her.

"Bring her to me," Jonas ordered.

Zack reached for her, but she jerked back her arm. One of the rocks shifted and she had to grip her bundle harder.

"Never mind, Brother Zack," Jonas called down. "Lola, I know you don't want to hurt the baby. Come up to my cabin. I promise I won't hurt you or the child."

As if she believed a word out of his mouth. But she walked slowly up the hill, holding the bundle of rocks protectively against her breast.

She listened to make sure that none of the guards had stumbled across Colt and Grace. But there'd been no more activity at the edge of the complex, no shouts, no gunshots. Jonas had sounded the all clear siren. His followers were slowly wandering back to either their beds or their guard duty.

Before she reached the steps to the cabin, Jonas told Zack to leave only a few guards on duty. The rest, he said, could go to bed for what was left of the night.

Clearly he thought that the danger was over and that Lola had acted alone.

She stopped at the bottom of the porch steps and looked up at Jonas. He had a self-satisfied look on his face. He thought he'd won. He thought he had her and he had Grace.

"How did you get here?" Jonas asked suddenly, looking past her.

"I stole his pickup."

"Colt McCloud's? I thought he was your hero?" he mocked.

"Some hero," she said. "But that doesn't surprise you, does it? You knew he'd believe you and not me."

Jonas almost looked sorry for her. "The man's a fool."

She hugged the bundle tighter.

"You should come in. It's cold out here," he said. "Is the baby all right?"

She knew he had to be wondering how Grace had been able to sleep through all of the racket. He had to be getting suspicious.

"She is so sweet," Lola said, glancing down for a moment to peel back of the edge of the blanket so only she could see what was inside. She smiled down at the rock. "She really is an angel." She wanted to give Colt as much time as possible to get away with Grace, but she knew she couldn't keep standing out here or Jonas was going to become suspicious.

"As I've said all along," he agreed as she mounted the steps. He reached for the baby, but she turned to the side, holding the bundle away from him.

"Please, let me hold her just a little longer." Tears filled her eyes at just the thought of the few minutes she'd had Grace in her arms and the thought that they might be all she was going to get.

Jonas relented. "Of course, hold her all you want. There is no reason you should be separated from your child. If you stay here, you will have her all the time. Imagine what your life could be like here with me."

"I have." She hoped she kept the sarcasm out of the voice as she moved to the middle of the room, giving herself a little elbow room.

"We could travel. Europe, the Caribbean, anywhere your heart desired. We could take Angel with us."

"Her name is Grace."

He ignored that as he started to close the door. He froze and cocked his head, taking in the bundle in her arms again. "It really is amazing she slept through all of that noise," he said again.

"She knows she's with her mother now. She knows she's safe."

Jonas looked out the still-open doorway as if suddenly not so sure about being alone with her. She saw Zack watching them.

Lola knew she had no choice. Zack was watching, expecting trouble, and Jonas was getting suspicious. She had no choice.

"Europe? I love Europe," she said, and saw Jonas relax a little. He waved Zack away and closed the door.

She looked around, remembering the last time she'd been brought here. Jonas had told her that he would make her his wife—one way or another. He'd tried to kiss her and she'd kicked him hard enough in the shin to get away and, apparently, given him a permanent limp.

Behind her, she heard him lock the door and limp toward her.

Chapter Eleven

Colt reached the pickup. All the way, he'd hoped that he would find Lola waiting for him even though he knew there was little chance of that.

Still, he was disappointed when he got there to find he was alone. Grace had quit crying not long after they'd left the compound. He was grateful for that since he was sure it had helped him get away.

He opened the passenger-side door, the dome light coming on as he laid the bundle Lola had given him on the seat to get his first look at his daughter.

A pair of big blue eyes stared up at him. He lost his heart in that moment. He touched the perfect little cheek, soft as downy feathers. She did resemble Lola, but he thought he could see himself a little in her, too.

"Hi, Grace," he whispered, his voice breaking. Tears welled in his eyes. He swallowed the lump in this throat. He had the baby, but what now?

He turned off the dome light, realizing that if someone had followed him, they would be able to see him through the pines. He stared into the darkness, willing Lola to appear.

He had to assume that Jonas had her by now. He'd heard the alarm go off and then another signal, which he'd assumed must be the all clear. Why would Jonas sound it unless he'd thought there was nothing more to fear?

Which meant he had Lola. She'd sacrificed herself to save her daughter. Their daughter.

He looked toward the dark trees, silently pleading for that not to be the case. He needed her. Grace needed her.

They had Lola. He couldn't leave without her. But he couldn't go back for her with the baby for fear of getting caught.

Nor could he stay there much longer. If Jonas suspected she hadn't come alone...

"What are we going to do, Grace?" he asked as he wrapped her in his coat and watched her fall back to sleep.

WITH HER BACK to Jonas, Lola reached into the baby blanket with her free hand and slowly turned to face him.

"What really happened to my parents?"

He had been moving toward her but stopped. "They were getting old, confused toward the end. Your mother came down with the flu. It turned into pneumonia. Your father stayed by her side. She was getting better and then she just...died."

She nodded, knowing that it happened at her mother's age, and not believing a word of it. "And my father?"

"I think he died of grief. You had to know how he

was with your mother. I don't think he could live without her."

That too happened with people her parents' age who had been married as long as they had. "You didn't have them killed?" She said it softly so he wouldn't think it was an accusation. It wasn't like she expected the truth.

"Lola." There was that disappointing sound in his voice again. He took a step toward her. "Why must you always think the worst of me? Your parents believed in me."

Well, at least her mother had—until he'd had her killed, Lola thought. She wondered if he'd done it himself and realized how silly that was. Of course, he hadn't. Her heart went out to her parents. She couldn't bear thinking about their last moments.

"I took care of your baby for you. I wouldn't hurt a hair on that sweet thing's head. Or on yours. Let me see her." He was close now, and she feared he would make a grab for the baby.

She loosened her hold on the baby blanket bundle a little and faced him, her hand closing tightly around the rock inside.

"Thank you for taking care of her," she said, letting her voice fill with emotion.

"I will take care of you, too—if you give me a chance." He was getting too near—within reaching distance.

She took a step toward him, closing the distance between them as she pretended to hold out the baby for him to take. She had to be close. She had to make it count. It was her only hope of getting out of here and being with Grace.

As Jonas opened his arms for the baby, she pulled out the rock and swung it at his head. He managed to deflect the blow partially with his hand—just enough to knock the rock from her hold.

But she'd swung hard enough that the rock kept going. It caught him in the temple. He stumbled back. She pulled out the second rock, dropping the baby blankets, as she swung again.

This time, he didn't get a chance to raise an arm. The rock connected with the side of his head. His blood splattered on the rock, on her hand. He stood for a moment, looking stunned, then he went down hard on the wood floor.

Lola didn't waste any time. For all she knew he could be out cold—or only momentarily stunned and soon sounding the alarm so the whole cult would be on her heels.

She ran just as she had before. Only this time, she wasn't leaving her baby behind.

COLT HAD NEVER had trouble making a decision under duress. He'd been forced to make quick ones flying a chopper in Afghanistan. But one thing he'd never done was leave a man behind.

He couldn't this time, either. He'd purposely not taken a weapon into the compound earlier. They'd needed to get Grace out clean, and that meant not killing anyone—even if it meant getting themselves killed.

Now he took the weapons he would need. He was changing the rules—just as he was sure Jonas was. Wrapped in his coat, he laid Grace down on the floorboard of the pickup. She would be plenty warm enough—as long as he came back in a reasonable amount of time.

Locking the pickup door, he turned back toward the woods and the SLS compound. He wasn't leaving without Lola. And this time, he was armed and ready to fight his way in and out of the place if he had to.

LOLA FELT A sense of déjà vu as she ran through the woods. Her pulse hammered in her ears, her breath coming out in gasps. And yet she listened for the sound of the alarm that would alert the SLS members to fill the woods. Jonas would not let her get away if he had to run her to ground himself.

If he was able.

She had no idea how badly he'd been hurt. Or if he was already hot on her heels.

She crashed through the darkness, shoving away pine boughs that whipped her face and body. Colt had said how important it was for them get in and out of the compound without causing any more harm than was necessary.

"We're the trespassers," he'd told her. "We're the ones who will get thrown in jail if we fail tonight. We need to get in there and out as clean as possible."

She thought about the blood on the rock and could see something staining her right hand as she ran. Jonas's blood. She hadn't gotten out clean. She might have killed him. A cry escaped her lips as her ankle turned under her and she fell hard.

She struggled to get up as she hurriedly wiped the

blood on the dried pine needles she'd fallen into. But the moment she put pressure on her ankle, she knew she wasn't going far. She didn't think it was broken, but she also couldn't put any weight on it without excruciating pain.

Grace. Colt. She had to get to them. They would have left by now, but she couldn't stay here. She couldn't let Jonas or one of his sheep find her. If Jonas was still alive. The thought that she might have killed him made her shudder. It had been one thing to wish him dead, to think she could kill him to save her daughter, but to actually know that she might have killed the man...

She crawled over to a pine tree and used the trunk to get to her feet. As she started to take a step, she saw a figure suddenly appear out of the blackness of the trees.

Lola felt a sob rise in her throat. She'd never been so glad to see anyone in her life. Colt. He seemed just as overwhelmed with joy to see her. She'd thought he would have left—as per their plan. But he couldn't leave her.

Another sob rose as he ran to her, grabbed her and pulled her to him, holding her so tightly she could hardly breath. "Lola," he kept saying against her hair. "Lola."

She couldn't speak. Her throat had closed as she fought to hold back the tears of relief. As he let go, she stepped down on her bad ankle and let out a cry of pain.

"You're hurt. What is it?" he asked, his voice filled with concern.

"My ankle. I'm not sure I can walk."

He swung her up in his arms and carried her through

the trees to the truck. She hadn't realized how close she was to where they'd parked it earlier.

She looked around, suddenly scared. "Grace? Where's Grace?"

He unlocked the passenger side of the pickup, opened the door and picked up a bundle wrapped in his coat. She heard a sound come from within the bundle as Colt helped her into the pickup and put Grace into her arms. The tears came now, a floodgate opening. No longer could she hold back.

Tears streaming down her face, she turned back the edge of Colt's coat, which was wrapped around the infant. "Grace," she said as Colt slid behind the wheel, started the truck and headed off the mountain.

Lola held her baby, watching her daughter's sweet face in the faint light as Grace fell back asleep. She thought she could stare into that face forever. For so long she'd feared she'd never see her again, never hold her. She wiped at her tears and looked over at Colt. He smiled and she could see the emotion in his face.

"Have you met your daughter?" she asked.

"I have," he said, his voice sounding rough. "We got acquainted while we were waiting for you, until I couldn't wait any longer and had to come looking for you."

"I'm so thankful you did."

"Let's go home," he said, his voice breaking.

Tears filled her eyes again as she looked from him to their daughter. She pulled Grace close as they left the mountain and headed toward the ranch. Home.

Chapter Twelve

Jonas came to, lying on his back in a pool of his own blood. His hand went to the side of his head and came away sticky. He stared for a few moments at his fingers, the tips bright red, before he tried to sit up.

His head swam, forcing him to remain where he was. He couldn't remember what had happened. Had he fallen? He'd been meaning to have one of the brothers fix that rug to keep the corner from turning up.

But from where he lay, he could see that the rug wasn't to blame. Not twelve inches from him sat a rock the size of a cantaloupe. A dark stain covered one side of it. Nearby was a baby blanket and another rock of similar size.

Memory flooded him along with a cold, deadly rage. The pain in his skull was nothing compared to the open wound of Lola's betrayal. His heart felt as if it had been ripped out of his chest.

He thought of those moments when she'd been holding what he thought was her infant in her arms. They'd been talking and she had made it sound as if she was weakening toward him. His heart had soared with hope that she was finally coming around. He had so much to offer her. Had she finally realized that she'd be a fool to turn him down?

He'd been so happy for those moments when he'd thought things were going to work out with her and even the baby. That other man's baby, but a baby Jonas was willing to raise as his own as long as Lola became his wife and submitted to him.

The shock when she'd pulled the rock from the baby blankets was still painfully fresh. It had taken him a moment, his arms outstretched as he'd reached to take her and the infant to his bosom. The shock, the disappointment, the disbelief had slowed his movements, letting the rock get past his defenses and stun him just long enough that she was able to pull out the second rock and hit him much harder.

He closed his eyes now. He was in so much pain, but a thought wriggled its way through. His eyelids flew open. His mind felt perfectly clear, making him aware of the quiet. He recalled the alert alarm going off. When Lola had come to him with the baby... Yes, he recalled. He'd sounded the all clear signal.

Why hadn't there been another alert? He had to assume that Lola had gotten away. Gotten away with the baby. If she'd been caught, she would have been brought to him by now. And if Sister Rebecca had checked the crib and found the baby missing...

For a moment, he thought the alarm must have sounded while he'd been unconscious. But if that was true, then Brother Zack would have come to check on him and found him lying here, bleeding to death.

Two things suddenly became crystal clear. Even through the excruciating pain, he saw now that Lola couldn't have acted alone. She would have had help to get the baby off the compound. And her showing up at his door with what he thought was the baby was only a diversion.

He let out a bitter laugh. As persuasive as he'd been, it was just as he'd feared. He hadn't convinced Colt McCloud that the woman was unbalanced, that their baby boy had died, that he should leave Lola while he could.

Apparently, she'd been more convincing than he had been. He grimaced at the thought. Admittedly, he had to give her credit—her plan had worked. Or had it been Colt McCloud's plan? He closed his eyes, cursing the man to hell. Colt was a dead man.

But so was he, he realized, if he didn't get help. He was still bleeding and even more light-headed. He felt around for his cell phone to activate the alarm.

He had to turn his head to find it. The pain was so intense that he almost passed out. He closed his hand around the phone and, leaving bloody fingerprints, hit the button to activate the alarm.

His hand holding the phone dropped to his side as the air filled with the shrill cry of the alert. Any moment Brother Zack would come bursting through the door. He could always depend on Zack.

Unlike someone else, he thought, remembering his second realization. If he was right, Colt had taken the baby while Lola had pretended to be acting alone. The alarm had sounded and she had known that she couldn't get away. So she'd come up to Jonas's cabin with the rocks in the baby blankets.

But wouldn't someone have checked the baby's crib? And then wouldn't Sister Rebecca, who was responsible for the infant, have realized the baby was gone and summoned help? Pulled the alarm again?

As Brother Zack burst through the front door and rushed to him, Jonas felt the steel blade of betrayal cut even deeper. One of his flock had betrayed him.

Chapter Thirteen

Colt woke to find Lola and the baby sleeping peacefully next to him. He felt his heart do a bump in his chest. The sight filled him with a sense of joy. A sense that all was right in the world.

Last night on the way down the mountain he'd felt like they were a family. It was a strange feeling for a man who'd been so independent for so long. They'd been exhausted, Lola barely able to walk on her ankle. He'd gotten them both inside the house and safe as quickly as he could.

With Grace sleeping in the middle of his big bed, he'd taken a look at Lola's ankle. Not broken, but definitely sprained badly. He'd wrapped it, both of them simply looking at each other and smiling. They'd done it. They'd gotten Grace back.

He had questions, but they could wait. Or maybe he never had to know what had happened back at the compound. He told himself it was over. They had Grace. That was all the proof they needed against Jonas should he try to take either the baby or Lola back.

They'd gone to bed, Grace curled between them, and fallen asleep instantly.

At the sound of a vehicle, Colt wondered who would be coming by so early in the morning as he slipped out of bed and quickly dressed.

Someone was knocking at his front door by the time he reached it. He peered out, worried for a moment that he'd find Jonas Emanuel standing on his front step.

"Sheriff," Colt said as he opened the door.

"A moment of your time," Flint said.

Colt stepped back to let the sheriff enter the house. Flint glanced around, clearly looking for something.

He'd been wondering how Jonas was going to handle this. He'd thought Jonas wouldn't call in the sheriff about the events of last night. He still didn't think he would. But this was definitely not a social call.

"What can I help you with, Sheriff?"

Flint turned to give him his full attention. "Jonas reported a break-in at the SLS compound last night. I was wondering if you knew anything about that."

"Was anything taken?"

Flint smiled. "Apparently not. But Jonas was injured when he tried to apprehend one of the intruders."

That was news. Colt thought of Lola just down the hall still in bed with Grace. Last night when he was wrapping her ankle, he'd seen what looked like blood on her sleeve. But he hadn't want to ask what she'd had to go through to get away.

"He see who did it?" Colt asked.

"Apparently not," Flint said again.

Just then the sound of a baby crying could be heard down the hall toward the bedroom.

Flint froze.

"So nothing was taken," Colt said. "Jonas's injuries…"

"Aren't life-threatening at this point," Flint said as Lola limped down the hall from the bedroom, the baby in her arms.

Lola spotted the sheriff and stopped, her gaze flying to Colt. She looked worried until Colt said, "You remember Lola. And this is our daughter, Grace."

Colt moved to her to take the baby. He stepped to the sheriff, turning back the blanket his daughter was nestled in.

Every time he saw her sweet face his heart swelled to overflowing. She was so precious. Having never changed a diaper in his life, he'd learned quickly last night.

Now he lifted the cotton gown she'd been wearing when Lola had taken her from the crib last night at SLS to expose the tiny heart-shaped birthmark.

"Our baby girl," Colt said. "We'll be going to the doctor later today to have her checked over—and a DNA test done, in case you were wondering."

Flint nodded solemnly, and Colt handed Grace back to Lola. As she limped into the kitchen with the baby, the sheriff said, "I'm not going to ask, but I hope you know what you're doing."

"That little girl belongs with her mother."

The sheriff met his gaze. "And her father?"

"I'm her father."

Flint sighed. "I was at the hospital this morning taking Jonas's statement. He isn't filing assault charges because he says he doesn't know who attacked him. I see Lola is limping."

Colt said nothing.

"You sure this is over?" the sheriff asked.

"It is as far as I'm concerned."

Flint nodded. "Not sure Jonas feels that way. Got the impression he's a man who is used to getting what he wants."

Colt couldn't have agreed more. "He can't have Lola and Grace, but I don't want any trouble."

The sheriff shook his head at that. "I'm afraid it won't be your choice."

He knew a warning when he heard one. Not that he had to be told that Jonas was dangerous. "He's brainwashed those people, taken their money and keeps them up on that mountain like prisoners."

Flint nodded. "A choice each of them made."

"Except for the children up there."

"You think I like any of what I saw on that mountain?" Flint swore. "But you also know there is nothing I can do about it. That's private property up there. Jonas has every right to keep trespassers off. Not to mention it is church property, holy ground under the law."

"I have no intention of going up there."

"I wish I thought it was that simple." The sheriff had taken off his Stetson when he'd come into the house, and now he settled his hat back on his head. Turning, he started for the door. "You know my number," he said over his shoulder. "I'll come as quickly as I can. But I fear even that could be too late."

"Thanks for stopping by, Sheriff."

At the door, Flint turned to look back at him. Lola had come out of the kitchen carrying the baby. She was smiling down at Grace, cooing softly.

Flint's expression softened and Colt remembered that Darby had mentioned the sheriff's wife was pregnant. "Have a good day," Flint said, and left.

JONAS LISTENED TO the doctor tell him how lucky he was. He had a monster headache and hated being flat on his back in the hospital when he had things that needed to be done—and quickly.

"You lost a lot of blood," the doctor was saying. "If your…friend hadn't gotten you here when he did…"

"Yes, it is fortunate that Brother Zack found me when he did," Jonas said. He didn't need the doctor telling him how lucky he was. He was very aware. But a man made his own luck. He'd learned that when he'd left home to find his own way in life.

Not that he discounted what nature had given him—a handsome, honest-looking face, mesmerizing blue eyes and snake-oil-salesman charm. But he was the one who'd taken those gifts and used them to the best of his ability. Not that they always worked. Lola, a case in point. They'd worked enough, though, that he was a very rich man and, until recently, he would have said he had very loyal followers who saw to his every need. What more could a man ask for?

"You're going to have a headache for a while, but fortunately, you suffered only a minor concussion. A fall like that could have killed a man half your age. Like I said, lucky."

"Lucky," Jonas repeated. "Yes, Doctor, I was. So when can I be released?"

"Your laceration is healing quite nicely, but that bandage needs to be changed regularly so I'd prefer you stay in the hospital at least another day, maybe longer."

That was not what he wanted to hear. "One of the sisters could change my bandage for me. Really, I would be much more comfortable in my own home. I have plenty of people to look after me."

The doctor wavered. Jonas knew that the hospital staff would be much more comfortable with him gone, as well. A half dozen of the brothers and some of the SLS sisters had been coming and going since his "accident." He'd seen the way the hospital staff looked at them, the men in their black pants and white shirts, the woman in their long shapeless white dresses.

"I'd prefer you stay another day at least. I'll give instructions to one of your…sisters for after that. We'll see how you're doing tomorrow."

"I'm feeling so much better. I promise that when you release me, I will rest and take care of myself." His head ached more than he had let the doctor know. He didn't want any medication that would make his brain fuzzy. He needed his wits about him now more than ever.

"Like I said, we'll see how you are tomorrow," the doctor said, eyeing him suspiciously. The man knew Jonas couldn't be feeling that good, not with his head almost bashed in. He also knew the doctor had to be questioning how he could have hurt himself like this in a fall.

Jonas just wished he would go away and leave him alone.

"I need to ask you about these pills you've been taking," the doctor said, clearly not leaving yet. "One of your church members told me they were for a bad heart, but that's not the medication you're taking."

"No, it's not for a heart ailment," Jonas had to admit. "I'd prefer my flock not worry about my health, Doctor."

"If you're suffering from memory loss at your age, then we need to run some tests and see—"

"I have early-onset Alzheimer's," Jonas interrupted.

The doctor blinked.

"It is in the beginning stages, thus the pills I'm taking. I can assure you that I'm being well taken care of."

The doctor seemed at a loss for words.

"I believe Brother Zack is waiting in the hall," Jonas said to the doctor. "Would you ask him to step in here? I need to talk to him."

Realizing he was excused, the doctor left. A few moments later, Zack stuck his head in the door.

Jonas motioned him in. "Close the door. Have you seen Sister Rebecca?"

"Not since last night."

"Who was on duty at the second nursery last night?" he asked.

Zack frowned. "Sister Alexa." His eyes widened as he realized what the leader was really asking. "Sister Rebecca was taking care of the...special baby."

The angel. That's what Jonas had told his flock. That he'd had a vision and Lola's baby was a chosen one.

"Sister Rebecca." Jonas nodded and closed his eyes for a moment. He'd known it, but had needed Zack to verify his suspicions. Rebecca had been with him since the beginning. If there was anyone he knew he could trust, could depend on, it was her. He slowly opened his eyes and stared up at the pale green ceiling.

Zack stood at the end of the bed, waiting. Rebecca and Zack had never gotten along. Jonas blamed it on simple jealousy. Both were in the top positions at SLS. He knew how much Zack was going to enjoy the task he was about to give him.

"Go back to the complex," Jonas told him. "I want Sister Rebecca—" if she was still there "—restrained. Use the cabin where Sister Lola stayed. Guard it yourself." He finally looked at Zack, who nodded, a malicious glint in his gaze even as he fought not to smile.

"I'll take care of it."

AFTER THE SHERIFF LEFT, Colt stepped to Lola and Grace and pulled them close. He knew the sheriff was worried and with good reason. Jonas was an egomaniac who enjoyed having power over other people. He ran his "church" like a fiefdom. He would be incensed to have lost Lola and the baby, but there was really nothing he could do. At least not legally. Once the DNA results came back, once they had proof that Grace was Colt's daughter...

He tried to put it out of his head. Jonas was in the

hospital. He'd lied to the sheriff. It was over. Hopefully, the man would move on with some other obsession.

Colt cooked them breakfast while Lola fed Grace. He loved watching them together. It made his heart expand to near bursting.

Their day was quickly planned. First the DNA tests, then shopping for baby things. Never in his life had Colt thought about buying baby things, but now he realized he was excited. He wanted Grace to have whatever she needed.

At the doctor's office DNA samples were taken, then Colt took Lola and Grace to the small-box store on the edge of town. He was amazed at all the things a baby needed. Not just clothing and a car seat, but bottles and formula, baby food, diapers and wipes.

"How did babies survive before all of these things were on the market?" he joked, then insisted they get a changing table.

"It's too much," Lola said at one point.

"It's all good," he'd said, wanting only the best for his daughter. At the back of his mind, like a tiny devil perched on his shoulder, a voice was saying, "What are you doing? You are going back on assignment soon."

He shoved the thought aside, telling himself that he'd cross that bridge when he got there. He still had time. But time for what? There hadn't been any offers on the ranch. It was another thought that he pushed aside. Instead, he concentrated on Lola and Grace, enjoying being with them. Enjoying pretending at least for a while that they were a family.

He didn't even need the DNA test. That was all

Lola. "We need it for Jonas should he ever try to take Grace again," she'd said. "Also, I don't want you to have doubts."

"I don't have any doubts."

She'd given him a dubious look. "I want it settled. Not that I will ever ask anything of you. And I will pay you back for all the baby things you bought. I called this morning and am having some money wired to me."

"That isn't necessary."

But she said nothing, a stubborn tilt to her chin. He hadn't argued.

Instead, he took them back to the Stagecoach Saloon where, the moment they walked in, he knew that Billie Dee was cooking up her famous Texas chili.

Lillie Cahill Beaumont just happened to be there visiting her brother, along with Darby and his wife, Mariah. They oohed and aahed over Grace and Lola did the same with their babies.

By the time they got home, Colt was ready for a nap, too. After Lola put Grace down, she came into the bedroom and curled up against him. He held her close, breathing in the scent of her. He'd never been more happy.

Chapter Fourteen

The next day, Jonas couldn't wait for the doctor to stop by so he could hopefully get out of the hospital. He knew that Zack was taking care of things on the complex, but he worried. He still couldn't believe that Rebecca would betray him. It shook the stable foundation that he'd built this life on. Never would he have suspected her of deceiving him.

When the doctor finally came by, he hadn't wanted to send Jonas home yet. It took a lot of lying to get the doctor to finally release him. It was late in the day before he finally got his discharge papers.

Elmer picked him up at the hospital and drove him to the compound. He liked Elmer, though he'd seen the man's faith in their work here fading. He and Lola's father had been friends. Jonas suspected Elmer only stayed because he had nowhere else to go. But that was all right. Jonas still thought that when the chips were down, he could depend on Elmer.

Once at the compound, Zack was waiting, Excusing Elmer, Jonas let Zack help him inside. He was weak and his head ached, but he was home. He had things that needed to be taken care of and had been going crazy in the hospital.

Three of the sisters entered his cabin, fussed over him until he couldn't take it any longer and sent them scurrying. The pain in his head was better. It was another pain that was riding him like a dark cloak on his shoulders.

As soon as he was settled, Jonas asked Zack to bring him Sister Rebecca. "She's still detained in the small cabin, right?"

"She is," Zack said.

"How is her...attitude?"

"Subdued."

Jonas almost laughed since it didn't seem like a word Zack would ever have used. "Subdued? Is she on anything?"

"No, but I've had the sisters chanting over her every few hours. I thought it was something you would have done yourself had you been here."

He was both touched and annoyed by Zack taking this step without his permission. But he needed Zack more than ever now so he let it go. "You did well. Thank you."

Zack beamed and Jonas saw something in the man's eyes that gave him pause. Zack wanted to lead SLS. The man actually thought he had what it took to do it. The realization was almost laughable.

"Bring Sister Rebecca to me," he said, and closed his eyes, his head pounding like a bass drum. He wondered if he shouldn't have put this off until he was feeling better.

Zack hurried out, leaving him peacefully alone with his thoughts. Lola had made a fool out of him by sleeping with Colt McCloud. To add to his embarrassment, she'd gotten pregnant. That child should have been his.

Instead, he'd put aside his hurt, his fury, his embarrassment and offered to raise the baby as his own. Still, she'd turned him down. How could she have humiliated him even more?

He let out a bark of a laugh. What had she done? She'd almost killed him—after giving him hope that she was weakening. The latter hurt the most. Offering hope was a poisonous pill that he'd swallowed in one big gulp. And now even his flock was turning against him.

Was he losing his mind faster than he'd thought? Could he trust his judgment?

He started at the knock on the door, forgetting for a moment that he'd been expecting it. "Come in."

The moment Rebecca walked through the door, he could see the guilt written all over her face. Brother Zack stood directly behind her. He started to step into the cabin, and Jonas could tell Zack thought he was going to get to watch this.

"That will be all, Zack."

The man looked surprised and then disappointed. But it was the flicker of anger he saw in Zack's eyes that caused concern.

Jonas watched his right-hand man slowly close the door, but he could tell he'd be standing outside hoping to hear whatever was going on. Was Zack now becoming a problem, too?

He saw Sister Rebecca quickly take him in. In her

gaze shone concern and something even more disturbing—sympathy, if not pity. His head was still bandaged, dark stitches under the dressing, but his headaches were getting better. Stuck in the hospital, he'd had plenty of time to think over the past two days.

It was bad enough to be betrayed by Lola, even worse by Sister Rebecca, because he'd come to depend on her. She had to have known that Lola's baby had gone missing. It would have been the first thing she would have checked. Seeing the baby missing, she should have come to him.

He was anxious to talk to her, but as he looked at her standing there, he felt a loss of words for a moment. He kept telling himself that he was wrong. Sister Rebecca had been with him for years. She wouldn't betray him. Couldn't. He'd always thought she was half in love with him.

Which was probably why she hadn't come to him to let him know the baby wasn't in her crib. Even if she'd seen Lola with that bundle in her arms entering his cabin, she should have come to him. If she had, his head wouldn't be killing him right now. But he suspected Rebecca had wanted to be shed of Lola and the baby he was so determined to make his.

Since Zack had locked up Rebecca, she would know she was in trouble. He wondered what story she would tell him and how much of it he could believe?

COLT ALMOST CHANGED his mind. Things had been going so well that he didn't want or need the interruption. He enjoyed being with Lola and Grace. If he said so himself, he'd become proficient at diaper changes and getting chubby little limbs into onesies. He liked the middle-of-the-night feedings, holding Grace and watching her take her bottle. Her bright blue eyes watched him equally.

"I'm your daddy," he'd whispered last night, and felt a lump rise in his throat.

So when Julia had called and said it was important that they meet and talk, he hadn't been interested.

"If this is about you needing me to forgive you—"

"No. It's not that," she'd said quickly. "I doubt you can ever forgive me. I know how badly I hurt you."

Did she? The news had blindsided him. Hell, he'd been expecting her to pick him up at the airport—not break up with him to be with one of his friends. He still couldn't get his head around how that had gone down. No warning at all. He'd thought Wyatt hadn't even liked Julia. He knew that Darby didn't think she was right for him. Not that Darby had ever said anything. But Colt had been able to tell.

He could laugh now. He used to think that Darby just had his expectations set too high. But then Colt had met Mariah and realized that his friend had just been holding out for the real thing. Darby had done well.

"Julia, I can't see what meeting you for coffee could possibly—" It had been Lola who'd insisted he meet with Julia. She'd walked in while he was on the phone. As if gifted with ESP, she'd motioned to him that he should go.

"Fine," he'd said into the phone. "When and where?" He had just wanted to get it over with.

Now he drove past the coffee shop, telling himself that there was nothing Julia could say that would change anything. But she'd sounded...strange on the phone. He suspected something was up. Did he care, though?

He circled the block, saw a parking space and pulled his pickup in to it. For a moment he sat behind the wheel debating what he was about to do. And why had Lola been all for him seeing his ex? Was she worried that he wasn't over Julia? Or was she hoping to hook the two of them up again?

He'd heard her on the phone calling a car dealership to order a vehicle. "You don't have to do that. You can use my pickup whenever you want."

"I need my own car, but thank you," she'd said.

He thought of the discussion they'd had after he'd hung up from Julia.

"I knew that was Julia on the phone," Lola had said. "I wasn't eavesdropping. You talk to her in a certain way." She'd shrugged.

"A certain way?"

"I can't describe it, but you owe her nothing."

"Then why should I meet with her?"

"Because it won't be over until you tell her how you feel," Lola had said.

He had laughed. She made life seem so simple, and yet could her life have been any more complicated when he'd met her? "Okay, I'll meet with her with your blessing."

"You don't need my blessing."

He stepped to her and, taking her shoulders in his

hands, pulled her close. "All I care about is you and Grace. You have to know that."

"So you'll talk to her. You'll be honest. You'll see if there is anything there that you might have missed. Or that you want back."

He'd wanted to argue the point, but she'd put a finger to his lips.

"You should go. She'll be waiting."

Let her wait, he thought now as he glanced at his watch. Let her think he wasn't coming—look how she'd treated him at the Billings airport.

Then, just wanting to be done with this, he climbed out and walked down to the coffee shop. It was midafternoon. Only a few tables were taken. Julia had chosen one at the back. Where no one would see the two of them together and report back to Wyatt?

As he pushed open the door, he saw her frowning down at her phone. Checking the time? Or reading a text from Wyatt?

She looked up as if sensing him and motioned him over. "I got you a coffee—just the way you like it."

Except he'd never liked his coffee that way. Julia had come out to the ranch when they'd first started dating with some caramel-mocha concoction. When he'd taken a sip, he'd had to force a smile and pretend he'd liked it. His mistake.

"It's good, huh. I thought you'd like it. You always have the same boring coffee. I thought we'd shake things up a bit," she'd said. And from then on, she'd decided that was the way he liked his coffee.

"Thanks," he said now, without sitting down, "But

I never liked my coffee that way. I'll get my own." He moved to the counter and ordered a cup of black coffee before returning to the table.

She looked sullen, pouting like she used to when he'd displeased her—which was often enough that he knew this look too well.

"So what is it you want?" he asked as he sat down but didn't settle in. He didn't plan to stay long and was regretting coming here, no matter what Lola had said. He couldn't see how this could help anything.

Julia let out a nervous laugh. "This is not the way I saw this going."

"Oh?"

She seemed to regroup, drawing in a long breath, sitting up a little straighter. He was suddenly aware that she'd dressed up. He caught a hint of the perfume she used to wear when they were together because he'd commented one time that he liked it. He frowned as he realized she hadn't been wearing it the day they'd accidentally run into each other.

"What's going on, Julia?"

She looked away for a moment, biting down on the corner of her lower lip as if nervous. He used to think it was cute.

"I've made a terrible mistake. I didn't mean to blurt it out like that, but I can tell you're still angry and have no patience with me. Otherwise, you wouldn't have been so late, you would have drunk the coffee I ordered you and you wouldn't be looking at me as if you hated me."

He wasn't going to try to straighten her up on any of that. "Mistake?"

Julia looked at him as if she thought no one would be that daft. "Wyatt. I was just so lonely, and it looked as if you were never going to quit the military and come home…"

"How did you two get together? I always thought Wyatt didn't like you."

She mugged a face at him. "You don't need to be cruel."

"I'm serious. He never had a good word to say about you. Or was he just trying to keep his feelings for you from me?"

"I have no idea. And I don't care. He probably didn't like me. Maybe that's why we aren't together anymore."

Colt realized he wasn't surprised. Julia hadn't gotten him to the altar. He remembered that had been the case with an earlier boyfriend, too. Looked like there was a pattern there, he thought but kept it to himself.

"That's too bad."

"I can tell that you're really broken up over it."

After the initial shock had worn off, he'd actually thought Julia and Wyatt wouldn't last. Julia was beautiful in a classic way, but definitely high maintenance. He could see that clearly after being around Lola. As for Wyatt, well, he'd never had a serious girlfriend. He'd always preferred playing the field, as he called it.

"I'm sincerely sorry it didn't work out. Is that all?"

"Colt, stop being so mean." She sounded close to tears. She glanced around to make sure no one had heard her. "I feel so bad about what I did to you."

"You shouldn't." He realized he meant it. For a while,

he'd hoped she choked on the guilt daily. Now he didn't feel vindictive. He realized he no longer cared.

"I know how hurt you must be."

"I was hurt, Julia. That was one crushing blow you delivered, but I've moved on."

"With that woman you were with the other day? Are you in love with her?"

Now there was the question, wasn't it? "It's complicated."

"It doesn't have to be." She reached across the table and covered his hand.

He pulled his free. "Are you suggesting what I think you are?"

She looked at him as if to say, *No one can be this dense.* "I want you back. I'll do anything." She definitely sounded desperate.

Colt had played with this exact scheme in his mind on those long nights in the desert after she'd dumped him. It had been like a salve that made him feel better. Julia begging to come back to him. Him loving every minute of it before he turned her down flat.

Now it made him feel uncomfortable because he no longer wanted to hurt her. If anything, he felt indifferent and wondered what he'd ever seen in this woman. He couldn't help comparing her to Lola. Julia came up way short.

"Julia, you and I are never getting back together. Truthfully, I doubt we would have made it to the altar."

"How can you say that?" she demanded. "You asked me to marry you."

"I did. But I didn't realize then how wrong we were

for each other. I overlooked things, thinking they would change once we were married. Now I know better. I'm sure it was the same for you. Otherwise, how could you have fallen so quickly in love with another man?"

She seemed at a loss for words.

"So I imagine we both would have realized we weren't right for each other before we made a huge mistake."

Julia stared at him as if looking at a stranger. "I don't believe this."

Had she expected him to take her back at the snap of her fingers? The flutter of her eyelashes? She really hadn't known him. Even if he'd never met Lola, he wouldn't have taken Julia back. She'd proved the kind of woman she was—not the kind a man could ever trust.

Colt got to his feet. "You should try to work things out with Wyatt. Now that I think about it, you two belong together."

Her eyes widened, then narrowed dangerously. "Do you realize what you're throwing away? And for what? That…that…woman I saw you with the other day?" She made a distasteful face.

"Easy, Julia," he said, lowering his voice. "You really don't want to say anything about the mother of my child."

"What?" she sputtered.

"Lola and I have a beautiful daughter together."

Openmouthed, she stared at him. "Lola? That's not possible. You can't have known her long enough to… Are you going to *marry* her?"

"I haven't asked her yet, but you know me. I like to

take my time. Also, I'm a little gun-shy after my last engagement."

Julia pushed to her feet. He'd never seen her so angry. It made him want to laugh because he realized, with no small amount of relief, that had he married her, he would have seen her like this a lot.

The one thing he did know was that he was completely over her. No hard feelings. No need for retribution. No need to ever see this woman again.

"This never happened," she said with a flip of her head. "You hear me? You're right. Wyatt and I are perfect together. We're going to get married and be happy."

He smiled. "So you and Wyatt aren't broken up." He let out a bark of a laugh. "Good to see that you haven't changed. Give Wyatt my regards."

Julia stormed out. Colt finished his coffee and threw away the cups Julia had left behind. He smiled as he headed for the door. He couldn't wait to get home to Lola and Grace.

Chapter Fifteen

Lola saw the change in Colt the moment he walked in the door. It was as if a weight had been lifted off his shoulders. He was smiling and seemed…happy.

"I guess I don't need to ask how it went." Her heart had been pounding ever since Julia's phone call. A woman knows. Julia wanted more than Colt's forgiveness. A woman like that would try to hold on to him, to keep him in the wings—if she didn't already want him back.

Colt met her gaze. "She wants me back."

It felt as if a fist had closed around her heart, but she fought not to let him see her pain. "That must seem like a dream come true."

He laughed. "I'll admit at one time it would have been. But no," he said with a shake of his head as he stepped to her. "It would never have happened even if I hadn't met you. But now that I have…" He leaned down to kiss her softly on the mouth. As he drew back, he saw that she was frowning.

"I don't want you giving up the woman you love because of me and Grace," she said quickly. "I told you. We can take care of ourselves."

"That wasn't what I meant." His blue-eyed gaze locked with hers and she felt a bolt of heat shoot to her core. "Julia is the last person on earth that I want."

She swallowed. "But you asked her to marry you."

"I did." He chuckled. "And I have no idea why I did. Honestly, I feel as if I dodged a bullet. But I don't want to talk about her. I want you," he said as he drew her close again. "Is Grace sleeping?"

While he'd been gone, Lola had practiced what she was going to say to him. But when she looked up into his blue gaze and saw the desire burning there, it ignited the blaze inside her.

She told herself that they could have a serious talk later. There was time. Colt was in such a good mood, she didn't want to bring him down. She cared too much about him. But that was the problem, wasn't it? She was falling in love with him. And that was why she and Grace had to leave before Colt did something stupid like ask her to stay.

LATER, AFTER MAKING LOVE and falling into a sated sleep, Colt heard Grace wake up from her nap and slipped out of bed to go see to her. "Hi, sweetheart," he said as he picked her up and carried her over to the changing table. As he changed her, he talked to her, telling her how pretty and sweet she was.

She was Lola in miniature, from her pert nose to her bow-shaped mouth to her violet eyes. And yet, he saw some of himself in the baby—and knew it might be only because he wanted it to be true. They hadn't gotten the DNA results, not that he was worried.

What bothered him was how much he wanted to see himself in Grace. How much he wanted to tell her about all the things he'd teach her as she grew up. What he wanted to do was talk about the future with Grace—and Lola.

Getting Lola's baby back was one thing, but seeing himself in this equation? He would have said the last thing he needed was a family. He was selling the ranch and going back into the service. That had been his plan and he'd always had a plan.

Now he felt rudderless and aloft, not knowing if he was up or down. What would he do if not go back to flying choppers for the Army? Ranch?

He stared into Grace's adorable face, feeling his heart ache at the thought of being away from her. He picked her up, holding her as he felt his heart pounding next to hers. Fatherhood had always been so far off in the future. But now here it was looking back at him with so much trust… He thought of his own father, his parents' disastrous marriage, how disconnected he'd felt from both of them.

He knew nothing about being a father or a husband. A part of him felt guilty for asking Julia to marry him. True, he'd put her off for years. It had come down to break up or marry her. He'd thought it was what he'd wanted.

Now, though, he knew his heart hadn't been in it. What he'd told Julia earlier had been true. He doubted they would have made it to the altar. After he'd put that diamond—she'd picked it out herself—on her finger, all she'd talked about was the big wedding they would have, the big house, the big life.

He'd let her talk, not really taking her seriously. He should have, though.

While Lola... Well, she was different. Her heart was so filled with love for their child that she'd risked her life numerous times. He'd never met anyone like her. And Grace... She smiled and cooed up at him, her gaze meeting his, and he felt her steal another piece of his heart if she hadn't already taken it all.

"Does she need changing?" Lola asked from the doorway.

"All taken care of. She just smiled at me."

Lola laughed. "I saw that." She'd been watching from the doorway, he realized. He wondered how long she'd been there. She was wearing one of his shirts and, he'd bet, nothing under it. She couldn't have looked sexier.

His cell phone rang. Lola moved to him to take the baby.

After pulling out his phone, Colt felt a start when he saw that it was Margaret Barnes, his Realtor, calling. He'd forgotten about her, about listing the ranch. All that seemed like ages ago.

"Hello?" he said as he headed out of the nursery.

"Colt, I have some good news for you. I have a buyer for your ranch."

For a moment he couldn't speak. He looked back at Lola and Grace from the doorway. Lola was rocking the baby in her arms, smiling down at her, and Grace was cooing and smiling up at her mother—just as she had done moments before with her father.

"Colt, are you there?"

"Yes." He saw Lola look up as if she heard something in his voice.

"You said to find a buyer as quickly as I could. If you have some time today, stop by my office. I can get the paperwork all ready. The buyer is fine with your asking price and would like to take possession as soon as possible."

He felt as if the earth was crumbling under his feet. Yes, he'd told her to find a buyer and as quickly as possible. But that had been before. Before Lola had shown up at his door in the middle of the night. Before he'd known about Grace.

"What is it?" Lola asked, seeing his distress as she joined him in the living room. "Bad news?"

He stood holding his phone after disconnecting. "That was the Realtor."

Lola hadn't asked about the for-sale sign on the road into the ranch and he hadn't brought it up. But Lola knew what his plans had been months ago. The night they'd met he'd told her he was going to accept another Army assignment rather than resign his commission, like he'd been planning before that night, to marry Julia.

"Does she have a buyer for the ranch?" Lola asked, giving nothing away.

He wasn't sure what kind of reaction he'd been expecting. His gaze went to Grace in her arms. He felt his heart breaking. Lately, his only concern had been protecting Lola, getting Grace back and making sure that horrible Jonas didn't have either of them.

He hadn't thought about the future. Hadn't let himself. "I think we should talk about—" His phone rang again. He checked it, hoping it was the Realtor calling again. He'd tell her he needed more time.

It was the doctor calling. He glanced at Lola and then picked up. "Doc?" he said into the phone.

"Your test results are back. You're welcome to come by and I would be happy to explain anything you didn't understand about DNA testing."

"Let's just cut to the chase, Doc."

Silence hung on the other end of the line for a long few moments. "The infant is a match for both Lola and you, Colt."

"Thanks, Doc." He looked to Lola, who didn't appear all that interested. Because she'd known all along.

"Are you all right?" she asked.

He nodded, but he wasn't. Grace had fallen back to sleep in her arms. Had there ever been a more beautiful, ethereal-looking child? No wonder Jonas had wanted her. Wanted her and Lola.

If he looked like a man in pain, he was. Lola and the baby had taken his already topsy-turvy life and given it a tailspin. All he'd wanted just days ago was to get out of this town, out of this state, out from under the ranch his father had left him and the responsibility that came with it.

Now, though, he no longer wanted to run. He wanted to plant roots. He wanted to make them a family. "I think we should get married." The words were out and he wasn't sorry to hear them. But he should have done something romantic, not just blurted them out like that.

To his surprise, Lola smiled at him. "That's sweet, but…it's too early, isn't it?"

Too early? Like in the morning or—

"We hardly know each other."

"I'd say we know each other quite well," he said as he picked up the tail end of his shirt she was wearing.

She laughed and playfully slapped his hand away as she headed for the spare room that they'd made into a makeshift nursery. "You know what I mean."

He followed her and watched as she put Grace down in the crib. "We have a daughter."

"Yes, we do. But we can't get married just for Grace. You know that wouldn't work."

"But neither can I let the two of you walk out that door," he said.

"Colt, that door will soon be someone else's."

She had a point.

"I won't sell the ranch."

She gave him a pointed look. "I owe you my life and Grace's. But I also owe you something else. Freedom. Grace and I can take care of ourselves now. Jonas is no longer a problem. He isn't going to bother us, not after the sheriff saw our daughter and knows that Jonas lied about keeping her from me. My parents set aside money for me should I ever need it and I saved the money I made teaching. Grace and I will be fine."

"But *I* won't be fine."

She looked at him, sympathy in her gaze.

"Lola, I need you. I need you and our daughter. I want us to be a family."

Tears welled in her eyes as she tried to pass him. "Colt."

He took her in his arms. "I know we haven't known each other long. But the night we met, we connected in a way that neither of us had before, right?" She nodded, though reluctantly it seemed. "And we've been through more than any couple can ever imagine, and yet we worked together and pulled it off against incredible odds. If any two people can make this work, it's you and me."

She smiled sweetly, but he could tell she wasn't convinced. "We're good together, I won't deny that. But, Colt, you don't want to ranch. You admitted that to me the first night we met. Now you're talking about keeping the ranch just to make a home for me and Grace? No, Colt. You would grow to resent us for tying you down. I see how your eyes light up when you talk about flying helicopters. That's what you love. That's where you need to be."

He wanted to argue, but he couldn't. She'd listened to him. She knew him better than even he knew himself. "Still—"

"No," she said as she moved down the hallway to the room that they now shared. She began to pick up her clothing. "This is best and we both know it."

It didn't feel like the best thing to do. He'd come to look forward to seeing Lola's face each morning, hear her singing to the baby at night and spending his days with the two of them.

"Promise you won't leave just yet," he said, panicking at the sight of her getting her things ready.

She stopped and looked at him. "I'll stay until the ranch closes so you can spend as much time with Grace as possible. But then we have to go."

"It isn't just Grace I want to spend time with," he said as he drew her close. He kissed her and told himself he'd figure out something. He had to. Because he couldn't bear the thought of either of them walking out of his life.

JONAS STUDIED THE woman before him, letting her wait. Sister Rebecca was what was known as a handsome woman. She stood almost six feet tall with straight brown hair cut chin-length. Close to his own age, she wasn't pretty, never had been. If anything, she was nondescript. You could pass her on the street and not see her.

That was one reason she'd worked out so well all these years. She didn't look dangerous. A person hardly noticed her. Until it was too late.

Studying her, Jonas admitted that he'd come to care very deeply for her. He had depended on her. Her betrayal cut him deeper even than Lola's. Fury gripped him like fingers around his throat.

Along with guilt, he saw something else in her face now. She knew that he knew what she'd done.

"Rebecca?"

She raised her gaze slowly. The moment she met his eyes, her face seemed to crumble. She rushed to him to fall to her knees in front of his chair. "Forgive me, Father," she said, head bowed. "Please forgive me."

He didn't speak for a moment, couldn't. "For almost getting me killed or for letting Lola get away with the baby?"

She raised her head again. While pleas for forgiveness had streamed from her mouth, there was no sign of regret in her eyes.

"You stupid, foolish woman," he said with disgust, and pushed her away.

She fell back, landing hard. He watched as she slowly got to her feet. Her dark eyes were hard, her smile brittle. Defiance burned behind her gaze, a blaze that he saw had been burning for some time. Why hadn't he seen it? Because he'd been so consumed with Lola for so long.

"I have done whatever you've asked of me for years," she said, anger making her words sharp as knives hurled at him.

"As you should, as one of my followers," he snapped.

She let out a humorous laugh that sent a chill up his spine. "I wasn't just one of your followers."

He felt for his phone and realized he'd left it over on the table, out of his reach. Zack had said he would be right outside the door. But would he be able to get in quickly enough if Rebecca attacked? Jonas knew he wasn't strong enough to fight her off. Rebecca probably knew it, too.

"Many times you were wrong, but still I did what you asked without question," she continued as she moved closer and closer until she was standing over him. "All these years, I've followed you, looked up to you, trusted that you were doing what was best for our community, best for me."

He swallowed, afraid he'd created a monster. If he was being honest, and now seemed like a good time for it, he'd let her think that one day the two of them would run SLS. He'd trusted her above all others, even Zack.

"You didn't sound the alarm when you found the crib empty," he said, trying to regain control and get the conversation back on safer ground.

She shook her head. "No, when I found Sister Amelia standing next to the empty crib, I told her to go back to bed and let me handle it. I thought about sounding the alarm, but then I didn't. In truth? I was overjoyed to see the brat gone, along with her mother."

"That wasn't your decision to make."

She smiled at that. "You would destroy everything for that woman? You would take her bastard and raise it as your own? I thought of you as a god, but now I see that you are nothing but a man with a man's weaknesses."

The truth pierced his heart and he instantly recoiled. "You will not speak to me like this or there will be serious consequences."

A chuckle seemed to rise deep in her, coming out on a ragged breath. "Will you have the sisters chant more over me? You've already locked me up. Or..." Her gaze was hard as the stone Lola had used to try to bash his head in. "Will you have me killed? It wouldn't be the first time you've had a follower killed, would it?"

The threat was clear in her gaze, in her words. Rebecca knew too much. She could never leave this compound alive, and they both knew it.

He grabbed for his phone, but she reached it first. She held the phone away from him, stepping back, daring him to try to take it from her.

"This is ridiculous, Sister Rebecca. You would throw away everything we have worked so hard for out of simple jealousy?"

She raised a brow, but when she spoke her voice betrayed how close she was to tears again. This was breaking her heart as much as his own. "I know you. After all these years, I know you better than you know yourself. You'll go after her and that baby. You'll have her one way or another even if it means destroying everything."

He stared at her, hearing the truth in her words and realizing that he'd let her get too close. She *did* know him.

She looked down at the phone in her hand, then up at him. She pushed the alarm. The air on the mountaintop filled with the scream of the siren.

When Zack burst through the door, she threw Jonas his phone and, with one final look, turned and let Zack take her roughly by the arm and lead her back to her prison.

She wouldn't be locked up there long, Jonas thought. He owed her that at least, he thought as he sounded the all clear signal. But things weren't all right at all and he feared they never would be again.

Chapter Sixteen

Colt had been worried that the sheriff was right, that Jonas wasn't going to take what had happened lying down. Hearing that Jonas had been released from the hospital, he'd almost been expecting a visit from the SLS leader.

He'd been ready, a shotgun beside the door. But the day had passed without incident and so had the next and the next.

The days seemed to fly by since he'd signed the ranch papers and deposited a partial down payment from the buyer. He'd kept busy selling off the cattle and planning the auction for the farm equipment. He tried not to think about the liquidation of his father's legacy, telling himself his old man knew how much he hated ranching. It was his own fault for leaving Colt the ranch.

He was in the barn when he heard footfalls behind him and turned to see Lola. "So the buyer doesn't want any of this?" she asked.

"No, I believe he plans to subdivide the property. It won't be a ranch at all anymore."

"And the house?"

"Demo it and put in a rental probably."

Lola said nothing, but when he saw her looking out the barn door toward the mountains, there was a wistfulness to her he couldn't ignore.

"I'm not leaving Montana. This will always be my home. I'm just not ranching. With what I got from the sale, I can do anything I want." But that was it. He didn't know what he wanted. His heart pulled him one way, then another.

"How long has your family owned this property?" she asked.

"My great-grandfather homesteaded it," he said. "I know it must sound disrespectful of me to sell it."

She shook her head. "It's yours to do with whatever you want, right?"

"Yes." He didn't bother to tell her that the three-month stipulation his father had put on it was over. "You were right. I'm not a rancher. I have no interest."

"But you're a cowboy."

He laughed. "That I will always be. I'm as at home on a horse as I am behind the controls of a helicopter. Ranching is a different animal altogether. Most ranchers now lease their land and let someone else worry about the critters, the drought, the price of hay. Few of them move cattle on horseback. They ride four-wheelers. Everyone seems to think ranching is romantic." He laughed at that. "It's the most boring job I've ever done in my life."

"That's why you're selling," she said with a smile. "It's the right thing."

He hadn't needed her permission, but he was thankful for it. As much as he denied it, there was guilt over selling something his father had fought for years to keep.

Nor had he contacted the Army about his next assignment, putting that off, as well. He still had plenty of leave, so there was time.

He'd also put off his Realtor about when the new owners could take possession. It sounded as if they hoped to raze the house as soon as he moved out.

He knew he couldn't keep avoiding giving a firm date and time, but once that happened Lola and Grace would be gone.

"Where will you go?" he asked Lola.

"Probably back to California. At least for a while." The car she'd ordered had come, and she'd been able to get to her funds and make sure Jonas couldn't access them. She'd had to get a new driver's license since Jonas had taken her purse with hers inside, along with her passport and checkbook and credit cards.

Colt had heard her on the phone taking care of all that. No wonder he could feel the days slipping away until not only this ranch and the house he'd grown up in were gone, but also Lola and the baby. He worried that once he went back to the Army, this would feel like nothing more than a dream.

Yet, he knew that he would ache for Lola and Grace the rest of his life—if he let them get away. He'd always see their faces and yearn for them.

He'd never felt so confused in his life. What would he do if not go back to the Army? He was almost thirty-three. He couldn't retire even if he wanted to, which he didn't. He wanted to fly. But he couldn't ask Lola and Grace to wait for him for the next two to five years. He couldn't bear the thought of her worrying about him, or the worst happening and him never making it back.

His cell phone rang. Margaret again. "I'd better take this," he said to Lola. As she walked back toward the house, he picked up. "Margaret, I might have changed my mind."

Silence. "It's too late for that and you know it. Colt, what is this about?"

A woman and a child. The rest of my life. Regrets.

"If you're having second thoughts about selling the ranch—"

"I'm not. I just need a little more time to get off the property."

More silence. "I'll see what I can do but, Colt, they are getting very impatient. I need to tell these buyers something concrete. I can't keep putting them off or they are going to change their minds or fine you, which they can under the contract you signed." She sounded angry. He couldn't blame her.

As he looked out at the land, he had a thought. "I'll be in first thing in the morning."

"What does that mean?" she asked after a moment.

"I have an idea."

She groaned. "Could you be a touch more specific?"

"I'm selling the ranch, but there's something I need."

"Okay," she said slowly. "Why don't we sit down with them in the morning, if you're sure you won't change your mind."

He pocketed his phone and watched Lola as she

slipped in the back door of the house. Taking off his Stetson, he wiped the sweat from his brow with his sleeve. "Do something," he said to himself. "Do something before it's too late."

"SHE'S STAYING ON the ranch with Colt McCloud," Zack told Jonas later that afternoon.

"Is the baby with them?"

"I've had the place watched as you ordered. They took the baby into town the next morning, bought baby clothes and supplies, and returned to the ranch."

So they were settling in. They thought it was over. "What kind of security?"

"No security system on the house. But I would imagine he has guns and knows how to use them since he's a major in the Army."

"I'm sure he does." That's why they would strike when the cowboy least expected it. He looked past Zack toward the main building below him on the hill. "You led church this morning?"

He nodded.

"What is the mood?"

Zack seemed to consider that. "Quite a few of them are upset over Sister Rebecca."

He'd suspected as much. "I'll lead the service tonight." Zack didn't appear to think that was going to make a difference. Jonas thought about the things that Rebecca had said and ground his teeth. He still had a headache, and while his wound was healing, it was a constant reminder of what Lola had done to him. Worse, she'd bewitched him, put a spell on him as if sent by the devil to bring him down.

Did he really want her back, or did he just want to retaliate? Did it matter in the long run? His memory was getting worse. The pills didn't seem to be working. He couldn't be sure how long he had until he was a blubbering old fool locked up in some rest home.

He shook his head. He wasn't going out that way. "I don't want Lola or the baby injured."

"What about McCloud?"

"Kill him and dispose of his body. I know the perfect place. If possible, leave no evidence that we were there."

COLT LEFT THE barn headed for the house, suddenly excited that his idea just might be the perfect plan. "Lola?" he cried as he burst through the back door.

"Colt?" She was standing in the kitchen wearing an apron that had belonged to his mother. He hadn't seen it in years. She must have found it in a drawer he and his father had obviously never bothered to look in.

"What?" she asked, seeing the way he was looking at her.

"You look so cute in that apron, that's all." He stepped to her. "I'm selling the ranch."

"I know."

"You were right. I'd make a terrible rancher, always did. This was my father's dream, not mine. I'm a helicopter pilot."

She nodded. "I thought we already knew this. So you're going to take the commission the Army is offering you."

"No."

She tilted her head. "No?"

"No," he said, smiling. "For years, my friend Tommy and I have talked about starting our own helicopter service here in the state. We're good at what we do. With the money from the ranch, I can invest in the birds we'll need."

"That sounds right up your alley. But are you sure?"

He nodded. "Come here." He put his arm around her waist and ushered her over to the window. "Look out there. See that."

"Yes? That mountainside?"

"Imagine a house in that grove of aspens and pines. The view from there is incredible. Now imagine an office down by the road and a helipad. The office would be just a hop, skip and a jump from the house. We'd have everything we need for Grace and any other children we have."

LOLA SMILED AT HIM, caught up in his enthusiasm. "Isn't that land part of the ranch?"

He grinned. "I'm going to buy it back."

"Aren't you being a little impulsive?"

"Not at all. I've been thinking about this for years." He seemed to see what she meant and turned her to face him. "And I've been thinking about being with you since that first night. With you and Grace here… Lola, I've fallen for you and Grace…" He shook his head. "It was love at first sight even before I knew for certain that Grace was mine. I want you to stay. I want us to be a family."

"Colt, do you know what you're saying?" But it was what he wasn't saying that had her stomach in knots.

She knew he wanted her and Grace, but she wouldn't let herself go into a loveless marriage just to give her daughter a home.

She said as much to him.

He stared at her. "Damn it, Lola, I love you."

She blinked in surprise. All their lovemaking, their quiet times together, those moments with Grace. She'd waited to hear those words. Well, maybe not the "damn it, Lola" part. But definitely the "I love you" part. Her heart had assured her that he loved her and Grace. And yet, she wouldn't let herself believe it was true until he finally told her.

"I love you," he repeated as if they were the most honest words he'd ever spoken. "I've only said those words twice to a woman. With Julia, it was over two years before I said them. I don't think it was a coincidence that I held off. With you... I've been wanting to say them for days now."

"Oh, Colt, I've been waiting to hear them. I love you, too."

He reached into his pocket and pulled out a small velvet box.

Lola gave a small gasp.

"This ring was handed down from my great-great-grandmother to my great-grandmother to my grandmother. When my grandmother gave it to me, she made me promise only to give it to a woman who was my equal." He opened the box.

She looked down at a beautiful thick gold band circled in diamonds. "Oh, Colt." Her gaze went to his. "I don't understand. Julia—"

"I didn't give it to her."

"Why?"

He shrugged. "I don't know. It didn't seem…right for her. She picked out one she liked uptown."

Her heart went out to him. Julia had hurt him badly in so many ways, only proving how wrong she was for him almost from the start.

"Now I realize that I was saving this ring so I could live up to the promise I made my grandmother," he said. "I want you to wear it." He dropped to one knee. "Will you marry me, Lola Dayton, and be my wife and the mother to my children?"

She smiled through the burn of tears. "Yes."

He slipped the ring on her finger. It fit perfectly. "Now what is the chance of that?" he said to her, only making her cry and laugh at the same time.

Swinging her up into his arms, he spun her around and set her down gently. "For the first time in so long, I am excited about the future."

She could see that he'd been dragged down by the ranch, Julia and the past, as well as his need to do what he did so well—fly.

Colt kissed her softly on the mouth. She felt heat rush through her and, cupping his face in her hands, kissed him with the passion the man evoked in her.

He swung her up in his arms again, only this time he didn't put her down until they reached the bedroom.

THAT EVENING, JONAS held church in the main building. He'd gathered them all together to give them the news. He could feel the tension in the air. There'd been a time when he'd stood up here and felt as if he really was a god sent to this earth to lead desperate people looking for at least peace, if not salvation.

As he looked over his flock, though, all he felt was sad. His father used to say that all good things end. In this case, the preacher was right.

"Brothers and sisters. I have some sad news. As you know, Sister Rebecca has chosen to leave us. It is with a heavy heart that I had to let her go." He wondered how many of them knew the truth. Too many of them probably. He was glad he'd had Zack bury her far away from the compound.

"But that isn't the only news. I have decided that it is time to leave Montana." His words were followed by a murmur of concern that spread through his congregation. "As many of you know, I'm in poor health. My heart… I'm going to have to step down as your leader."

The murmurs rose. One woman called out, "What's to become of us?"

He'd bilked them out of all their money. A lot of them were old enough now that they would have a hard time getting a job. He didn't need this crowd turning on him as Sister Rebecca had.

"Brother Zack will be taking those who want to go to property I've purchased in Arizona. It's farmable land, so you can maintain a life there. Each of you will be given a check to help with your expenses."

The murmur in the main building grew louder. "If you have any questions, please give those to Brother Zack. I trust him to make sure that each and every one of you will be taken care of." That quieted them down, either because they were assured or because they knew how Zack had taken care of other parishioners who'd became troublesome.

"It is with a heavy heart that I must step down, but I know that you all will be fine. You will leave tomorrow. Go with Godspeed." He turned and walked away, anxious to get back to his cabin and pack. The sale of his property would be enough to pay off his followers—not that he would be around to hear any complaints after tonight.

He rang for Zack. Since he'd told Zack of his plan, the man had been more than excited. Jonas had recognized that frenzied look in Zack's eyes. He'd seen it in his own. Zack would be Father Zack. God help his followers.

"I need you to pick about six brothers and a few sisters for a special mission," he told Zack. It would be one of their last missions under him.

Zack nodded, clearly understanding that he needed to pick those who would still kill for their leader.

"Make sure one of them is Brother Elmer."

"Are you sure? I mean—"

"Already questioning my authority?" he asked with a chuckle.

"No, of course not."

"Good. I have my reasons."

"I'll get right on it," Zack said, and left him alone.

Jonas looked around the cabin. He'd had such hopes when he'd moved his flock to Montana. He couldn't get maudlin now. He had to think about his future. He stepped to the safe he had hidden in the wall, opened it and took out the large case he kept there full of cash and his passport. Next to it was Lola's purse.

He took that out, as well, and thumbed through it even though he knew exactly what was in it since he'd often looked through it. He liked touching her things. He found her passport. Good, it was up-to-date. He'd deal with getting the baby out of the country when it came time.

After putting Lola's passport beside his own into his case, he closed the safe. There was nothing keeping him here after tonight. He would have everything he'd ever dreamed of, including a small fortune waiting in foreign banks across the world.

He thought of his father, wishing he could see him now. "Go ahead, say it. You were right about me, you arrogant old sanctimonious fool. I was your worst nightmare and so much more. But you haven't seen anything yet."

Chapter Seventeen

Colt woke to the sound of both outside doors bursting open. The sudden noise woke the baby. Grace began to cry in the room down the hall. Lola stirred next to him and Colt, realizing what was happening, grabbed for his gun in the nightstand next to him.

Moments before he had lain in bed, with Lola beside him.

They were on him before he could draw the gun. They swept into the room, both men and women. Colt fought off the first couple of men, but a blow to the back of his head sent him to the floor and then they were on him, binding his hands behind him, gagging him, trussing his ankles and dragging him out of the house.

He tried to see Lola, but there was a group of women around her, helping her dress. In the baby's room, he heard Grace quiet and knew they had her, as well.

The strike had been so swift, so organized, that Colt realized he'd underestimated Zack—the only ex-military man in SLS. Clearly he had more experience at these kinds of maneuvers than Colt had thought.

Still stunned from the blow to his head, he was half carried, half dragged to a waiting van.

"Take care of him, Brother Elmer," he heard Zack say, the threat clear in the man's tone. Zack must have known that Brother Elmer was a weak link. "Brother Carl will go with you to make sure the job is done properly."

The van door slammed. Elmer started the engine and pulled away. The whole operation had taken less than ten minutes.

"DON'T HURT HIM!" Lola had cried as Colt was being dragged from the bedroom. Three women blocked her way to keep her from going after the men.

"Dress!" Sister Caroline ordered.

"My baby?"

"Grace will be safe as long as you do what we ask," Sister Amelia said. But there was something in Amelia's tone, a sadness that said not even she believed it.

Lola had no choice. They had Colt. They had Grace. She dressed quickly in a blouse and jeans, pulled on her sneakers and let the women lead her outside to a waiting van.

Sister Shelly was already in the van and holding Grace.

"Let me hold her," Lola said, steel in her voice.

The women looked at one another.

"Give the baby to Lola," Sister Amelia said and Shelly complied.

She sat holding the now-fussing Grace as the van pulled away. "Where are they taking Colt?"

No one answered. Her heart fell. Hadn't she feared

that Jonas would retaliate? He'd be humiliated and would have to strike back. Isn't that what the sheriff had warned them about?

But what could he hope to achieve by this? The sheriff would know who took them. The first place Flint Cahill would look was the compound.

She remembered something she'd overheard while a prisoner at SLS. Some of the women had been worried that Jonas wasn't himself, that his memory seemed to be failing him. He often called them by the wrong names, got lost in the middle of a sermon. They questioned in hushed voices if it was his heart or something else, since they'd seem him taking pills for it.

"What is going on?" Lola asked, sensing something different about the group of women.

"We're leaving Montana," Sister Amelia said, and the other sisters tried to hush her. "She'll know soon enough," Amelia argued. "Father Jonas announced it earlier. He's selling the land here. Some are going to a new home in Arizona. Others..." Her voice broke. "I don't know where they're going."

Lola realized that their leader wasn't here. "Where is Sister Rebecca?" The question was met with silence. "Amelia?"

"She's gone."

"Everyone is leaving," Sister Shelly said, sounding near tears. "Father Jonas... He's letting Brother Zack lead the group in Arizona. He will be Father Zack now."

Lola couldn't believe what she was hearing as the van reached the highway and headed toward the compound. "He's putting Zack in charge?" She knew that the women in this van must feel the same way she did about Zack. "Did Jonas say what he is planning to do?"

Silence. Lola hugged Grace to her, her fear mounting with each passing mile as the van turned onto the road up to the mountain. Lola saw no other taillights ahead. No headlights behind them. Where had they taken Colt?

COLT COULDN'T SEE OUT, but he could tell that Elmer and Carl weren't taking him to the compound. He had a pretty good idea what their orders had been when Zack had told Elmer to take care of him.

He was furious with himself. He'd thought Jonas would have no choice but to give up. He should have known better. He should have taken more precautions. Against so many, he knew he and Lola hadn't stood a chance.

When they'd gone to the compound and rescued Grace, he'd thought this could be settled without bloodshed. It was why he hadn't taken a gun to the compound the first time that night. He didn't want to kill one of Jonas's sheep. They were just following orders, though blindly, true enough. But he hadn't wanted trouble with the law.

Now, though, he saw there was no way out of this. Jonas had taken Lola and Grace. Nothing was going to stop him. He was going to end this once and for all no matter whom he had to kill.

Colt rolled to his side. They'd bound his wrists with plastic ties. He worked to slip his hands under him. If he could get a foot into the cuffs, he knew he could break free.

As he did, he watched the men in the front seat. Neither turned around to check on him. He got the feeling they didn't like being awakened in the middle of the night for this any more than Colt had. And now they had been ordered to kill someone. They had to be questioning Jonas and the SLS. He already knew that Brother Elmer had a weak spot for Lola and her baby.

He managed to get his hands past his butt. He lay on his back, catching his breath for a moment before he pushed himself up. Once he had his hands in front of him…

The van slowed. Elmer shifted down and turned onto a bumpy road that jarred every muscle in Colt's body. Colt caught a glimpse of something out the back window and realized where they were taking him. The old gravel pits outside of Gilt Edge. He caught the scent of the water through the partially opened windows up front. It was the perfect place to dump a body. Weighted down, there was a good chance the remains would never be found.

He felt his heart pound as he worked to free his wrists. The plastic restraints popped—but not louder than the rattle of the van on the rough road. Colt went to work on the ones binding his ankles.

As the van came to a stop, he resumed his original position, his hands behind him, feet together as he lay on his side facing the door.

Both men got out. He waited, wondering if either of them was armed or if the plan had been simply to drown him.

The van door opened noisily. "Can you get him out?" Elmer asked his companion.

Carl grunted but reached for him.

Colt swung his feet around and kicked the man in the chest, sending Carl sprawling in the dirt. He followed with a quick jab to Elmer's jaw. The older man stumbled and sat down hard on the ground.

So far, Colt hadn't seen a weapon, but as he jumped out, he saw Carl fumbling for something behind him. The man came up with a pistol. Right away, Colt saw that he wasn't comfortable using it. But that didn't mean that Carl wouldn't get lucky and blow Colt's head off.

He rushed around the back of the van to the driver's side. Grabbing open the door, he leaped in and started the van. As he threw the engine into Reverse, he saw Carl trying to get a clear shot. Elmer had stumbled to his feet and was blocking Carl's way—either accidentally or on purpose.

Colt didn't try to figure out which as he hit the gas. The van shot back. He cranked the wheel hard, swinging the back end toward the two men.

Carl got off two shots. One bullet shattered the back window of the van. The other took out Colt's side window, showering him with glass, and just missing his head before burying itself in the passenger-side door.

Elmer had parked the van close to the edge of the gravel pit, no doubt to make unloading his body easier.

As Colt swung the van at the two men, they tried to move out of the way. But Elmer was old and lost his footing. He was the first to go tumbling down the steep embankment and splash into the cold, clear water.

Carl had been busy trying to hit his target with the gun so he was caught unaware when the back of the van hit him and knocked him backward into the gravel pit. He let out a yell as he fell, the sound dying off in a loud splash.

Colt shifted into first gear and tore off down the bumpy road, thankful to be alive. He hoped both men could swim. If so, they had a long swim across the pit to where they would be able to climb out.

If either of their cell phones still worked after that, they might be able to warn Jonas. Not that it would matter.

Colt sped toward his house to get what he needed. This time he was taking weapons—and no prisoners.

For Lola, walking into Jonas's cabin with the bundle in her arms felt a little like déjà vu. Only this time, there was a precious sleeping baby instead of rocks in her arms. As she entered, propelled by Brother Zack, she told herself that she would die protecting her daughter. Did Jonas know that, as well?

"Leave her," Jonas ordered. Zack started to argue, but one look at their leader and he left, saying he would be right outside the door if he was needed. The sisters scattered, and the door closed, leaving Lola and Grace alone with Jonas.

He still had a bandage on the side of his head, but she knew better than to think his injury might slow him down.

"You are a very difficult woman."

"Only when someone tries to force me into doing

something I don't want to do or they take my child from me."

He glanced at the bundle in her arms. "May I see her?"

Lola didn't move. "What do you hope to get out of this?" she demanded.

"I thought I was clear from the beginning. I want you. It's what your parents wanted—"

"I don't believe that. I heard from my father before he...died. He wanted out of SLS. He was trying to convince my mother to leave. I believe that's why you killed them both."

Jonas shook his head. "Are we back to that?"

"You're a fraud. This is no church. And you are no god. All this is only about your ego. It's a bad joke."

"Are you purposely trying to rile me?"

"I thought maybe it was time you heard the truth from someone instead of Sister Rebecca telling you how wonderful you are."

"Sister Rebecca is no longer with us."

"So I heard. Did you kill her yourself or make one of your sheep do it?" She knew he could not let Rebecca simply walk away. She'd been with him from the beginning. She'd done things for him, knew things.

"Why do you torment me? I cared about Rebecca."

"And yet you had her killed. I don't like the way you care about people."

At the sound of vehicles and activity on the mountain below them, Lola moved cautiously to the window, careful not to turn her back on Jonas.

She frowned as she saw everyone appearing to be

packing up and moving. Fear coursed through her. "What's going on? I thought they weren't leaving until tomorrow?"

"Our time in Montana has come to an end. We are abandoning our church here."

What Amelia had told her was true. "So they're scurrying away like rats fleeing a sinking ship. You're really going to let them go?"

"All good things must end."

She thought of Colt as she had on the ride to the compound. Something told her that he hadn't been brought here. "Where is Colt?"

Jonas shook his head. "As I said, all good things must end."

Tears burned her eyes. "If you hurt him—"

'What will you do? Kill me? They will put you in prison, take away your baby. No, it is time you realized that you have never been in control. You are mine. You will always be mine. I will go to any lengths, including having Grace taken away so you never see her again if that's what it takes to keep you with me."

Fear turned her blood to ice as she looked into his eyes and understood he wasn't bluffing.

"You have only one choice. Come with me willingly and Grace will join us once we are settled."

No, she screamed silently. She didn't trust this man. But she also knew she couldn't keep someone like Zack from ripping Grace from her arms. Just as she knew that Jonas wasn't making an empty threat. She'd known this man was dangerous, but she hadn't realized how much he was willing to give up to have her—and Grace.

"You have only a few minutes to make up your mind, Lola." He had his phone in his hand. "Once I push this button, Zack will take Grace. If you ever want to see her again, you will agree to go with me."

"Where?" She knew she was stalling, fighting to find a way out of this. Colt. If he was dead, did she care what happened to her as long as she had his baby with her?

"Europe, South America. I haven't decided yet. Somewhere far away from all this. I have money. We will live well. We will be a family."

She thought of the family Colt had promised her and felt the ring on her finger.

Jonas's gaze went to her left hand. His face contorted in anger. "Take that off. Take that off now!"

Chapter Eighteen

Colt dialed the number quickly, knowing he had no choice even if he ended up behind bars. It would be worth it as long as Lola and Grace were safe from Jonas Emanuel once and for all.

"I need to borrow a helicopter," he said, the moment his friend answered.

"Mind if I ask what for?" Tommy Garrett asked, sounding like a man dragged from sleep in the wee hours of the morning. Tommy worked as a helicopter mechanic outside of Great Falls. Colt had served with him in Afghanistan and trusted the man with his life—and Lola's and Grace's.

"A madman has the woman I love and my baby daughter."

There was a beat of silence before Tommy said, "You planning to do this alone?"

"Better that way. I'll leave you out of it."

"Like hell. Tell me where you are. Outside my shop I have a Bell UH-1 Huey that needs its shakedown. The old workhorse is being used to fight forest fires. I'm on my way."

Colt knew the Huey could do up to 120 mph. But a safe cruising speed for helicopters was around a hundred. Without having to deal with traffic, road speeds or winding highways, the response time in a helicopter was considerably faster than anything on the ground. It was one reason Colt loved flying them.

So he wasn't surprised when Tommy landed in the pasture next to Colt's house thirty minutes later. The sun was coming up, chasing away the last of the dark. He could make out the mountains in the distance. Within a matter of minutes, they would be at the compound. He tried not think about what they would find.

"How much trouble is this going to get you in?" Colt asked his friend as he loaded the weapons in the back and climbed into the left seat, the crew chief seat.

"You just worry about what happens when we put this bird down," Tommy said in the adjacent seat at the controls.

As they headed for the mountaintop in the distance, Colt told him everything that had happened from that moment in the hotel in Billings to earlier that night.

When he finished, Tommy said, "So this woman is the one?"

For a moment, Colt could only nod around the lump in this throat. "I've never met anyone like her."

"Apparently this cult leader hasn't, either. Tell me you have a plan." He swore when Colt didn't answer right away.

"There will be armed guards who are under the control of the cult leader, Jonas Emanuel. But we don't have time to sneak up on them. You don't have to land.

Just get close enough to the ground that I can jump," Colt said as he began to strap on one of the weapons he'd brought. "Did I mention that these people are like zombies?"

"Great, you know how I love zombies. Except you can't kill zombies."

"These are religious zealots. I suspect they will be as hard to kill as zombies."

"This just keeps getting better and better," Tommy joked.

Colt looked over at him. "Thank you."

"Thank me after we get out with this woman you've fallen in love with and your daughter." He shook his head. "You never did anything like normal people."

"No, I never did. There's the road that goes up to the compound."

Tommy swooped down, skimming just over the tops of the pines, and Colt saw something he hadn't expected.

"What the hell?" As they got closer to the mountain, Colt spotted the line of vans coming off the mountain. He felt a chill. "Something's going on. Fly closer to those vehicles," he said to Tommy, who immediately dipped down.

Inside the vans, he saw the faces of Jonas followers. There were a dozen vans. As each passed, he saw the pale faces, the fear in their eyes.

"Where do you think they're going?" Tommy asked.

"I have no idea. Leaving for good, from the looks of it. What is Jonas up to? Are these people decoys or are they really clearing out?" He thought of Lola and the baby. How crazy was Jonas? Would he kill them and then kill himself, determined that Colt would never have either of them?

"Up there," Colt said, pointing to the mountaintop. Tommy swung the helicopter in the direction he pointed. Within a few minutes, the buildings came into sight. Colt didn't see any guards. He didn't see anyone. The place looked deserted. Had everyone left?

Not everyone, he noticed. There was a large black SUV sitting in front of Jonas's cabin.

"Think you can put her into that clearing in front of the cabin?"

"Seriously?" Tommy said. "You forget who you're talking to. Give me a dime and I can set her down on it." Colt chuckled because he knew it was true.

LOLA LOOKED DOWN at the antique ring that Colt had put on her finger. She swore she would never take it off. It felt so right on her finger. Colt felt so right.

Jonas moved faster than she thought he could after his injury. He grabbed the baby from her arms and shoved her. She fell back, coming down hard on the floor. "I told you to take if off. Now!"

"Give me Grace."

"Her name is Angel, and if you don't do what I say this moment…"

Lola pulled off the ring. She knew it was silly. Colt was probably dead. She'd lost so much. What did a ring matter at this point? The one thing she couldn't lose was Grace, and yet she felt as if she already had in more ways than one. Jonas had them captive. He could do whatever he wanted with Grace. Just as he could do whatever he wanted with her now.

"Happy?" she asked, still clutching the ring in her fist.

"Throw it away." He pointed toward the fireplace and the cold ashes filling it.

She hesitated again.

"Do as I say!" Jonas bellowed at her, waking up Grace. The baby began to cry.

Lola tossed the ring toward the fireplace. It was a lazy, bad throw, one that made Jonas's already furious face cloud over even more. The ring missed the fireplace opening, pinged off the rock and rolled under the couch. She looked at Jonas. If he really did have a bad heart, she realized his agitation right now could kill him. She doubted she would get that lucky, though.

He seemed to be trying to calm down. Grace kept crying and she could tell it was getting on his nerves.

She got to her feet. "Let me have her. She'll quit crying for me."

He shook his head. "I'm not sure I can trust you," he said slowly.

Colt was gone. The ring was gone. But Jonas had something much more precious. He had Grace. But Lola wasn't giving up.

"How do I know I can trust *you*?" she said.

The question surprised him. He'd expected her to cower, to promise him anything. She knew better than to do that. Jonas was surrounded by people who bowed down to him. Lola never had and maybe that's why he was so determined to have her.

She approached him. "You hurt my baby and I will

kill you. I'll cut your throat in your sleep. Or push you down a flight of stairs. Or poison your food. It might take me a while to get the opportunity, but believe me, I will do it."

He chuckled as his gaze met hers. "I do believe you. I've always loved your spirit. Your mother told me what a headstrong young woman you were. She wasn't wrong."

It hurt to have him mention her mother. Was it possible that Jonas could get away with the murders he'd committed? She feared it was. She thought of Colt and felt a sob rise in her throat. She forced it back down. She couldn't show weakness, not now, especially not for Colt. She had to think about Grace.

"We seem to be at an impasse," Jonas said. "What do you suggest we do?"

"I suggest you give me my baby and let me leave here."

He shook his head. "Not happening. Neither you or your baby will be leaving here—except with me."

"So what are you waiting for?" she demanded.

Jonas chuckled as he tilted his head as if to listen. "We're waiting for Colt. I just have a feeling he will somehow manage to try to save you one more time."

Lola listened as her heart thumped against her rib cage. Colt? He was alive? She thought she heard what sounded like a helicopter headed this way.

"I believe that's him now."

COLT FOUGHT THE bad feeling that had settled in the pit of his stomach. Jonas was playing hardball this time.

He wasn't going to let Lola and Grace go—not without a fight to the death. That's if they were still alive.

"Change of plans," he said to Tommy. He felt as if time was running out for Lola and Grace. "Put us down and wait for me," he said, fear making his voice sound strained as he passed Tommy a handgun. "I hope you won't have to use this. It appears that the guards have left, but I've already underestimated Jonas once and I don't want to do it again. I'm hoping this won't take long."

As Colt started to jump out, Tommy grabbed his sleeve. "Be careful."

Colt nodded. "You, too."

"I'll be here. Good luck."

Colt knew that if there was anyone he wanted on his side in a war it was Tommy Garrett—and this was war. These soldiers would die for their leader. They were just as devoted to dying for their cause as the ones he'd fought in Afghanistan.

The moment the chopper touched the ground, he leaped out and ran up the mountainside to where a large black SUV sat, the engine running and Brother Zack behind the wheel. Behind him, he heard Tommy shut down the engine. The rotors began to slow.

Colt looked around. The only person he'd seen so far was Zack, but that didn't mean that another of the guards hadn't stayed behind.

As he approached the SUV, he could hear the bass coming from the stereo. Closer, he saw that Zack had on headphones and was rockin' out. He must have had the stereo cranked, which explained why he hadn't heard the helicopter land. Nor had he heard him approach.

Colt yanked open the door. A surprised Zack turned. Colt grabbed him by his shirt and hauled him out. Unfortunately, Zack was carrying and he went for his gun. Zack was strong and combat trained. But Colt was fighting for Lola's and Grace's lives.

Colt managed to get hold of the man's arm, twisting it to the point of snapping as they struggled for the weapon. When the shot went off, it was muffled— just like Zack's grunt. Blood blossomed on the front of Zack's white shirt. The gun dropped, falling under the SUV.

As the man slumped, Colt shoved him back inside the vehicle, shut off the stereo and slammed the door before turning to Jonas's cabin. He'd seen suitcases in the back of the SUV and suspected the sheep weren't the only ones fleeing.

Colt pulled his holstered gun and climbed the steps. He had another gun stuck in the back of his jeans under his jacket. He always liked to be prepared—especially against someone like Jonas Emanuel.

He could still hear the sweep of the helicopter's rotors as they continued to slow. The wooden porch floor creaked under his boots. He braced himself and reached for the doorknob.

Before he could turn it, Lola opened the door. Her face had lost all its color. Her violet eyes appeared huge. He could see that she'd been crying. The sight froze him in place for moment. What had Jonas done to her? To Grace?

"Where is Jonas?" Colt asked quietly. Suddenly there wasn't a sound, not even a meadowlark from the grass or a breeze moaning in the pines. The eerie quiet sent a chill up his spine. "Lola?" The word came in a whisper.

"I'm leaving with Jonas," she said.

"Like hell." He could see that Jonas had put the fear into her and used Grace to do it. He'd never wanted to strangle anyone with his bare hands more than he did the cult leader at this moment.

"Please, it's what I want." Her words said one thing; her blue eyes pleaded with him to save Grace.

He pushed past her to find Jonas sitting in a chair just yards away. He was holding Grace in such a way that it stopped Colt cold.

JONAS RELISHED THE expression on Colt's handsome face. It almost made everything worth what he was going to have to give up. The cowboy thought he could just bust in here and take Lola and the baby? Not this time.

"Lola is going with me and so is her baby," he said as he turned the baby so she was facing her biological father and dangling from his fingers. He wanted Colt to see the baby's face and realize what he would be risking if he didn't back off.

"I don't think so," Colt said, but without much conviction. Jonas was ready to throw the baby against the rock fireplace if Colt took another step. The cowboy wasn't stupid. He'd figured that out right away. But he'd been stupid enough to come up here again. The man should have been dead.

Idly, Jonas wondered what had gone wrong at the

gravel pit. He'd known he couldn't depend on Elmer, but he was disposable. Brother Carl had inspired more faith that he would get the job done. Jonas had assumed that Carl would have to kill both Elmer and Colt. Clearly, the job had been too much for him.

"Has he hurt you?" Colt asked Lola.

She shook her head.

Jonas was touched by the cowboy's concern, but quickly getting bored with all this. "Elmer and Carl?" he asked, curious.

"Swimming, that is, if either of them knows how," Colt answered.

"And Brother Zack?"

"No longer listening to music in your big SUV."

So he couldn't depend on Zack to come to his rescue. Another surprise. Everyone was letting him down. Just as well that he was packing it all in. He'd grown tired of the squabbling among the sisters and the backbiting of the brothers. Human nature really was malicious.

Still, he would miss Zack. And now who would lead his people to the promised land of Arizona? He chuckled to himself since he didn't own any land in Arizona. But they wouldn't know that until they got there, would they?

He saw the cowboy shoot a look at Lola. She was standing off to Colt's left as if she didn't know what to do. He could see the tension in her face. She wasn't being so smart-mouthed now, was she? As much as he was enjoying this, he didn't have to ask what she was hoping would happen here.

But, this time, she'd been outplayed. The cowboy

was going to lose. It was simply a matter of how much he would have to lose before this was over. Did he realize that he wasn't getting out of here alive? At this point, Jonas wasn't sure he cared if Lola and the baby survived either, though he still wanted the woman, and damned if he wouldn't have her—dead or alive. The thought didn't even surprise him. His father used to say that one day he would reach rock bottom. Was this it?

"Why would you want a woman who doesn't love you?" Colt asked conversationally, as if they were old friends discussing the weather—and took a step closer.

"Because I can have her. I can have anything I want, and I want her. The baby is optional. I guess that's up to you."

"How's that?"

"You can't reach me before I hurl your baby into the rock fireplace. But if you try, I will, and then we will only be talking about Lola. The thing is, I don't think she will love you anymore, not after you got her baby killed," Jonas said. "Want to take a chance on that? Take another step…"

COLT COULD SEE that Jonas's arms were tiring from holding Grace up the way he was. He was using the baby like a shield. There was no way Colt could get a shot off with Jonas sitting and the baby out in front of him. Nor could he chance that, as he fired, Jonas wouldn't throw Grace into the rocks.

One glance at Lola and he knew that what they both feared was a real possibility—Jonas could drop the baby at any moment. Or, worse, throw Grace against the rock fireplace as he was threatening.

"Colt, I'll go with him. It's the only way," Lola pleaded as she stepped to him, grabbing his arm.

It was a strange thing for her to do and for a moment he didn't understand. Then he felt her reach behind him to the pistol he had at his back. She must have seen the bulk of it under his shirt. She freed the gun and dropped her hands to her sides, keeping turned so Jonas couldn't see what she held. Then she began to cry.

"You heard her," Jonas said. "Leave before someone gets hurt. Before you get hurt." His arms were shaking visibly. "If you care anything about this child…"

Jonas knew Colt wasn't leaving without Lola and Grace. Saying he could walk away was all bluff. Did he have a weapon handy? Colt suspected so.

Lola was still halfway facing him so she could keep the gun in her hand hidden. Colt feared what she planned to do, but he could feel time running out. Jonas was losing patience. Worse, his arms were shaking now. He couldn't hold the baby much longer—and he couldn't back down. Wouldn't.

"Tell him, Jonas," she cried, suddenly running toward the cult leader and dropping to her knees only feet from him after sticking the gun in the waist of her jeans. "Tell him I'm going with you, and that it's true and to leave."

The cult leader hadn't expected her to do that. For a moment, it looked as if he was going to throw the baby. Before he could, Lola grabbed for Grace with her left hand. At the same time, she pulled the pistol from behind her with her right. She had hold of Grace's chubby little leg and wasn't letting go.

Everything happened fast after that. Colt, seeing what Lola had planned, took the shot the moment Lola managed to pull the baby down and away from Jonas's smug face. Colt had always been an expert shot. Even during the most stressful situations.

He missed. Jonas had fallen forward just enough that the shot went over his head and lodged in the back of the chair. Before he could fire again, he heard Lola fire. She'd taken the shot from the floor, shooting under Grace to hit the man low in the stomach. He saw Jonas release Grace as he grabbed for his bleeding belly.

Lola dropped the gun and pulled Grace into her arms. They were both crying. As Colt rushed to the cult leader, his gun leveled at the man's head, Lola scrambled away from Jonas with Grace tucked in her arms.

Jonas was holding his stomach with one hand and fumbling for something in the chair with the other. Colt was aiming to shoot, to finish Jonas, when he saw that it wasn't a gun the cult leader was going for. It was the man's phone.

He watched Jonas punch at the screen, his bloody fingers slippery, his hands shaking. It took a moment for the alert to sound. Jonas seemed to wait, one bloody hand on his stomach, the other on his phone. He stared at the front door, expecting it to come flying open as one of the guards burst in.

Seconds passed, then several minutes. Nothing happened. Jonas looked wild-eyed at the door as if he couldn't believe it.

"They've all left," Colt said. "There is no one to help you."

Jonas looked down at his phone. With trembling fingers he made several attempts to key in 9-1-1 and finally gave up. "You have to call an ambulance. It's the humane thing to do."

"This from the man who was about to kill my baby daughter?"

"You would let me bleed to death?"

Colt looked over at Lola, huddled in the corner with Grace. Their gazes met. He pulled out his own phone and keyed in 9-1-1. He asked to speak to the sheriff.

When he was connected with Flint, he said, "You were right. Jonas hit us in the middle of the night. He sent two men to kill me. I left them in the old gravel pits. He took Lola and Grace, but they are both safe now. Unfortunately, one of his guards tried to shoot me. He's dead outside here on the compound and Jonas is wounded, so you'll need an ambulance and a—" He was going to say *coroner*, but before he could get the word out, the front door of the cabin banged open.

He spun around in time to see Zack bleeding and barely able to stand, but the man could still shoot. He fired the weapon in his hand in a barrage of bullets before Colt could pull the trigger.

LOLA SCREAMED. GRACE WAILED. It happened so fast. She'd thought it was all over. Finally. She'd thought they were finally safe. And so had Colt. He hadn't expected Zack to be alive—let alone come in shooting—any more than she had.

Colt threw himself in Grace's and her direction. As he did, he brought up the weapon he'd been holding on Jonas. The air filled with the loud reports of gunfire.

Lola laid her body over Grace's to protect her, knowing that Colt had thrown himself toward them to do the same. It took her a few moments to realize that the firing had stopped. She peeked out, terrified that she would find Colt lying dead at her feet.

Colt lay on his side, his back to her. She put Grace down long enough to reach for him. He was holding his leg, blood oozing out from between his fingers. He looked up at her.

"Are you and Grace—"

"We're fine. But you're bleeding," Lola cried.

"It's just a flesh wound," Colt said. "Don't worry about me. As long as you and Grace are all right..." He grimaced as he tried to get to his feet.

In the doorway, Zack lay crumpled on the floor. Lola couldn't tell if he was breathing or not. Her gaze swung to Jonas. He had tumbled out of his chair. He wasn't breathing, given that the top of his head was missing. She looked away quickly.

Grace's wailing was the only sound in the room. She rushed to her. As she did, she saw Colt's cell phone on the floor and picked it up. The sheriff was still there.

"We need an ambulance. Colt is wounded. Zack and Jonas are dead."

"Tommy," Colt said, trying to get to his feet. "He would have seen Zack heading for the cabin..." He limped to the door and pushed it open. Beyond it, he saw Tommy slumped over the controls of the helicopter. "There isn't time to wait for an ambulance. Tell the sheriff we'll be at the hospital."

As she related to the sheriff what Colt had said, she hurried to the couch. Squatting down, she fished her ring from under it. Her gentle toss of it hadn't hurt the ring or the diamonds. She slipped it on her finger, feeling as if now she could face anything again. Then, holding Grace in her arms, she ran after Colt to the helicopter sitting like a big dark bird in the middle of the compound.

COLT IGNORED THE pain as he ran to the helicopter. When he reached Tommy, he hurriedly felt for a pulse. For a moment, he thought his friend was dead, and yet he didn't see any blood. He found a pulse and felt a wave of relief. He'd dragged his friend into this. The last thing he wanted to do was get him killed.

On closer inspection, he could see a bump the size of a goose egg on Tommy's head. He figured Zack must have ambushed him before coming up to the cabin to finish things.

"Is he...?" Lola asked from behind him. She held a crying Grace in her arms and was trying to soothe her.

"He's alive, but we need to get him to the hospital. Come around the other side and climb in the back with Grace." Colt helped them in and then slid into the seat and took over the controls. He started up the motor. The rotors began to turn and then spin. A few minutes later, he lifted off and headed for Gilt Edge.

The helicopter swept over the tops of the pines and out of the mountains. Colt glanced over at Tommy. He seemed to be coming around. In the back, Lola had calmed Grace down and she now slept in her mother's arms.

He told himself that all was right with the world. Lola and Grace were safe. Tommy was going to make it. But he was feeling the effects of his blood loss as he saw the hospital's helipad in the distance. He'd never lost a bird. He told himself he wasn't going to lose this one—especially with the precious cargo he was carrying.

Colt set the chopper down and turned off the engine. After that, everything became a blur. He knew he'd lost a lot of blood and was light-headed, but it wasn't until he'd shut down the chopper and tried to get out that he realized how weak he was.

The last thing he remembered was seeing hospital staff rushing toward the helicopter pushing two gurneys.

Chapter Nineteen

Colt woke to find Lola and Grace beside his bed. He tried to sit up, but Lola gently pushed him back down.

"Tommy is fine," she told him as if knowing exactly what he needed to hear. "A mild concussion. The doctor is having a terrible time keeping him in bed. We're all fine now."

Colt relaxed back on the pillows and smiled. "I was so worried. But everyone's all right?"

She nodded. "I was worried about you." She pushed a lock of hair back from his forehead and looked into his eyes. "You lost so much blood, but the doctor says you're going to be fine."

He glanced over at the IV attached to his arm. "I remember flying the chopper to the hospital but not much after that." He took her hand and squeezed it. "How is Grace?"

"Sleeping." Lola pointed to the bassinet the nurses had brought in for her. "I refused to leave until I knew you were all right." They'd also brought in a cot for Lola, he saw. "I've just been going back and forth from your room to Tommy's."

Colt smiled, took her hand and squeezed it. "I almost lost you. Again."

"But you saved me. Again. Aren't you getting tired of it?"

He shook his head. "Never." He glanced down at the ring on her finger. When he'd come into the cabin, he'd seen her rubbing the spot on her left hand where it had been. He hadn't been surprised Jonas hadn't liked seeing the ring on her finger. "When are you going to marry me?"

"You name the day. But right now you're in the middle of selling your ranch and holding an auction, and the doctor isn't going to let you out of here for a while. The bullet missed bone, but your leg is going to take some time to heal. Also, I believe you missed your appointment with your Realtor."

Colt grimaced. "Margaret. She is going to be furious."

"I called her. Apparently, ending up in the hospital bought you some time."

"I need to talk to Tommy, but I want to talk to him about my plan for the future, for *our* future."

The hospital-room door opened and Sheriff Flint Cahill stuck his head in. "Our patient awake? I hate to interrupt, but I need to talk to Colt if he's up to it."

Colt pulled Lola down for a kiss. "I'll talk to the sheriff. You can leave Grace. If she wakes up, I'll take care of her."

She nodded. "I know you will." She said hello to the sheriff. "I'll just be down the hall."

Flint took off his Stetson and pulled up a chair. "I've already spoken with Tom Garrett and Lola. I have their statements, but I need yours. I have two dead men up on the mountain, two suffering from dehydration and two more in the hospital. Elmer and Carl have been picked up. They both said they were the ones who almost got killed, not you." He pulled out his notebook and pen. "Said you knocked them into the gravel pit."

Colt nodded. "After they took me from my house in the middle of the night, tied me up and planned to kill me and dump me in the pit. They probably didn't mention that."

"Actually, Elmer confessed this morning. They're both behind bars." The sheriff sighed. "Just give me the basics. You'll have to come down to the office when you're released."

Colt related everything from the time he was awakened by the cult members breaking into the house until he landed the helicopter at the hospital.

"It would have been nice if you'd given me a call," Flint said.

"Jonas would have killed them. He was so close to hurting Grace…" His voice broke. "If Lola hadn't acted when she did…"

"Jonas had one bullet in him from a gun registered to you, but all the others were from a gun registered to Jonas himself. We found it next to Zack's body. Why would Zack kill his own leader?"

Colt shook his head. "He came in firing. When I jumped out of the way, he kept firing…"

"He's the one who wounded you?"

"Yes. And the one who knocked out Tommy, but he might have already told you that."

"Actually," the sheriff said. "He didn't see who or what hit him."

"Zack was the only guard left. Everyone else vacated the property."

"Lola said that most of them were headed to Arizona, where Jonas had promised them a place to live, but we can't find any property owned by him or SLS," Flint said. "We did, though, find a variety of places where he has stashed their money, a lot of it. I would imagine there'll be lawsuits against his estate."

"Lola thinks he murdered her parents. They're buried on the compound."

The sheriff raked a hand through his hair. "We saw that there is a new grave in the woods. We were able to contact a couple of SLS followers who didn't make it any farther than town. They said they think he killed Sister Rebecca and that she is buried in the new grave." He shook his head. "He had me fooled."

"Me, too. For a while," Colt admitted.

Grace began to whimper next to his bed.

The sheriff put away his notebook and pen as he rose. "I'll let you see to your daughter." He tipped his Stetson as he left.

THE STORY HIT the local paper the next day. SLS members were spilling their guts about what had gone on up at the compound. A half dozen had already filed lawsuits against the fortune Jonas had amassed.

The article made Colt and Tommy sound like heroes. Colt figured that was Lola's doing since she'd told him she'd been interviewed by a reporter. She'd said she

was anxious for her story—and that of her parents—
to get out.

"Maybe it will keep other people from getting taken
in by men like Jonas," she'd said. "He caught my parents at a vulnerable time in their lives. But if they could
be fooled, then anyone can."

Lola picked him up after the doctor released him
from the hospital.

He sat in the passenger seat of the SUV she'd had
delivered to his house. The woman was damned independent, but he liked that about her. Grace grinned at
him from the car seat as they drove out to the ranch.
Drove home. Well, home for a while anyway. All he'd
been able to think about was getting back to that old
ranch house that had felt like a prison before Lola. Now
it felt like home.

Not that he was going to get sentimental and hang
on to the house. Or the ranch. He wanted a new start
for his little family.

They'd been home for a while when Tommy stopped
by the house to see how he was doing before taking his
helicopter home.

"You've met Lola," Colt said.

Tommy nodded.

"We got to know each other while we were waiting
on you to get well. I had to thank him for all he did in
helping us." She turned to the man from where she was
making cookies in the kitchen. "We owe you. If you can
stick around for twelve minutes, I will have a batch of
chocolate chip cookies coming out of the oven. It's not
much, given what you did for us."

"I'm just glad you're all right," Tommy said, looking bashful. "Anyway, I owe your husband. He saved my life. I'd do anything for him. I got to tell you, I think our boy Colt has done good this time," his friend said, grinning at Lola, then Colt. "You got yourself a good one," he said with a wink. "So what's this plan you wanted to talk to me about?"

"You're not mad at me for almost getting you killed?" Colt asked.

Tommy looked embarrassed. "I let some cult member sneak up on me."

"Zack was ex-military."

"That makes me feel a little better, but let's keep it to ourselves, okay? So what's up?" he asked as he took the chair he was offered at the kitchen table. Lola checked the cookies. Grace was watching her from her carrier on the counter. Colt liked watching Lola cook. He just liked watching her and marveling at how lucky he'd gotten.

"Colt?" Tommy said, grinning as he drew his attention again.

He laughed, then got serious. "Remember all the times we talked about starting our own helicopter service?" Colt and Tommy had spent hours at night in Afghanistan planning what they would do when they got out of the Army. Only Colt had stayed in, so their dream of owning their own flight company had been put off indefinitely.

"You still thinking about it?" Tommy asked.

"I know you're doing great with your repair business. I know you might not be interested in starting a company with me, but I've sold the ranch. I have money to invest. You don't have to answer right now. Take a few days to—"

"I don't need a few days. Absolutely," his friend said. "Where were you thinking of headquartering it?"

"There's a piece of land close by I'd like to build a house on. Right down the road from it would be the ideal place for the office, with lots of room for the shops and landing any number of birds."

Tommy laughed. "You really have been thinking about this." He glanced past Colt to Lola, who was busy taking the cookies out of the oven. "What about the military?" he asked, his gaze shifting back to Colt.

"I've decided not to take the upcoming assignment and resign my commission. I'm getting married. I have a family now. I don't want to be away from them."

"I get it," Tommy said as he took the warm cookie Lola offered him. "How soon?"

"I can make an offer on the land and we can get construction going on the shops and hangers—"

"How long before you get married?" Tommy asked with a laugh and took a bite of the cookie, before complimenting Lola.

"In three weeks. That was something else I needed to talk to you about," Colt said. "I need a best man."

LOLA WANTED TO pinch herself. She couldn't believe she was getting married. She'd never been so happy. She was glad they'd put off the wedding for a few weeks. There'd been a lot of questions about everything that had happened up on the mountain. The investigation, though, had finally ended.

It had taken a while for the bodies of her parents and Sister Rebecca to be exhumed. Just as she'd suspected, autopsies revealed that both of her parents had been poisoned. So had Rebecca. Lola made arrangements to have their remains flown to California and reinterred in the plots next to her sister's.

"You have nothing to feel guilty about," Colt had assured her.

"But if I'd come straight home after university and tried to get them out of that place—"

"You know it wouldn't have done any good. They were determined that you join them, right?"

She'd nodded. "But if I'd come right home when I got my father's letter, maybe I could have—"

"You know how Jonas operated. It wouldn't have made a difference. You said yourself that your mother adored Jonas. You couldn't have gotten her to leave and your father wouldn't have left without her, right?"

She'd known he was right. Still, she hated that she hadn't been able to save them. She was just grateful to Colt. If it hadn't been for him...

Lola looked down at her sleeping daughter. Yes, if it hadn't been for him there would have been no Grace.

COLT WANDERED THROUGH the days afterward, more content than he had ever been. He and Lola went horseback riding. She took to it so well that she made him promise he would teach Grace when she was old enough.

"I'll teach all of the kids."

"All of the kids?" she'd asked with one raised eyebrow.

He'd smiled as he'd pulled her to him. "Tell me you wouldn't mind having a couple more."

"You want a son."

"I want whatever you give me," he'd said, nuzzling her neck and making her laugh. "I'll be taking all girls if that's what you've got for me."

Lola had kissed him, promising to give him as many children as he wanted.

"And I'll teach them all to fly. Which reminds me, anytime you want to go for a ride… The helicopters will be coming in right after the wedding."

The new owners of the ranch had allowed Colt to stay on with his family until he was able to get a mobile home put on the land he'd bought back from them. "We'll live in it until the house is finished, then maybe use it for the office until the office building is done."

Lola seemed as excited as he was about the business they were starting with Tommy. She kept busy with her new friends Lillie and Mariah. They were actually talking playdates for the kids.

He ran into Wyatt a couple more times in town. He hadn't wanted to slug him. Actually, he'd wanted to thank him. The thought had made him laugh.

Also, Colt hadn't been that surprised when Julia called. He almost hadn't answered. "Hello?"

"Colt, it's Julia. I saw your engagement announcement in the newspaper not long after that story came out. What a story."

He didn't know what to say.

"Wyatt and I are over. I know you don't care, but I wanted you to hear it from me first."

"I'm sorry." He really was. He no longer had any ill will toward either of them and said as much.

"I won't bother you again. I'm actually leaving town. But I had to ask you something..." She seemed to hesitate. "It's amazing what you did for this Lola woman. You really put up a fight to save her and the baby."

He waited, wondering where she was going with this.

"Why..." Her voice broke. "Why didn't you put up a fight for me?"

It had never crossed his mind to try to keep Julia from marrying Wyatt. She was right. He hadn't put up a fight. He'd been hurt, he'd been angry, but he hadn't made some grandiose effort like riding a horse into the church to stop the wedding—if it had ever gone that far.

"I hope you find what you're looking for," he said, because there wasn't anything else he could say.

"And I hope you're unhappy as hell." She disconnected.

He looked over at Lola and laughed.

"Julia," she said.

"Yep, she called to say she liked the article."

Lola smiled. "You're a terrible liar."

"She's leaving town."

"Really?" She didn't seem unhappy to hear that.

"She wished us well."

"Now I know you're lying," she said as he pulled her close.

THE WEDDING TOOK PLACE in a field of flowers surrounded by the four mountain ranges. Colt had purchased the property just days before. He'd had to scramble to get everything moved in for the ceremony.

What had started as a small wedding had grown, as old and new friends wanted to be a part of it.

"Lola, I know this isn't what we planned," Colt had apologized. They'd agreed to a small wedding, and somehow it had gone awry.

She had laughed. "I love that all these people care about you and want to be there. They're becoming my friends, as well." Lillie and Mariah had given her a baby shower, the three becoming instant friends.

He kissed her. "I just want it to be the best day of your life."

"That day was when I met you."

Colt couldn't believe how many people had helped to make the day special. Calls came in from around the world from men he'd served with. A dozen of them flew in for the ceremony. The guest list had continued to grow right up until the wedding.

"Let us cater it for you," Lillie and Mariah had suggested. "Darby insists. And the Stagecoach Saloon is all yours for the reception, if it rains."

Lola had hugged her new friends, eyes glistening and Colt thought he couldn't be more blessed. Lola had accepted their kind offer and added, "Only if the two of you will agree to be my matrons of honor."

So much had been going on that the weeks leading up to the wedding had flown by. Colt wished his father was alive to see this—his only son changing diapers, getting up for middle-of-the-night feedings, bathing the baby in the kitchen sink, and all the while loving every minute of it.

Tommy always chuckled when he came by and

caught Colt being a father. "If the guys could see you now," he'd joked. But Colt had seen his friend's wistful looks. He hoped Tommy found someone he could love as much as Colt loved Lola.

She'd continued to amaze him, taking everything in her stride as the ranch auction was held and the sale of the ranch continued. She'd had her things shipped from where they'd been in storage and helped him start packing up what he planned to keep at the house.

He'd felt overwhelmed sometimes, but Lola was always cool and calm. He often thought of that woman he'd met in Billings—and the one he'd found on his doorstep in the middle of the night. Often he didn't feel he was good enough for her. But then she would find him, put her arms around him and rest her head on his shoulder, and he would breathe in the scent of her and know that this was meant to be.

Like standing here now in a field of flowers next to Lola with all their friends and the preacher ready to marry them. If this was a dream, he didn't want to wake up.

LOLA COULDN'T BELIEVE all the people who had come into her life because of Colt. She looked over at him. He was so handsome in his Western suit and boots. He was looking at her, his blue eyes shining. He smiled as the preacher said, "Do you take this woman—"

"I sure do," he said, and everyone laughed.

Lola hardly remembered the rest of the ceremony. She felt so blissfully happy that she wasn't even sure her feet had touch und all day.

But she remembered the kiss. Colt had pulled her to him, taking his time as he looked into her eyes. "I love you, Lola," he'd whispered.

She'd nodded through her tears and then he'd kissed her. The crowd had broken into applause. Cowboy hats and Army caps had been thrown into the air. Somewhere beyond the crowd, a band began to play.

Lillie hugged her before handing her Grace. Lola looked up from the infant she held in her arms, her eyes full of tears. Colt put his arm around both of them as they took their first steps as Mr. and Mrs. Colt Mc-Cloud.

* * * * *

THE SHERIFF'S
SECRET

JULIE ANNE LINDSEY

Dedicated to Tina.

Chapter One

Tina Ellet checked her watch for the tenth time in half as many minutes. Two of her seven patients had missed the entire group session, without so much as a text to let her know they weren't coming. Dedication and accountability to personal recovery was a must in her program, and the group had always taken the requirements seriously. Until now. So what were those two up to?

She rubbed goose bumps off her arms. Trouble was coming, she was sure of it. She just wasn't sure what form it would take. She approached her wide office windows and gave the empty sidewalk outside another long look. The forest of brightly colored trees across the lot swayed with a wicked wind. It wasn't autumn in Kentucky until a storm tried to knock you down. "Please take it slow on your way home or to work." She turned to face the group with a forced smile. "It doesn't look good out there."

The men and women nodded in easy agreement.

"If any of you hear from Carl or Tucker, please let them know they were missed." Tina was certain many of them were worried, too, but there was nothing to be done about it for now. Instead, they flattened folding chairs and dropped disposable cups into the trash, making fast work of the cleanup and sending faint scents of cigarette smoke and coffee into the air. The scents of her childhood, minus the distinct sting of alcohol.

When the room was righted, she shouldered her handbag and collected the empty tray from her home-made blueberry muffins. Early morning sessions were popular with her group, and Tina tried to send a little hope and encouragement with each member when they left. At least enough to help them face whatever the day might bring. So far, this day had brought plenty of rain. The forecasted showers had come right on schedule, successfully soaking everything in sight. "I suppose we might as well make a run for it. The rain doesn't appear to be giving up anytime soon." In fact, the rain hadn't slowed since it began more than an hour before. "Does everyone have a ride?"

Steven, the newest member of her group, looked away as the others raised their car keys.

"Steven?" She tipped her head toward the sheeting rain. "Would you like a ride home? I'm sure someone would be glad to drive you. No one should walk in this."

Several members chimed in with offers, and Steven dipped his chin in agreement to the one made by Carol, an older woman standing near the door. Carol winked at Tina. She'd see Steven home safely.

Sometimes heading a recovery group for PTSD and trauma survivors was tricky. What one member saw as comfort, another saw as a threat, and so far, Steven saw most things as a threat. He'd joined the group after receiving an other-than-honorable discharge from the army last month. His severe emotional trauma had led to unbecoming behavior that garnered him a quick boot from the service, complete with truncated benefits and nowhere to turn for the support he needed. Luckily, Tina had found him, and she was certain she could help, if she didn't scare him away first.

"All right. Here we go." She swung the door open and held it for the group to pass. Together, they moved onto the sidewalk and waited beneath the large metal awning while Tina locked up. Hopefully, wherever Carl and Tucker were, they were safe, not caught in a flash flood or car accident or worse. She blamed her "mother's mind" for the number of scary scenarios scooting through her head. Since the birth of her precious daughter four months ago, she'd begun to see potential danger everywhere and longed more than ever to wrap her arms around the entire world in protection.

Slowly, a few brave souls ventured into the storm, plodding through puddles toward their vehicles and prompting the others to follow. The lot was nearly empty this time of day, making Mountain Medical Plaza the perfect location for her private morning sessions.

Tina followed Carol and Steven toward a massive pickup truck whose lights flashed and locks popped up upon approach. Tina's car was the small sedan two spots away. Steven slowed his pace as he neared Carol's truck, suddenly unconcerned by the rain and wholly focused on a distant point in the morning sky.

"Steven?" Tina lifted her handbag overhead, a makeshift umbrella, and squinted through the rain. "Everything okay?"

He raised an arm, finger pointed at the building's rooftop. "Do you see that?"

The fine hairs on the back of Tina's neck raised to attention. She forced her eyes to focus through the downpour. "What do you see?"

A small shadow rocked into view. What appeared to be the long barrel of a rifle stretched out before it.

Ice coiled in Tina's gut. *It couldn't be...*

"Gun!" Steven yelled. "Get down!" He turned for Tina, arms thrown wide as one loud blast of gunfire cracked the air. Steven's head whipped back and his gait fell short. His legs crumbled beneath him and his body collapsed onto the rain-battered asphalt in a silent thud. Group members screamed and hollered around her, scattering between vehicles and running for the building. Shattered glass rained over Steven, falling from the truck window at his side.

Tina's lungs burned as she struggled to breathe. She fell to the ground, barely perceiving what had happened. Wind whipped through her hair and mingled with the ringing in her ears. Voices warbled around her, distorted by the storm and panic beating through her head. "Stay down!" she screamed. "Get down and stay down!" She forced her eyes to search for the shadow once more, but it was gone.

Where did it go? She craned her neck in every direction, as if the shooter could be anywhere, beside her, behind her. Her chest ached and her mouth dried. How could she know who the next bullet would hit? Would there be another? Was the man finished shooting, or was he reloading? She dug her phone from her purse and dialed 911.

"911. What's your emergency?" a tinny voice echoed in her ringing ear.

Tina scrambled under the truck, counting pairs of feet moving through the lot toward the building. Four. Good. The rest were safe and together now.

"Ma'am? What's your emergency?" the voice repeated.

The world snapped back into focus then, the tragedy becoming unbearably clear. "There's a gunman at

Mountain Medical Plaza." The words fell clumsily off her tongue, a line memorized for a play. Impossible to be real. "One man is down. I don't know." She stared at Steven's motionless form. "He's not moving. I don't know where he was hit. There's so much blood."

"Where's the shooter now?"

"I'm not sure. He stopped, I think." Tina willed her mind into focus. Her group needed her. Steven needed her.

"Are you somewhere safe now, ma'am? Is there somewhere you can find shelter until emergency responders arrive?"

Her office door seemed miles away, but two group members were already there, crouched against the wall, and two others were steps away. She could help them. Get them inside.

Screaming tires drew her attention across the lot. A faded red pickup truck roared recklessly in the distance and fishtailed onto the county road beyond, barreling away like the devil was chasing it.

Tina pulled in a long gulp of oxygen to clear her brain. "I think the shooter is gone now. There was only one shot. Maybe two minutes ago. And someone's racing away in a pickup." She forced herself from beneath the truck and onto her knees, crawling over the broken glass to Steven's side. "A man's been shot. He's not moving." She stared at his motionless chest. "Not breathing." Tina pressed shaky fingers to his neck in search of a pulse that didn't beat, then tried again. "No, no, no, no." She set the phone on the ground at Steven's side, pressed the speaker option, then laced her fingers against his chest and said a silent prayer. Tina filled his lungs and pumped his heart for him until her arms shook uncontrollably from terror, grief and effort. "He's not breathing," she cried. "His heart isn't beating. CPR isn't working."

Behind her, the group bellowed for her to come to them. Above her, the thunder rolled.

Tina grabbed her phone and pushed onto her feet. In a torrent of desperation, she forced herself away from Steven. A round of ugly sobs pressed through her tightened lips as she hurried back to the group collecting outside her office once more. She wiped her hands on her shirt, smearing it with blood, then jammed her key into the lock and ushered the others inside. "One man is dead," she reported to the woman on the phone. "The rest of us are..." Are what? *Fine?* None of them were fine. A man had just been murdered in front of their eyes. "No one else was physically injured."

She wiped her eyes and nose, fighting the wave of panic determined to lay her in a useless ball. How many times had she called 911 as a kid? How many times had her drunken father taken his frustrations out on a mother too depressed to get out of bed? Broken limbs and noses. Cuts and bruises. Nothing like this. Never like this, and yet she'd felt exactly this way. Desperate. Afraid. And guilty. Always guilty. "I'm so sorry," she wept. "So very sorry."

The soft cry of an approaching ambulance registered in the distance, refueling her hope and drive. "I hear them now," she told the dispatch operator. "Help is almost here." She made the second announcement more loudly, aiming her words at the terrified group before her.

Tina slid her suit jacket from her shoulders. "You will survive this," she told them, falling back on her training. "Understand?" They stared in variations of shock, anguish and despair. "You are survivors." She forced the words from between clenched teeth, as much for her own benefit as theirs. "Help is almost here now. You're going to be okay."

Except Steven. Steven would never again be okay.

When she could find no more words, she carried her jacket through the raging storm and placed it over Steven. Fresh out of faux strength, Tina fell onto her bottom beside him, cell phone in hand, and bawled. What was wrong with this world?

CADE COUNTY SHERIFF West Garrett pressed a wide-brimmed hat over his head and levered himself out of the cruiser. A carousel of red-and-white lights illuminated the gruesome scene at a local counseling practice. Blood and glass covered the lot beside a newer model pickup truck. EMTs spoke with a cluster of people near one building.

A man lay motionless and partially covered by a tiny, bloodstained woman's coat. This must have been the fatality Dispatch had announced. Presumably, the coat belonged to the woman curled up at the man's side. Her arms were wrapped around her knees and her face was buried in the material of her ruined suit pants. Only the top of her blond head was visible, and it was shaking with each new sob she released.

West made his way, slowly, toward the woman.

The coroner dropped a black bag on the ground opposite the deceased.

"Ma'am?" West tugged the material of his pants and crouched beside her. "I'm Sheriff West Garrett. I'm afraid I need to ask you a few questions."

The woman stilled. Her sobs ceased.

West rested his forearms on his thighs, allowing his hands to dangle between his knees. Rain dripped from the brim of his sheriff's hat and the sleeves of his slicker. "Are you hurt, ma'am?"

She slowly raised her tearstained face, catching his gaze in hers. "No."

"Tina." His heart clenched and his gut fisted at the sight of her after all these years, her clothes smeared in blood.

"Hi, West," she croaked. Her rain-soaked hair hung in clumps over her shaking shoulders.

The sound of his name on her tongue was a painful slap of nostalgia. "Hi." West struggled to make her presence at the crime scene something other than ludicrous. "What are you doing here?"

"It's my practice."

West rubbed a rough hand over his mouth. He'd heard she worked at the medical center but had refused the details. This wasn't the same girl who'd stolen his teenage heart and eventually destroyed it. That girl had left Cade County long ago. This was someone else. Someone he no longer knew. He pulled in a long breath and refocused on the job. He gave her a more critical exam. "Is any of this blood yours?"

"No." Tina pushed onto her feet with a whimper and wrapped trembling arms around her middle. "I'm not hurt. I want to help."

He stood, as well. "All right. You can start by telling me what happened." He motioned to a section of the sidewalk covered with an awning. "Let's step out of the storm."

She complied, shuffling toward the building, peeling clumps of sopping hair off her cheeks and forehead. "We were leaving the building. It was just after eight, and there was a shadow on the roof." She stopped short and swallowed several times.

"We?"

"I have a weekly support group for PTSD and emotional trauma survivors." She rolled her shoulders forward and squelched a sob. "Steven saw the figure on the roof. He told us to get down. He tried to get to me." She pressed the heels of both hands against her eyes. "The gunman shot him before he reached me."

West nodded toward the man on the pavement. "That is Steven?"

She removed her hands from her face with a sigh. "Steven Masters. He was discharged from the army about a month ago. He has a wife and little girl." Her voice broke on the last word. "Oh, Lord. His poor family," she whispered. Tina spun away from West, walking aimlessly into the lot, obviously in shock despite her efforts to look otherwise.

"Hey." West jogged to her side and wrapped an arm around her shoulders. "Why don't you have a seat while we talk?" He led her to a bench beneath the awning and released her at once. The instinct to comfort her was unprofessional and wildly outdated. "Better?"

She didn't answer.

"Tina?" West knew firsthand that she wasn't a sharer, but this time he needed her to open up. "I know this is tough," he began.

Tina rolled glossy blue eyes up at him. "Someone shot Steven from that rooftop. I don't know who. I don't know why." She shook her head roughly. "It's just nonsense."

"West?" His baby brother and current deputy, Cole Garrett, strode to his side. Cole was four years younger than West and twice as smart, but he'd been bitten by the law enforcement bug like the rest of the Garrett men and refused to go out and change the world like West and their older brothers had suggested. "I'm going to head out and see if I can get a bead on this guy."

"What do you have so far?" West asked.

Cole gave Tina a wayward look. "Not much. Witnesses heard a car hightailing out of here. I'm going to head up the road and see if anyone saw a vehicle taking the state route in a hurry."

"It was a pickup truck," Tina said.

Cole's sharp gaze locked on hers before drifting back to West. "Isn't she—"

"Don't," West warned.

Cole whistled the sound of a falling missile and walked away.

Tina rolled her head against the wall behind their bench. "I suppose I'm not exactly the Garrett family's favorite local."

West grunted. That was a conversation he never wanted to have. The past was the past. He'd like to leave it there. "I need to know which member of your group could've made someone mad enough to do this?"

Tina's soft expression hardened. She glanced at the coroner's van. "The only person to blame is the maniac who did it."

West raised an eyebrow. "I'm not blaming. I'm looking for bread crumbs. Which one's the loose cannon?"

"All my patients are serious about their recovery. They're employed. Paying bills. Contributing to society. They wouldn't be here every week, carving out time before work, if they weren't dedicated to the process."

"Uh-huh." West nodded. "I understand why you'd say they're doing well, seeing as how you're their therapist." He gave a little smile, knowing he walked a fine line. "You look for the best in people, and that's admirable, but can you tell me honestly that if one of your patients had gotten into trouble, you'd know? How can you be sure? Because I'm sitting outside an office where people suffering from emotional distress come for treatment, and one of them is dead. You want me to believe the location is a coincidence?"

She scowled. "Of course it can't be a coincidence because you don't believe in those."

West regrouped and tried again before she shut him out completely. "You're right. You know these guys. I don't. I'll admit that, but I'm thinking distraught individuals tend to make poor decisions, and maybe one of them got tangled up with someone capable of doing this."

"No."

"No?"

She shook her head. "You're wrong about my group."

"How do you know?" West asked. "What do you talk about in your sessions? Has anyone shared anything out of the ordinary lately? Did they meet someone new? Make a friend? Take a trip?"

Tina rubbed her forehead. "That's all covered under counselor-patient confidentiality."

"Are you kidding me?" West bristled.

"You know I can't tell you any of those things."

West ground his teeth. "Even in the aftermath of all this, you still want to keep secrets?"

Tina looked away. "You can ask them anything you want to know. I'm sure they'll tell you. And I'll tell you anything I can about my day. About the moments before and after the shooting. About the figure. Anything that won't break my patients' trust, but I owe them that. I took an oath."

West braced himself for a long day. Prying secrets from Tina was a task he'd never had any success with, and frankly she was right. What he wanted to know was covered under confidentiality laws, unless she'd suspected criminal activity. In that case, she had an obligation to report it, but she'd already declared the group's united innocence and probably wouldn't change her story. "Okay," he conceded. "Fair enough. I'll ask my men to question the group members. What do you say about coming with me to the station while they do that? It sounds like you spoke to the victim just before the incident, and it seems you were also the closest to him by proximity." His gaze slid over the bloodstains on her rain-soaked blouse and pants. "I need to get an official report from you, and I'd like to continue the interview while the details are fresh. I imagine you'd like to get away from here for that."

"Yeah."

"Well, then, Miss Ellet, let me walk you to my car."

Chapter Two

Tina climbed inside the sheriff's cruiser, shaking off memories of similar rides as a girl. Every time her dad had caused a scene at a park or ball game and was hauled in for a night in the drunk tank, Tina was escorted home by a nice deputy, often by the former sheriff. West's dad. Eventually, she'd smartened up and steered clear of her dad before he could insist they go anywhere together.

She buckled in and winced as the condition of her hands and clothes registered. "Oh." She rubbed her stained fingers against the ruined material of her pants, but it was no use. A tremor rocked through her as memories of the gunshot came rushing back. Tina shook her hands out hard at the wrists and released a shuddered breath. "Can…" She swallowed against the painful lump in her throat. "Can we make a pit stop at my house? I'd like to get a dry change of clothes before we go to the station. I don't think I can concentrate like this." She bent and stretched her fingers in the air above her lap. "Please."

West gave the gas pedal a break, seemingly torn between giving her what she wanted and following his protocols. West had always been a stickler for doing the right thing, and that probably didn't allow for a trip to an old girlfriend's home before taking her formal statement.

"Which way to your place?" He dropped his sopping wet hat between them, then ran a hand through his hair.

She raised her brows in surprise. Maybe she wasn't the only one who'd been changed by time. "Left on Canyon Drive. We're in the River Park neighborhood." She balled her shaking hands into fists and set them on her lap.

"Who's we?" West asked, sweeping his gaze to her naked ring finger.

"Just Lily and I," she said. "My daughter." A hot tear stung the corner of one eye. Lily had come too close to being an orphan today. She pushed her focus beyond the passenger window. "And Ducky."

"Ducky?"

She sighed. "The dog."

"No Mr. Ellet?" he asked. "Or maybe you have a new last name?"

Tina touched the bare skin where a wedding ring had briefly dared to dream. "We weren't married long enough for me to get it changed. I hadn't realized there was a hurry." She turned her stricken face to his, chin up, jaw tight. "I met him about two years ago, right after I moved back to town. We were married after a few months, and he died four weeks later. I never got to tell him about Lily." She silently cursed her chattering teeth for betraying her show of strength.

West gave her a long, silent look. "How old is Lily?"

"Four months." Tina had seen the expression West was giving her before, though never from him. *Pity.* "It's fine. We're okay. He was here and gone like a dream. Sometimes, I think if it wasn't for Lily, I'd wonder if he was real." The pain was real. The loss. But it was true: her short time with Thomas had felt more like a movie she'd seen long ago than an adventure she'd truly been part of.

"I'm sorry about your loss. Lily's, too. Is she home now?"

"No." She batted stinging eyes. "She's at Mary's. That's the sitter." Somehow West's condolences to her daughter meant more to her than anything else he could have said.

"What happened?" West asked. "I'm not trying to pry. I'm just getting caught up. It's been a long time."

"I don't mind." It was strange being on the other side of a confessional for a change. Her spilling her troubles and someone else nodding patiently as the story unfolded. "Hunting accident."

"You didn't know him long before you married." A hint of agitation edged his voice. "Then he just died?"

"Basically," she answered. "He went up to the mountains for the weekend and never came home." He'd asked her to go along on that trip, but she wasn't feeling well enough to make the hike to the cabin. It wasn't until after he'd left that a pregnancy test confirmed the reason for her fatigue and nausea. Lily was on her way. Tina had had big plans for springing the news when Thomas returned, but fate had other ones. "Two State Highway Patrol officers came to my door."

"I'm sorry," West said again, before she went any further. "I wish you hadn't had to go through that."

"Me, too."

When he glanced her way again there was curiosity on his brow. "How'd you meet him? If you don't mind me asking."

"It's okay," she said. "He spoke to me at the garden center a few days after I moved back here. I was buying redbud trees." A small smile touched her lips. "He helped me plant them in my backyard."

West grunted. His eyes narrowed, but he kept them focused on the road.

"I asked him once if he knew you," she said, feeling a little guilty for having asked one man in her life about another.

"And?"

"He laughed. He said he'd never had any reason to run into the sheriff."

"Lucky guy," West muttered.

Tina tried not to wonder if there was a dual meaning behind his words.

The pair rode in silence for several long blocks. West turned sharp blue eyes her way from time to time, rubbing the dark shadow of stubble on his cheeks without speaking.

"What?" she asked.

He shot her a small smile. "I shouldn't be surprised you've done so well despite it all. Remember that time you dared me to jump off that old rope into the swimming hole on New Year's Eve?"

"Like it was yesterday." She'd goaded West endlessly, daring and challenging him to be reckless, testing his stock. But West wasn't reckless, not even as a teen. He'd been the first man to show her they didn't all become monsters when the mood struck. West was as sensible as the day was long and a Garrett through and through. Hell-bent on saving the world. Garretts were soldiers and law enforcement officers. If rumor served, one of West's brothers was a federal agent and the other was a US marshal.

The cruiser took a slow turn into her neighborhood and stopped at the first crossroads. The rain had stopped, and muted sunlight streamed from behind thick gray clouds. Emerald green lawns stretched before them, lined in newly blooming mums and anchored in elaborate pumpkin arrangements showing off for Halloween. Lily was too small to know, but she was going to be a princess this year. Every year, if Tina had any say in it.

River Park had been an up-and-coming neighborhood when Tina was young. She'd stared through dirty school bus windows for years as classmates poured on and off with clean clothes and new shoes every fall, and she'd dreamed of living there. Now, the homes were older and in her price range as long as she budgeted. Lily would have safe streets to ride her bike on and neighbors who knew her name. Maybe even a few folks who cared where she went and who she was with.

"Here?" West asked at the next intersection.

"Two blocks up, on the left. The white farmhouse."

West accelerated to the posted speed limit. "I think you should see a doctor before we go to the station."

"No." She watched her unsuspecting neighborhood crawl past. Did the neighbors have any idea what had happened today? Was it on the news? Steven was dead. Pointlessly murdered by a coward with a gun. How did a community move on from that?

"I'll swing by the hospital on our way to the station. Better to be safe."

"No," she repeated, a little more forcefully this time. "I wasn't hurt, just shaken, and every minute counts right now. I want to be helpful."

West huffed, but didn't argue.

"Here. This one," Tina said as her little home came into view, all country with a wraparound porch and a tree in the front. "I won't be more than five minutes."

Confusion pinched her brow as Ducky, her golden retriever pup, jogged toward the car, tail flopping.

"You know that guy?" West asked, watching the happy dog outside his window.

"He's mine," Tina whispered, "but I left him in his crate when I went to work this morning." Her heart jammed into her throat, making it impossible to swallow. "Someone let him out."

THE CRUISER JERKED to a rocking stop. West was on his feet and striding toward her home a moment later. He notified Dispatch of a possible break-in, then unholstered his sidearm. A break-in and a shooting involving the same woman on the same morning wasn't a coincidence.

Tina was on his heels, teeth chattering intensely behind him.

He stopped her at the front door. "Wait in the car. Lock the doors."

"I can't."

The terror in her voice tugged his heart, and West weighed his options. Taking her along could be dangerous. Leaving her alone could be deadly. He turned the knob, and her door opened. "Stay behind me."

Her small fingers slid against the material over his back, and he hated the pleasure it gave him to be near her again.

Inside, the house was silent and spotless. "Cade County Sheriff," West announced, edging past about a hundred pairs of shoes by the front door.

"Woof!" Ducky called from Tina's side.

West reached around Tina and let the dog in.

Ducky barreled through the house, barking and protesting. He slid around a corner and out of sight.

West motioned for Tina to wait as he followed Ducky down a short hallway toward the back of the home. The dog stopped in the mudroom, pawing and barking at a narrow closet door.

"Cade County Sheriff," West announced again, stepping carefully into the small room. He moved into position, gun drawn and faced off with the door. "Come out with your hands up."

A blinding pain split the back of his head and loosened his grip on the weapon. Flashes of light splintered his vision. His knees buckled and he tumbled forward against his will. One palm landed against the floor in support.

The back door swung wide and a figure dressed in black bolted into the yard.

"Damn it." West shoved onto his feet and forced himself through the door. He slid in the wet grass on uncooperative legs. "Freeze!" he hollered.

A fresh blast of pain punched through his skull at the sound of his booming voice. He pressed one hand to the back of his head and groaned. The goose egg was already forming, and his palm slid against something warm and slick. A quick look confirmed the substance as his blood.

West angled between the next set of homes, hoping to get a glimpse of the getaway car or a look at the man's face. The figure had doubled the distance between them, clearing the next hill and vanishing before West could manage to gain any speed.

West holstered his sidearm and radioed Dispatch. "Suspect is fleeing on foot, moving southwest toward Main from River Park Estates." He'd be lucky if a deputy was anywhere near his location. The Cade County Sheriff's Department was small, just six including himself, and not everyone was on duty. Those who were had their hands full with the shooting.

He paused to curse and allow his vision to clear. What the hell had he been hit with? And what was the dog barking at if not the intruder?

West climbed the steps to Tina's front porch slowly and with a little effort. "He got away," he said, sliding inside and forcing his posture straighter. "Got any ice?" He scanned the empty living room. "Tina?"

Ducky jumped at his feet, a leash in his mouth. "Now you want to go out?" He sidestepped Ducky and fought an irrational wave of fear. "Tina?"

"West." Her trembling voice sent him in the direction of her kitchen.

He cut through the living room, taking in as many details as possible. Everything smelled like Tina. Vanilla and cinnamon, warm and inviting. There wasn't much in the way of furniture, but the baby seemed to have more than any one child could ever need. Infant seats, swings and play sets dotted every inch of space he passed, accompanied by a barrel of stuffed animals in the living area.

Tina stood alone in the kitchen's center. The table had been set for two, complete with hot pads in the middle, as if standing in anticipation of a meal yet to come. She shook her head, clearly baffled. "I didn't do this."

West's muscles tightened. "Don't touch anything." He dialed Cole as an icy swell of fear rose through him. West knew exactly the kind of person who'd break into a woman's home and stage a scene like this. A dangerous one. Maybe even someone capable of shooting a man right in front of her just to get her attention. He turned away from Tina as he relayed the situation to his brother. The pain in his head grew by the second. West checked again to see if the blood flow had slowed.

Tina gathered ice into a dish towel and pushed it his way.

He gave her a sour face, but accepted the offer. "This is the opposite of not touching anything."

"Yeah, well, you're hurt," she said. "Don't bleed on my carpet." The attempt at levity was lost with the crack in her voice.

Tina was scared, and West needed to fix that.

He cleared the rest of the house, room by room, then took a break to let the ice do its work. "Any idea who'd pretend to make you dinner?" He winced as the towel slid against his hair.

"None."

"Are you seeing anyone?"

"No."

"I think you'd better pack a bag. I need to get a team out here to pull prints off the dog's crate, your doors and everything in the kitchen." He gripped the back of his neck. "As soon as they finish at the medical center parking lot."

Tina followed him into the bathroom and retrieved a first-aid kit from under the sink. "The house is clear. Now hold still and tell me what happened."

"Ducky was barking at the closet door, and someone jumped me while I was distracted."

The pup appeared at the sound of his name. *"Woof."*

Tina took the lead from his mouth and set it aside. "We keep his leash in the closet. I take him for a walk when I get home."

West rolled his eyes and regretted it. "Ow."

"Here." She tossed a bloodied cloth into the sink and

handed him a bottle of aspirin. "I don't think you'll need stitches."

"Great. I wasn't planning on getting any." He tossed a pair of pills into his mouth and scooped a handful of water from the bathroom sink.

He led her to her bedroom and made a slow circle through the room. "We know someone has been inside. We don't know for how long or how often." West peered through the curtains into the back and side yards. "Crimes like this are predominately orchestrated by men. Are you sure there isn't anyone you can think of who might have some fixation on you or infatuation you weren't aware of?" He ignored the fire burning in him at the thought. He couldn't let this get personal. Couldn't afford to have clouded judgment.

"I haven't dated since I met Thomas. That was two years ago. There was nothing serious before that."

West ignored the strike to his chest. He thought that they had been plenty serious once, but then again, she'd already made it clear he was wrong.

Tina wrinkled her nose. "There was a man at the hospital who asked me out a few times while I was pregnant. I thought that was weird, but he eventually took no for an answer."

"Who was that?"

"Chris something. He worked at the pharmacy on the main floor."

West released the curtains in favor of his cell phone. "Go ahead and gather whatever you need," he instructed, tapping the tiny screen. "You can shower and change at the station if you'd like. Your soiled clothes will need to be bagged as evidence. We can come back for Ducky once we finish there."

"How long will I be gone? How much should I

pack?" Her mind raced with questions. Where should she and her daughter go? Was anywhere safe?

"Take enough to last you a couple days, Lily, too."

Tina braced her hands against the bed's edge. "Do you think the shooter did this?" Her ivory skin whitened further.

West sent a quick string of orders to his deputies via text message before turning his attention back to Tina. "We can't know for sure. Not yet."

"Was it him?" She choked. "Could the shooter from my office have been *here*? Inside my home?"

"That's what we're going to find out."

"Damn it, West!" A flush of frustration bled across her pale cheeks. "Stop dancing around and just tell me what you really think happened here."

West wedged his hands against his hips, struggling to deliver the impossible truth. As if playing witness to murder wasn't enough horror for her to experience today, the psychopath had to invade her home and do *who knew what* while she was trying to save the life of her patient. "I don't think this is a coincidence."

She nodded her head, an expression of disbelief on her brow. "So, this is about me? The shooting, too? Steven died because of me somehow? It's insane! He'd barely begun his recovery." She stopped. "I think I'm going to be sick."

"You're probably in shock." West offered a hand to help her onto the bed. "Sit back. Put your head between your knees and breathe." He waited for her to comply. "You okay now?"

"No."

West turned to lean against the bed at her side. "None of the things that have happened today are your fault. None of them. Whoever's doing this is unstable. Deranged. He could've picked anyone to unleash his anger on. It had nothing to do with you. It could just as easily have been the neighbor, or the grocery clerk, or the librarian. Understand?"

She sobbed against the back of her hand, but nodded her agreement.

West stepped away from the bed. He needed to get her out of there. "Do you want me to pack the bag?"

Tina slid onto her feet. "Don't you ever get tired of bossing people around?" she grouched.

"No. Where are your bags?"

"Oh, my gosh! Lily!" She dug into her purse and brought out her phone. "I have to call the sitter. If this is about me, then Lily's in danger!"

West moved into her line of sight. "That's not a guarantee, and I've already sent a deputy to check on her."

"How did you know where she was?"

He smiled. "There's a giant pink heart on the refrigerator with Lily's schedule and Mary's contact information. I saw it when you got me the ice."

Her lips lifted into a small smile. "Right. Thank you." She adjusted the phone against her cheek. "Mary? This is Tina. How's Lily?" Tina's voice cracked on the last little word. Tears rolled over her cheeks as her smile widened and turned to laughter. "Thank you. Okay. Thank you." When she disconnected, Tina looked weightless, as if everything awful in her day had been forgotten. "Lily's okay. Mary saw what happened on the news. She's been worried about me, but they're both fine. They're eating applesauce and blowing bubbles. She said I should take as long as I need. She knows I have things to sort out, but I just want to end this awful day and pick up my baby. The sooner I have her back in my arms, the sooner something might make sense again."

She stuffed her things into a bag from the closet then looked at the bathroom door. "Should I bring a towel for the shower?"

"No." West marveled at the way the promise of seeing her baby had rejuvenated and refocused her. "We have towels at the station."

"Okay." Tina rolled her shoulders back and hiked the bag over one shoulder. "Let me grab Lily's things, and we can go."

Chapter Three

Tina touched her hair nervously as she entered the bustling sheriff's department. West hadn't made a big deal out of her appearance, but she knew exactly what she looked like. Death.

The cluster of deputies and administrative staff huddled around a desk straightened to welcome their leader. Cole broke away from the group as West and Tina approached. The others stopped to stare.

"Tina Ellet," West said, "I'd like you to meet the Cade County Sheriff's Department. Team, this is Miss Ellet."

The group offered warm smiles, but their gazes traveled the circuit from her to West and then to Cole. He'd clearly filled the group in on her history with their sheriff. Ridiculously, her cheeks heated.

Cole greeted West with a handshake, then turned an apologetic expression on Tina. "I'm sorry this is happening to you." He barely resembled the gangly teen she remembered. No more acne or braces. His undeniable Garrett genes had brought him through puberty with a gold star. Exactly like his brothers.

She pulled the bag higher on her shoulder and gripped it with one hand. "Thanks."

Tina scanned her new surroundings with curiosity.

Miraculously, she'd never been inside the station before. It wasn't the way she'd imagined. Based on the horror stories her father had told, she'd assumed the place was dark and scary. Full of people like him in handcuffs. Instead, the building was open-concept, bright and clean. The walls were lined in diplomas, Don't Text and Drive posters and a cluster of community boards with fundraising flyers pinned to them.

West lifted a hand in Tina's direction, but dropped it quickly with a frown. "There's coffee and hot water for tea in the break room, and there's normally something to eat on the counter. Fruit. Bagels." He stepped away from the little group, and she followed.

She hurried behind him down a long hallway lined with closed doors. Her stomach twisted into painful knots at the thought of food. "Just a shower, I think."

He stopped at a door marked Locker Room. "We'll need to put your clothes into an evidence bag, so leave them out when you're done." He pushed the door open and held it for her. "I'll flip the in-use sign so no one bothers you. Small building. Everything's coed."

Tina hesitated. Police station or not, the empty room was frightening. "Will you be here when I get out?"

West looked over his shoulder. "I'll try. I need to touch base with my team and see what's been done. If no one's visited the two men who missed your group this afternoon, then I'd like to get over there myself. I've got a limited number of deputies and a vested interest in this case."

Tina tried not to wonder if that "vested interest" was her. "Has anyone tried calling the men who missed the meeting?" Why hadn't she thought to do that? "I have their numbers in my phone." She dug nervously through the giant bag on her shoulder and nearly dumped the contents.

"Hey." West's steady hand fell upon her fluttering one. "Stop." He gripped her fingers until she looked his way.

She pulled in deep breaths, borrowing strength from his touch. "What if the gunman visited them before coming to our session? Maybe that's why they weren't in group today."

"It's unlikely," West said, "but we're going to find out. Plus, I have questions for them. We really don't know what's going on in the big picture yet." He lowered his face to her level and searched her with kind eyes. "Can you think of any connection between the victim and yourself beyond your recent professional relationship?"

Tina considered the way she'd found Steven asleep at a bus stop outside the hospital last month. They were strangers until then, and had only seen each other at group sessions since. "No. None. Why?"

"I'm still trying to figure out how the shooting and the break-in are related. The crimes are vastly different, but the timing has my flags up. If the shooter is the same man who attacked me at your home, understanding the link between the three of you would be helpful. I'll be back once I drop in on your absentees, then we can finish our interview. I still need a formal statement from you."

Tina straightened. "Take me with you."

He followed her lead, returning to his full height with a snap. "I don't think that's a good idea."

"West."

His expression changed, ever so slightly.

"Please." The stubborn sting of emotion bit at her eyes and nose. "I need to know the rest of my patients are safe. If they don't answer their phones, I'm going to pay them visits myself. Seems like I'd be safer with you."

"I need you here making a formal statement."

"I'll write it while you drive. I promise." She hoped the desperation in her heart came through in her tone. "Please don't leave me behind."

West ducked his head and gripped the back of his neck. "You shower. I'll try to reach the men by phone before I leave. We already have their numbers." He turned on his heels and walked away.

"Does that mean I can go with you?" she called after him.

"You've got ten minutes."

Tina ran for the shower. Ten minutes wouldn't have seemed like long enough time to get wet before Lily was born. Since then, Tina had learned to do almost anything in a quarter of the time it had once taken.

She folded her stained clothes and stacked them on a bench for evidence, tucking her underthings carefully between the pieces, unsure if she was meant to turn those in, too. These were things a person should never have to wonder. The things that had happened today didn't belong in Shadow Point, Kentucky. They were fodder for television crime shows or the headlines of a city she'd never visit.

Tina doused her hair with shampoo and lathered her body from neck to toes in seconds, scrubbing harder than necessary, until the water ran clear. Ironic, because she doubted the stains from her day would ever truly be gone. She shook off the heavy wave of emotion and concentrated on the ticking clock. The damp towel was in the communal hamper and she was re-dressed with four minutes to spare. Tina grabbed her things and yanked open the locker room door. Hopefully, West had really waited. If he hadn't, she wouldn't blame him.

She'd always hated the way she'd left things with him after high school. When the college scholarship she'd applied for came through, she'd packed up and asked him to understand. It wasn't an opportunity anyone could pass up, certainly not her. She'd needed to get out of Shadow Point like she needed oxygen. West had wanted to get married. He'd wanted a house and some land, a perfect replica of what his parents had, but Tina didn't believe in fairy tales, and at eighteen, she couldn't see past her escape. She'd picked up the phone a thousand times over the years to tell him the truth about why she had to leave. Her family was a train wreck. Her father was in jail now, probably for the rest of his life, and her mother had run away in his absence. Tina was broken because of it, and West deserved better. Without her to hold him back, West had enlisted in the military, served overseas and come home to be the county sheriff. She had been baggage for him, but she could never find the strength to say those things out loud, so she didn't. Pride was vindictive that way.

WEST PRESSED HIS palms to the desk, scanning the map before him. Cole and the other Cade County deputies had compiled a list of viable reports about a man in a dark jacket and jeans spotted near the crime scene. Though no one outside Tina's group had witnessed the attack, several had heard the gunshot and called to report it. A handful had confirmed Tina's claim about the old pickup truck. "You can't throw a stone without hitting an old pickup in this county," West groaned.

"Someone thought it was a faded red Ford," Cole said. "That's something."

West rubbed his eyes. Let Cole be the optimist for a change. Someone had to be because West wasn't finding a lot of hope in the reports he had in front of him. The descriptions were in agreement, but the locations were all over the place. "So he either went north or south?"

Cole sighed. "Yep."

West strained upright and shook his head. "Did we catch a lead on the assailant at Tina's home?"

"No." Cole lifted his brows. "How's your head?"

West frowned. "Hurts. What else do you have for me?"

"We found a standard 30-06 shell casing on the building's roof at the crime scene."

"I guess that's something."

Cole didn't look hopeful. "It's the same ammo we'd find in half the homes in Cade County. Hell, I've got the same stuff at my place."

West adjusted his hat over the tender lump. If Cole saw it, he'd try to administer first aid, and he'd had enough of that from Tina. "See if ballistics can get a match. Maybe the gun's been used in another crime. We might be able to find him that way." He pulled his shoulders back, trying and failing to alleviate the tension there. "Have we been able to reach either missing group member?"

Cole pressed his lips and shook his head. "No. When I couldn't reach them at their home numbers, I called their places of employment. One man went to work on schedule last night and left this morning without incident. The other called off before breakfast."

West grabbed his keys. "So, both whereabouts are unaccounted for. I'm heading out to see what kept them away from the meeting. Let Tina know—"

"Let Tina know what?" Her voice startled him into

a spin. "By my watch, I have two minutes left on the ten you gave me."

Cole smiled against one fist, then failed to cover his humor with a cough. "You want to split the work, boss? I'll hit one, you take the other?"

"I'd like to speak with them both," Tina said.

Cole cast a quizzical look in West's direction.

West shook his head. "Why don't you take the guy who went to work last night? I'll take the guy who called off this morning."

Cole ducked his chin and made for the door.

West turned to address the remaining deputies. "Call me direct with anything new. I want to be kept up to the minute on this, and when they're done collecting prints over at Miss Ellet's home, have someone stay put until I get back."

A round of "Yes, sirs" drifted through the electrified air. West's chest puffed with pride. His deputies were the best in the state. He'd made a habit of reaching out to the most dedicated and promising rookies as early as possible, and when positions arose within his team, he gave those men and women a call. It was a practice he'd learned from his father, the sheriff before him. Stacking the deck in Cade County's favor was a Garrett family tradition, and one more reason the son of a gun who did this would soon be sorry.

He shoved the front door open and held it for Tina to pass.

She stopped to face him in the narrow threshold. "You were going to leave me?" Her steel blue eyes nailed him to the wall.

West swallowed long and slow. The energy building between them in the small space was more of a distraction than he could allow. A fitted sweater and jeans clung to her youthful figure, reminding him of the many times he'd personally helped her out of them. He extended one arm into the dreary day. "You're here now, so let's go."

THE RIDE TO Carl Morgan's house was long and slow. The heater vents circulated scents of Tina's shampoo and perfume around his head in a hurricane of distraction. "Tell me about this guy," West said, flipping his headlights on to illuminate the gloomy road.

Tina shifted in her seat, angling toward him. "Carl's a nice man. He's about our age, originally from Florida. He works at Franklin's Garage. Lives alone. He's quiet and a little detached. It's common with trauma survivors. Tender hearts hurt deeply, and we live in a world where growing tough skin is practically a survival requirement."

"Could he have gotten himself into trouble? Maybe ticked off a homicidal maniac?"

Tina's head was shaking before West stopped talking. "No. Carl's a people-pleaser, but he'd avoid intimidating individuals."

"Not every shooter is an intimidating individual. Look at school shooters and others who've committed similar crimes. They're a lot of things, but dangerous-looking isn't one of them."

She glanced his way, then back at the road.

"Given that you are well aware of the profile for someone who'd pull a stunt like this, can you tell me unequivocally that neither Carl Morgan or Tucker Bixby fit the mold?"

"No, but I can tell you there isn't a mold, and that the number of patients in therapy is far smaller than the number of folks who need it but aren't getting it. There are probably a hundred people in Cade County who psychologically fit the bill that we don't know about. So you have no hard evidence to support your theory that the shooter is connected to my group."

West gripped the wheel tighter, unable to argue and unwilling to upset her further by playing devil's advocate. The truth was, he had no idea what was going on in his county today. "Is there anything else you can tell me about Carl before we get there?"

"No. Just that he's doing phenomenally in group, so please don't upset him if you can help it. News of the shooting will be tough enough—badgering him could set his progress back, and I don't want that."

The country road rose and fell before them under a covering of gray clouds. Green reflections of little eyes blinked along the roadside, considering a test of their fate.

It was late in October and nearing lunchtime already. Barely six hours of sunlight remaining. West had enjoyed autumn as a kid, but he'd learned to see it as a hindrance after joining local law enforcement. Shorter days meant fewer hours to look for clues and missing people. It also gave criminals more time to hide under the cover of night.

Tina fidgeted with the hem of her sweater. "Where do you think the shooter is now? Do people like that just go home and have dinner? Do they kill themselves? Leave the state?"

"Depends." West slowed the cruiser to a crawl at the end of a narrow dirt road. Peeling numbers on the battered mailbox suggested that they'd arrived. "This it?"

"I don't know. I've never been here."

West spun his wheel, navigating a sharp right into the unknown. No Trespassing signs were nailed to posts on either side of the road. A trailer stood fifty feet back, bookended by trees and a picnic table. An aged blue car sat in a bed of gravel out front.

"That's his car," Tina said, unbuckling her belt.

"Wait." West stretched a hand across her middle like a guard gate. "It's dark under all these clouds and trees. I want you to stay put until I give you a signal."

"Why?" She dropped her voice to a low, ragged whisper. "Do you think the killer's here?"

He gave the dark trailer another long inspection. "Not necessarily. There's only one vehicle, and it's not a pickup, but I'd rather be safe, so wait here until I give you an all clear. Understand?"

"Okay."

He popped his door open and flashed her a warning look when the interior light came on. "I mean it this time."

She made a show of fixing her hands on her lap.

West flipped his bright lights on and locked her in the car. The cruiser's headlights illuminated a path to the trailer. West scanned the ground for signs of a struggle as he moved. Nothing unusual, no fallen items, drag marks or drops of blood. He stepped with care onto the makeshift wooden deck outside the front door, and a motion light snapped on.

West's heart rate sprang into overdrive. He reseated his sidearm, unleashed on instinct at the unexpected flick of the light, and rapped on the trailer door. Surprisingly, the shock hadn't increased his headache. The aspirin must've finally taken effect. He braced his free palm against the butt of his gun. "Cade County Sheriff, Mr. Morgan," he boomed.

The trailer rocked slightly. Interior lights flashed

on one by one from the back to the front. West moved away as the silver door swung open.

A heavy-lidded man in worn jeans and a faded blue T-shirt squinted at the cruiser's lights. "Hello?"

"Over here, Mr. Morgan," West said. "Do you know why I'm here?" He examined Carl slowly for signs of a weapon.

Carl blinked long and slow, scrubbing calloused hands over his thick brown hair. "Was there an accident on the road?"

"No, sir." West took a more relaxed stance, but kept the distance. "You want to tell me why you aren't at work?"

"I had a migraine." He pressed a palm to one side of his head in evidence. "I've been in bed."

"You get migraines often?"

"Sometimes." Carl's gaze drifted back to the cruiser. "Is someone else in there?" He shielded his eyes with one hand.

West ignored the question. "You've been home all morning?"

Carl dipped his chin, still preoccupied with the cruiser's lights.

"Any visitors?"

"Not until you. Why? I don't understand what's going on."

"You missed your group session. Don't you usually call ahead if you're not coming?"

"I—I've never missed. I d-didn't know I had to call."

The stutter gave West pause. Tina's words came back to mind. Much as he'd like to continue questioning Carl alone, he didn't want to be the reason the man relapsed or whatever Tina had just warned might happen. He lifted a hand without taking his eyes off Carl and opened and shut his palm, beckoning Tina from her place of safety. He changed positions as she approached, putting the trailer's wall at his back and everything else within his line of vision, peripheral or otherwise.

The passenger door opened, and Carl took a step backward, arm extended toward the trailer door.

"Stop," West ordered, and both people froze. He motioned to Tina again, attention fixed on Carl. "Keep your hands where I can see them, Mr. Morgan."

He didn't have to guess when Tina came into focus for Carl. The man's eyebrows stretched into his hairline, and his mouth dropped open. It was the reaction he expected most men had when they first saw her. Having been the onetime recipient of her rejection, West might've felt bad for the guy if there wasn't a shooter in town with his sick mind set on Tina. As far as West was concerned, all men were suspects until proven otherwise.

Chapter Four

"Hi, Carl." Tina spoke carefully as she climbed onto the wooden platform outside the trailer. Water dripped from the ragged awning stretched overhead, remnant drops from the recent storm. "I missed you at group today."

Carl's eyes darted between her, the headlights and the brooding sheriff at his side. "I—I'm a little surprised you felt the offense required an intervention by l-law enf-f-forcement." His expression softened with the joke.

Tina smiled, thankful to see Carl at ease. She flicked West a meaningful look. "Maybe we can cut the spot-light."

West leveled Carl with a no-nonsense expression before finally stepping away.

Carl moved closer to Tina the instant West abandoned his position as watchdog. "This isn't really about me. Is it?"

"Not at all." Tina shook her head, hoping to look less on edge than she felt.

"Are you okay?" Carl asked. "Did something happen to you? To Lily? Is there anything I can do? If you need a place to stay, I—I have plenty of room."

"No. Nothing like that, exactly. Something happened after group today, and we wanted to check on you. Make sure you were okay."

His mouth curved into a small smile. "You were worried about m-me?"

"Yeah." Memories of the moments outside her office flashed back to mind, stinging her eyes and drying her mouth.

The blinding headlights extinguished, and Tina blinked several times to readjust her vision. "There was a shooting."

West returned to them slowly, watching with careful cop eyes, one hand resting on the butt of his gun. Tina doubted that he missed much as town sheriff. He'd missed very little as a teen. She could only imagine his power of perception had grown keener with training and maturity.

Carl's gaze traveled quizzically over Tina. "You weren't hurt."

"No. Not me."

West shifted his weight, drawing Carl's attention. "Another member of your group was murdered today. Steven Masters. How well did you know him?"

Tina narrowed her eyes on West. He could've been a little tactful about announcing a person's death.

Something in his expression said he'd been intentionally harsh. Too much tightness in his jaw and rigidity in his stance. West didn't trust Carl. Why?

Carl pointedly ignored him. "I only kn-kn-knew Steven from gr-gr-group."

"You don't seem too choked up," West said.

"I guess I'm stun-stun-stunned."

Cold wind whipped through the trees and rattled the tattered awning over their heads. West was right. Carl didn't seem to care at all. She fell back a half step. Did it truly not matter to him that a man he knew was murdered, or hadn't the shock registered yet?

Carl stepped closer, erasing the bit of distance she'd created. "Are you cold? Do you need a c-coat?"

"No. I'm fine. We're here to check on you."

"Yeah, but this must b-be awful for you." He angled his back to West. "You and Steven were getting p-p-pretty close."

"How so?" West asked, moving into the space at Tina's side and blatantly hovering over her patient.

Carl stiffened. "They spent extra time together before and after sessions. She does that with new members." He touched Tina's sleeve gently. "If you n-need someone to talk to…"

Tina wrapped shaky arms around her center and attempted to stifle her recoil. How well did she know the members of her group? Could one of them truly be a killer? Could Carl? "Thank you. I'm sure this is something we'll be talking about for months to come at our sessions."

His eyebrows tented and he shoved both hands deep into his pockets. A flicker of something dark flashed in his eyes, and Carl's suddenly heated expression fell on West. "I'm still not sure why you're here. I wasn't at group today, s-so I can't give a statement."

"Carl," Tina started softly, "can you think of anyone who'd want to hurt Steven? The shooter only took one shot. I've seen the two of you talking before. Did he tell you about anyone who was upset or holding a grudge against him?"

"No."

West sucked his teeth and continued to eyeball Carl. "Can anyone verify your whereabouts between seven and nine this morning?"

"No." Carl grinned. "I've been here all day." He

opened his arms, as if to showcase the trees and silence around them.

"Is that right?" West asked. "My deputies tried calling. You didn't answer."

"I had a m-migraine. The ringer was off."

Tina's phone buzzed with Mary's signature tone. She peeked at the incoming message. A photo of Lily wearing a fancy hat with feathers and the caption *Playing dress up*.

Her eyes teared at the sight of her daughter's bright, toothless smile. The day had been too dark. She needed to cuddle Lily against her chest, inhale her sweet scent and feel her strong little heart beating against her own. Tina had told West that she wanted to visit both Carl and Tucker, but now she just wanted to be with her baby girl.

West pulled a buzzing phone from his pocket and barked a few monosyllables into the receiver, startling her from her thoughts.

"Carl—" Tina shot him a pleading look "—can you think of anything that might help us find the person who did this?"

"No."

"Okay." She nodded her acceptance. "I'll arrange a new location for next week's meeting while we all work through this loss. We'll talk more then."

West stretched his hand out to Carl, a business card stuck between his fingertips, cell phone put away. "Thank you for your time, Mr. Morgan." He caught Tina's hand in his. "If you think of anything that might be useful, give me a call."

Carl fixed his attention on West's hand over Tina's. "Will d-do."

Tina turned for the cruiser, thankful for the escape. She wasn't cut out for questioning people as if they were

criminals. And Carl's response to her news wasn't at all
what she'd expected. It left her feeling confused and un-
easy. She could only hope his apparent indifference was
a result of shock and not something far more gruesome.

WEST KEPT HIS eyes on Carl as he closed the passenger
door for Tina, shutting her safely inside. The fragile
and uncertain man she'd described wasn't the one who
stood outside the trailer. His smooth transition between
hostility toward West and concern for Tina set off all
West's internal alarms. Not to mention how precisely
his behavior had mimicked the day's crimes. A cold-
blooded murder outside the medical complex, and a
thoughtfully planned meal at Tina's home.

West folded himself behind the wheel and radioed
their position to Dispatch.

He reversed down the gravel drive and pulled onto
the country road, making plans to run a thorough background check on Mr. Morgan.

"Was that phone call back at the trailer more bad
news?" Tina asked. "Did something else happen?"

"No. That was one of my deputies. Mary and Lily
are doing fine. He's patrolling the neighborhood until
you can get there, making a circuit and keeping watch
on the streets around her home. If you don't see him
when you arrive to pick Lily up, wait for him. He'll be
back on his next loop, then he can follow you to your
place and wait while you get Ducky."

Tina nodded slowly. "Will the deputy stay with me
until I decide where to go? How much time do I have
to decide?"

"I asked him to process your home while he's there,
so you can take a minute to breathe, but limit the number of things you touch. I'm hoping he can get a good

print from that dinner setup in the kitchen. My other men are finishing up at the medical complex, then following leads on the shooter and faded red pickup seen leaving the scene. Tucker Bixby wasn't home when Cole got there, so Cole's looking into his whereabouts. I imagine you'd like to get to your daughter now."

Tina blew out a long, labored breath. "Yes. Very much."

"I'll take you back to your car now," West said. He fished a handkerchief from his pocket and passed it her way.

She accepted the offering and pressed it to the corner of each eye. She twisted the thin white fabric in her hands. "I can't believe you still carry this."

"Grandpa's handkerchief? We all do. I'm a little surprised you remember it."

Tina rolled wide eyes in his direction. "I remember that funeral like it was my own grandfather's. I remember each of your brothers with these hankies in their jacket pockets. Four brokenhearted pallbearers." She balled the fabric in one hand. "Hundreds of people came that day and filled every moment with love and kindness." She swiped a tear off her cheek. "It was beautiful. He would've been so proud."

"I'm sure he was." West turned his face to the road. "Grandpa told us regularly how important it was to build relationships. He touched a lot of lives." Next to his father, West's grandfather was the best man he'd ever known. His brothers and uncles came in a tight cluster for third. Love, pride and honor were always on tap at the Garrett house. "You okay?"

"I will be."

He tapped his thumbs against the steering wheel. "I hate to push this, but I still need a formal statement.

You promised to write it while we were en route, and we're nearly back to your car."

Tina pulled the notepad and pen from her purse and began to write. Tears fell in fat drops onto the page as she worked.

West kept his mouth shut as long as possible, but he hated seeing her cry. "How did you feel that interview with Carl went?" he asked. "Is he always so…" What was the word? She surely wouldn't approve of *creepy*.

She wiped the wet paper with his hanky. "I don't know."

"Based on your description before we got there, I'd expected a television-grade nerd or a little harmless guy afraid to make eye contact." Not the lean and borderline hostile man who'd answered the door.

"Whose fault is that?"

He ignored the question. West had heard it from her before, and the answer was always *West's*. Making assumptions might not have been his best attribute, but as a sheriff the practice had proven indispensable more times than he could count. "Do you think he had a problem with you spending extra time with Steven?"

"No. That's standard practice. Carl's been with the group long enough to know that."

"Do all the members have the same problems?"

Tina shot him a knowing look. She'd already made it clear she wouldn't divulge her patients' personal information. "They're all dealing with PTSD and severe emotional trauma for various reasons. Some members are former military. Some are abuse survivors."

"How did you spend the extra time you had with Steven?"

Tina sighed. "Occasionally I'd use the time to educate and encourage. Other times, he'd tell me things he wasn't ready to share with the group. It was all very up-and-up."

West repositioned his grip on the wheel, relaxing his hands and leaning back against the seat. "I didn't mean to imply otherwise."

"You didn't. I just want it stated for the record."

He cocked a brow. "This isn't going on a record. We're just two old friends talking."

She turned her face to his, a sad smile on her full pink lips. "Is that what we are, West?"

"I'm not sure what we are now," he admitted, "but I was engaged once to a girl who looked a lot like you."

She dropped her gaze to the handkerchief briefly before pinning him with a powerful stare. "I'm not that girl anymore."

"No," he agreed. "Clearly, that girl has been upgraded by time and experience." He reached across the seat to give her knee a playful push. "I think the girl I knew would be proud."

A smile bloomed on her lips. "Thank you for saying that."

"I meant it."

She caught his fingers in hers and squeezed. "I know."

West released her to pull his cruiser into the lot outside her office.

The crime scene was roped off now, and two members of his team worked their way through a rain-soaked lot, careful not to miss anything that might lead them to the shooter's identity. Plastic yellow teepees with bold black numbers anchored the shattered glass and polka-dotted the surrounding area.

Tina shuddered beside him.

"I'll be by to check on you and Lily as soon as I can, but I'm going to pay the hospital pharmacist a visit now." The one who'd asked her out multiple times during her pregnancy. "What did you say his name was?"

"Chris."

West itched to tighten his fingers around hers once more, but he wasn't sure how many times he could force himself to let go.

Tina rolled her head against the back of the seat, turning sharp blue eyes on him. "Tell me this wasn't because someone thought I was spending too much extra time with Steven." Her body tipped slightly toward his. The change was small, nearly imperceptible. So much so, Tina probably didn't even realize. But West did.

He felt the too-familiar pull at his core, an urge to meet her in the middle.

No amount of time would change that about them. He and Tina were human magnets in need of connection. Being near her without being *hers* was a new and ugly sensation. He didn't like it.

West cleared his throat. "We'll know more soon." His thoughts drifted back to Carl Morgan. The timing of Carl's absence with the shooting today was highly suspicious, and West didn't like the way Carl had looked at Tina. Definitely not the way a patient should look at his therapist, and it had taken all of West's self-control not to smack Carl's grubby hand away when he'd reached for her arm. The look in Carl's eyes when she recoiled was satisfying, but delivering the weirdo a solid right hook would've been even better. "We'll see what my team turns up and what Tucker and Chris have to say once we find them. We've got to follow the facts." Lucky for Carl, being creepy wasn't against the law, and West's gut instinct wasn't grounds to hold him.

Tina rolled her eyes, instantly looking a decade younger. She nudged his arm with a grin. "You still do that, huh? Answer my questions with random truths when you don't want to lie or upset me with the one I'm asking for."

Her hand lingered on his arm, warming him to the core.

West fought a budding smile. "Would you prefer I lie?"

"As if you could." She cracked the door open and swung her legs into the brisk autumn wind.

He circled the car and met her halfway to hers, toting the bags she'd packed at home earlier. "Slow down." He caught her wrist in his fingers, cursing himself instantly for the thrill it gave him. "Hey. Take a minute before you drive. You've had one hell of a day. You're worried about your baby, your safety, your group."

She stopped to face him. Her shoulders drooped. "I'm okay to drive."

"Okay, then tell me you have a plan before you shoot out of here. If you're planning to get a hotel room, you'd better change cars and register in cash under a different name. I'm going to need your contact information regardless, in case we have reason to believe you're in danger."

Her face went slack. "Maybe I could take Lily to Disneyland for a week. Or the beach. We can go somewhere far away for a while."

"Maybe." He'd like to think he'd have the son of a gun behind bars before dawn, but the odds certainly weren't in his favor, and he couldn't promise he'd have him caught in a week, either. "How long can you afford something like that?"

"I don't know." Her voice ratcheted an octave as fear changed her expression to something panicked and feral. "I've never been stalked, or hunted, or anything like this before, if that's even what this is. You're the expert. What are we supposed to do?"

West couldn't give her an answer. He didn't have one.

He ached to fold her into his arms and kiss her head like he used to. He wanted to fix this. All of this. He'd never wanted anything more than to keep her safe and make her smile. And ten years apart hadn't changed a damn thing.

Tina groaned and rubbed her eyes. "I need coffee. I need to fix my face, paste on a smile and make sure Lily doesn't pick up on any of the horrific things rolling through my head."

She pried her keys from her handbag and beeped her car doors unlocked. "I'll get Lily and Ducky, then I'll figure out where we're going before your deputy leaves my place. I'll call you as soon as I know."

He shifted his weight. "I'll head over to your house as soon as I can." He passed her the bags, and she tossed them onto her passenger seat.

Tina slid her hand down the length of West's arm, catching his fingers in hers. "I'm glad you're here."

"Always," he said, returning the gentle squeeze.

They stood in palpable silence for a long moment, evaluating one another, it seemed. There was obviously something more Tina wanted to say.

She didn't.

Instead, she dropped behind the wheel of her car and motored away.

They were beginning to make a bad habit of this.

Her leaving, and him watching helplessly from behind.

Chapter Five

Tina turned onto the main road with a sigh of relief, thankful to put a little distance between herself and the man causing her already shocked and broken heart so much unnecessary confusion. She dialed Mary and set the phone to speaker.

Thankfully, the call connected on the first ring. "Hi, Tina," Mary answered. "How are you? Is everything okay?"

Tina checked her mirrors and adjusted her defrost vents. "I've been better. How are you and Lily?"

"Lily's sound asleep, and a strapping young deputy is patrolling my neighborhood, so I'm not doing too bad, either."

"Great." A smile edged over Tina's lips. Mary was Tina's first friend after moving back to town. She wasn't much older than Tina's mom, and she missed caring for children, so the arrangement with Lily was perfect all around. "Well, I'm finally on my way. Can I bring you anything?"

"You don't need to do that. You've had an awful day. Besides, Lily and I ate lunch before she went to sleep." Mary gave a sad laugh. "Considering what you've been through, I should probably be making you lunch." She paused. "Do you want me to make you lunch? Maybe pour you a glass of wine? I'm a great listener if you need someone to talk to."

"No." Tina almost laughed. She didn't drink, and it was barely past noon, but after the morning she'd had a glass of wine didn't sound half bad. "How about I buy you a fancy coffee instead? Cup of Life is on the way to your place from here."

"Fine," Mary agreed. "I will accept your coffee, but only if you agree to stay a few minutes before you take off again. I worry about you. Sometimes I think you get so busy taking care of everyone else that you forget to take care of yourself."

Tina didn't have the energy to argue or confess all that had happened today. Like the possibility she may have been the reason for Steven's death. Or that, even if she wasn't, someone had still been in her home. Touched her things. Pretended to make her dinner.

An involuntary shiver coursed down her back. "I've got to go. I'll see you soon."

Tina disconnected, then loosened her grip on the wheel, bending and stretching her fingers in a futile attempt to relax. She needed a better headspace before holding her baby again. Lily was sure to pick up on the anxiety pouring off her mother in buckets.

Tina closed her eyes at the red light, and West's deceptively gruff image appeared. She popped her lids open and cursed herself internally. Given all that had transpired today, it was ludicrous she couldn't concentrate on anything but memories of his determined face.

She eased her foot off the brake as the light turned green.

She'd been back in town for nearly two years, and had managed to date, get married and have a baby, all without running into a single Garrett. Now, after just a few hours at his side, she was seventeen all over again, wondering when she would see him next, and if his heart still beat as fast as hers when they touched. More important, could he forgive her for the way she'd left things between them all those years ago?

West's opinion of her had always mattered. As much today as it had when they were young and wildly in love. She groaned inwardly at the thought. It had been unfair for her to let him love her then. Back when she had been a lie. She'd put up a nice show. Smoke and mirrors to distract from what she really was. He gave her his all, but she'd never really let him in. She'd kept the real things to herself.

She'd known what people said about her, of course. She fed on the gossip, imagining her life was something other than it was, letting people believe anything, so long as it wasn't the truth. She'd pretended to be rail thin by choice, instead of half starved, pretended to wear too-short shorts for attention, when the truth was that she kept getting taller, and clothes were expensive.

No more.

Now, she had a stack of jeans in her closet, all the right size, and Lily had more clothes than one child could ever want, whatever the season. Tina would never be that helpless child again, and her daughter would never know the humiliation of a life without a mother's love.

Possibly the only thing she loved more than knowing how much she had changed was knowing that West hadn't changed at all. He was still strong and certain, reliable and steadfast. All the things she'd fallen in love with long ago. Even being with him again for a short time had made her miss the family she never had and long for a husband to cradle their daughter. She wanted someone she could find strength in when hers was gone.

The coffee shop came into view, and Tina shook off the useless thoughts and childish fantasies. She pulled up to the window at Cup of Life and freed some money from her wallet. "I'll take two medium lattes, please. And I'd like to pay for the car behind me."

Tina inched forward, waiting her turn, but eager to get moving once more. She traded cash for coffee and waved in her rearview mirror at the couple behind her who was about to get a nice surprise. Paying for the next person in line was something Tina had done throughout her adult life. It was an act of kindness that someone had performed for her family on a night they'd planned to dine and ditch because there wasn't enough money for food, and they hadn't eaten in two days. It didn't seem logical, but there were tougher things than living with an alcoholic father and depressive mother. Consistently going hungry was one of them.

Mary's house came quickly into view from there. Only three short blocks from Cup of Life, nestled in a mostly rural neighborhood with more livestock than people. Electric candles burned in the windows, but the porch light was off.

Rolling thunder growled in the distance as Tina shifted into Park and squinted at the darkened doorstep. Maybe it was the day she was having, but something felt off. Instinct crawled over her skin like a nest of baby spiders, and she worked to pull herself together. There was no need to worry Mary any further or upset her sweet daughter.

It's fine, she told herself, *just breathe.*

She shored her resolve and palmed her keys.

A massive bolt of lightning slashed the gray sky, illuminating Mary's open front door before dropping the house back into darkness.

A block of fear lodged in Tina's throat. She fumbled for her phone, dialing West as she flung off her seat belt. Her car door jerked open with help from the raging wind, and she lunged into a sprint.

"Sheriff Garrett," West's voice boomed through the receiver at Tina's ear.

"West. I'm at Mary's house and the front door is open. Everything is dark." She took the porch steps two at a time.

"Mary! Lily!" she called, praying this wasn't what it seemed. Anything but a crime involving her daughter.

"Go back to your car and lock the doors," West ordered. An engine growled through the speaker at Tina's ear. "I'm on my way. I'm notifying Dispatch. Do not leave the car for any reason, and do not hang up."

"My baby…" She leapt across the threshold, blindly smacking the wall beside her in search of light switches, unable to voice the horrific and bloodcurdling things that raced through her mind. "Mary!"

"Be careful," West growled. "You need to slow down and think. This could be a trap."

"I don't give a damn, West Garrett!" she screamed. "I need to find my daughter!"

Tina sprinted through the old farmhouse toward the room where Lily normally slept, sliding over hardwood floors and knocking into walls as she took the corners at full speed.

She clutched the stairwell and used the spindles to propel her faster than her feet alone could move her onto the second floor. "Lily!" She'd give anything to hear that sweet cry. Anything to know she was safe in the crib where Mary had laid her. Hot tears rolled over her cheeks as she tore down the silent hallway, toward the dark room with the open door at the end. Images of tiny pink lambs and clouds floated dreamily over the walls and ceiling, cast from a domed night-light.

She came to a stop in the room's center. Her collapsing heart nearly dropping her onto the floor. The crib was empty. "She's not here." The words clawed their way free from her tightening throat.

"And Mary?" West asked.

"I don't know." Tina stumbled from the room, gasping for air through a tightening chest. One by one she checked the rooms for a sign of her friend and babysitter. Maybe Mary had taken Lily someplace safe. Maybe they were hiding together.

"I'm just five minutes away now," West said. "The deputy patrolling her neighborhood should be back any minute. He'll handle things until I get there. Please go back to your car."

"I can't," she cried. "What if they're here? What if they're hurt?" Tina flung open closet doors and screamed until her throat burned raw.

She slid to a halt in the first-floor mudroom, heart hammering and stomach twisting.

Mary lay sprawled on the floor, hands outstretched toward the wide-open back door.

Tina screamed until black dots raged in her periphery and the world slanted beneath her.

WEST ARRIVED MINUTES LATER, having listened to the silence for far too long. It was as if Tina had died on the spot after delivering that scream. He'd soundly broken every traffic law on record to get there from Tucker's neighborhood, where he'd rendezvoused with Cole to knock on doors. Neighbors confirmed that Tucker hadn't been home since the night before. West hadn't even had time to visit Chris, the questionable pharmacist.

He crammed the gearshift into Park and jumped free of his cruiser, leaving it at a hasty angle in Mary's front lawn. The deputy, formerly patrolling the neighborhood, now spoke with a growing crowd of neighbors along the roadside. EMTs rolled a woman through the grass on a gurney.

Somewhere in the distance, thunder cracked.

West bypassed everyone, charging into Mary's home in search of Tina. "Tina?" he called, both into the phone and into the air. "Where are you? I'm here." She'd stopped talking minutes ago, but he'd refused to hang up. He wouldn't leave her alone and in pain ever again. Not even for a second.

"Here." Her ragged voice echoed over the line and through the empty farmhouse from above.

He stuffed the phone into his pocket and raced to the second floor.

Gentle sobs rolled from the room at the end of the hall where Tina sat, doubled over, on the floor, hugging a teddy bear to her cheek. "She's gone."

The words ripped at West's gut. The agony on her face and in her voice shredded his heart. He fell into place at her side and curled her against his chest like he'd longed to do since he'd first laid eyes on her again. "Hey." He stroked tear-soaked hair from her cheeks and cradled her head against his collarbone. The cell phone clattered from her grip. West swept it away and pulled her body closer. "An Amber Alert has already been issued. It came across my phone and onboard computer. My deputy is talking to Mary's neighbors now, following protocols. We're on top of this. My guys are the best, and we're going to get Lily back. It's everyone's first priority, and we will bring her home to you."

Tina covered her face with both hands and cried harder.

"Tina." He angled his head, straining for a look at her hidden face. "I know this is awful, and I'm an ass for saying so right now, but I need you to pull it together."

Tina stiffened in his arms. She rocked away from him with betrayal in her eyes. He deserved the heated look. It wasn't like her to let her guard down, and he'd told her to knock it off, but he had good reason.

West returned her stare with what he hoped looked like compassion. He had a job to do, and he needed her help. "Your sitter is out cold. I saw her being taken on a gurney. She's my only witness, and she's useless to me until she regains clarity. The neighbors might've seen something. I don't know yet. What I have here and now is you, and I need you."

Tina's eyebrows relented their angry stance. "Me?"

"Yes. Can you tell me if anything other than Lily is missing? A favorite blanket or doll. A diaper bag. Anything like that. Is there anything that should be here right now but isn't?"

"Everything," she cried. "It's all gone, as if he tried to erase her from existence. He even stripped the bedding from her crib. He took her toys. The spare outfits. Anything Mary kept in reserve for her is gone. All he left was this bear." Her voice cracked, but she handed the animal over.

West turned the plush toy around. The bear's tiny T-shirt had bright golden letters that formed the word *Thomas*. "Thomas was your husband's name."

She chewed her bottom lip roughly, never taking her eyes off the small brown bear.

West considered the newest disturbing fact. The one who stole her daughter had left the bear named after Lily's father. West was no profiler, but it seemed to him the person responsible for this probably planned to replace Lily's father completely. No need to bring a memory of him along.

"What are you thinking?" she asked in a whisper, pushing herself away from him. "I'm missing something. I can see it in your eyes. And don't you dare hold back. I need all the facts right now, West. Don't treat me like a stranger."

West stretched onto his feet and circled the room's perimeter, deciding how to approach the conversation. If there was a bright side, he had to lead with that. Tina needed hope more than ever. "I think it's good that the abductor took all of Lily's things." He opened and closed an empty drawer. "He needs all that stuff to take care of her. He wants Lily to have all the things she needs and loves."

Tina's face brightened. "He plans to care for her."

"Yeah."

"That would be slightly more comforting if he hadn't shot a man today. There's delusion and then there's downright dangerous." Her face crumbled. "I don't want my baby in the hands of a killer."

West returned to her and pressed steady hands to her quivering cheeks. "We don't know who took her. We need to get all the facts before we lose focus. Okay?"

"Okay."

Outside, the cry of an ambulance broke through the night.

West dropped his hands. "They're taking Mary to the hospital. Someone will be in touch when she's able to answer questions."

Tina squared her shoulders, regaining herself. "Mary had a weak pulse, but it was there. I don't know what happened. I didn't look for the injury." She cupped shaky fingers over her lips. "I left her on the floor. I kept looking for Lily. Oh, my gosh. I'm a terrible person."

West scoffed, then pulled her against him. "I don't know a better person than you. No one blames you for leaving Mary. Not the EMTs, not Mary. No one. You were worried for your baby. What else could you do?"

"Lily's so tiny," Tina choked out. "She's so fragile. If he drops her. Or shakes her."

"He won't," West interrupted. He held her close and stroked her hair. "We're going to get her back, and we're going to find her in the same perfect condition you last saw her in. I swear it."

West's gut fisted at the promise. He meant it, 100 percent, but he couldn't will it to be true, and if he broke this promise, there was no coming back. He'd lose Tina forever. She'd survived a lot of things, but he didn't see her recovering from the loss of her child. Everything about her said that Lily was her life raft. The reason Tina had kept her head up through it all, and someone had taken that from her. West couldn't allow her pain to go on a moment longer than absolutely necessary. He wouldn't.

His heart blistered with empathy as a new round of Tina's sobs broke against his chest.

What was happening today? In his town? To his... *his what*? The mental shock jarred him speechless. Tina wasn't *his* anything. He tightened his arms around her, hating the truth of the thought.

Chapter Six

Tina leaned against West's side as they descended the farmhouse stairs. Her mind flooded with pictures of her baby crying in a stranger's arms, frightened as he ripped her from her safe haven. The images were accompanied by horrific scenarios in which Mary had probably tried to save her by escaping through the back door, only to be violently incapacitated after Lily was wrenched from her hands.

Unlike when Tina had arrived, every light in the house was now on, blinding her sore eyes and illuminating any nook or cranny where the most microscopic piece of evidence might have landed. A smattering of men and woman worked the crime scene inside and out, some deputies, some unknowns, all scouring the immediate area.

Three men huddled near the porch looked up at them as they passed.

"Does that jacket say FBI?" she asked.

"Yes," West answered.

She struggled for a look at West's face. "Why are they here?" Not that she didn't appreciate the help, but... "Has something else happened?"

He held her tight against his side until they reached

his cruiser, cocked half in the driveway and half on the lawn.

Tina nearly fell over when he released her in the driveway. She hadn't realized how much she'd been relying on his strength, in every way, to keep going.

He turned to face her, hands hovering as if she might tip over. His eyes busily scanned the dismal afternoon crime scene. "Child abductions are often handled by the FBI. My brother Blake is FBI. I'm sure the patrolling deputy reached out to him as soon as he knew Lily was gone."

"Blake?"

"Yeah. He lives in town now with his fiancée, Marissa. Blake's a damn good agent. Looks like he's already rallied a few of his team members from Lexington."

Tina scanned the blue coats for Blake. He was always so much older. More grown-up. Her eyes landed on a near replica of West talking to a woman on Mary's porch. He was a little broader than West, with too much hair, but that was definitely him. Her former surrogate big brother was now a federal agent. "I can't believe he did that. That's wonderful," she whispered.

"We've got a good network. We'll find her, Tina."

Tina envied the pride in his voice. She longed for a day when she could feel proud of her family. With a runaway mom and father in prison, she'd be waiting a very long time.

Blake jogged down the porch steps and cut across Mary's muddy lawn, now lined with nosy neighbors.

"West." He stretched a hand out to his brother. "Tina." He nodded in her direction, eyebrows crouched between sharp blue eyes. It was much the same look Cole had given her outside her office after the shooting.

"Got anything?" West asked.

Blake stared into his brother's face for several long beats, unable or unwilling to answer.

A pile of gruesome thoughts clogged Tina's mind once more, and she curled frozen arms around her middle to keep from falling apart all over again.

West slid immediately out of his sheriff's jacket and pulled it over her shoulders. He snaked a broad arm around her waist and dragged her to his chest. "Do you want to sit in the car? I can turn on the heater."

Tina's heart broke at the gesture. To be cared for was wonderful and amazing, but to be so vulnerable was terrifying and nearly intolerable. She pursed her lips and shook her head. What she needed was a way to get in control of her frantic emotions before she went wholly insane from the severity and endless confliction.

West rubbed the chill from her arms and back with one broad palm. "What?" he prompted Blake, who still hadn't answered his question.

Blake walked away, moving slowly toward the back of West's cruiser. West followed, pulling Tina along beneath his wing.

Successfully distanced from the other investigators, Blake leaned his backside against the car's bumper and lowered himself into Tina's line of sight. "I called in a favor and got some background information on the two members of your group who were missing during the shooting. Your guy Tucker has a long history of addiction problems and erratic behavior."

Tina chewed her bottom lip. She'd never seen that side of him, but survivors were like that. Either they wore the pain around their necks like an albatross, or they hid it so well no one would ever suspect what they'd been through. "That's not uncommon for some-

one like Tucker," she said, snapping into business mode.
Law and order might be in the Garrett blood, but ad-
vocacy ran hot in hers. "PTSD patients often look for
a way to escape the pain. Drugs and alcohol make easy
and unfortunate outlets for folks trying not to deal with
their past. Why are you bringing this up? Do you think
he fits the profile for this, or are you suggesting he's
on a bender?"

"I'm suggesting he's got a history of instability. Sharing facts. Nothing more. It's still early."

West released Tina to stand on her own again. "What
about Carl Morgan? Find anything on him?"

Blake raised his heavy brows. "You like him for
this?"

"I don't like him at all."

"He wasn't surprised to hear Steven was shot," Tina
blurted. "It's been on my mind, niggling in the background, since we spoke with him." She'd wanted West
to follow the facts, not her paranoia, but it felt good to
finally voice the concern.

"She's right," West agreed. "I thought the same thing.
I assumed the lack of response could be a side effect of
his mental health issues, but he didn't even pretend to
care about the victim."

Tina cast a pleading look at West. "I'm not accusing
him of anything. I just wanted to put it out there." Carl
didn't normally talk much. Whether that was because
he's ashamed of the stutter or just hiding his demons,
she couldn't say. Either way, he might not have reacted
to Steven's death because he simply didn't make a habit
of reacting. "Indifference doesn't mean he's a murderer.
Right?" She slid her gaze from West to Blake. She knew
the answer. Indifference could mean many things to a
troubled heart and mind. Though, the more she thought

about it, she wasn't sure which specific problems Carl attended her group to resolve. He'd mentioned abuse during his entrance interview, but he'd been stingy with the details. Still was. In group, Carl preferred to be an encourager while others shared, and he watched Tina closely when she spoke. Given the circumstance, she couldn't help wondering if he might've misconstrued her interest in his well-being as personal interest in him. Romantic interest.

Could Carl Morgan be a stalker? A child abductor? And what about Tucker Bixby? Had she somehow given one of them the wrong idea?

Blake shifted his weight. "So far we know Carl grew up in Pine Hurst. That's about ten miles from here, just outside the Cade County lines. He moved to town about sixteen months ago when his mother went to live in the nursing home downtown."

West yanked his phone from his pocket. "Pine Hurst's a pretty good-sized place. They've got a police department over there. I may not have cause to petition for psychiatric records, but police reports are public. Let me see if they've got him in the system, and if so, why." He stepped away from Blake and Tina.

Tina threaded her arms into the too-long sleeves of West's coat. The material was still warm from his body heat and scented by his cologne and body wash. She zipped the front to cover the chill left in his absence.

The rain had stayed at bay since the morning's storm, but wind continued to beat against the trees and everything in sight. Thick gray clouds hung low in the murky afternoon sky.

Tina lifted her eyes to Blake. "Do you think Carl or Tucker could've done this?" She struggled to put the quiet, guarded men she knew into the context of child abductor, someone obsessed with her and possibly also a murderer. Could either man have created silent fantasies about making her dinner or being the father figure in her little family of two?

She struggled to swallow the acidic burn of bile rising up her throat.

"Maybe." Blake watched her carefully, seeming to scrutinize her every breath, as if deciding whether or not *she* was a suspect in his investigation.

"What?" she snapped, sounding exactly as impatient as West had minutes before.

His eyes flicked to West, busily speaking with someone from Pine Hurst on his phone, then back to her. "How long have you and my brother been talking again?"

She looked at her watch. "About five hours. He came to the office after the shooting."

"What about before that?"

"You probably heard about the time before that." Her chin inched higher, prepared to defend herself for the inexcusable behavior. She had been wrong not to open up to West about her reasons for leaving back then, but she was also very young and broken. She'd needed more than a boyfriend to heal her pain.

"You bought a home here," Blake said. "When did you move back?"

"About two years ago." She struggled to remember the exact date, but Blake was clearly looking for more. "A few months after Dad went to jail, I guess." Her father should've gone to jail long ago, but he was making up for it with ten to life now. His drunken outbursts had finally hurt him almost as much as his victim.

Blake's eyes jumped again to West. "Yeah?"

"Yeah." Shame and guilt plugged her throat. According to police reports, someone half her dad's age had mouthed off to him at a bar, and her dad couldn't let it go. He lit into the guy, but age and alcohol had slowed him, and for once his victim wasn't afraid. When the young guy got the best of him, her dad had hit him with a broken bottle, then stabbed it into his side. The victim lived, but he pressed charges, and somehow every call the police ever made to her childhood home came crashing down on him, sealing her father's fate with a maximum sentence.

Tina had come home when her mom stopped answering the phone. She'd worried about the frail woman who'd spent most of Tina's life hiding in bed, nursing fresh wounds delivered by the hands of her husband. Sadly, without her father to hold her hostage, her mother had fled. Tina had laid down new roots in Shadow Point, praying for her return.

West pocketed the phone and turned back to Tina and Blake. "Pine Hurst PD is willing to cooperate. They're searching their database for anything they have on Carl. They'll get back with me as soon as they have something."

Blake nodded. "We're looking for the pharmacist. He wasn't home or answering his phone."

West widened his stance and crossed his arms. "All right. Anything else?"

Blake's eyes were locked on Tina. "West said your husband was in a hunting accident?"

Tina's mouth opened, but words failed her. Rehashing the loss of Thomas was more than she could manage, and she felt her mind shutting down.

Blake dragged his pointed gaze to West. "Shooter used a 30-06 today."

Tina slid her eyes closed. A hunting rifle. *Like the one that killed Thomas.* Her world shifted beneath her.

"That was more than a year ago," she said, fear and panic churning in her soul, cracking her voice and composure in one fell swoop. "What you're suggesting is impossible. I'm not stupid. I haven't been stalked for a year."

Blake was watching her when she opened her eyes. He didn't speak.

Tina covered her mouth, muffling a strangled sob. The ache in her throat spread to her eyes and pounded in her head. It couldn't be true. Her husband's death couldn't have been murder. It was an accident. Wasn't it? She clenched her fists to stop the tremor rocking through her hands, and willed her legs to hold her upright as the weight of the revelation did its best to knock her down. "Why is this happening?"

"Garrett?" a distant voice called. Someone in a blue jacket waved one hand overhead.

Blake walked away.

"We don't know," West said. "This is the part where we run down every scenario. Even the ugly ones." He guided her to his passenger door and helped her inside. "Let's get Ducky and head to my place for the night. You can stay there for as long as it takes us to find the person who's doing this. I guarantee you no one will come near you there."

Tina swung her feet inside, and the door shut hard enough to rattle her teeth. He grabbed the bags from the passenger side of her unlocked car and tossed them onto his back seat. She'd never seen West angry before, but he looked fit to kill, and she didn't doubt his promise of safety for a second.

WEST PULLED INTO Tina's drive, ready to collect her puppy and get her to safety. The deputy hadn't had a chance to process and sweep Tina's home. He was still on Mary's lawn talking to federal agents. It was just West and Tina now.

"Listen," he said, "I'm sorry about Blake. If he made you uncomfortable. I can only guess what he was saying while I was on the phone. If he overstepped, you have my apologies. He's not thinking like an old friend right now. He's thinking about nailing the son of a gun who took your baby."

"Blake was fine," she said softly. "He didn't say anything about our past, if that's what you mean." She tugged the cuff of her sleeve, fidgeting with an invisible thread. "I am sorry, though. About the way I ended things."

He angled to face her in the warm front seat. "Then why did you?"

"I loved you," she said. "That was never the problem. I left because my family was a nightmare, and I thought I was destined to be one, too. You deserved better, and I needed out. It seemed like the right thing to do at the time."

West bit back his opinion on the way things should have been. "That was a long time ago," he managed. "I've never held a grudge."

"No. You wouldn't." She deflated against the back of the seat. "None of this day feels real. It's like the worst dream ever."

"That's the stress," he said. "Your mind's putting distance between you and the horror so you can process it." He stopped short. "Of course, you already know that."

"Yeah, but it's good to hear. Do you really believe Lily's okay? He didn't take her so he could hurt her or…" She exhaled a long, quiet breath.

"He's not going to hurt her." West hovered a hand

over hers, but pulled it back. He had to be the sheriff, not some old flame, consumed with her presence or re-kindling the past. He had a job to do. And truthfully, getting too close to Tina right now would make losing her again all the worse when he put her life back together and she walked away.

Tina unlocked the door to her home, and West led the way inside.

Tina flipped every light switch she passed until the house was fully lit.

West cleared the rooms. "We're alone," he said, hol-stering his sidearm. He hadn't expected to find the killer waiting on her again, but it was better to be prepared than surprised.

Ducky whimpered in his cage, waiting impatiently where they'd left him hours before. West crouched to unhinge the latch. "I bet you need to go out."

"Woof!" Ducky wagged his tail and attempted to hop and pounce in the locked crate.

"If you need anything else, now's the time to get it," West advised Tina. "I'll take Ducky out and walk your perimeter before we load up. Keep the doors secured while I'm gone."

"Thank you for doing this," she said.

He caught her weary stare and forced a tight smile. "Anything and always."

He opened the door for Ducky, and chastised him-self for using their old words of endearment now. What had possessed him? Hadn't he just told himself to back off five minutes ago? The woman had lost everything, yet there he was trying to get back into her heart. As if he wasn't the reason her dad got a maximum sentence and her mother was in the wind. West shook his head. He hadn't predicted her mother's reaction to her father's sentence. If he had, he never would have pushed. Now it was too late, and once Tina understood the role West had played in her family's disintegration, she'd never speak to him again.

Ducky chased smells on the wind and through the grass with gusto, running full speed, then stopping repeatedly to jam his nose into the rain-soaked lawn.

West flicked his flashlight beam over the shadowed ground. He'd assumed the primary crime scene was inside when they'd arrived the first time. Strange how quickly things could change.

He kicked a boot through the tall grass at the back of Tina's property. The tree line stood thick and foreboding, less than a dozen yards from her home.

From his new vantage point, West had a clear view of Tina's kitchen, living room and bedroom. The windows of her home glowed like a television screen against the night. He watched, mesmerized, as she ghosted past the glass, a silent movie to which any lunatic could add his own script.

West went back to work, only to discover something far worse than the view. His heart thudded dangerously at the discovery of a large matted section of grass. A thermos and cooler were masked by the low-hanging cover of an evergreen branch. The remnants of a sandwich wrapper rustled in the wind, caught on the edge of a hardened shaft of a weed.

West lowered into a crouch and marveled at the view of Tina's home. Someone had scouted the property line and chosen the best spot for his twisted voyeuristic games.

West needed someone out here to collect and process the evidence before another storm came and washed it all away. He snapped photos and forwarded them to his team with the directive to get over there as soon as possible, then he checked the cooler and thermos contents. Water in the latter, packaged jerky and melted ice in the former. The grass was dead beneath the cooler. Whoever came here did so often enough that they'd stopped hauling supplies back and forth. It was the equivalent of having a drawer for your things at your girlfriend's house. If your girl was an unsuspecting single mother you stalked from the property line.

A tight knot wound in West's gut as he watched Ducky roam the yard. Ducky knew his territory. He knew every scent. What belonged. What didn't. Ducky hadn't attacked the intruder earlier because he knew him.

She'd gotten the dog following the loss of her husband.

The psycho had always been a part of her dog's life. How many times had the killer been inside Tina's home? Played with her dog? Her daughter? Was Tina ever there when he crept through her rooms?

West raised his eyes to the graceful silhouette floating through a golden backdrop of lamplight. His muscles tightened, balling both hands into fists. Tina Ellet had been his first true love, and like it or not, his heart had never fully released its claim on her. Whoever had done these things was going to pay, and when he knew she was safe, West was going to win her back.

Chapter Seven

Headlights drew Tina's attention to the front window. West was in the backyard with Ducky, and she had no intention of opening the door to anyone without him. Whoever had just arrived could walk around the house and meet him out back. Not to be rude, but she simply couldn't face another lawman right now. Her daughter was missing, and Tina was in no mood to play hostess.

She pressed the soft fabric of Lily's favorite blanket against her cheek and fought another round of heart-wrenching sobs. The sweet scent of baby wash pinched her chest and stung her eyes.

Where was her baby?

The headlights continued to shine against her window without blinking out. No slamming car doors. No footfalls upon her porch stairs. Just a gloomy October afternoon and a set of blinding headlights.

Tina hugged the blanket to her chest and pulled the curtain back for a peek. She dropped the little quilt, having been nearly blinded, and blinked her vision back to normal. No one was in her drive. The light was coming from a truck parked on the curb across the quiet intersection from her home.

Fear pressed her back a step.

Was she overreacting, or was some other horrible thing about to happen?

She freed the phone from her pocket, then peeked outside again. What if the shooter was in that truck? Or her stalker? Or her daughter? What if Lily was only a few yards away, and Tina still couldn't reach her? "Pick up," she whispered to the ringing phone.

"Garrett," West answered.

Tina wet her lips and willed her voice to come. "There's someone out front," she whispered. "A truck with its bright lights on, and they're pointed into my living room."

"Stay inside," he snapped.

The call disconnected.

Tina rolled her shoulder against the wall. She lifted her head for one more glance through the window. A familiar shape streaked across the yard and into the flood of light. *No.*

"Ducky!" Tina swung the door open with bumbling hands.

The driver's door opened and a man stepped out, scooping her dog into his arms and dropping him into the pickup's bed before returning to his place behind the wheel.

Panic welled and boomed in her, beating between her ears and pounding in her chest. "Ducky!" She scrambled into the yard. "Come!"

An arm stretched through the open driver's-side window and motioned her closer, but her dog stayed.

With a stranger?

"Stop!" West's voice echoed through the air. He moved into Tina's peripheral vision, weapon drawn. "Cade County Sheriff," he announced, moving steadily toward the truck. "Get out and put your hands up!"

The pickup's engine growled and roared. Powerful amounts of torque tilted the faded red pickup with each press of the gas, successfully drowning West's demands for subordination.

Ducky barked and paced the truck bed, tail wagging.

Tina's stomach rolled. It was the pickup that she'd seen fleeing the shooting this morning. Her dog knew this man? Chose to ride in the truck over returning to her? How often had Ducky seem him? How well did Tina know the truck's driver? Had she invited him to her home? Had he made the trip on his own more often that just this day?

Who would do something like this? What had she done to him that had caused this? Her baby wasn't enough? He'd even come for her dog? She pressed desperate palms to the sides of her head, protecting her ears and attempting to hold her mind together.

West continued his approach, gun up, wrists locked. He stepped slowly and confidently into the blazing light. His mouth moved, but the words were smothered by the revving truck.

Slowly, the doors on neighboring homes began to open. Folks spilled onto their porches, only to take note of the armed sheriff and dash back inside.

The engine reduced to a steady purr, and West moved into the light. "I won't say it again. Get out now."

The truck's tires barked, and the vehicle lurched forward with a roar.

"West!" Tina screamed as the pickup careened onto the sidewalk, heading straight for the sheriff.

West dove out of the way, colliding with the pavement in a wild roll as the truck fishtailed back onto the street.

"West!" Tina slid to a stop against his side, grinding

pebbles from the sidewalk into her knees and shins. The truck had escaped with her dog and another piece of her broken heart. "West!" She fell onto his chest, pressing her cheek to his motionless torso. "No!"

A low groan rumbled against her ear. Heavy arms wrapped around her trembling frame. "I'm okay."

Tina pulled back for a closer look at his filthy, bloody coat and face.

"I'm all right." He shoved into a sitting position, dusting his arms and stretching his neck with a wince. He ran a fist under his bloodied nose and grimaced. "Ow."

Tina brushed dirt from his stubble-covered cheek. "I thought you were dead."

He shot her a disbelieving look. "Please. I'm not that easy to kill."

She pulled him to her again and squeezed. "Thank goodness because I can't lose you, too," she whispered, utterly horrified by the possibility. Someone as truly good and selfless as West Garrett was not the sort of man a woman should ever let go. She'd already done that once, and she preferred not to let it happen again.

He rubbed her back and cleared his throat. "I'm not going anywhere."

"Good." She hooked her flyaway hair behind one ear and tried not to be sick. "Do you think Lily was in that truck?" Her stomach knotted as she imagined her infant in a vehicle driven so recklessly. One mistake. One small error. She couldn't bear to think of the potential consequences.

West ran a gentle palm along Tina's cheek. "I don't know."

"Woof!"

Tina jumped at the blessed sound. "Ducky!"

The retriever hobbled toward her, tail beating behind him. *"Woof!"*

She released West and pulled the dog onto her lap.

Beside her, West pressed onto his feet and reported the truck situation to Dispatch.

Tina held Ducky tight and promised herself Lily would soon be in her arms again, as well.

WEST FINISHED HIS call while checking his limbs and appendages for range of motion and functionality. Everything seemed to be in working order, though his ribs and nose were a little worse for wear. "I put a bulletin out on the truck," he told Tina. "I missed the plate, but I got a real close look at the vehicle, so I think I nailed the description. It was the one you saw this morning. Wasn't it?" She nodded.

"I figured." He limped several steps, testing his legs and ankles with a hearty grunt. Between that roll on the pavement and the recent knock on the head, West was nearing his daily capacity for physical beatdowns. "Damn. I'm not twenty-five anymore." He rolled his shoulders and shook out his arms. Nothing was broken, but he felt like maybe he'd have been better off getting hit by the truck.

West pulled Tina onto her feet. "Come on. Let's get Ducky's things and get out of here." He needed to go somewhere he could rest and heal.

"Shouldn't we wait for the ambulance? You need to let a medic take a look at you."

"Nah." West urged her toward the front door. "I didn't call an ambulance."

"You were just hit by a truck!" She struggled to slow him down as he nudged her forward. "You need an exam at least."

"I wasn't hit. I've been hurt worse, and most of this mess will come off in the shower. Now, move."

Ducky hopped along at their feet until they reached the steps, but stopped without attempting the climb.

"You, too," West told him. "Let's go." He pulled the retriever into his arms and nodded at Tina and the house. "A little help?"

She rushed inside, bracing the door for them to pass. "I don't understand why no one's coming here? A madman just sat outside my home while we were inside. He tried to steal my dog, nearly killed my..." Her mouth snapped shut. Her chest rose and fell with several short breaths. "You."

West wished like hell she'd have finished that sentence, but that would have to wait. "I've got limited resources, and this nut is everywhere today. Blake's sending a man out to talk to your neighbors. He'll get here as soon as he finishes at Mary's. Meanwhile, if you give your vet a call, I'll see if being the sheriff can get Ducky seen immediately. Then we'll head to my place, where I can clean up and review all the data we gathered today. It'll probably take me until dawn to wade through everything. Maybe you can get some rest."

Tina stared through her front window. "I'll go to your place tonight, but I won't sleep." Not until Lily was home safely. "Maybe I can come up with some characteristics for a profile on the kind of person who'd do this, then form a list of every person I've ever met who fits the bill. Maybe something I think of will help Blake's team find this guy."

West smiled. There was fire in her eyes again. That was the woman who had tossed his teenage world into upheaval, and he was mighty proud to be back at her side. "Atta girl. This guy didn't live in a bubble before today. He has friends, coworkers, relatives, neighbors. One of those people will be willing to assist in his capture and the safe return of your daughter."

West loaded Tina and Ducky into the cruiser.

He gave Tina a long look at the first stoplight. Even with a background in counseling, he couldn't imagine how anyone could deal with all she'd been put through today. "Hey."

Tina turned unseeing eyes on him; exhaustion and grief twisted her pretty face.

"What did you do while you were away all those years?" he asked, hoping to be a distraction from her sorrow.

"College," she answered flatly, a note of disappointment in her tone. "Undergrad. Grad school. Internships. After that, I shared a chic little apartment above a yoga studio with a New York City transplant named Elise. She grew sprouts in a window box and blended them into smoothies with kale and bananas." Tina offered West a small smile. "I know what you're doing."

"What?" He feigned innocence. "I'm curious. Can you blame me? I missed out on a third of your life."

"You're trying to keep me from going into shock or completely over the mental edge. I know. I do it with patients in crisis."

He motored through the green light and took the next turn toward the local veterinarian on Main. "Sounds like you had an interesting time. The only thing I put in my blender is margarita mix."

"We did that, too."

"Did you ever get homesick?"

She leveled him with a pointed look. "The only thing I've ever missed about this place was you."

West pressed his lips tight. The only thing she'd

missed was him? What the hell was that supposed to mean? She hadn't missed him enough to come home. Not even for one night. Not in a decade. She hadn't missed him enough to make a phone call and say so or return an email. He'd kept the same account open since high school, hoping that one day she'd reach out to him. He'd checked for that message every day while he was overseas, hoping she'd realize what they had was special. Worth fighting for. "Why'd you come back?" he finally asked. It certainly hadn't been for him. She'd been home two years without ever saying hello.

"My mom," she answered softly, then turned her face toward the windshield, shutting him out all over again.

West gripped the wheel tighter. It was his fault her mom had run. He needed to tell her the truth about that, but now wasn't the time. She needed some good news today, not more things to break her heart. And he'd prefer to remind her why they'd been great together, not give her more reasons to run.

"What'd I say?" she asked. "You're grinding your teeth hard enough to break them."

He jerked his head back. "Nothing."

She huffed and crossed her arms. "You always sucked at lying. You want to keep it to yourself? Go ahead."

He would.

He swung the cruiser into the lot outside the vet clinic and climbed out. He needed to get his head in the game and off his battered heart.

He shut his door a little more roughly than necessary and opened the back for Ducky.

The whole thing was ridiculous, to be thinking about her like that at a time like this. He hefted the dog into his arms and jammed the back door closed with one hip. Maybe *he* should get some therapy when this was over.

A narrow hand poked into view and pulled the clinic door open for him. Tina stood back so he and Ducky could enter the building. "You didn't think I was going to wait in the car, did you? With a lunatic stalking me?" She marched to the desk and smacked one palm against the little silver bell on the counter.

West lowered Ducky onto the floor and found a seat. He positioned himself for the best view of the clinic's window, door and empty lot.

A man in a white lab coat spoke softly to Tina before handing her a clipboard and pen.

A moment later, she lowered herself into the chair at West's side. "I'm really angry." She scribbled her contact information onto the paper, a look of frustration on her brow. "I want to just go crazy, blow up and fight, but there's no one to fight. None of this makes sense. It's not real."

"You can fight with me, if it helps." He tapped the toe of his boot against her sneaker.

Her cheek kicked up. "I don't want to fight with you."

"You sure?" He shifted in his seat and grimaced. His ribs were more sore than he'd thought, and sitting still was only making it worse. "I'm tougher than I look."

"You look like crap." She rolled her eyes and deposited the clipboard on the floor with Ducky. "Let me see your ribs." She reached for the hem of his shirt.

"Hey, now." He pressed the fabric back over his tender flesh.

Tina scoffed. "Baby. Move your hands."

"Excuse me?" He frowned. "I was hit by a truck."

"If that truck had connected with you, you never would've gotten up." She pushed his hands away and dragged the shirt up for a better view of his torso.

West stopped fighting when she made a little sound.

The expression on her face was perfection. "See something you like, doc?"

She blinked, then dropped the shirt as if it had burned her. "Just bruising. A hot shower, aspirin and ice will help."

"Are you sure?"

She nodded and gathered the clipboard back into her hands.

"You can look again if you want."

She shook her head and went back to writing on her paper. "Shut up." Her cheeks darkened under his stare, reminding him of other times he'd coaxed a rush of color into her skin. She slid her eyes his way, then put them back on the task before her.

There was something she wanted to say, but she was fighting it. He could see it in her eyes when she'd moved her gaze in his direction. The look was there when he'd returned her to her car earlier, and it was there again now.

He hoped she'd change her mind this time. He couldn't take being shut out again, and he didn't want to let her go. West returned his attention to the world beyond the clinic window, but damn it if his heart wasn't seated in the chair right beside him.

Chapter Eight

Tina watched with rapt curiosity as the cruiser wound along desolate country roads. She'd never given much thought to where West hung his hat, but now that they were on their way to his place, she couldn't stop thinking about it. Clearly, he hadn't chosen a traditional neighborhood. Those were all behind them now, tucked closely together near the center of town. She imagined if he had his choice, he'd live on a small farm or in a cabin. West was an outdoorsman through and through. It was his love of nature that had drawn her to him, and his love for people that held her there to the very end. Amazing how she appreciated those qualities all the more as a grown woman.

The cruiser slowed near a bend in the road, and West turned onto a narrow drive nestled between ancient oaks and evergreens. The forest rose into the sky on either side, tangling their limbs in leafy patches overhead. "Here it is."

"Talk about secluded," Tina marveled. "Don't you get lonely?"

He smiled through the windshield. "Not with all this."

They rocked down the gently pitted drive in silence, listening to songbirds and crunching gravel before a handsome log cabin came into view. A wide expanse of lawn extended in every direction, seemingly cut from the hills just for him. No, West wouldn't be lonely here, surrounded by nature and just minutes from all the friends and family a person could want.

West gathered her bags and swung Tina's door open. "You're smiling."

"This is beautiful."

"Thanks. I bought the land when I came home from the service. Dad, Cole and I restored the house. It was pretty well run-down, dilapidated, collapsed roof, but it was part of Shadow Point's story, so we gutted it and started over inside. It needed just about everything replaced, but the bones were solid, and I like living in a piece of our town's history." He led the way toward his home, saddled with her things. "This used to be the office of an old mining company. I found some pictures at the library and framed them for the mantel. The house is small, but it's been plenty big enough for me."

The sun had set while they'd waited for Ducky to be seen and treated. A while longer still for paperwork when she'd decided he was safer being boarded with her trusted veterinarian than going home with her and West.

Tina followed him along a flagstone path to the porch, admiring his landscaping and the tire swing suspended from a massive oak in the front yard. It was like having a deeper look inside the man West had become. "That swing is just like the one at your folks' house."

"Yeah. Didn't seem like home without one, though I'm not sure anyone's ever used it. I don't get much company and Cole stopped swinging years ago." He flashed her a mischievous smile.

"Good to know." She gave the tree another long look before moving on. She hoped that one day Lily would swing on a tire like that, happy and carefree, oblivious that childhoods like Tina's existed.

West shoved the cabin door open and flipped on the lights. A cozy living space sprung into existence before her eyes. "Wow."

"Thanks." West locked the door. "We put the loft and stairs in. It'll be my office once I get the electrician out here to wire it, but it could also be a guest room with a little work. I'm going to put your things in my bedroom. I'll take the couch, and you can do whatever you'd like. I don't plan on sleeping, but you should try."

Tina followed him down a wide hall to a pair of doors facing off with one another.

He pointed to the left. "That's the bathroom, and this—" he turned to the right "—is the bedroom." He hit the light switch, then delivered her bags to the bed.

Tina wandered inside, admiring the comfortable-looking bed and trying hard not to let her mind wander to where Lily was sleeping tonight. Allowing her thoughts to wander was the worst sort of torture, and she needed to hold it together a little while longer.

She had solid plans to cry herself to sleep at the first opportunity. "This is beautiful."

"I made it from trees on the property. We had to take them down to make room for my pole barn." Thick, polished limbs and logs were twined together to form the headboard and bedposts. The mattress was nearly waist high and covered with a pale gray duvet.

West watched her curiously as she took it all in.

She'd felt the way he looked not long ago, when West had gone through her home, room by room. She'd been irrationally anxious, wondering what he thought of her life, and if he knew how important it was to her that he approved. She couldn't be sure about the second part, but West was undoubtedly feeling as exposed as she had while he'd plucked through her personal space.

She circled the room, taking in the details. Everything smelled like aftershave, leather and spice. A row of belts hung from the open closet door, and a line of boots stood against it. Stacks of blue jeans and T-shirts climbed the closet interior, supported by a framework of wooden shelves. He'd probably made those, too.

A photo of several men in fatigues sat on his dresser. Most of the group members were shirtless. All were tattooed. West included. Dark lines of india ink wrapped their arms, chests and sides. She turned curious eyes on him.

"Army buddies," he said.

"You got a tattoo?"

"Couple." West cleared his throat and leaned against the doorjamb. "It was nice of the vet to keep Ducky, but I didn't mind bringing him here."

A change of subject? West didn't want to talk about the tattoos. Why? She bit her lip against the nosy question, and went with his new subject instead. "Dr. Flanders's wife is a friend of mine. I know he'll take good care of Ducky while I'm away, and I have no idea what comes next for me, so I think he's better off there than here. I'm just glad he only needed a bandage." Ducky was lucky that leap from a moving vehicle hadn't done worse than some muscle strain. "Speaking of injuries." She walked back to West. "You need to clean your scrapes and cuts, and put a butterfly bandage on your chin or you could wind up with a scar. You'll also want to put some ice on your worst bruises, or they'll hurt like hell in the morning."

West shook his head, clearly amused by her list of orders. "Yes, ma'am."

His slow Southern drawl sent her back to high school, when those words had been his standard response for personal requests, like a toe-curling kiss or a rendezvous under the bleachers after class. Heat bled across her cheeks.

West grabbed a small stack of clothes from his closet, then turned for the door. "Give me ten minutes to shower, then I'll make coffee and we can get started on the killer's profile. I don't need ice or bandages." He glanced at the bed. "If you'll try to rest, I'll try to hurry."

Tina watched as he dropped his things on the bathroom counter across the hall and stared into the mirror. He unbuttoned his uniform shirt and let it fall onto the floor before grabbing the hem of his white undershirt and stripping it off over his head. Thick, taut muscles worked across his back and chest as he removed the material and tossed it aside, leaving a clear view of his sharp, lean torso. West had always been fit, but now... wow. Expertly detailed tattoos lined his ribs, arm and shoulder. The words were dressed as badges, painted on military choppers and replica dog tags. Words like *Ranger. Airborne.* And *All Gave Some. Some Gave All.*

She pressed a palm to her stomach, no longer lean from youth and hunger, in an attempt to stop the butterflies. Her body had changed as much as West's, though not in the same ways. He was broader and thick from military training and an outdoorsman's life. She was softer, curvier from the effects of maternity and a regularly filled stomach. Sure, her hips were wider and her bottom more round, but she'd never felt as beautiful. She couldn't help wondering if West had noticed the physical changes in her, too. If he had, what did he think?

West turned to look across the hall at her, as if he'd somehow heard her unspoken question. He unbuckled his belt and slid it from the loops. His hands lingered at his waist, and his soulful blue eyes fixed hungrily on her.

Tina's heart hammered and her chin dropped. "Oh, my God. I'm so sorry." She was caught staring. Caught watching the man undress. "I didn't… I wasn't…" She waved her hands helplessly between them. She wasn't what? Imagining what his new body would feel like pressing down on hers? "Oh, Lord." She marched to the open bedroom door and swung it shut before she died of humiliation.

WEST CHUCKLED SOFTLY and rubbed a heavy palm over his cropped hair. He'd been caught in the midst of a fantastically filthy fantasy. Worse, he'd been caught by the woman who was starring in it. If Tina's expression was any indication, the images he'd unintentionally conjured were painted on his face. He'd been enjoying the imagined reflection of her bare backside in the bathroom mirror while she sat on the counter, legs wrapped tightly around his waist.

And *damn*.

He'd looked across the hall to find her staring back. Her face was six shades of red, and he couldn't muster a single explanation. Though, she'd panicked enough for the both of them.

He rushed through his shower and re-dressed in his favorite blue jeans and old army T-shirt, hoping she wouldn't ask what he'd had on his mind when their eyes had met. He wasn't a fan of lying, and she probably wouldn't like the truth. Luckily, the steaming hot water had cleared his mind and helped him refocus.

West wrenched the bathroom door open and padded

into the kitchen on bare feet. Scents of black coffee and scrambled eggs rose to meet him.

Tina sat cross-legged on a stool at his island, sipping from an old mug. "Sorry. I realized I was starving, and figured you were, too." She cringed. "I should've asked before I made myself at home in your kitchen."

West ignored the warmth blooming in his chest. The view before him was one he'd always wanted, but it wasn't real. They weren't sharing a meal, coffee and conversation because they wanted to. They were here because she was in danger, and it was up to West to protect her. Nothing more.

He poured some coffee and shoveled eggs onto a plate. "You don't have to ask. You're a guest. What's mine is yours." He opened his laptop on the counter and printed the new findings from Tina's case and the shooting. "I've got enough work here to keep me busy. The shower's free and so's the bed. Help yourself to whatever you need. I'll be here in my temporary office for a while."

Tina set her cup aside and dusted her palms together. "Okay. First, do you mind if I take a look at those bruises?"

West concentrated on his email. "I'm fine." He could probably use some ice or aspirin like she'd suggested earlier, but he definitely didn't need her hands roaming over his skin. He was only human.

She slid off the stool and approached him behind the counter, where his printer expelled page after page of documentation.

He gathered the papers from the printer and tapped them against the counter, creating a tight stack. "Look at all this." He dragged his phone from his pocket and swiped the screen to life. "Three new texts and a voicemail. How long was I in the shower?" Couldn't have been more than a few minutes. He'd made sure of it. West scrolled through the texts, hoping for some good news, then dialed into his voicemail and put it on speaker.

"West." Cole's voice rang into the air. "We got our hands on the other patient. Tucker. He was on a bender, out camping in the national park. I'm hauling him in for questioning, but he's a mess. By the look and smell of him, he hasn't been in any condition to shoot or drive for a couple days. No word on the truck or baby yet, and no indication an infant or anyone else was with Tucker out here. I'll keep you posted." The message ended and West pocketed the phone.

Tina frowned. "So, it wasn't Tucker. That's good, but I wish he wasn't using again. I wish I could talk to him. Find out what's going on."

"You've got enough to worry about. Let Tucker worry about himself right now." West rubbed his cheek, lost in thought. "Hopefully Chris the pharmacist turns up with an alibi tomorrow. Blake tried to reach him at home and work, but Chris wasn't at either place."

Tina studied the floor. "I didn't consider Chris a serious person of interest until someone took Lily. Now I keep thinking how adamant he was that I join him for dinner or coffee while I was pregnant. He's left me alone since then, more or less, but that's strange, right?"

"Maybe." West couldn't help but understand any man's desire to know Tina better, pregnant or not. What he thought was strange was the encounter he'd had with her other patient, Carl. That guy might not have been a killer, but he was weird, and something told West that Tina should stay away from him. Though, he doubted she'd take that advice since she was on a quest to save the world.

The heel of his hand caught on his aching chin and he sucked air.

"West." Tina crammed into his personal space, pressing herself between him and the row of cabinets at her back. "Let me see that cut." One small hand landed on the stubble of his cheek. Her thumb fanned over the swollen section of his jaw and lingered near the cut on his chin. "It's bleeding again. You need a bandage. Do you have one?"

He wiped a napkin against his chin, capturing a tiny drop of blood. "This ain't bleeding. This is nothing."

"It isn't nothing," she argued. Her gaze slid from his chin to his lips and lingered. "You need to treat that cut."

"Yes, ma'am." The words were out before he'd intended. He'd used the old line on her earlier to see if it ruffled her feathers, but this time the context was right and so was the mood. The words had come on instinct.

Tina's face drifted closer to his and her free hand curled against his collarbone. The world stilled as the fragrance of her engulfed him. Scents of vanilla drew him nearer, and he pulled his head down to hers. Tina's eyelids dipped closed and her breath washed over his lips. He clamped greedy hands over the curves of her full, sexy hips and groaned at the warmth of her breasts pressed firmly against him.

"Tina," he started, his voice sounding far too husky. He rested his cheek against hers and shored up his restraint. "You've had one hell of a day. I don't want to play a part in making it any worse once you're thinking clearly."

"Hey," she whispered, tipping her mouth to his. "Shut up and kiss me."

How could West resist an order like that?

Chapter Nine

West pressed his mouth to hers, savoring the moment. He ached to deepen the kiss, but refused to complicate their already complicated reunion any further. He ran his palms down the length of her arms and twined their fingers together on both hands before breaking the chaste kiss.

Uncertainty pinked Tina's cheeks as she opened her eyes. "Oh." She tried to step away, but West held her fast. "It's okay if you don't want me that way anymore," she said. Her voice was strong and even.

He liked that a lot, but she couldn't have been more wrong. "Tell you what." West formed his most challenging smile and released her hands in favor of skimming his palms over the deep curves of her waist and gripping her sexy hips once more. He pulled them tightly against him and held her there.

Tina gasped. Her lids fluttered and the sound from her lips was nearly enough to undo him.

"I'm going to be a perfect gentleman until this is over," West vowed, "but if you're still interested after that, I'll make sure you know exactly how I want you."

She caught the thick of her bottom lip between her teeth and smiled. "Deal."

"Deal."

TINA SETTLED ONTO the couch and pulled her feet up with her. She balanced a notepad on her lap and tapped a pen to the paper. She needed to distance herself from West and refocus on finding the man who'd stolen her baby and demolished her life. West moved past her toward the fireplace, and the sting of rejection pinched her cheeks. He was right, of course, to put her off. She was in no condition to make decisions, and in her experience sex had always complicated things. She'd trusted very few men with that kind of access to her, and had been un-equivocally disappointed in the long run, if not sooner. She put that blame on herself. Physical intimacy still meant too much to her, even in the age of cell phone apps made for hooking up with strangers. Sex required a lot of trust, and trust mattered. Which was exactly why she'd behaved so impulsively. At one time, West had been her rock and her comforter. She'd taken all her broken hearts to him, and he'd made her forget her tears. West Garrett was her protector, and no matter how much time had been lost between them, a part of her had hoped he would work his magic again. Make her believe that everything was going to be okay, and that he'd protect her from anything or anyone who dared say otherwise. If West had accepted her advances, she would've been comforted for a while but devastated to lose him when this was over.

Then again, maybe he knew that. Maybe that was his reasoning.

West pushed logs around inside the fireplace, send-ing embers into the flue. "I keep asking myself what kind of nut would do all these awful things, and I've got nothing." He swiveled to face her, replacing the poker in an iron rack before taking a seat beside the hearth. "I mean, I know crazy is crazy, and the reason probably makes perfect sense to him, but I don't get it."

Tina wasn't a fan of words like *crazy* or *nut* when referring to mental health, but the anger inside her had found a few much worse things to call the man attacking her from every angle. "I'm not sure," she admitted. "I didn't study profiling, and most of my education and experience centers on trauma survivors. If you're looking for speculation, however, I'd say this person is trying to merge our lives. He's attacked my job. Inserted himself into my home." She paused to force images of a cooler in the tall grass behind her home out of her mind. West had shared his awful findings with her while they waited for Ducky to be seen by the vet. Unthinkable as those photos had been, this lunatic, whoever he was, had done much worse. "And he's taken my baby—" she cleared her thickening throat and pushed ahead "—and come for my dog." She cupped a hand over her mouth, certain she'd be sick. It had been a mistake to try to eat at a time like this, even something as mundane as scrambled eggs.

"Then why you?" West asked. He bent his knees and draped steel arms over them. "Is it because you're you, or because you're a widow? A single mom? A counselor?"

"I don't know."

The muscle in his jaw popped and clenched. "Do you think this guy followed you here from your old town, or is a citizen of my county doing this?"

Tina wrinkled her brow. "You take personal responsibility for thousands of people? That's a heavy burden."

"Kind of comes with the job." A small smile formed on West's lips. "I guess I feel as protective of them as you do of your patients, which is why I'm going to ask this carefully. Could this be the work of one of your group members? Past or present?"

Tina's knee-jerk response was "No, of course not," but she hadn't stopped considering the possibility since the shooting, and the more pointed crimes she'd witnessed today, the more she'd wondered if this was someone she knew. Even Ducky seemed to know the man somehow. Was he someone she'd talked to about her life? Had she unwittingly presented a killer with casual details about Lily and the sitter, her house, dog and job? No. She was guarded by nature, and she hadn't had many people over since Thomas died. Even fewer since Lily had been born. "I've considered it, yes. Abuse survivors could swing wide, exchange feelings of intense grief for action. Form a working plan to re-create a life lost." She released a slow breath for stability. If that theory was true, then she had to face an even more heinous one. "If ballistics can match the shooter's bullet to the one that killed Thomas, then this behavior goes back a year. It's had time to percolate and grow in the killer's unstable mind."

"Walk me through the timeline following your return to Shadow Point."

Tina stroked the soft fabric of her jeans, drying sweat-slicked palms on her knees. "It started when Dad went to jail."

"About two years ago," West said.

"Right." The solemn look in his eye puzzled her. Maybe his father had told him her secrets after all. She flinched at the possible betrayal to her younger self.

"What then?" West pressed.

"Well." She searched for the right details. "I started calling home again. I knew he couldn't beat her to the phone anymore. I'd finally be able to talk to Mom. Except, she rarely picked up. I thought she'd flourish in his absence, but instead she crawled deeper into herself. It was only then that I came to realize that her depression and detachment had nothing to do with me and everything to do with him. His incarceration hadn't set her free—it had set her afloat without an anchor."

West shifted on the floor, resuming his fuss with the growing fire. "So, he wasn't the tyrant and warden I thought he was?"

"No," Tina scoffed. "He was worse." She closed her eyes against the violent memories racing to her mind's surface. "I think that without him, she was too humiliated to face her life. She'd hidden behind his abuse for so long. Letting him control everything. Including her. Mom and I tried to keep it quiet, but I can see now that everyone knew. Maybe not the specifics, but enough, and she'd built her sad life around the abuse and codependency. When that was taken from her, she bailed."

West's jaw set.

Did he know more than he said about her past? How could she ask without giving it all away?

Tina dragged a pen across her paper. "Dad was arrested, and I put my house on the market when Mom stopped taking calls. I came to visit, and the house was empty. Mail was piled in the box. I had to stay and try to find her." She tipped her head back in exasperation. "Not *find her*, find her. I didn't plan on going on an expedition or anything. I assumed if I kept watch, she'd eventually come home, probably in terrible shape, and I'd be here to help her get back on her feet."

West's face turned stricken. "I looked for her."

"What? When?"

"She wasn't gone more than two days before a neighbor reported it. Mail in the box confirmed the timeline. I thought she'd gone on a vacation. Needed time to think. I checked every day after that. Made calls. Contacted extended family and known acquaintances."

Tina bristled. "You didn't call me."

"How?" He gasped, half laughing at the absurdity, half angry that she didn't think he'd tried. "It's not like she had you listed as an emergency contact. She didn't even have an address book in that house. No computer. Nothing. The letters I sent to your last known address came back unforwarded. Your dad wasn't talking when I went to him. You'd vanished."

Tina tipped her chin higher. She'd made a point of starting a new life because the pain from her old one was more than she could bear, and probably the reason she'd chosen her profession. She couldn't save herself or her family, but she could help someone else if they'd let her.

"When you came back, I assigned a new deputy to look after the case and advise if she turned up. I figured you wouldn't be in a hurry to see me or talk about it, and if you were, I'm not too hard to find."

Tina ignored the jibe. Yes, she could've run to West for help, but according to the deputy, her mom was all but a cold case. So, Tina paid her mom's property taxes and hoped for the best. "Then you know I got here, found a job, bought a house and met Thomas a few weeks later."

"I'd heard that, yes," West admitted. "I tried not to keep up with the details, but I heard anyway. Price of living in a small town, I suppose."

She imagined a thread of hurt in West's voice. "We were married on a whim, the most impulsive thing I've ever done. Stupidest, too. Not that I wouldn't do it again," she corrected. "I got Lily out of the deal, but he was never the one. You know?" She flicked a sheepish gaze at him. "Not the one I'd dreamed of marrying."

West's Adam's apple bobbed long and slow, but he didn't speak.

"I had my suspicions about the pregnancy," she babbled on, wishing she'd kept that last comment to herself, "but I wanted to wait to tell him after I confirmed with the doctor. Then he went on his annual hunting trip. Something he said he did with his dad and brothers growing up in Missouri. He went last year in solidarity, even if he couldn't be with them in person. Driven by nostalgia, I suppose. I don't think he'd actually killed anything in years."

Tina wiped a renegade tear from her cheek. It was awful that he'd died alone in the woods, trying to hold on to a special time from his past when she was waiting at home with news about the future. "His family was torn up at the funeral. Bitter and angry. They blamed one another for not coming back here to hunt with him. It was absurd. As if anyone could've stopped his death." She shook her head. "His dad sent flowers to the hospital when Lily was born, but that was it." She'd stupidly thought that Thomas's family would become her family, even in his absence. They hadn't, and that made two families who didn't want her.

West moved to the couch and tugged her against his side. "You and your daughter deserve more than some crappy flowers and angry, uninvolved in-laws. You know that, right?"

"I know that Lily deserves the world."

"And you do, too." He pressed a kiss against the side of her head that felt a lot like a promise, though she didn't dare dwell on what that promise might be.

She forced her thoughts past the moment and back to

the subject at hand. "If this is the work of someone from my therapy sessions, past or present, then you should know I run an open and rolling group. That means anyone can request to join during certain months. When I get a request or referral, I like to do a quick evaluation of the candidate to see if they will benefit from what we do and if they will fit the existing dynamic. I look at the source of their trauma, their current situation and personality. It's important that the group can work together. So, for example, a rape recovery group would be exclusively divided by gender, but abuse survivors can be mixed, especially in situations of parental abuse. Same for former military or law enforcement."

West pulled his arm away and angled to look at her face. "What happens in the sessions? How much do you reveal about yourself?"

"My sessions are process based. Members lead the sessions. They share and give feedback among themselves. I'm more of a moderator."

"Anyone ever express any desires to do something like this? Maybe comment on how much they'd like a family like yours?"

"Never."

He turned his attention to her notepad. "So, what's on your list?"

She flipped the page over to reveal a line of names. "These are all the men I've met and the places I've been since returning to town."

West quirked a brow. "That's a huge list."

"I've been here awhile."

"Cashier at coffee shop? Postman?"

She smiled. "I don't know the whole town by name."

"Park. Gas station. Church."

"I'm trying to be thorough." Tina pulled in a jagged breath. "West?" The thing that had been tearing her apart inside finally forced its way onto her tongue. He would tell her the truth, even if it wasn't what she'd hoped to hear. "Why do you think I never knew anything was wrong before today? How could I have no idea someone was fixated on Lily and me like this? I didn't know we were being watched. Followed. How could I not realize my baby was in danger? Shouldn't that be my instinct?" She pressed a palm over her heart. "Am I a bad mother?"

West's expression crumbled. "No. It means you're sane and human. It means you trust people, you expect good things, and you were busy enjoying your life while a predator was watching." He cocked a knee on the couch between them and leveled her with a flat, no-nonsense gaze. "You said yourself that these people can be chameleons. What kind of mother would you be if you spent all your time looking for them, expecting the worst? That's no way to live, and you had no reason to do that. So, let's stick to the positives here."

Tina nodded.

West lifted a finger and ticked it off with his opposite hand. "We know criminals who do the kinds of things we saw today, like stalking their victims and setting up a deluded romantic dinner, and they probably do those things because they imagine a relationship with the victim. That's a good thing for right now. It means he's unlikely to do anything he thinks might ruin it. He's going to take good care of Lily to show you that he can. The next time he makes contact, he's going to want you, and I think that will be soon. He came for Lily and Ducky in the span of a few hours. Another good thing because if he tries to get near you, he's mine."

Tina blinked. A dangerous thought was solidifying

in her mind. Being abducted would mean getting her hands on Lily. If she could somehow slip into the abductor's grasp and fulfill his fantasy, then she could get Lily and find a way to escape. Another sign she was on the edge of losing her mind. She didn't think reckless things like that anymore. Especially when the recklessness would involve Lily.

West would hate that idea. It was dangerous. And crazy. She'd have to keep it to herself for now.

"May I?" West pulled the notepad onto his lap and reached for the pen. "I know some of these people. I can strike a few off. What kind of guy wouldn't do this?"

"Anyone with a stable home life. Someone with a consistent and predictable work history or strong ties to the community." She heaved a sigh. "There isn't a specific profile. We all process differently, and some people just blend in."

West began to draw lines through the names.

"What are you doing?"

"I grew up with some of these guys. A few are friends of Dad's. Others are regular volunteers at the church or live in a neighborhood I'm familiar with. Little League coaches. Married to their jobs. Wives. Mortgages. Two-point-two kids."

She nodded. Someone juggling the typical American dream was an unlikely candidate for this sort of crime spree, but she was slow to discount anyone. Tina knew firsthand how much people could hide.

West returned the notepad to her and headed to the kitchen. He carried his laptop and a stack of files from the printer back to the couch. "Let's see what we have here. Maybe we can narrow your list down a little further."

He worked diligently for a long while, reading and

marking papers. Tucking some between himself and the arm of the couch, tossing others onto the coffee table. He checked his phone regularly, as if it might've buzzed, but he'd missed it. He seemed as equally unhappy when there were messages as when there weren't.

Slowly, Tina's interest in West's progress dimmed. Her stinging eyes grew blurry from fatigue, and her lids drooped in exhaustion. When she reopened them, the pile of papers on the coffee table in front of West had quadrupled.

He dug the heels of his hands against his eyes.

"Are you okay?" she asked.

"Yep. I've gone through every page, account and report. Now I'm just waiting for more, and contrasting what we know versus what we need to know. Wondering how to get the latter." He dropped his hands away from his face and moved the laptop to the coffee table, sending an avalanche of papers onto the floor. "I'll send your completed lists to Blake."

He carried her notepad to the kitchen. A moment later, his printer buzzed to life, scanning and saving the pages. West returned with a thumb drive and a determined look. "Time for bed."

"What?"

"Come on, get up. You can't get any rest on a couch." He extended his hand to her.

"No," she protested. "I should stay up with you. What if something else happens?"

West pulled her onto her feet. "You need your sleep. I've got this." He tucked her against his side and squeezed. "We're going to get Lily back in your arms, then she can steal your sleep. How does that sound?"

Her throat clogged with emotion. "Perfect."

"I promise to wake you if anything significant comes

up." He led her to his room and turned down the covers. "Now rest. Tomorrow is a new day."

Tina slid between the sheets, immediately and immeasurably thankful for West's stubborn streak. His bed was perfect—warm and inviting. Her muscles unwound on contact.

"Sweet dreams." He pulled the blanket up to her chin and cut the lights on his way out.

Alone for the first time since losing Lily, Tina's heavy heart ached anew as she closed her eyes to the silence of a home without her baby.

Chapter Ten

West jolted awake. He blinked heavy lids at the orange spray of sunlight filtering through the window. Was it dawn? When had he fallen asleep? His phone buzzed on the coffee table beside his laptop and a mountain of useless reports. He lurched for the vibrating cell phone and snatched it up in one hand. "Garrett," he croaked.

"West?" Cole's voice blew through the line. "I'm at the hospital. Tina's sitter just woke up."

Electricity raced over West's skin as he processed the words and their potential meaning. Mary could potentially provide a description of the man who took Lily. "We're on our way."

He cleared his scratchy throat and called for Tina. A moment later, he was at his bedroom door. "Knock, knock." He rapped his knuckles on the wall before stepping into the room.

Tina was upright in bed, eyes wide. "What happened?"

"Mary's awake. We've got to go." He left Tina to get ready, then headed for the living room. He grabbed a fresh uniform from the closet and ducked into the bathroom to change. A moment later, he pocketed his keys, stuffed his wide-brimmed hat over unkempt hair and winced at the tender lump on the back of his head. West would *really* like to return the favor when he found out who'd jumped him inside Tina's mudroom. He threaded his arms into the soft sleeves of his Cade County Sheriff's jacket and turned back for Tina.

She flew down the hallway, passing him on her way to the front porch, still rubbing sleep from her eyes. "What did Mary say?"

"I don't know. Cole only said she's awake. I want to talk to her before the doctors take her for testing, wear her out or drug her up and leave her too exhausted to answer my questions."

Tina hopped along beside him through the brisk dewy morning, tugging the backs of untied shoes over her heels. "The medical team wouldn't do that," she protested. "They have to know we need her before they take her away. My daughter's life is at stake."

West stopped to unlock the doors to the cruiser. "They don't do it to get in the way. They've got a job to do. We've got a job to do. Problem is, they don't care if we solve our case today or six months from now. Assessing Mary's full medical status is their priority. Getting answers from her is mine. Get in."

West gunned the car's engine to life. He stuck to the speed limits as he headed back into town. The sun scorched a path through the sky before them, blinding and reminding him anything could happen. It was a new day. The shocking emotional charge of yesterday's crime spree had worn into a flat collection of facts. West's mind was clear and focused, thanks to a few unintended hours of sleep, and today was the day West would reunite Tina with her baby. Mary's description of the intruder might even be what makes that possible.

Cole met them in the hospital atrium with an unshaven face and tray of disposable coffees. His uniform shirt was partially unbuttoned and tucked crookedly into his waistband.

Tina greedily accepted the coffee. "Thank you." She wound her fingers around the cup and looked at Cole. "How is she?"

"She's going to be fine." He led the way to the elevator and abused the button with his thumb. "No one's been in to see her yet. Just a nurse making rounds to check vitals." He shifted from foot to foot as he watched the floor numbers illuminate and darken.

West frowned. "Have you slept?"

The doors swept open and Cole dove inside. "A little. Yeah. Come on."

"Have you been home?" Tina asked, parental concern bleeding through her tired voice.

West smiled. He liked this look on her, and it was always fun to aggravate Cole a little.

Cole stiffened. He hated being fussed over. As the youngest of four Garrett brothers, he'd spent more time than he should have trying to prove he wasn't a baby. "I stayed here in case whoever did this decided to keep Mary quiet." He hit the button for the fourth floor and leaned his back against the wall.

"Good work," West said. "How'd it go? Anyone come by who seemed out of place?"

"No, but I caught up with the pharmacist, Chris, this morning. He was at his girlfriend's house last night. Turns out he didn't stop asking Tina out because the baby was born. He stopped asking her out when he started dating this woman."

The doors rattled open, releasing them onto Mary's floor. They followed Cole along a silent hallway, bypassing the nurses' desk with quick nods and a flash of Cole's badge.

He knocked on Mary's door before walking inside. The room was dark despite the morning sun.

"Cole?" Mary's voice was soft and groggy.

"I'm here," he answered, flipping on a dim row of lights along the edge of the room.

She rolled her bandaged head against the pillow and squinted. "Tina." A tear rolled over her ruddy cheeks. "I'm so sorry. I tried to run."

"She's got a concussion," Cole explained. "Light hurts her eyes. Sounds hurt her ears. Movements hurt her head. When she's not sleeping, she's puking."

Tina sat on the edge of Mary's bed and lowered herself to hug the woman. "It's okay. I know you did everything you could, and I'm so sorry you were hurt." She released her with a sniffle. "We're going to find him and get Lily back. These guys will make sure he pays for all these horrible things. I promise. Can you tell us who took her? Or describe him so they can contact the media and get his image out there publicly?"

"No." A sob broke on Mary's lips. "I was watching for you to arrive, and a truck pulled into the drive. It had its bright lights on. I could barely make out the shape of it. I knew something was wrong, so I didn't answer the door. I went to get Lily and wait for the deputy to come back. He was making rounds through the area. I planned to tell him about the truck when he returned, but I heard the front door open." Her chest bounced with shuddered breaths. "I hid in my bedroom closet with Lily. When I thought I heard him leave, I made a run for the back door, but he grabbed me by my hair." Her hand moved higher, stopping at the crown of her salt-and-pepper hair, as if she still felt his fingers there.

West approached the bed, hat in hand, hoping to convey respectful urgency. "Is there anything you can recall about the man who grabbed you? Even the smallest detail can make the difference."

Mary bit into the thick of her bottom lip and shook her head in one tiny move. Her tear-filled eyes locked onto Tina's gaze and the drops rolled freely onto their joined hands.

"It's okay," Tina said. "You might remember something else. Something that's significant, but you don't even realize. How did he smell? Like cigarette smoke, or a familiar cologne? Maybe a topical medicine or a certain food? Anything?"

Mary's lips quivered. "No."

Tina released Mary's hands and gathered her unbrushed hair into a fisted ponytail. "When he grabbed your head, you were holding Lily. Were you holding her when he took her? Did you get a look at his hands or shoes? Were there tattoos on his arms? Was there anything significant about his clothes?"

Mary's head continued to swing infinitesimally from left and right. "No. I'm so sorry." She gasped. "I can't believe I let him take her. I didn't save her."

Tina slid off her bed and turned to pace the room, hands knotted at her middle.

Cole redirected her to an empty but rumpled bed in Mary's semiprivate room. "Mary's going to be fine, and so is your little girl," he promised.

From the looks of it, Cole had made himself comfortable in the spare bed last night. The guy was nothing if not dedicated, and West was damn lucky he'd chosen to become his deputy. Cole could've done anything he wanted with his life, but he'd chosen the same frustrating, heartbreaking, dangerous work as the rest of them. The nut.

Mary sobbed, drawing West's attention back to her.

He dragged a chair to her bedside and lowered himself into it. "Can you walk me through what happened when you reached the back door? Step-by-step."

Mary's eyes darted regretfully to Tina's. "I had one hand on the knob when I heard him behind me. He said, 'Don't make me shoot you,' and I knew he'd do it. I figured he was the one who shot Tina's patient, and maybe he'd meant to shoot her but missed. Maybe he'd gone to my place to wait for a second crack at her. I panicked. I begged him not to shoot. I told him I was carrying a baby." Her words broke into sobs. "If he shot me, then he'd hit her."

West leaned his elbows against his knees, bringing himself closer to Mary's weeping face. "How did he take Lily from you without you seeing him?" Surely he hadn't knocked her out while the baby was in her arms.

Mary plucked tissues from the box at her bedside. "He told me to kneel and close my eyes. I thought he'd kill me, but he told me to lay her on the floor, and that's the last thing I remember."

"Okay," West said. "So, he knocked you out, then took Lily from the floor." He had every opportunity to kill Mary, but didn't. Why? The killer hadn't hesitated to shoot Tina's newest patient, and possibly her late husband, but he'd spared the sitter. Was Mary part of the larger plan to re-create Tina's life somewhere else against her will?

West groaned inwardly. Mary was probably lucky she wasn't abducted to care for Lily, but then again, that would've been a better scenario for Tina and the baby.

Mary pressed wadded tissues to her eyes and choked on a new round of sobs.

"Tell me about the man's voice," West pressed. "Was it especially deep or high? Soft or harsh? Did he have an accent? A drawl? Anything significant to the cadence of his speech?"

Mary cried harder, and West's patience thinned. Yes, Mary had been through a horrific ordeal, but so had Steven, the dead guy; Tina, the grieving mother; and poor Lily, an infant in the hands of a maniac. "Mary," he pressed.

"West," Cole warned. "Give her a minute."

West's fingers curled tightly over his knees. His jaw locked, and his muscles tensed. How could the only witness to the kidnapping have witnessed nothing?

The second hand on the wall clock ticked loudly overhead, punctuating the passage of time, marking the moments lost in their race to save Lily.

West pinched the bridge of his nose and tried to formulate a new plan for intel. Maybe canvassing Tina's neighborhood would help. Neighbors had come onto the porches at the sound of the truck revving its engine. Maybe someone had seen something else useful recently. A man lurking in the trees or yard, playing with the puppy or entering the house. Maybe they recognized the truck, or had seen it before.

Mary pulled another tissue from the cardboard dispenser. "There was one thing," she whispered.

"What?" Tina's voice sounded from behind him.

The air inside the room thickened with anticipation.

"It's probably nothing," she hedged.

"What?" West prodded.

Mary wrinkled her nose. "He didn't say much. Just those few short sentences, but when he told me to put the baby on the floor...he stuttered."

West's chair scraped against the floor, nearly knocking into the nightstand in his haste. "Get someone to Carl Morgan's trailer. Now." He pointed at Cole, who was suddenly on alert. "Get a warrant. Get someone over to see his mama at that nursing home and get his picture all over the damn news!" He strode toward the doorway, still barking orders. He knew that squirrely bastard wasn't right.

Tina gushed her goodbyes to Mary and followed Cole through the door.

Cole contacted Dispatch as they hustled down the hall.

"Tell the first man on location to haul Carl in for questioning and detain him," West said. "We need to get inside that trailer. Talk to the neighbors. He's got that baby."

West's gut clenched. Anger and adrenaline coursed over his skin and pounded in his veins. He'd stood two feet from Carl Morgan yesterday, and he'd walked away. That was before he'd assaulted Mary and kidnapped Lily. "Get his photo added to that Amber Alert along with a description of that pickup truck." West could've prevented this. Now Mary was lying in a hospital bed, injured and sobbing her apologies to Tina for something he'd allowed. It was on him to make this right.

Tina jogged down the hallway behind two puffed-up lawmen. The space around them had burst to life since their arrival. Nurses and orderlies marched purposefully in every direction, flipping charts and pushing carts. Families poured through the double doors, toting balloons and flowers past the nurses' station.

It seemed unfathomably surreal that none of these people had any idea about what was happening to her. They didn't know that hope had just filled her empty heart until it ached inside her chest.

Cole headed back to Mary's room once the elevator opened.

She and West climbed aboard, waited through a painfully slow descent, then sprinted to the parking lot.

Tina's thumping heart twisted and jumped in her chest. Images of her little girl flooded her mind as she climbed into West's cruiser and buckled up beside the uncharacteristically quiet sheriff. This was the part where he should be thrilled. Proud, even. Saying things like, *Everything is going to be okay.* The nightmare was over. She was safe. Lily was safe. The bad guy was going away for a very long time.

He jammed his foot against the gas pedal and peeled through the parking lot. A drastic contrast to the care he'd taken on their way to the hospital.

Tina watched his face turn slowly redder as he drove. "I've never invited Carl to my house," she said. "I don't talk to the group about my personal life. I don't know how he knew about Mary. None of it makes any sense. How could he have been lurking in my life without me knowing?" The notion sent chills over her skin. Could they be wrong? Could the killer be someone else, and her hope of holding Lily again soon be in vain? "What's wrong?"

Trees and traffic whipped past the window, blurring in a seasonal smear of orange and gold, dotted with irrelevant vehicles and the occasional pedestrian.

"Talk to me, West," she pushed. "Something's bothering you and you have to tell me what it is. I don't think my heart can take any more bad news or surprises."

West flicked his heated gaze her way. "I had him, and I let him go." He flexed and tightened his grip on the steering wheel. "I should've listened to my instinct and taken him to the station for questioning right then.

I should've kept him there until I could prove he was the shooter."

Tina stared. In all the years they'd known one another, she had never been the rock he needed. Their relationship had always been a series of her crisis and his comfort. Though she'd never given him all the facts, he'd kept open arms for her. Never pushing, and never needing her strength in return. She was the victim. He was the hero.

Yet, here he was, opening up to her. Admitting his feelings of failure and frustration.

He shot a look her way. His handsome face scrunched in turmoil.

"You had nothing to go on," Tina blurted, praying her training would kick in while her mind scrambled to appreciate the new change between them. "Carl was behaving oddly, but being strange isn't against the law. Assault is, by the way, so you can't go unleashing a lifetime of pent-up frustration on him. He's not worth losing your career or ruining a thirty-year track record of good choices."

"I didn't always make the right choice." West gave her an apologetic look, and reached for her hand on the seat between them. "You're right. I did the best I could with the information I had. Now that I know Carl's behind this, I won't let him go a second time." He gave her a closer look. "How are you holding up?"

"I'm terrified," she admitted. "I feel half paralyzed with fear of all the unknowns. Part of me wants to leap from the car when we get there and tear the door down to get to her, but the rest of me is just really frightened. We don't know if we're right about Carl, and it makes me afraid of the letdown if she isn't there. If we're right, and she is there, I have no idea what condition I'll find her in. Sure, he might plan to make a happy family, but that doesn't mean he knows how to care for her. Does he even know how to prepare her bottles? Did he remember to buy formula? What if he got tired of her crying and…" A lump formed in her throat, silencing the words. "My mind has conjured the absolute most unthinkable scenarios. Whatever we find can't be worse than the things I've thought."

West's cell phone rang in his pocket, and he freed it as they hit the county road at full speed. "It's Deputy Loman," he said before swiping the screen to life. "Garrett," he answered. "You're on speaker with Tina Ellet."

"Are you en route to the Morgan home?" Loman asked.

"We are. I just hit the county road."

"ETA?" the deputy asked.

West's serious expression turned sour. "Maybe five minutes. Why?"

Tina's nails bit into the tender flesh of her palm. Her stomach rolled against her spine. The hope that had carried her from the hospital to the cruiser was suddenly gone. Eviscerated by the tone of the deputy's voice and expression on West's face.

"What's going on, Loman?" West growled.

"He's not here, Sheriff," the deputy responded. "No one's here. No truck. No baby. No Carl Morgan."

The No Trespassing signs posted at the end of Carl's drive appeared in the distance, and West pressed the gas pedal harder before slowing at the gravel drive.

Tina collapsed forward, sucking in shallow breaths and trying not to pass out. Her baby was there. She had to be. That was why they'd come. She could practically feel the weight of her in her arms again, and smell the shampoo on her sweet head. She was losing her all over again.

West rocked the vehicle to a stop and released a few venomous curses.

She forced herself upright with a guttural moan.

The deputy's cruiser sat outside her window.

West rounded the car's hood. A man in uniform waited on Carl's porch, hands on hips.

She watched in disbelief as West tried the trailer's front door and peeked in every window before circling the home and returning to the deputy for a handshake and departure.

He climbed back behind the wheel, already on his cell phone. The device now pressed to his ear. "Where are we on the warrant?" he asked. "I want into that trailer. Now. Loman's keeping watch in case Carl comes back."

Carl's trailer grew smaller in the distance as West reversed down the narrow drive, erasing Tina's hope of holding Lily again today. "Why are we leaving?" she asked. "I don't understand." She swiped a deluge of tears from her cheeks. "Why aren't we waiting for him to come home?"

"Loman's staying. I'm going to find Carl's closest neighbor."

Tina gripped the dash for stability as the cruiser spun back onto the county road in a shower of loose gravel and mud. Her body ached with a void where Lily belonged. She cradled her center with a weak, desperate arm.

She'd counselled her baby's kidnapper for more than a year without a single clue about what he had planned for her family. West blamed himself for what was happening, when in truth this was her fault. She should've seen Carl for what he was and stopped him. Instead, she'd assumed he had a rough past to work through. She'd thought he would open up eventually. If she was patient. If she didn't push. Now, she just wondered if Carl had ever needed her help at all. How much of what he'd let her see was even real? And why hadn't she been able to tell the difference?

Tina had failed her job as mother and therapist.

Now, her poor baby was in the clutches of a madman, and no one had any idea how to find her.

Chapter Eleven

West jammed his brakes and skidded to a stop near an elderly woman checking her mailbox at the edge of the winding road. Her eyes went wide at the sight of the sheriff's cruiser tossing gravel into the trees and over the berm. He crammed the gearshift into Park and turned to Tina. "Wait here."

The woman stepped back as he approached.

West tapped a finger to the brim of his hat. "Morning, ma'am. I'm West Garrett, Cade County Sheriff, and I have a few questions about the man who lives down the road about a quarter mile. His name's Carl Morgan. Do you know him?"

She narrowed her milky eyes on West and cocked her head. "I don't make a habit of gossiping."

"It's not gossip. A little girl's gone missing, and I think Carl Morgan has her, but he's not home. You'd be assisting in an investigation."

She shifted her gaze to Tina in the cab. "I don't know anything." She cleaned out her mailbox and turned to walk away.

"Wait!" Tina's door flew open, and she ran for the old woman. "Please," she pleaded. "My name is Tina Ellet. I was in the parking lot with my patients yesterday when one man was shot and killed. Did you hear about that? Did you see that on the news?"

The woman straightened. A gleam of recognition lit her face. "I remember you. They play that clip every few minutes. Your daughter's missing. I know because there's an Amber Alert, and they play that, too."

Tina seemed to shrink at the sound of her words. "Please help me."

The woman's weary expression faded into something kind and motherly. "I'm Celia Hickman." She extended a hand to Tina, who shook it gratefully. "My husband knows more about Carl than I do. Carl keeps to himself."

"Thank you," Tina said, breaking the handshake and stuffing her fingers into her pockets.

Celia motioned for them to follow her up the lane, and Tina matched her pace.

West brought up the rear, keeping watch on the woods around them.

"Celia?" A man in bib overalls rocked in a chair on the porch. He planted his boots on the floor and sat taller at the sight of them.

"That's my husband, Frank," she told Tina. "These folks want to know about the neighbor," she called to her husband.

"Neighbor?" Frank struggled to stand. His gray beard and hair fluttered in the growing breeze. He unhooked a cane from the porch railing and met them in the yard. "Everything okay?"

A small, ratty-looking dog pranced into view. It gave a dismissive bark before retreating, uninterested.

West offered the man a hand. "Sir, I'm Sheriff Garrett."

"Sure you are," Frank answered. "I knew your daddy. You look just like him."

West forced a smile. "We have reason to think your neighbor, Carl Morgan, was involved in a series of crimes yesterday." He rested a palm on Tina's shoulder. "We think he has her daughter."

Frank's expression fell. "He said he was babysitting."

"What?" West asked. "When? Did you see the baby?"

The women turned on Frank with wide eyes and slack jaws. Shock jolted from Celia, and hope rose in waves from Tina.

"Frank," Celia screeched. "You didn't tell me he had a baby over there! I could've called the police."

"Well." Frank stroked his beard, looking a bit frightened. "I didn't see the baby. I only heard it, and I didn't think nothing of it anyway. Babysitting is babysitting." He swung his attention back to West. "The dog took off last night, and I tracked him all the way over to Carl's trailer. Dog was on Carl's porch barking up a storm. I got there at about the same time Carl came outside to complain. I apologized, tucked the mutt under my arm and said good-night. Then I heard the baby crying."

Tina clutched her hands to her chest. Terror bleached her face. "Was she okay?"

Frank looked past her to West. "I don't know. I didn't see her. He said he was babysitting for the night, then taking the little one home first thing in the morning."

Tina seemed to age before West's eyes. "Could they be at my house? Waiting?"

West worked the cell phone from his pocket and tapped the screen. "I'll ask Blake to get over there." He refocused on Frank and Celia. "Is there anything else you can tell us?"

"Afraid that's all." Frank frowned at Tina. "I know you probably don't think you should, miss, but you ought to lie down before you fall over." He shot West a pointed look. "She's not well."

West wound one arm around Tina's back and nodded. "Thank you. If you think of anything else, please call the sheriff's department. Tell them what you remember. They'll see to it that I get the message."

Celia leaned into Frank's side and rested her head on his chest. "We're going to be praying for you and your baby girl," she said.

Tina coiled in on West, releasing silent sobs against his ribs as they made their way back down the lane to his cruiser.

TINA WANDERED BACK to the cruiser, guided by West's strong arms. She'd done plenty of wrong things in her life. She probably deserved the pain and heartache she was feeling, but Lily didn't. Lily was pure and innocent and perfect. Why was this happening to her? Tina had no idea what her baby was going through, but whatever it was, she deserved better.

West zoomed through town toward her neighborhood, honking at intersections and waving apologetically at folks with gaping mouths. He arrived outside her home in half the time it would've taken to get there legally. Maybe there was a rule breaker under his perfect, upright facade. Or maybe the last twenty-four hours were wearing away everyone's composure.

Blake and two men in navy FBI windbreakers stood beside a large black SUV in her drive. No sign of the red pickup truck anywhere.

West charged forward to meet his brother and the other men.

Tina bumbled along on unsteady legs. Why weren't the agents inside? Where was Lily?

"No one's here," Blake announced. "Windows and doors are locked. Perimeter's secure."

Tina fell back a step. "He told his neighbors he was taking her home."

Blake offered a sad smile. "Wasn't his home. Wasn't yours."

West turned in a slow circle. "What do we know about Carl Morgan? Who are his people? Where else might he consider home?"

Tina collapsed onto the bottom porch step. Defeated. Drained of hope for the second time in an hour. "He moved here to be with his mom when she went into the assisted living facility."

Blake nodded. "We talked to her. She's got no love for her son. Says he's a thorn in her side. Always has been. Never happy. Always acting out."

West looked to Blake. "Any word from his home-town police department?"

"Yeah." Blake braced his hands over his hips. "I got ahold of them on my way here. They had a file on the mom, nothing on Carl, but he was in the older reports. As a minor, he was present at the time of multiple police calls to the home. Mostly noise complaints by neigh-bors with an occasional drunk and disorderly for Mom. Home conditions were described as cramped and un-clean. Neighbors speculated abuse and neglect, but I don't have any arrests to back that up." He angled his back to Tina. "I sent some men around last night to ask her neighbors about the truck you saw. I didn't get any-thing concrete."

West folded his arms. "Cole added the vehicle de-scription and Carl's photo to the Amber Alert. He can't get far with this kind of coverage. Folks are going to recognize him, and someone's going to turn him in."

He gripped the back of his neck. "I read all the reports and findings last night."

"Dead ends," Blake said.

"Yeah. Any chance Carl kept the family home in Pine Hurst? Maybe that's where he went."

"Nope," Blake answered. "Sold to pay for the nursing home."

"Right." West turned to face Tina. "I think you should talk to the neighbors. They know you. They're going to be more at ease talking to you than to some federal agent. Maybe if they're really trying to help, something useful will shake loose."

Blake dipped his chin. "Agreed. I can be intimidating."

Tina tried to laugh, but the sound was lost to despair. "I'll do it."

Blake turned toward his vehicle. "I'll reach out to the Pine Hurst Police Department again."

West took Tina's hand. "And check on the warrant. We need inside that trailer."

Tina moved beside him on numb legs, the late morning chill seeping into her bones. Her heart was empty, as hollowed out as the jack-o'-lanterns on her neighbors' doorsteps.

West rang the doorbells one by one. He explained the horrific situation to every homeowner on her street, while Tina stood dumbly at his side. She'd begun to disconnect from the day, from the pain. Her emotions pulled back, shut down to protect her. The tingling in her limbs was dreamlike, as if she might soon wake up from the nightmare. The neighbors' faces blurred into one abstract frown.

They moved methodically along her street. Up one side, then down the other, collecting the same information. Everyone had heard the truck last night. No one had gotten a look at the driver or the license plate. No one knew if her baby was in the vehicle.

"This isn't working," Tina said as they climbed the steps to the last house on her block. "We have to do something else."

West rang the bell and waited, tapping his palms against his thighs. "We're planting seeds. That's important. If nothing else comes from this, you'll at least have reinforced your home with a personal neighborhood watch. One that's educated about the situation and aware of what to do if they see something unusual happening at your place. If Carl comes back here, we're guaranteed to hear about it now."

A moment later, the door opened several inches, and a woman Tina knew as Darcy peeked out. "Yes?" Darcy was a young mother of two. She had a husband who mowed the lawn and chased their kids through the sprinklers all summer. They seemed like a nice family, but they'd never spoken to Tina.

Tina edged around West, finally finding her voice. "Darcy?" Humiliation swirled in her gut. Tina didn't have a husband or a partner of any kind in this. She was Lily's only protector, and she'd failed her. "I'm Tina. I live across the street. This is Sheriff Garrett. Can we talk to you?"

Darcy gave West a long look, then pulled the door open and motioned them inside. "I thought you looked familiar."

West gave a limp smile. "How are the kids?"

"Good. Napping."

Tina held her questions. It was a small town. Of course they'd come across people who knew West and his family.

Darcy led them to the kitchen, where plastic toys peppered the floor and dry cereal dotted the table beside brightly colored bowls. "You have to excuse the mess. I wasn't expecting company."

"It's fine." Tina forced the words through gently chattering teeth. Excess adrenaline and stress were leaking from her in every form. She'd fallen asleep just before dawn, certain today would be better, but she was wrong. Yesterday was packed with shocking news, but there was still hope. Today, her hopes had been repeatedly crushed. Her heart along with them.

West took a seat at the cluttered table and dusted a space in front of him with one hand. "Darcy dated one of my brothers a while back," he announced. "Blake?"

"Ryder," she corrected.

"Right." West nodded.

Tina tried to control her expression, which was surely twisting into anger. She didn't care who Darcy dated. She cared where her baby was.

West tapped his cell phone to life and turned the screen to Darcy, as he had to every neighbor before her. "Do you recognize this man?"

"Sure." She cast a curious look at Tina.

Tina blinked. "You know him?"

"No." Darcy dragged the word out for several syllables. "I don't, but I recognize him. I've seen him at your place a bunch of times. I thought you two were a thing. Or related."

"Related?" West asked.

"Yeah. I started seeing him after your husband…" She trailed off, a look of remorse on her brow. "After the funeral, there were lots of folks coming and going. Bringing you food and looking after you. I assumed he was one of them. He came a lot. Addison had colic then, and I'd pace the house all day and night, hoping he'd fall asleep and wouldn't disturb the neighbors."

West leaned across the table. "Have you ever seen him go inside?"

"No. I don't think so. I've seen him go around the house, and I've seen him leave flowers." She shifted her gaze to Tina. "That's why I thought you two might be dating."

West's expression crumbled in disbelief. "He gave you flowers?"

"No," Tina protested. "Of course not."

Darcy scoffed. "He did. I saw him do it plenty of times. Big wildflower bouquets." She mimed the size with her hands. "I had the kids out in a stroller one morning after your baby was born. Everyone on the block had gone to work, and he was there. He saw me looking, so I told him how much I admired the flowers. He said they were a surprise, so I shouldn't tell. I swear I had no reason to think that was weird. I thought it was kind of sweet." She let her lids fall shut. "I should've known."

"You couldn't have known," West interrupted. "Did he say anything else? Anything at all."

Darcy reopened her eyes. "I asked how you two met, and he said you bought him a coffee when he needed it most. He said he knew then that you understood him, so he joined your group, and the two of you became quite close."

Tina's stomach dropped. "I always pay for the car behind me at the Cup of Life drive-through. Is that what he meant?" She replayed Darcy's words. "Oh, my goodness. Carl was following me before he joined my group? Everything he's told me was a lie." Tina pressed a cool palm to her burning face. "Buying coffee for strangers is an act of kindness. That's all." She cast her gaze at West. Her lips began to tremble. "He's stalking me because I was kind when he needed kindness, and this is my punishment."

West took her hand in his and squeezed. "Do you remember getting wildflowers?"

Words lodged in her throat. Images of the beautiful arrays burst through her mind. She'd loved the wild-flowers. Even looked forward to them. "I received the first bundle on the day of Thomas's funeral. I get them every month now."

Darcy leaned against her counter. "Are you telling me I stood there with my kids and talked to a killer?"

Tina rolled her eyes up to meet Darcy's. "I'm sorry."

West tugged her hand in his. "Was there ever a card with the flowers? Did you keep it?"

"No," Tina answered. "Never. They were just flow-ers." Her tongue stuck to the roof of her mouth as all the facts of the day snapped into place, like a sick, de-mented puzzle. "He's been stalking me all this time. Through my pregnancy. All through Lily's life. I feel sick."

Darcy sprung away from the counter. She pointed around the corner, beyond heaping baskets of unfolded laundry. "Bathroom is opposite the laundry room."

Tina darted inside and pressed her forehead to the door. She'd been violated, deceived and plotted against for more than a year by someone who wanted to steal everything she'd worked all her life to earn. And why? Because she'd bought him coffee? She wanted to scream. To cry. To crawl into bed and let the heavy sheet of darkness, now nipping at her conscience, pull her under and take her away.

"No." She smacked her palms against the door and

went to splash cold water over her burning face. She stared at her haggard reflection. *I will find my baby*, she vowed.

And she knew what she needed to do next.

She needed to talk to Carl's mother.

Marriage...Surprise...

..

..

..

..

Chapter Twelve

West scanned the lot outside the assisted living center in town. The sun had finally gotten a grip on the day, drying puddles and dew from the roads and grass. No signs of Carl, Lily or the red Ford pickup.

Tina popped her door open and headed for the building in long, purposeful strides.

"Wait." West caught her wrist in his hand and stopped her progress. "Slow down. You can't go in there hot, pouring everything we know out for her inspection and demanding answers. We don't know what kind of relationship Carl has with his mother, or if she's as strange as he is. Take a breath."

Tina pulled free. Something new and feral burned in her eyes. "That woman's son has my daughter. What do you want me to do? Play coy? Make small talk while he holds her hostage?"

"No." He planted his feet and dragged her to him, until her heart raged against his own. "I want you to remember Carl spent more than a year planning this. You need to choose your words carefully. Don't tell her more than she already knows from watching the news. If she has any information beyond that, we'll know it came from Carl." He rubbed his forehead, hoping it wasn't a complete mistake to bring Tina on this interview. He'd hoped her presence would add emphasis and encourage Carl's mother to share, but Tina's heated state of mind could do more harm than good. She needed to pull it together before she ruined the potential lead.

Tina made it to the welcome desk first and asked to see Mrs. Morgan.

The receptionist shook her head. "I'm sorry. We don't have a Mrs. Morgan here. There's a Mr. Morgenstern."

West pushed himself into the small space beside Tina. "Hello. I'm Cade County Sheriff West Garrett. We'd like to talk to Ms. Baxter."

Her wide brown eyes opened impossibly farther. "She's in suite three twelve."

"Thank you." West led the way to the room, taking long, purposeful strides and noting the exits. "Here it is."

"How did you know she had a different last name?" Tina asked.

West smiled. "Late-night reading."

The warm, buttery scent of fresh baked rolls clung to the air outside her door. A sign for the cafeteria pointed to the end of the hall. According to West's watch, and his gut, the time was nearing noon, and he'd already missed breakfast. West ignored the pang of hunger and knocked on the door. "Ms. Baxter?"

A woman in a hot-pink sweat suit answered. Long gray hair hung to her narrow waist and slippers covered her feet. "Who are you?"

"I'm West Garrett, ma'am, and this is Tina Ellet. We're friends of your son."

She opened the door, then headed for a small couch pushed against the wall and picked up her remote control. The room was decorated like a tiny dorm room. Bed. Mini fridge. Love seat and television. Small, homey items lined the walls and every flat surface. She poked the remote into the air like a sword, at a television mounted high on the opposite wall. "Carl doesn't have any friends. You're here like the others this morning, hoping I'll turn him in."

West worked his jaw. This trip suddenly felt like another dead end. A frustrating one. "We have reason to believe Carl shot a man in cold blood yesterday, then kidnapped an infant." The civility in his tone was failing.

She stopped channel surfing and flicked her gaze quickly to him. The Amber Alert for Lily lodged firmly in the corner of the television. Carl's face was posted side by side with one of a baby wearing a pink quilted jacket.

Ms. Baxter powered the television off.

Tina froze near the coffee table, where a mass of wildflowers erupted from a stout vase. "Did Carl give you these?"

Ms. Baxter rolled her eyes. "Yeah. He comes here all the time, trying to make up for all the trouble he caused me growing up."

"Growing up in Pine Hurst?" Tina asked.

The woman shot her a sour face. "I don't have to answer your questions. You think Carl did those things, then you figure it out. Leave me out of it."

Tina moved cautiously toward the love seat. "Carl brings me flowers like this, too."

West locked his jaw against a number of rude clarifications. He pretended, instead, to examine a collection of photos taped to the closet door. Blake told him this was a dead end.

"So, you're the girlfriend?" Ms. Baxter laughed. The raspy sound turned quickly into a deep and uncontrollable cough that took more than a minute to quiet and another to recover from. She lifted a glass of water from the table to her lips; a tremor wobbled the liquid inside her glass. Eventually, she turned her ashen face back to Tina. "He wasn't lying. You are pretty. He says you're a doctor."

"I'm a clinical psychologist," Tina corrected.

Ms. Baxter made a deep throaty noise that led to another, less aggressive, round of coughing. "Figures. I told him no doctor would want him."

"Why not?"

The woman crinkled her nose in distaste. "Why not? Have you met him? He practically flunked out of high school. Was rejected for the military. Makes no money. He barely talks, and when he does it's with a st-t-t-tutter," she mocked. "He was always a mama's boy."

"How so?" West asked, unable to stay out of it any longer.

"He stayed inside all the time, clinging to my hip. Worrying about me. Fussing over me. 'You drink too much. Don't smoke. That man's not nice to you.'" She mimicked her son in a whiny childlike voice. "He didn't like fighting or hunting or sports or getting dirty. All I had to do was yell a little and he'd run off. Anytime I hit him, he'd hide under the bed like a damn injured dog. Don't think I didn't try to make a man of him. I had plenty of boyfriends who tried to toughen him up, but it never took. Even dated a cop once." She gave West a pointed look. "Didn't matter. Carl just curled into a sad little ball and did nothing with his life. He spent more time with those wildflowers than he ever did with any woman."

"Carl needs help," Tina whispered, "and so does my baby."

Ms. Baxter looked her over. "He only likes you because you bought him coffee. Just like that little girl with the lemonade stand. Any woman so much as looks his way and he's falling over himself to love her. Ridiculous. If women wanted pets, they'd buy a dog."

"What happened to the little girl with the lemonade stand?" West asked, suddenly worried that Carl had a lifetime of missing women in his wake.

Ms. Baxter scoffed. "She broke his heart. What do you think happened to her? Then I poured that lemonade over his head and told him to be a man! No woman was ever going to love a weak, clingy cupcake like him."

This was getting them nowhere. West hated to admit it, but that was exactly what Blake said had happened to his men when they visited her earlier. He'd failed to mention, however, that she was a mean, spiteful old woman. He couldn't imagine being raised by someone so hurtful and vindictive. No wonder Carl was warped. Whatever was wrong with him may or may not have been there from the day he was born, but living with Ms. Baxter certainly couldn't have helped matters. He widened his stance and set a hand on Tina's shoulder, hoping to offer her a bit of his strength when hers was clearly wearing thin. "This kid sounds like a real thorn in your side. Why not tell us what you know so we can punish him for what he's done?"

Her eyes flashed hot. "Because he's mine and you can't have him."

Well, that solidified it. She was as insane as her son. "Any idea where he'd go with a baby? He told a neighbor he was taking her home."

She shrugged, attention glued to West's hand on Tina. "Like I said. You're the detective. You figure it out."

"Ms. Baxter, if you know where he is and intentionally withhold that information, you can be charged with aiding and abetting."

She stuck her wrists out. "What are you gonna do? Haul me in for protecting my son? Take me from this prison and lock me in another one?" Her voice grew louder with each word, and she began to cough. "If he took that baby, it wouldn't surprise me."

A nurse poked her head through the open door. "Everything okay in here, Ms. Baxter?"

"No," the old woman choked out between coughs. "These two are pissing me off."

The nurse looked to West. "Sir," she started.

West waved a hand. "We're leaving, but we'll be back, so make sure Ms. Baxter doesn't go anywhere." He wrapped a protective arm around Tina and guided her back through the building, the woman's cough echoing down the hall behind them.

TINA FELL ONTO West's couch. Thankful to be somewhere she could lie down, and equally guilty for wanting to rest at a time like this. What was wrong with her to think of such a thing when her daughter was missing? Was Lily able to sleep? Was she cold? Hungry?

Tina forced her eyes wider and gave her cheeks a few sharp pats.

West's stomach growled loudly for the tenth time since they'd arrived at the assisted living facility. "Are you hungry?" he asked. "Because I need to eat something before we have to take off again."

"I think toast or crackers is all I can manage," she said.

West opened a cupboard, then tossed a sleeve of saltines across the room to her. "Anything else?"

She snorted. "Water or coffee. Probably coffee." Her body felt fifty pounds too heavy. Even keeping her head upright had become a chore on the ride back to West's home. She situated herself on the couch so that she could watch West in the kitchen. It was hard to fit the man before her into the context of high school sweetheart. The angles of his face were sharper, his voice a little deeper and his heart was still as big as ever, but he wasn't a kid anymore. Odd to think that while she was away becoming an adult, he'd been doing the same and she'd missed it.

He busily unloaded the contents of his fridge onto the counter and arranged it all in layers on a hoagie bun until he had the equivalent of a Scooby-sized sandwich. "What'd you think of sweet little Ms. Baxter?" he asked, sarcasm dripping from the words.

Tina peeled the cracker sleeve open and pursed her lips. She'd been plagued by a terrible thought since meeting the angry woman who showed no love or concern for her son. "I think Carl wants me to replace her."

West froze. A horrified look screwed over his face. "He wants you to be his mother?"

"No, but I think he wished someone had been." She took her time trying to find the right words for what she thought was happening. The visit with Carl's mother was extremely disturbing. And eye-opening. "I think he wants a woman in his life to be the mother he never had. I don't think he wants me to *be* his mother, as much as he wants me to be *a* mother who belongs to him. She said this all goes back to the coffee I bought him, and the little girl who'd done something similar when he was younger. When I gave him the coffee, he attached himself to the kindness of a woman. As awful as his mother is to him, they were new here over a year ago, and their already broken dynamic was changing. She's sick. If he's going to lose her, he'd better be prepared. Then, he watched me go through a pregnancy and care for a newborn. The kind of woman he wished his mother had been literally become a mother."

"He wants a normal family," West said, wiping a dollop of mustard from the corner of his lip.

"I think so. Unfortunately, that's not in the cards for everyone." Herself included. "It scares me because he's hobbling a family together, thinking it's all going to be glorious, but this situation can't possibly live up to his expectations, and he'll be angry all over again. The failure of his efforts will exacerbate his feelings of inadequacy, and he'll need to be rid of us, so he can try again."

West watched her for several long beats. "He doesn't have you."

Tina stared at the cracker pinched between her fingertips. "No, but he has Lily, and that's the same thing."

"It's not the same to him. You're the endgame here."

Tina set the crackers aside and scooted forward on the couch cushion. She curled her fingers around the edge and refocused her attention on West. It was time to share her crazy idea with him. "We need to find him so I can go with him. Then I can be sure Lily's okay and try to get her away from him."

"First of all, no," West said. "Absolutely not. And second of all, we *will* find him. After that, we'll take him down. We will *not* turn you over."

Tina bit her tongue. If West could arrest Carl without Lily being harmed in the process, fine. But if things went south, and she saw an opportunity to save her baby, that's exactly what she'd do. Regardless of the risk. Protecting Lily was all that mattered.

Chapter Thirteen

Tina hovered over her third cup of coffee and waited for West's phone to ring. He'd insisted on working from his laptop, instead of hitting the road again, and they'd already been sitting still for more than an hour. If it was up to Tina, she'd knock on every door in Cade County until someone recognized Carl's picture.

She'd already tried and failed to rest, despite the glaring physical effects of sleep deprivation. Images of Lily's sweet face flashed repeatedly into her mind, only to morph quickly into red-faced cries of desperation. Tina's nerves were shot, and every precious memory of her baby was slowly becoming twisted in her absence. Was Lily hurt? Was she cold? Sick? Scared? Was she hungry? Was she being changed and fed? Did he have formula for her? Did he know how many ounces to feed her?

Tina ground the heels of her hands against her sore and puffy eyes. She tipped her head from side to side, stretching the bunched-up muscles of her neck and shoulders. Her limbs were heavy and slow to respond when she wanted to move. Worst of all, the ceaseless worry had sent her on a downward spiral of emotional states. Most recently, she'd passed from heart-wrenching desperation into complete detachment. West was kind

enough to pretend not to notice. One minute she was in
mental hell, and the next minute there was a void where
all her internal suffering had been. The seemingly endless tears and tormented thoughts had simply vanished.
Her mind was blank. Her emotional capacity stunted.
When she tried to think of the horrible things she'd been
dwelling on, her mind simply rejected them. The whole
thing was unsettling, but she couldn't seem to change it.

She set the empty mug aside and forced herself upright. "Care if I use your shower while you do whatever
it is you're doing?"

West pulled his eyes from the laptop screen. "I'm re-
viewing reports taken by my men and Blake's. Hoping
something will stand out." He curled his mouth into a
smile that didn't reach his eyes. "Go ahead. Take your
time. If I find anything useful while you're in there, I'll
come knocking."

"Thanks." Tina headed for West's room, where she'd
left her overnight bag, trying not to think of some more
pleasant reasons he might interrupt her shower.

The scalding water did nothing to snap her out of her
stupor. She slid to the shower floor and drew her knees
to her chest, letting the water flow over her, wishing for
her sense of self to return. This was the perfect time for
a breakdown. She had privacy and white noise to drown
the cries, hot water to mask the tears and explain the
flush of her skin. Unfortunately, her tears seemed to
have dried up with her emotions. The detachment she
felt was textbook self-protection, but she hated it. She'd
met dozens of people in therapy who spent all their energy trying not to feel, but that wasn't who she was.
Tina normally felt everything. For everyone. Her heart
ached for strangers' losses and rejoiced with their victories. Neighbors. Friends. People on television shows

and commercials. Tina lived with enough emotion to power the universe, and she'd never seen it as a burden. It meant she was human.

She gave up on the shower and toweled off. She powered up her travel blow-dryer and wiped a hole in the steam on West's bathroom mirror. So far, he hadn't knocked. Which meant there was no news on Lily or the monster who'd stolen her. She'd give anything to know where they were right now, and how she could get to them, but Carl had never said much about his present circumstances. When he had opted to talk in therapy, which wasn't often, he'd focused on stories from his childhood. Instances that had hurt or angered him. He'd vaguely discussed his mother's insensitivity and the harshness of her boyfriends without saying anything substantial. He'd nodded along as others group members recalled being beaten or locked in rooms, humiliated and taunted, but Carl had never given any indication of where he might go under duress.

Re-dressed in yoga pants and a fitted, long-sleeve top, she tied her hair into a messy bun and went back to sit on the couch, where she would presumably stay until something motivated West to leave.

He gave a double take when she walked in, blinking sharp blue eyes before turning back to his computer and setting it aside. "Feel any better?"

"Cleaner."

"Refreshed?"

"Sure." She pulled her feet up on the couch and re-opened the cracker sleeve. Might as well get a little something in her stomach while she wasn't too nauseated to eat.

He narrowed his eyes. "Anything I can do for you?"

"Actually." She squared her shoulders and dusted crumbs from her palms.

West swiveled to face her fully, curiosity clinging to his handsome features. "What?"

"I'm not one to talk about my personal baggage," she began.

West made a sarcastic expression. "That is brand-new information."

She rolled her eyes. She also wasn't one to feel detached from herself, but that was exactly what was happening. Being with West helped. She had never spent a second with him and not felt something. Her chest was already beginning to swell and tingle. She was coming back to herself just by speaking to him. "What you don't know is that I don't talk about those things because I can never find the right words. The stuff that has weighed me down since we first met was so much bigger and more complicated than I could describe that I kept it inside. I pushed it down." Tina paused. This wasn't an easy conversation, and maybe the timing was awful, but at least she was beginning to feel again, and if she wasn't numb, then maybe she'd be okay. "I pretended my home life didn't affect me, but it did. It was unbearable, so I looked for ways to enjoy the other parts of my life. I tried to pretend the rest wasn't real. I should have told you a long time ago. I'm sorry I didn't, but I'd like to tell you now."

Her words seemed to pull the humor from West's face. He fixed her with those soulful eyes and waited.

She'd mentally rehearsed this conversation for years. So, why now, when the opportunity was before her, did she want to run away? She worked the fabric of her shirt's hem between her fingers. "My dad was horrible. To me. To Mom. To everyone. He was abusive verbally, emotionally, physically." She peeked up at him for a response.

There was fresh hurt in West's eyes. "I could've protected you."

"We were in high school, West. No, you couldn't. No one could."

"I could have. We were young, but what we had was powerful. If we'd stayed together, nothing he did would have mattered."

Tina felt a guttural roar building in her center. "You think his behavior didn't matter?" It didn't affect them? Was he kidding? Maybe the town didn't know as much about what went on behind the Ellet doors as she'd thought. "My dad hurt us. Can you understand that? My mom got the worst of it, but I was ruined. He shamed us, belittled us, denied us every single thing we needed from food to affection. He drank up all his paychecks, when he bothered to hold a job long enough to get one. He blamed us when he couldn't. He blamed Mom for everything, and she took it lying down. Literally. And I—I was alone. And broken."

West inched closer with an unfathomable expression. "You were never alone."

Her skin crawled with humiliation. She hated baring herself to anyone, particularly her worst self, and especially to him. "Forget it."

"Hey," he said carefully. "I get why you wanted out of that house, even out of town, but it didn't mean we couldn't be together. You didn't have to cut me off and act as if I'd never mattered. Like *we* hadn't mattered." His haunted expression teetered between regret and heartbreak. "I would've waited for you. For college. Whatever you needed to do. You knew that and you still left. You changed your number. Returned my letters. Why?"

She raised her hands in the air and let them drop lifelessly to her lap. "I had to." She batted stinging eyes. "I did it because I loved you and you deserved more. Something better. More honest and less toxic than what I was." She released a humorless laugh. "What I am."

He narrowed his eyes. "You're not toxic."

"Of course you don't think so. You refuse to see me for the mess that I am. I'm a train wreck waiting to happen. The people I love either hurt me, like Dad did, run from me, like Mom, or die, like Thomas."

"That's only three people, Tina, and it's not everyone who loved you. I loved you." He ground the words through his teeth, shredding her heart with each syllable. "I never left or ran away. Hell, I'm still right here where you left me ten years ago."

He'd loved her. Past tense. A long time ago. Another lifetime. She ignored the painful churning in her chest. She had to be logical and calm. Had to make him understand. "Look." She exhaled slowly and began again. "Do you think my parents started out all messed up and wasted? That one day, long ago, some young, drunk version of Dad saw a young depressed version of my mom, thought to himself, *I'd like to trash her life*, so he slapped her across the face, told her it was her fault that he never had anything nice and she married him?"

West recoiled.

"Every couple starts out happy," she said. "Young. In love. Hopeful. Even them, and look what happened. I didn't want to wind up like them, and I sure as heck wasn't going to drag you down with me."

He caught her hand in his and smoothed his palm

against hers. "You aren't your mother, and I'm not your father. *We* are nothing like them."

"You're exactly like your dad," Tina argued. "Just like your brothers. Your uncles. I would expect you of all people to know that it's true what they say about apples not falling far from the tree."

West blew out a long, angry laugh. "I turned out like my family because I chose to. It was my goal." He pounded a fist to his chest. "I decided who I became. Just like you did."

Tina nearly choked on a sharp intake of breath. The emotions that had been hiding away and making her numb came back with a crushing blow. She wanted to believe him, but she'd never seen herself the way West had. Strong and independent. In control of herself and her life. Those were just more things she wished were true, but weren't. "If I decided how my life would turn out, then why am I here like this now?" Her hands balled into fists on her lap. She pulled them away from him. "A madman, who I counseled—" she swallowed back the cracker attempting to reemerge "—stole my baby. He killed one of my patients."

"I know."

"Don't do that," she warned. "Don't try to smooth this over. Not everything that goes wrong in the world can be fixed with a little Garrett charm and a few waves of your magic badge. I did this. I let Carl get close to me, and I ruined everything I worked for with my ignorance."

A crippling sense of loss flattened her will to fight, and she fell into West's waiting arms. Pride demanded she get up and walk away, but she couldn't bring herself to care about pride anymore. "All I ever wanted to be was a good mother," she whispered against his chest. "And I failed."

WEST FOLDED TINA against his chest. He hated the pain she was in. Hated Carl for putting her through this now, and her dad for everything he'd put her through before. Most of all, he hated himself for not telling her that he was the reason her mom had vanished.

He pulled in a deep breath and peered down at the top of her troubled head. "Tina." He cleared his throat, choosing his words carefully, despite the awful timing. If he didn't tell her soon, the truth would seem like something he'd intentionally kept from her, instead of something he'd hoped to bring up when they weren't in the middle of a crisis.

Tina twisted in his grip and stared back at him with wide, red-rimmed eyes. "Yeah?"

His phone buzzed on the table, halting the words on his tongue.

She shifted away from him, wiping her eyes against her sleeve. "What is it?"

"Hold that thought." West snatched the phone off the table and checked the text. His stomach soured at the stream of photos arriving in succession.

"What's wrong?" she asked, craning her neck for a better look at the unthinkable.

A small pink pacifier lay under the edge of a worn-out couch. The small plastic nub was speckled with dirt, dust and hair from the yellowed linoleum floor. "Blake and his men are inside Carl's trailer."

"Oh, God." Tina ran for the bathroom. Her retch was audible as West responded to the text. He'd accept that response as a positive ID of Lily's pacifier.

THEY RODE IN silence to Carl's place.

Tina had threatened to walk when West tried to convince her to stay at his house until the search was com-

pleted. They'd compromised with her agreement to wait
in the cruiser. As anxious as she was to get a look at
the location where Lily had been held, the trailer was a
crime scene and she was forbidden from entering. The
best West could do was report back and share photos
as he explored the space. Part of him was glad to have
her there. Leaving her alone anywhere too long was a
risk he wouldn't take.

He parked behind a line of cruisers and government
vehicles filling the space between Carl's trailer and the
county road. "Sit tight," he said. West climbed out, but
waited for Tina to nod in agreement before closing the
door.

He headed up the gravel lane in search of Blake. By
the looks of it, all the Cade County deputies were aiding the search party, as well as a significant influx of
federal agents. A bubble of pride puffed his chest.

Blake's FBI team crawled over the trailer in matching navy jackets with yellow block letters, shining
black lights, snapping photos and bagging evidence.
One agent dug through an overturned trash can beside
the wooden porch. The putrid stench of spoiled food
and loaded diapers peppered the air. West pressed one
wrist against his burning nose. The agent's thin latex
gloves and medical mask didn't seem like nearly enough
protection.

West lifted his chin when Blake took notice of his
approach. "What have we got?"

Blake braced his hands against his hips. "This place
is a pigpen. I don't know how anyone lives like that. I
hate to think of what that baby went through."

West repositioned himself, forming a wall between
Blake and his cruiser at the end of the driveway. As if he

could somehow protect Tina from what was happening before him. Thankfully, she couldn't hear Blake's words.

"We've got dirty diapers and empty formula cans in the trash," Blake said. "There's paths everywhere. Boot prints and ATV tracks crisscross the whole property. I can't say for sure yet if the prints are Carl's or not. We're making casts of the impressions."

"What else?"

A line of hounds weaved their way through the surrounding underbrush, eagerly chasing scents on the breeze. West knew they weren't all trained to search for the living. He fought the blast of anxiety squeezing his chest. He wouldn't accept the possibility of finding Tina's daughter in an unthinkable condition.

"Well, wherever he went, he didn't take his bathroom stuff. So either he's planning to buy new, or he's planning to come back. The second one would be stupid, so I'm going with the first. We've flagged his credit cards and put his face on every form of news media. We will flush him out. It's only a matter of time. He can't go anywhere in three counties without someone recognizing him and that baby. We're expanding the Amber Alert as time goes on."

"What about the cadaver dogs? Tell me they're just doing their due diligence."

"For now, yes. I figured I'd get some out here with the search team. Cover all the bases. See what turns up. The trackers were given items from Tina's home to catch the baby's scent, and we pulled Carl's clothes from the trailer."

A flick of instinct pinched his gut. "How far have the search teams gone?"

"Not far. They're just getting started."

West turned in a small circle, scanning the surrounding hills and trees. Something felt off about the scene before him. "Did you head over here after the search warrant came in?"

"Nah. The neighbors called the station. Said you spoke with them earlier, and they could hear the baby crying again."

West twisted at the waist for a look over one shoulder. The Hickman's home was barely visible through the trees. Tina's silhouette was motionless inside his vehicle. He waved and waited. When she waved back, he sighed in relief. This whole case was getting to him. "Why didn't you call me after you spoke with them?"

Blake dragged his gaze over West from head to toe. "When was the last time you slept?"

"Last night."

"For how long?"

He glanced at Tina once more. West wasn't sure how long he'd slept, but it was probably longer than Tina, and he wasn't going to stop working this case until she had Lily back in her arms. She surely couldn't take much more of this. His heart was nearly torn in two and he'd never even met Lily. He couldn't imagine what Tina was going through. "I need you to keep me in the loop on this. All of it. I'll decide when I sleep. Got it?"

Blake sucked his teeth and stared. "Yep."

"Anything else you haven't told me?"

"No. How about you? Did you make a trip out to see Ms. Baxter like Tina suggested?"

West groaned.

Blake snorted. "She's a real piece of work, and her file's a mile long. No wonder her kid is messed up."

"I thought the same thing. I read the file. Didn't see anything on Carl, though. Means he's good. Smart. He's never been caught." West knew there was no way a guy went from being an upright citizen to a killer and child abductor in one day. He'd probably committed dozens of crimes over the years, all leading up to this. "Good news is he probably thinks he's untouchable. That means he'll get brave and stupid. When he does, I'm going to be there to…"

A sharp and sudden crack of gunfire echoed through the trees. The air rushed from West's chest as Blake plowed into him, smashing him against the wooden porch. Together, they rolled onto the muddied ground and ducked around the trailer's edge. A large hole splintered the boards just inches from where West had stood moments before.

The hounds went wild, barking and howling into the sky. The echoes of their laments soared through the hills as a dozen lawmen drew their weapons and took cover.

"West!" Tina's voice rushed into the mix. She ran in the trailer's direction, blind panic ravaging her face.

"Get down!" West launched himself toward her.

The next crack tore through his flesh. He'd no sooner heard the sound than felt the searing pain rip through his arm. A bulging rain barrel burst behind him with a loud snap. Water gushed onto the ground, splitting into rivers at his feet and slicking the already mushy earth.

West's hand flew to his wound on instinct. He dove back to where he'd come with a rampaging heart rate and blinding pain. "Get down," he called again, unable to reach Tina where she stood frozen in fear.

She swung her head toward the cruiser, then back to West, apparently torn between making a run for him or returning to the car, already several yards away. Her wide eyes locked on the blood flowing over his fingers where they wrapped his bicep.

"Now!" Blake barked at Tina. His voice was low and authoritative. "Move it!"

An irrational bout of anger rose in West's chest at the sound of his brother speaking to her that way.

She winced, but found her feet and ducked behind the nearest cruiser. She pressed her back to the tire and covered her head with both hands.

"You okay?" Blake asked West, attention trained on the hillside.

"Flesh wound." He peeled his fingers away and shook his jacket off for a better look. "Where's that nerd Cole when we need him?" Cole would know how to stop the blood in an instant. He'd know how serious the injury was, and how soon West could climb the hill and stop Carl Morgan.

"He'll be around in a minute," Blake answered, still searching the trees for signs of the shooter. "He can smell an injury six counties away."

West tried to tear his shirt across the hem and failed. The pain in his right arm kept it still at his side, and he couldn't do much with his left.

"I can't see a damn thing," Blake complained. He inched out from behind the trailer and sent a round into the woods.

No return fire.

Blake swore. "You know the nut is up there in camouflage with a rifle and a scope, laughing at us with our peashooters and no advantage."

West moved in the opposite direction from his brother, scanning the trees for a glint of sun off the rifle scope. "*We* aren't crazy. That's our advantage."

"Is it, though?" Blake deadpanned. "Because right now he's got us in a barrel, and we're working blind while he tries to kill you."

The words rang in West's ears.

Carl wasn't shooting at authorities for going through his trailer or interfering with his plan. He was trying to get rid of West like he had Steven from group therapy, and probably Tina's husband. West wouldn't be surprised if Carl had arranged this, intentionally allowing Lily to cry so the neighbors would make the call that brought him there.

The roar of an ATV engine echoed through the hills. West squinted into the distance, struggling for a glimpse at the vehicle hidden behind a million red and gold leaves. "He's got an ATV. Just like the tracks you found." He pulled his grandpa's white handkerchief from one pocket and stretched it out in plain view of the hillside. He wiggled his fingertips, swinging the flag in surrender.

The engine's roar grew soft and distant as West repurposed his handkerchief from little flag to bandage, wadding and pressing it against the gunshot wound on his arm.

Hounds rushed into view on long red leashes tied to trainers' wrists, racing toward the disappearing sound.

Blake holstered his weapon, deflated. "He's gone." He marched toward the open trailer door, where an agent poked his head out. He ordered his team to stop what they were doing and look for fresh ATV tracks. "Find them, then follow them. We need to know where he's hiding."

West made a run for Tina. His head swam slightly with pain and adrenaline.

Cole appeared in the driveway, jogging straight for him with the medical supply bag he never left home without. "Sit down before you fall down, you moron," he scolded.

West chuckled, but kept moving. He must look like he felt.

He waved the nearest pair of deputies over in his direction. "Pull up an aerial view of this property. Find out what else is around here. There's got to be another building. An old barn. Abandoned home. Someplace he could hide a baby, a truck and an ATV." That would explain how he'd been able to disappear so quickly and thoroughly following the Amber Alert. Maybe he and Lily hadn't gone anywhere at all. Maybe they were still right there in Cade County waiting for the chance to kill West or take Tina.

He landed in the gravel at her side, and his men dispersed.

Tina clung to West's chest and kissed his cheek with fervor. "I thought I was about to lose you all over again."

Cole squatted beside them, pulling latex gloves over his hands and prepping his medic supplies.

West stroked her hair and placed a kiss against her head. "I'm not that easy to kill."

Cole cast a mischievous look in Tina's direction. "Believe me. I've tried."

West pulled her tighter and winced as Cole put pressure on the wound. Carl wasn't getting anywhere near Tina. Whatever his plan was, it was going to fail because the next time Carl Morgan came within striking distance, West would be ready.

Chapter Fourteen

Cole drove West to the hospital in his cruiser. Tina followed in West's, unapologetically running every light Cole did. He used sirens and flashers. Tina used a heavy hand and horn.

She locked the car and raced through the emergency room doors, desperate to see if West was still okay. That nothing had gone horribly wrong since she'd been forced to leave his side. Cole had insisted the wound was superficial, but the way he'd driven implied something more.

Tina scanned the nearly empty waiting area. No Cole. No West. Only half a dozen people in a room with three dozen chairs. Where were the Garretts? They'd only been a minute ahead of her.

The room swayed, and she forced herself to fight another brewing round of panic. She rubbed a hand against the pain in her chest as she approached the admittance desk. "There was a deputy," she told the nurse. "He came in right before me. The sheriff was with him. He had a gunshot wound to the arm." She slapped her bicep to clarify the injury location.

The nurse nodded. "Deputy and Sheriff Garrett. They never wait. They went right back and told me to send you ahead, as well." She lifted a pen in the direction of two swinging doors.

Tina broke into a sprint, trying not to think too long or hard about the nurse's words. *They never wait.* How often were they here? And why?

Her hands met the double doors with only one thing in mind. "West!"

The impact reverberated through her palms and wrists. Locked.

A moment later, the barrier parted. Cole stepped into view, motioning her back. "Come on. He's fine. I was just on my way to meet you."

She followed him to a pale green curtain drawn around a bed and two silhouettes.

Tina darted through the flimsy veil. Her heart soared at the sight of the only man she'd ever truly loved. "West."

A doctor on a rolling chair jammed a curved metal needle into West's arm. He gave a tug and shot West a pointed look before tipping his head in Tina's direction. "She's with you?"

"That's right," West said, his voice low and scratchy. His cocky smile nearly made her grin. "She's with me."

The doctor pinched West's puckered skin and laced another round of suture thread through. His white lab coat dusted the stool where he worked, shifting over his thighs with each move of his blue-gloved hands. He paused for a longer look at Tina. "You hurt anywhere?"

"No." Her heart and lungs needed to be reminded regularly of their duties, but other than that? "I'm fine."

Cole planted a hand on her shoulder. "Let's get out of here so he can finish." He nudged her back. Away from West's side. "He'll be fine. Carl's rain barrel took the brunt of that shot."

Tina lifted a hand to West and the doctor, completely at a loss for words. Was it the lawmen in them that allowed them to speak so casually about things that crushed her lungs? She absently shook her head. Maybe it was the *Garrett* in them.

She followed Cole into the waiting room and fell onto a chair. "This is my fault."

"Yeah," Cole said sadly.

She jerked her head around to find the same goofy smile on Cole's face that West had worn a few minutes before. She dropped her head against the wall behind her chair. "What is wrong with you people? Your brother was shot. Why aren't you more upset?"

Cole took the seat at her side and placed one ankle over the opposite knee. "I don't know. Probably because he lived."

Tina groaned and sunk low in her seat. "He was shot."

Cole hooked his elbow over the arm of his chair. "I'm sorry about what's happening to you. No one's trying to make light of it. It's just our way of getting through. Gotta claim the victories, you know? Today, Carl Morgan set us up so he could try to kill my brother, but he lost." He turned his hopeful face to hers and leveled her with the trademark Garrett stare. "It won't be the last time we beat him at his game. Yeah?"

She forced her swollen, sticky tongue to work. "Yeah."

"Good." Cole rolled onto one hip and freed his phone from his pocket. "It's Blake." He walked several paces away to take the call.

Tina twisted for a look at the motionless double doors separating her from West. She longed to return to him, or maybe sneak up on Cole and eavesdrop, but her legs felt like noodles. She refocused on the deputy, trying and failing to read his lips. His body language seemed at ease, maybe even disappointed, but his expression was stiff. Whatever had left him feeling let down, wasn't anything too concerning. Definitely nothing to do with her directly. He hadn't glanced her way once since taking the call.

"Ready?" West's voice sounded at her side.

She spun in her chair. "You're done?"

"Yep." He reached for her. The sleeve over his opposite arm was torn and dark with blood. "It's going to hurt like hell tomorrow. You okay to drive?"

She shrugged heavy shoulders. "I don't know. I guess I'm in better shape than you."

"Sold." He wound his good arm across her back.

"I can't believe I just watched you get shot."

He headed for the automatic doors. "You watched me get grazed. That rain barrel was the one who got shot."

"Right. I almost forgot. You're perfectly fine," she deadpanned.

"Well, I mean, I am kinda bummed my jacket has a hole in it."

Tina released a heavy breath. The more she protested, the harder West would work to convince her there was nothing wrong. They'd done this dance before.

"Wait up!" Cole jogged to West's side before they reached the exit. "FBI tracked the ATV to a main road. They're running on the theory he used the truck to transport the ATV, but that road isn't regularly traveled. No cameras. Maybe he's staying nearby and using the ATV for transportation. No one's looking for him on a four-wheeler."

"What about the property?" West asked. "Any barns or other structures on the map?"

"No. The dogs and search team have finished walking the area. No additional buildings or shelters were found. They're moving into neighboring parcels now."

Tina watched as West processed the new information. His jaw clenched and popped. A vein pulsed in his temple. She wrapped herself tightly with trembling arms. "What about Lily?"

The men turned their eyes on her.

"Is he riding around on a four-wheeler with my infant? Or leaving her alone somewhere?" She pulled her shoulders up to her ears, fully ready to explode from the pressure in her heart. "If he's out joyriding and taking shots at the sheriff, then who's watching my baby?"

Cole tucked the phone back into his pocket and pulled out his keys. He gave Tina a sad smile.

No one knew. She understood that. But the concerns were valid, and she could only hope Lily was still alive to be watched at all.

Vomit rose in her throat.

Cole moved his full attention to West without responding. "Carl's trailer is sitting on a hunk of ground that isn't listed as his on the auditor's site, so I'm going to see what I can find out about the owner."

"Good idea," West said. "Maybe the owner can give us some insight. Emergency contact info, prior addresses, anything we don't already have on Morgan."

"I'll keep you posted." Cole saluted and left.

Tina touched West's fingers where they rested on her hip. "Can we check on Mary before we leave? I've been worried about her tests." She'd feel a lot better knowing Mary was healing, and that she wasn't any more injured than the doctors had originally suspected.

She'd also like to know if Mary had thought of anything else that could help them find her daughter.

"Sure." West dropped his arm from her waist and

led her down the hallway toward an elevator bay. He leaned against the wall inside the car.

Tina scrutinized the blank cop expression on his face. His skin had lost its healthy glow. He was being brave for her sake. Even if he wasn't scared or worried, he was hurting. Just too stubborn to admit it. "You lost a lot of blood. You should eat and rest. I'll bet that's exactly what the doctor said before he let you go. Isn't it?"

West forced a weak smile. "The doctor said if I didn't get your number and ask you out, then he would."

She smiled. "Did not." Handsome as he had been, the doctor had seemed far more interested in West's injuries than in her.

"True," he admitted, "but when I saw him looking at you that way, I set him straight before he got any gutsy ideas."

Tina laughed. She gave West her most enticing smile, enjoying the unexpectedly flirtatious moment before life came at her again. "How was he looking at me exactly?"

West's smile faded. His gaze heated her skin and parted her lips. A set of chills coursed over her, rousing a blush on her cheeks. "Like I do."

Her toes curled inside her sneakers. She looked at him like that, too.

WEST SLID INTO Mary's room on Tina's shadow. He waited while the ladies hugged, then pulled up a chair and reintroduced himself.

"I remember," Mary said. She latched her drifting gaze onto West's damaged sleeve. "What happened to you?"

"Flesh wound." He smiled. He and his brothers had used the phrase all their lives. Those two little words had stopped their mom from worrying and their dad from digging too deeply into whatever shenanigans they'd been into when the injury occurred. It was a wonder they weren't all as good with a bandage as Cole. They'd all taken their share of licks on ill-fated Garrett boy adventures. "Have you had any other visitors since we left?" he asked Mary.

"No. None. Why?"

Tina set a hand on her friend's arm. "We're just checking in."

West had seen her encourage and uplift lots of people when they were young. It was a trait he appreciated even more today. When he'd told her he blamed himself for letting Carl get away, Tina hadn't agreed, but she'd let him say it anyway. She'd let him put it out there without chastising him for a moment of lost composure. It was nice to be real with her, no pressure to put on the Good Sheriff Show. She'd always taken him as exactly who he was. Junk parts and all.

He rolled his shoulders in search of a comfortable position for his aching arm. "Have you thought of anything else?" he asked.

Tina's attention snapped to him. "I was going to ask her that."

He smiled. "Then ask."

Mary pressed her lips into a thin white line. "I've been mentally replaying the attack and those moments when he was in my home. Something that keeps going around in my scrambled thoughts is how he seemed so confident and casual about the whole affair. If not for the stutter, I'd have thought he was perfectly at ease breaking into my house and stealing a child. Who does that?"

"A very troubled man," Tina said.

West shifted in the chair and winced. Between his bruised ribs, knot on the head and a fresh gunshot wound, he was a mess. Thankfully, neither woman seemed to notice. "We think he's been planning this for a while. Was there anything else? Additional physical description. Clothing. Scent. Anything like that?"

Deep creases ran over Mary's brow. She chewed her lip for a long moment before answering. "I've seen the news. Saw the reports. The photos of Carl Morgan." She wet her lips and shifted her gaze from West to Tina. "I think I recognize him." Her voice was barely audible, even in the silent room. "I've seen him in your neighborhood and at the park where I take Lily for stroller rides."

That, too, fit perfectly with the scenario they'd developed. Carl had been plotting his actions. Choosing when and where to strike. West could only hope that he'd become overconfident and would make a mistake soon.

"Sometimes he was with another guy," Mary said. "The other one has red bushy hair and a beard. He wore old band T-shirts and looked like someone out of the 1960s."

Tina gasped. "Did he wear glasses? Round wire rims?"

"Yes."

West felt his blood pressure rising, heating his muscles and pounding in his head. "You know him?"

She lifted her hand from Mary's and set it on his chair. "I think she's describing Tucker."

The other patient who'd been suspiciously absent from her group on the day of the shooting.

West dialed Dispatch. His fingers curled tightly around the phone, thinking again of all the ways he'd like to make someone pay for this stress and heartbreak. Tina didn't deserve any of this, and neither did that poor sweet baby. "Tell me you still have Tucker Bixby in detainment."

"Um." The deputy fielding calls at the station hesitated. The telltale sounds of a keyboard clicked in the quiet background.

Maybe the stars had aligned to deal them a good hand for once today.

The keyboarding sounds ended. "No, sir," Dispatch reported. "He sobered up and Deputy Neely drove him home a little while ago."

"Get someone to his place. Right now. Pick him up and hold him there until I arrive." West disconnected and sent texts with the new information to his team and Blake's. They'd hear it from Dispatch, but he wanted to be sure they knew it came from him and he wanted to be kept apprised.

He pushed onto his feet, feeling stronger by the minute. "I'm sorry to run, Mary, but we've got to go. You've been very helpful."

Together, he and Tina fled the hospital. She drove like a NASCAR driver all the way to Tucker Bixby's place and jammed it into Park beside a deputy's cruiser.

The home was small and yellow. A bungalow with a hibachi grill on the front porch and two camping chairs leaned against the railing. It wasn't much to look at, and a few years late on a much-needed coat of paint.

The front door opened, and Deputy Neely poked his head out. He cast a weary gaze at West and Tina, then motioned them inside. "This way." He led them through the silent home to the kitchen, then lowered to the floor beside a motionless Tucker.

Tina gasped. "Is he dead?"

"No." The deputy's Adam's apple bobbed slowly. "We released him not too long ago. He'd sobered up, and I brought him home. He was drunk when I found him at the park. Maybe high. He had a tent all set up. Said he wanted to be alone." Deputy Neely rechecked Tucker's vitals as he spoke. "When I drove him home he said he didn't want to be here. I didn't ask why. What if he was trying to tell me something? You know. Like a cry for help."

West circled the room, taking inventory of the scene. "And now?"

The deputy turned his attention toward the budding sound of a distant ambulance cry. "He's nonresponsive. Breaths are shallow. Pulse is slow and thin but there." He rubbed his forehead. "Possible overdose. Suicide attempt. I'm not sure. I checked his vitals, got him on his side and called 911."

Tina's knees buckled. She slid onto the floor with a thud. Mouth open. Eyes heavy with tears. "I don't understand. He's been doing so well. Making so much progress. He hasn't struggled with drugs in a long while, and he told the group that his drinking was under control. He was proud of his positive strides. He was changing his life. Why would he do this?"

West wasn't sure if she meant the overdose, the potential involvement in Carl's scheme or both. As for the overdose, West wasn't convinced it was intentional. It'd been a long couple of days, especially for someone already suffering from anxiety and instability. "I'd like a look around."

The deputy stepped away. "There are bottles and paraphernalia on the table. Nothing at first glance to determine the time of the OD. I got here about four minutes ahead of you. Door was open. I didn't touch anything except him, looking for vitals. I called the ambulance a minute later when I found him."

West dashed the toe of his boot against the floor. "Door was open when you got here. Why?"

The deputy raised his brows.

West swore. "Carl had something to do with this." He lifted his eyes to the deputy. "Radio Dispatch. Get people out here looking for evidence of foul play and some way to prove Carl Morgan was here. If Tucker was part of Carl's plan and he went rogue, tried to run off or back out, then I'm willing to bet Carl would've had an opinion about it."

The ambulance pulled onto the curb with one final cry.

West led Tina back to his cruiser and helped her inside. "I'm going to take a look around the house, talk to the EMTs and wait for the crime scene folks."

Then, he and Tina could head back to his place where he could take some more aspirin and wait for prelims and toxicology on Tucker.

Tina sat limply in the passenger seat and palmed his keys. "I think it's your turn to drive."

He accepted the offer. "I'm sorry this is happening to another member of your group."

She blinked a tear loose.

The near-death of Carl's possible partner in crime was far too convenient to be anything other than attempted murder.

Chapter Fifteen

Tina stripped out of her clothes inside West's bathroom, her body running more on autopilot than intention. Steam hovered over the surface of her bath like
an apparition, as if the ghosts of her day had gathered
in one spot to torture her. She sunk deep into the water
until only her face remained dry. Her thoughts returned
to Tucker. Had he been involved in the things that had
happened to her? Had he wanted to die and failed? How
long had he been using again, and how had she missed
the signs?

Tina closed her eyes. Slipped completely beneath the
surface. And the world went silent. She counted slowly
to ten, releasing small bubbles of air, and reorganizing
her thoughts before reemerging. Sadly, she couldn't live
underwater, so she'd have to figure out her problems
on land. She filled her lungs with oxygen, then coiled
wet hair into a knot on top of her head.

She needed to talk to Tucker as soon as he woke up.
There were so many questions to be asked. Most important, did he know where Lily was?

She rested her back against the smooth white surface of West's tub and prayed Tucker wouldn't die. For
his sake and for hers.

She couldn't help wondering what else would go

wrong. How much worse would things get before they got better? She kept thinking the worst had come, then something else would happen. A patient would overdose. The man she loved would be shot. Her heart ached at the thought. She loved West. Had denied it for years, but the reality of that love was too much to ignore, and she was tired of walking away from the thing she wanted most for herself. *Him.*

Thankfully, the sun had set, and this wretched day was coming to an end. West needed to rest. He played a good game, but she could see the pain in his eyes, in the way he moved a little slower now, and when his brows crowded sharply together at the slightest jostle of his injured arm. Why did he try to hide it from her? What was the point? She could always see through him, even before she'd pursued a career in human behavior. She didn't need a degree to know he was a terrible liar.

She'd have to deal with him later. Until then, the plan was to let the water wrinkle her skin and unknot her muscles. She skimmed her arms over the water's steamy surface and let her legs tip against the tub's side.

A set of quick knocks rattled the bathroom door. "Tina?" West asked.

She forced her eyes open. *Unbelievable.* "What happened now?"

She hated the unintentional bite in her voice. It wasn't his fault she was so tense, but surely he could see she was barely holding herself together. She needed this break. A moment to relieve the tension.

"Everything's fine," he called back.

"Then why are you knocking?" She hoisted herself from the water. That didn't make any sense. "Never mind. I'm coming. Just a minute." Tina wrapped a giant towel around her heated skin and padded quickly across the room. She opened the door with one hand and supported her towel with the other. "Are you sick?" She looked at his bandaged arm. The blood hadn't come through since he'd last changed the gauze.

His eyes met hers with a look of shock. "I didn't mean to interrupt," he rushed. "I just know how the last couple days have gone for us, and I figured we should talk before something else went wrong. I'm making coffee and maybe some food if you think you can eat. When you're finished."

"We should talk?" Tina didn't like the sound of that. In her experience, arranged talks usually ended in bad news, hurt feelings or a fight. The exact opposite of how she'd wanted to spend whatever quiet time the day would give them. "Let me get dressed."

West seemed to notice then that he'd literally pulled her out of the bath for this. His gaze dropped from her eyes to her exposed shoulders, then skimmed her neck and collarbone, where drops of water were beginning to cool her flushed skin. He didn't stop there. He continued to take her in, head to toe, without apology, and she widened the door several inches to give him a better view. *Too bad he was so determined to be a gentleman.*

His eyes returned to hers with an expression she'd seen on him many times before. The look was heated, raw and sexy as hell. Desire painted his skin and tensed his frame. He was clearly struggling not to reach for her, when all she wanted in that moment was to be touched by him.

"West." He'd rejected her advances last night, but he hadn't looked at her like this in years. She pushed the door open wide. Cool air rushed into the room, tightening her skin into gooseflesh and drawing her closer to the heat of him. Surely he felt it, too. Whatever this thing was that crackled and burned in the air between them. It wasn't just attraction. Not just chemistry. She'd had those things before. This was different. Palpable. Indescribable. Powerful. If this was all in her head, then she was in serious trouble because it felt 100 percent real to her. Like she and West had never truly been apart, as if their bond had never been broken, only stretched by distance and the hands of time.

And it was snapping back with bone-jarring intensity.

She set a hand on his chest and marveled at the pounding of his heart beneath her fingertips. He felt it, too.

Confliction pursed his lips and lined his brow as she traced a slow path over his shoulder, enjoying the feel of chiseled muscle beneath her fingers, watching closely for signs she'd gone too far.

Desire darkened West's eyes. He dropped his head forward, pressing his forehead to hers and wrapping her in the strength of his body, as if he thought she might disappear.

She inhaled the scent of his cologne, intoxicated by the moment. West was everywhere. His hands on her skin. His heart next to hers. She tipped her head back, savoring the moment she'd waited so long for. "Tell me this is real," she whispered breathlessly.

"This," he whispered back, tugging her closer and gripping her tight, "this is everything." His voice was velvet on her aching heart, and his hold arched her back sensually.

The towel lost its grip, but didn't fall. Much like Tina, it was captured in the moment, held tight by the press of their bodies.

She moved her gaze to his lips, longing to feel them

on her, to watch them trace paths over her skin and pull moans from her core. "Kiss me." She stared into his stormy eyes. "I don't need a protector right now," she whispered. "I don't need a gentleman or a sheriff. I need you."

West pulled back an inch, emotion warring in his eyes.

"Please." The anticipation of rejection scorched her cheeks and knotted in her stomach. Was this really where she was now? Begging for physical comforts from a man she'd never stopped loving, one who couldn't even decide if he wanted to kiss her?

She dropped her chin and slid her arms away from his neck. Better to catch the towel before it fell completely and she died naked of humiliation.

West wrapped strong fingers around her wrists and returned them to his shoulders. Her towel loosened further, but his hot blue eyes never left hers. "You're sure about this?"

"Yes."

He lowered his mouth to hers, vanquishing the fear of rejection on impact. His kiss warmed her soul. It filled her with nostalgia for what they had and new hope for what they could become, if he still wanted her when the nightmares were over.

He broke the kiss far too soon with a growl and a pant. Tina's towel fell, and she was glad to be rid of it. There was no time to watch him toil over whether or not this was the right thing to do. She needed him. Now. She shoved his T-shirt upward, away from her. Over his head. The moment it hit the floor, his hands were back on her body, lifting her off the ground and onto the countertop. Her legs wrapped his waist on instinct and locked against his back. The new position pressed her fully against the length of him. She curled her fingers in his hair and dissolved into the effects of his divine and practiced attention.

Finally, in the moment she needed it most, West devoured her in hungry head-to-toe kisses until there was nothing left for her to do but fall apart in his hands.

WEST CREPT OUT of the bedroom where he'd held Tina until she was soundly asleep. Making love to her had been the last thing on his mind when he'd knocked on the bathroom door. He'd only been thinking of losing her again. He'd wanted to let her know that he had something to tell her, and that they should talk before they were interrupted by a new catastrophe.

He shuffled to the kitchen and poured a glass of ice water. He rolled it against his forehead before gulping it down. That woman made it impossible to keep his hands off her. His will was strong enough to survive three brothers, a war and every criminal in the county, but she looked at him sideways, and he was putty. Never mind when she *asked* for something. As if he could tell her no. As if resistance was possible. It had nearly killed him to step away the last time she'd confronted him with her desire. At least then she'd had her clothes on.

He poured another glass and tried to remember he was only human. Sure, he'd promised her he'd behave like a professional until Carl was caught and her life was right-side up again, but she'd said please. *Please.* He finished the second glass of water and set the empty cup in the sink. He leaned over the counter, bracing his hands and hanging his head in shame.

Deeply satisfied shame.

She was going to be doubly pissed when he told her

what he'd been trying to tell her. It was his fault her mom was in the wind.

"Everything okay?" Tina stood in the hallway wearing nothing but his T-shirt. Her hands curled around the corner of the kitchen wall as if she wasn't sure she should come in.

West tried not to stare at the way his shirt slid off her shoulder, revealing the creamy expanse of skin along her collarbone and dusting the ivory flesh of her thighs with its hem. "I thought you were sleeping."

"I was until you left. Did something happen?"

"No. I'm going to make some coffee, review the files on Carl and see if I can think of something we missed. Can I pour you a mug?"

Tina shook her head. "Just water for me. I'm hoping to fall back asleep soon." She dragged a palm across his bare abdomen on her way to the cupboard for a glass.

His muscles tightened with recent memories of similar caresses. "We have to talk," he blurted. Not exactly how he wanted the unfortunate conversation to begin, but if he didn't tell her soon, and she touched him like that again, they'd be back in bed and he'd be in deeper trouble.

Tina froze. The cup stopped inches from her bee-stung lips, still pink and full from the tug of his teeth and brush of his stubble. A playful smile curved her cheeks. "Are you breaking up with me?"

He took the cup from her and set it aside. "This is serious."

Her mouth pulled down at the corners. "Please don't look so guilty. I know you think you took advantage of me, but you didn't. I'm a big girl, and I asked for it."

The gleam in her eye nearly derailed his concentration. "It's not that." He scrubbed a hand over his face. "I didn't mean for that to happen."

Her eyes went soft and round. Her hands traced the curves of her sides with uncertainty. "I know I'm different now. Older, but I thought I did okay in there." A bashful smile lifted her cheek.

"Stop." Images of all Tina's new curves sprang back to mind. That little smile didn't help, either. "You've got to stop talking to me about your body, or I'm putting you over my shoulder, and we're going back to bed. Then I'll never get to say what I'm trying to say."

She gave his shoulder a long look. "Okay. What's this about?"

"Your dad. You know what? Maybe we should sit down." West led her to the couch and started at the beginning. He laid it all bare from the arrest to the hearing. "I pushed for the maximum sentence. I did it because I blamed him for you leaving. I blamed him for hurting you. I knew you hated him, but I hadn't understood until then." He swallowed a brick of anger wedging in his throat. Could feel his temper slipping at the memory of what that monster had put Tina through. "I knew things were bad at your house, but I had no idea until I read his file. Once I knew, I made sure his charges stuck. I volunteered as a character witness. I personally delivered the files to the prosecutor and pretty well offered your father up on a silver platter to be sure he got the worst he could get." West gave her his most pleading look and prayed for the right words to make her understand. "I thought I was doing the right thing. I finally understood why you'd wanted to leave so badly, and even if it was years too late and you were already gone, I wanted to protect you like I should have all along."

Tina blinked, but didn't speak. She relaxed against the couch.

"I've felt awful ever since," West said. "He was on trial for the bar fight, but my help had made it more like he was being charged with dozens of crimes all at once. His history of violence left the jury beyond words. They gave him the maximum sentence for what he did to that guy at the bar. The victory I felt disappeared once he was led away. That wasn't how our courts should work. Your dad's trial was unfair because his own sheriff had a finger on the scales. I think that's why I didn't visit your mom." He dared another look in her direction.

Tina looked as if he'd slapped her.

"Say something." *Yell. Scream. Anything.* He deserved it, and he could take it.

"You let me confess my deepest family secrets to you yesterday, and you already knew? You'd read his file with all our bloody details. Literally. And you let me go on. Do you know how hard that was for me? I've never told anyone about the things I went through."

West rolled her complaint around a few times. "You're not mad because I had a hand in your dad's extensive sentence or your mom's flight? You're mad I didn't interrupt you yesterday and blurt out that I already knew the things you were telling me?"

She crossed her arms.

"I wanted to hear them from you. I want to hear everything you have to say. If this is going to work—" he motioned from his chest to hers "—then you're going to have to keep talking, Tina. You have to let me in, all the time, not just when you've had a decade to think it over."

"Me?" She poked her chest. "Me! What about you? You just finished confessing a secret of your own. Why? Is it because we had sex?"

His jaw dropped. Was she out of her ever-loving mind? "You think I'm trying to pay you off with secrets for sex?" Maybe her dad had messed her up more deeply than he'd realized. "I don't want anything from you."

Tina's cheeks went white. Her arms dropped limply to her sides.

He recognized the misunderstanding at once and closed the distance between them. He wrapped her in his arms, despite a mild protest on her part before she returned his embrace with fervor and tears. "I'm sorry I didn't tell you sooner. I knew you were back in town the minute you got here, and that's when I should've come to you with the truth. I told myself I was respecting your boundaries by not showing up on your doorstep. You were the one who'd left, and you didn't look me up when you came back. I assumed you didn't want to see me, and I let that be my excuse for not knocking on your door." He cupped her face in his hands and stared into her distrusting eyes. "Please don't let what happened between us today confuse you. That was done out of love."

She looped her arms around his neck and buried her face into the curve of his neck.

"Come on." He kept her tight against his side as he led her back to his room.

She climbed into bed and rolled away without a word.

The steady throb of pain from his gunshot wound was nothing compared to the iron fist squeezing his heart. West hit the lights on his way out, reminding himself to breathe. He'd just gotten her back, and he wasn't ready to lose her again.

He never would be.

Chapter Sixteen

West jogged through the house toward his ringing phone and snatched it off the kitchen countertop. Blake's face lit the screen. It had been hours since West had received any new leads, and West was beginning to feel the grip of fear in his gut. "Tell me you've got good news," West said. His muscles tensed in anticipation of the answer. They'd had a lot of news these past two days, but none of it had been good, and West needed a break, or at least a viable lead to keep his mind off the angry woman in his bed.

"I'm not sure if it's good news," Blake answered, "but I'm at the hospital with the OD victim, and he's awake."

"He lived?" Maybe West's luck was starting to turn around after all. Tucker's pulse was barely existent when the EMTs loaded him into the ambulance. "Is he coherent? Talking?"

"He's something," Blake said.

"Well, what's that supposed to mean?" West ground his teeth. "Did he make a statement or not?"

"He's not talking."

West lifted a hand in exasperation. "Then make him talk."

"Can't. I showed him my badge, and he demanded I

arrest Carl Morgan for trying to kill him. When I asked about his own role in the shootings and kidnapping, he shut down and asked for a lawyer."

"Of course." West had never met a criminal who wouldn't drop their demands in a heartbeat to cover their own ass. "Try getting the information another way. Refocus on Carl as a killer. We can arrest Tucker later. Right now we just need to know where that baby is."

"No can do," Blake said. "He's refusing to speak without the lawyer, and for the record, I tried to make him talk, but he pushed the little help button at his bedside and told the nurse I was harassing him. I got kicked out by a woman in scrubs with little bears on them."

"Try again."

"She's guarding his door. There's nothing I can do now but wait. The federal public defender will be here first thing in the morning."

West swore. So much for administering the Garrett charm. He rolled his head between his shoulders. Blake had always been a bit of a battering ram, but he normally got things done that way. Cole was the sweet talker, but West suspected calling him in wouldn't make a difference on Tucker. That guy was done talking to law enforcement tonight. "Maybe Cole can distract the nurse and you can get another shot at our accomplice."

Tina crept into view. She'd traded his T-shirt for soft cotton pants and a sweater. She'd been in West's room for several hours. Had she not been able to sleep, or had the phone woken her? "Let me talk to him."

West pulled the phone from his ear. "Blake?"

"Tucker," she corrected, apparently having eavesdropped on the conversation. "He'll talk to me. I know him, and being involved in this must be killing him. It's not who he is. He's sensitive and overthinking. He's not a bully. Far from it."

West pressed the phone back to his ear. "Did you hear that?"

"Yeah. Get her over here," Blake said.

West disconnected and pocketed the phone. He stepped closer to Tina, longing to pull her back into his arms.

She stepped away with a deep frown, as if she could read his mind. "You should get dressed. I'll grab my coat and shoes."

TINA WAS OFFICIALLY sick of this hospital and a growing number of other things. Like people who kept big secrets, for example, herself included. Keeping secrets was a terrible decision, destined to end in tragedy. No one ever kept happy things to themselves. They only swallowed the dark, damaging things, and those bitter truths had a way of coming back up eventually. From now on, she was only interested in the immediate truth.

Blake was easy to spot in the long white hallway, a tall, dark presence in an otherwise blinding wing. He spoke softly with an old woman in teddy bear scrubs who didn't appear to be taking any of his orders. The hospital was her turf. Just like West had told her before they visited Mary. Blake's badge would only do so much good here. The low tenor of his voice ricocheted off the bare walls in waves of murmured agitation. Tina couldn't make out the words, but his brow was pinched. His posture was stiff, and his hands moved fast enough between them to set him into flight.

"She won't let him back in the room," West interpreted, keeping pace at her side. "Tucker says Blake's upsetting him."

Blake took notice of their approach and turned to face them.

The nurse blocked the threshold to room three fifteen. "Evening, Sheriff." She nodded at West before turning to Tina. "Miss."

"This is Tina Ellet," West explained. "She's your patient's therapist. She insisted on seeing him when she heard the news."

The woman gave Tina a hard look. "What sort of therapist?"

Tina pulled a business card from the pocket of her coat and handed it to the woman. "I'm a licensed clinical psychologist specializing in trauma recovery."

The nurse pocketed Tina's card. "He's had a trauma, but that's new. How can he already be your patient?"

Tina's client list was confidential, but she still needed to see Tucker. "I'm also a concerned friend," she said, trying to sound cordial instead of angry. "I came as soon as I heard he was here." None of the things happening to her were the nurse's fault. It wasn't fair to take them out on her.

The nurse didn't look convinced.

"You can come inside with me," Tina suggested. "See for yourself if he wants me to leave." She crossed her fingers that Tucker wouldn't be too much of a coward to face her after his involvement in her hellish nightmare. She was certain his gentle nature would make him bubble over with guilt and shame at the sight of her. If he didn't send her away, he'd talk, but there was a good chance those same characteristics would make him want to hide. In which case, she'd be booted back into the hall with the Garretts. Not a place she wanted to be at the moment.

Her heart was still stewing from West's confession.

He'd known about her childhood traumas for more than a year. Residual humiliation burned her cheeks. It had nearly killed her to finally voice those very painful, private memories, and he'd sat there, letting her ramble on like an idiot, confessing things he'd already known. It was an unexpected blow to her pride after what had happened between them physically. Though, in his defense, he had come to tell her they needed to talk before she begged him to take her. Her head fell slightly forward, and she pressed hot fingertips to her forehead.

The nurse huffed. "I can see you're truly troubled. Not like the agent over there." She pushed the door open and gave it a gentle knock. "Tucker? There's a friend here to see you."

"Who?" Tucker's voice was surprisingly sharp.

Tina pushed her way into the room. "Me."

Tucker's eyes went wide. "Ms. Ellet. What are you doing here?" His reddish hair was mussed and tucked behind both ears. His beard was ragged and unkempt. He sounded well, but he looked every bit the part of a man who'd recently been near death.

She tried not to bite her tongue completely off. "I came to check on you. I heard what happened, and I was really worried." The sugary sweetness of her voice rang false and fairly malicious in her ears.

"You were?" He flicked his gaze from Tina to the nurse and back. "I didn't do that heroin," he said. "I took some pills and blacked out, but I shouldn't have done that."

Tina took a tentative stop forward. "I'm just glad you're okay now."

"You are?" Disbelief colored his tone.

"Yes." She was also glad to see he was clear of thought. That would help her tremendously as soon as she ditched the nurse. "You look really good, too. I expected you to be asleep after everything you've been through."

The nurse took a step toward the hallway, letting the door swing with her. "If everything's okay, I guess I'll let you two visit."

"Yeah. Thank you." Tucker nodded. He straightened in the bed, adjusting his pillows and arranging the puddled blankets more smoothly over his legs. "Come on in. There's a chair. Do you want water?"

"No." Tina lowered herself into the bedside armchair, concentrating on her breathing and composure. A piece of her worried about Tucker. She'd guided and counseled him for nearly a year. How long had he been using drugs? How much of that time had he spent with Carl? How long had he known about Carl's plans?

"Are you okay?" Tucker asked.

She raised her eyes to him. "No. I'm not. Someone took my baby."

His mouth opened. He shut it without a sound.

"You missed our last session. Did you know that Steven is dead now? That someone shot him in the parking lot? He was right beside me. It was terrifying."

Tucker's cheeks darkened, and he looked away. "I heard about that. I'm sorry."

"Thank you. I'd thought it was the worst thing I would ever experience, but then I learned someone has been stalking me, breaking into my home, watching my baby and me." Images of her late husband's face washed into mind beside fresh memories of West being shot. Had Carl done the same thing to Thomas? Hidden in the woods to end his life with the curl of one finger?

"I didn't know that he'd—" Tucker clamped his lips tight. "I'm sorry."

"Didn't know what?" she asked, training her gaze on his. Tina tried to make herself seem smaller and less threatening. The guise should've been easy given her circumstances, but at the moment she struggled not to tell him exactly what she thought of a grown man playing the "innocent" card. He might not want to admit it, but he'd known something was monstrously wrong, and he'd done nothing to stop it. At the very least, Tucker was complacent, but he was not innocent. "What didn't you know?" she pressed. "Is it something about my daughter? If it is, then you have to tell me." She leaned toward him and gripped the safety railing along his bed. Traitorous tears blurred her vision. "I don't care about anything else. I just need to get my baby back."

Tucker looked at the door behind her. "I don't want to go to jail."

Tina nearly choked on her disgust. "Would you really let an infant die because you want to protect yourself? Is that who you are? Who you want to be?" She shoved off her chair hard enough to send it scraping loudly across the floor.

The door swung open and West barged inside. He moved between Tina and Tucker, evaluating the situation before turning to her with an expectant look.

She reached for him, and he locked his protective arms around her.

"My baby is out there somewhere," she told Tucker. "She's scared. She could be hurt. Maybe worse. And you're in here, all tucked into your little hospital bed, being guarded by a nurse from the big bad lawmen." Her voice climbed in decibels with every new word. "What is wrong with you?" She pushed away from West and fell back onto her chair, wiping frantically at the falling tears. "I'm so sorry." She batted blurred eyes at Tucker. "I didn't mean to yell."

Tucker leaned away as if she'd slapped him.

She'd probably ruined everything by screaming at him. Wasn't that exactly the kind of behavior she and Tucker had both grown up fearing?

The door opened once more, and the nurse arrived with a scowl. "Out."

"Wait," Tucker said.

Tina held her breath. She said a prayer.

"It's okay. I want to talk to these two."

Air whooshed from her burning lungs when the nurse retreated, closing the door behind her.

Tucker tugged his ratty beard and fixed his gaze on Tina. "Carl talked about a lot of crazy stuff, but he never did any of it. I told myself he was just nuts."

"What?" West stormed Tucker's bedside. "You didn't think to report it? Not even to Tina, if not to the sheriff's department?"

"No."

West gripped the back of his neck and took a lap around the room, presumably to keep himself from giving Tucker another reason to be in the hospital.

Tina shook her head in disbelief. "He talked with you about murder and kidnapping. You should have told someone. Told me. I could've stopped him. None of this had to happen."

"What else does he have planned?" West asked, stopping at Tina's side. "And where did he take the baby?"

"I don't know." Tucker released his beard. A look of resolution narrowed his eyes. "I was with Carl last year when your husband died."

Tina gasped. "What?" She forced herself to breathe.

To make sense of the admission. "What do you mean?" she asked. Her stomach lurching at the implication.

"Off the record?" he asked West.

"Hell no." West's hand found Tina's, and he squeezed.

Tucker dipped his chin in a stiff acceptance. "Carl showed up at my place that night with a case of beer, wanting to go camping. He didn't have any gear, and he knew from group that I'm an outdoorsman. At first I said no, but after a few drinks, I agreed to go. He drove my truck so I wouldn't get pulled over. I set up the tent where he wanted, built the fire. Had a few more beers, then I passed out. Carl woke me the next day. He'd packed up the truck, and he was in a big hurry to go home. He said his mom's living facility called. She'd fallen, and we needed to go. I slept on the ride home. I didn't think anything of it until word got around about your husband. I remembered all the things Carl had said about him, and when I asked where we went camping, he got angry. He said we could never tell anyone we were camping that night or they'd link us to you and accuse us of murder. He said the sheriff wouldn't care if it was true—he'd just want to close the case and punish someone for a man's death. Our histories of instability, and my problems with substance abuse, made us the perfect scapegoats."

"You bought that?" West snapped.

"Yeah. I mean, you hear that stuff all the time on the news."

West's body went rigid. "You had to know it was Carl who shot him."

"I didn't. I was out cold until he woke me to go home. I still can't remember exactly where we camped, and he never told me. It wasn't as if we were at an official campground. We just pulled off somewhere, walked a bit and set up for the night. He seemed to know where we were going, so I went with it. All I knew was that his sudden desire to camp on the night of your husband's death was a heavy coincidence."

Tina was officially numb.

West released her hand to cradle his injured arm against his chest a moment before crossing the free arm over it. "We've got ballistics out on that case now. If it was the same gun, we'll know. For the record, Carl was wrong about me arresting anyone just to close the case, but I'll damn sure charge him with murder if those results come back as a match, and you're going down as an accessory."

Tucker frowned. "When do I get my lawyer?"

"Public defender will be here in the morning. You can wait for representation, or you can start putting someone else first for once and help me save this baby's life. You have to know something we can use to find her."

Tucker seemed to weigh West's words. "I don't know where they are. Carl and I aren't friends like that. We drink together sometimes. Usually when he arranges it. He's obsessed with Tina. Has been since I met him in group, but he was following her before that. She bought him a coffee, or something, and he couldn't get over it. He said he asked about her at the drive-through window when the cashier told him his order was paid for. He was so happy, he followed her home that day. He's never stopped. After her husband died, I tried to put some distance between us, but he was insistent. He kept me close. I could tell he was watching me in case I decided to talk. Then, one night we went to play pool. He drove. When we left, he couldn't find his keys, so we walked to his house, but without his keys we couldn't get in. I picked the lock on the back door for him." Tucker's face turned red. "We'd talked about that a few days before. I learned it growing up. My dad would lock me in the basement." He shook his head hard, as if he could somehow erase the memory. "The door opened, but he didn't invite me inside. I had to walk home alone from there. I woke up on my lawn. A few weeks later, I picked him up to go fishing, but the address he gave me was a trailer."

"Not the house you broke into," West finished.

"No," Tucker said. "The farmhouse wasn't his. He'd tricked me into breaking into it."

Tina forced another round of vomit back down her throat. Was she sleeping while two drunks had broken in? What had Carl done while he was inside?

Tucker turned tired eyes on her. "That was your house, wasn't it?"

She nodded. "What about my dog? Did he bark or growl?"

"No dog."

Tina's mind scrambled back, thankful that Ducky wasn't there. That meant that Lily wasn't born yet, either. "I lost my keys last spring," she said. "I was struggling with Thomas's death and the pregnancy. I forgot things. Slept all the time. I bet Carl took them when he came in." Then he could let himself in anytime he wanted, as if her home was his home, too.

"Why didn't you report the break-in when you realized it was Tina's house?" West asked.

Tucker made an ugly noise. "He had me, man. On both counts. I was drunk and doing stuff I wasn't supposed to. I'd have wound up in jail right beside him."

Tina smacked her palms against the arms of the uncomfortable chair. "What do you think is going to happen now? All you've done is put off the inevitable. You could've at least saved Steven's life and spared my baby by doing the right thing a long time ago."

Tucker flopped against his pillow. "I wish I could help you find your baby. I've tried to think of where he might be, but Carl never gives all the facts. He talks in circles. Never completes a story. He just gives enough detail to drag you in and shove you under."

"Think," West growled. "Give it your best try. We're running blind out there."

"All I know is that he's obsessed with Tina. Her home, baby, dog, everything. He thinks she's the perfect mother, and he really hates his."

Tucker's deflated expression broke Tina's heart. He'd trusted the wrong person. Let substance abuse cloud his judgment. "You told Agent Garrett that Carl tried to kill you. Is that true?"

"Yeah. I don't do heroin."

West scoffed. "Are you saying Carl forcefully injected you with the drug? And you couldn't stop him?"

"I'm saying I was stoned. Out cold on oxy and I woke up in here. They pumped my stomach, dosed me up with Narcan and told me I tried to kill myself. I don't do needles." A shiver wiggled down his frame.

The door swung open and Cole blew inside. "West." The look of excitement on his face snapped Tina back to life.

"What'd you get?" West asked.

"I just spoke with the man who owns the property where Carl's trailer sits." A wide smile pulled over his lips. "He said Carl called him yesterday and asked to use his cabin near the lake for a few nights. The man agreed."

Tina popped onto her feet. "You know where they are?"

Cole nodded. "I think we do."

West wrapped a strong hand around her wrist and led her toward the door. "Hang tight, Tucker. There'll be a deputy outside your door standing guard with the nurse. Don't get any ideas about leaving early."

"Good luck," Tucker said. "I really do hope you find him."

Cole followed West and Tina into the hallway, where Blake joined their ranks.

They filled Blake in as they hurried to the waiting elevator. The exact words were lost to Tina, whose ears were ringing loudly with hope.

They finally knew where her baby was.

Chapter Seventeen

The sheriff's department buzzed with activity. Men and women in various uniforms poured in and out of the door like bees to a hive. They spoke hurriedly into walkie-talkies and cell phones, ramping up Tina's already sprinting pulse.

This could really be it. The moment she got her hands on Lily again. This time she might never let her go.

West caught the door and held it as the next group of officials spilled into the night. "Ladies first."

Tina passed into the busy department, squinting against the harsh glow of fluorescent lights. Her heart thundered against her ribs, aching to burst from exertion or just break free.

"Look who beat us here," West said. "Mom, you remember Tina."

A familiar face broke free from the crowd. "Of course." Her sweet voice tugged at Tina's heartstrings. She pulled Tina against her chest with strong, motherly arms and gently stroked her hair. "Oh, how I've missed you."

Tina held her tight. She smelled exactly the same. A perfect blend of cookies and mountain air.

His mother pulled back for a thorough look at Tina. A bright smile graced her face. She'd gone gray since they'd last met, but that was no wonder surrounded by Garrett men and their thirst for danger.

Tina fought a wave of tears and nostalgia. Even after the way she'd left West, his mother looked as happy to see her as if she was a long-lost daughter of her own. She wasn't sure she'd be as understanding if someone hurt Lily.

"She and Dad are here to help," West said. "Dad will be working the desk, aiding Dispatch, should something unexpected arise. He knows the job as well as I do. He did it for twenty-five years. Mom's the moral support."

His mother extended an arm, finger pointed, and swept it in front of her, indicating the mass of busy officials. "I keep them in line."

Tina dragged her attention from the woman she'd often pretended was her mother and fixed it on West. "What do you mean by unexpected? Like what?"

The corner of West's mouth curled up. "We don't know. That's what makes it unexpected." He moved into Tina's personal space and planted a kiss on her head. "We've got this, and you don't need to worry. We're taking a trained team to scout the area and confirm Carl's presence. Once we've got that, we'll move in silently and follow Blake's lead on hostage extraction. Carl will never know we're there until Lily's safely away and we all move in."

Tina considered the possibility. A horde of men, trained or not, marching up to and entering a cabin with only one man and a baby inside. How could Carl *not* know they were there? The cabins along the lake were all old, weathered and creaky. Fairly dilapidated as well, if memory served. Those buildings were good for camping and shelter, but not exactly the kind of place a bunch of federal agents could descend upon silently.

Then there was Lily. To think she wouldn't wail at the sight of a strange man in SWAT gear, or whatever they would be wearing, was naive at best. Though, dumb seemed more fitting.

"We've got this," West repeated. He pressed the pad of his thumb to the space between her brows and smoothed the deep frown that had gathered there.

"You keep saying that, but it doesn't make it true." She glanced at West's mom, suddenly self-conscious at the way he freely touched her in public. Did everyone know what had happened between them? If they didn't before, they must now. Heat rose into her cheeks, and she forced her thoughts back to what mattered most. Lily. "What if this is all a ruse? He could have set the whole thing up just to lead you into danger. He could have the cabin booby-trapped. What if he's really staying at the owner's home, holding him hostage? He might have forced him to make that suspiciously helpful and conveniently timed call to Cole."

West hung his head and peeked up at her through thick dark lashes, a look of humor and humility on his face. "You know, your lack of faith in us is a little insulting."

His mom rubbed his back and grinned. "You can take it. Chin up. I'm going to go check on your father." She winked in Tina's direction and was gone.

Tina stepped back, out of West's reach. "It's not that I don't think you can do what you say you can do. It's that this isn't the first time you thought you had him, and the last time you followed a lead on Carl, you were shot. Then Tucker was nearly killed. And that was just today."

"I'm going to be fine."

She shook her head. "It's more than that. I don't know if I can handle another crushing blow. Every time I think I'll get Lily back—" she pressed her hands against the aching void in her chest "—something goes very wrong, and that hope is torn away."

West's expression turned sober. He moved in closer and dragged her back to him. "C'mere." He lowered his cheek until it lined with hers. His breath washed over her ear. "No one else is getting hurt. Not Lily. Not me. Maybe Carl." She felt his cheek pull into a smile against hers.

West was clearly in his element, on some kind of adrenaline high, like athletes before a big game. His broad palms found the deep curves of her waist. "My deputies are already patrolling. Deputy Neely is positioned on the main road closest to the cabin. The others have eyes on every route in and out, including anything passable by four-wheeler. If Carl's there, he won't get away." West pressed a kiss against her temple and straightened with a crooked smile. "Cole's out there with a drone for aerial surveillance. If all that hasn't put your mind at ease, let me show you something that will."

He pulled her in the direction of his parents. "Dad's staying right here until it's over." They stopped at the desk where Dispatch fielded calls. "He'll be able to hear our chatter, process all the information and make decisions as needed in the event my comms go out or I have to go radio silent."

His dad saluted as they approached. "It's nice to see you again, Tina. It hasn't been the same around here without you."

She forced a smile through quivering lips. "Thank you." West's dad had apparently kept all her family's dirty little secrets. As the former sheriff, he knew the Ellets well. Part of her had always wondered if he'd filled West in on just how damaged his girlfriend really was. Based on West's confession today, his father had never told. He'd hauled her dad home more times than she could count, drunk, angry or both, and he'd warned him never to lay a hand on her. The former sheriff had promised to rain hell on him if he ever saw a mark on Tina. The sad memory evoked a strange smile. West really was like his father, and both men were ones she wanted in hers and Lily's lives.

He patted the arm of the chair at his side. "I set you up a chair right here. This way if you hear anything you don't understand, I can translate."

"Thank you," she said, as much for the chair as for the hundred times he'd given her teenage heart hope for a better future. Tina folded her arms, but couldn't bring herself to sit. A stubborn bubble of optimism filled her chest. Logic told her not to get too excited. *Remember*, she warned herself, *you keep getting punched down*. And finding her footing again had been harder after every new hit.

West pressed a button on the spread of radio equipment before them. White noise and distant voices piped through the speaker. "If you sit here and listen, you'll know everything that's going on. You won't have to wait for us to come back to know what we found. It'll be like you're right there with us. Only here. Safe."

West and his dad traded pointed looks.

She didn't ask. Listening from a safe distance seemed a solid compromise to stealing a cruiser and trying to follow them unnoticed. If Lily was out there, Tina wanted to be there to comfort her frightened little heart. She could only hope that if things went exactly as West described, he would return for her and bring her immediately to see her daughter. Until then, the waiting would be unbearable. There were too many unknowns.

Too many variables and what-ifs. More than that, there was too much at risk.

West wiggled the empty chair.

"Thanks." She forced her wooden legs to bend and fell onto the seat at his father's side.

Blake's head popped up from the huddle around a broad metal desk. "Sheriff."

West gave her a confident smile and went to join his brother.

"I've got eyes on the cabin." Cole's voice rang loud and clear through the speaker in front of her.

The room stilled. Conversations and movement instantly halted. They'd been waiting for this moment.

West was back at her side, pressing a button on the radio. "Do you see any movement down there?"

"Negative. It's too dark and ground cover is heavy."

"What about a vehicle?" West asked, casting his attention toward his father. "Do you see the red pickup truck?"

Silence beat in her ears. A chill of suspense beaded her skin into gooseflesh and stood the fine hairs along her arms and across the back of her neck at attention.

The crowd seemed to hold its breath in collective anticipation.

"Affirmative," Cole finally announced. "I have eyes on a late-model Ford pickup. License plate unreadable."

The mass of frozen officials burst into action.

"Good job, brother," West said, pushing and releasing the button once more. "Stand down for backup." A broad smile split his face as he leaned in to kiss Tina's lips. "I know you're still mad at me for not telling you I knew about your past."

She stiffened in his grasp. Half embarrassed to hear the words spoken in a crowded room.

He planted another quick kiss. "I won't let you down like that again, and I'm about to make you forget I screwed up at all." He pinned her with a sexy, heated kiss before turning away without a goodbye.

He stretched one arm overhead, circling his wrist. "Roll out."

Tina watched breathlessly as the room emptied and the darkened lot beyond the windows was illuminated in headlights.

West's mom moved to the door, watching as her boys and their teams drove away. Her eyelids slipped shut for several moments before reopening with a look of pride that Tina had seen on her countless times before. When the last set of taillights had gone, she turned for the desk. "Now, we wait. Can I get you a distraction from the break room, sweetie? Some cold water or hot tea?"

"No, thank you." Tina pressed unsteady hands against her middle, attempting to crush the nerves and keep the last food she'd eaten in place.

A dozen quiet voices flooded the speaker, chattering to one another in some sort of code made of slang and foreign acronyms. West's dad tapped his fingers against the table and whistled, completely at ease.

A miserable thought presented itself then, coiling regret through Tina's heart. She hadn't said goodbye to West. If anything happened to him, if she lost him again, he'd never know how much he meant to her, or that she wasn't mad like he thought.

She understood why he did what he did to her father. If she thought it would have made a difference, she'd have testified, too, but no one asked. Maybe that was also part of West's doing. Either way, her dad had always breezed through his arrests. A night in jail here. A week there. Inevitably released due to overcrowding or some other nonsense. Then again, he'd always been a drunken menace, never a violent offender. That had surely made the difference this time, and West had done the right thing. She also wished she'd told him that he wasn't responsible for her mother's disappearance. Tina should've made him understand that instead of pulling away to stew about her own burned pride. It had been her mother's choice, and hers alone, to leave without so much as a phone call or forwarding address, and truth be told, her mother had left Tina a long time ago.

Her phone buzzed against her leg, and she flipped it over with haste. If it was West, then she'd respond with the words she wished she'd have said sooner. *I love you.*

Surprisingly, the text was from an unknown number. She swiped her thumb across the screen to read the note. Maybe West used another phone during an operation like this one.

The message was mixed media. A picture of Lily in her winter coat, strapped in a car seat, plus a line of text.

Side lot. Now. Or it's the last time you'll see your baby. Come alone. Tell no one.

She gasped, turning quickly to West's dad.

He raised his bushy brows. "Everything okay?"

She returned her eyes to the little screen. The time on the dashboard clock behind Lily read 10:10. The same time her phone had in the corner. The picture was taken now. In a car. Not at a cabin.

Now or never, Tina.

She stretched to her feet. "Fine," she answered West's dad belatedly.

He puckered his brow. "You sure?"

She nodded too quickly, feeling suddenly unsteady

and flushed. "Yeah. I'm just going to— I changed my mind about the water." She bumbled away from the seat.

He narrowed sharp, knowing eyes. Twenty-five years as the sheriff had apparently given him an intuition about liars that Tina had failed to achieve. After all, if she'd seen Carl for who he was, none of this would be happening.

She pointed at the speaker, where voices continued to spout cop lingo and military jargon alongside map coordinates for a cabin that they would soon find empty. At least West was safe, barring any booby traps. "I'll be back before they get started." She turned for the hallway to the break room and rear exit. "I'll hurry."

She jogged away, looking repeatedly over her shoulder in case Mr. Garrett followed her.

"Whoa." West's mother sidestepped a near collision as she exited the break room with two steaming mugs. "Everything okay? You look ill."

"Yes. Bathroom."

"Oh." The woman frowned. "I was just bringing you tea. Do you want me to go with you?"

Tina shook her head. Tears welled and stung in her eyes. "No, thank you."

Mrs. Garrett offered a sad smile. "Let me go set these down, and I'll be right there to check on you."

"'Kay." Tina ducked into the bathroom under Mrs. Garrett's loving watch. She listened as the woman's footsteps faded in the distance. Then she quickly texted West. It was her last chance to help bring Lily home. Carl would surely take her phone the minute he saw her.

West—He came for me. He has Lily & I'm going.

She hurried from the bathroom to the rear exit. A

big blue pickup waited in the gravel at the building's side, out of the parking lot cameras' range. Tina hit the record button on her video app and leaned the phone against the wall on top of a five-drawer filing cabinet in the hallway. She pointed the camera at the door's rectangular window.

This was it.

No more time to waste. West's mother would soon discover she wasn't in the bathroom. Carl would drive away with her baby.

She shoved the back door open with resolute determination and hustled into the darkness, hoping the angle on her phone was right, praying that West would find the video of the truck as they pulled away and follow it wherever it would take her. It was the only hope she had left.

Behind her, her phone began to ring.

Chapter Eighteen

The truck was in motion before Tina could fasten her seat belt, tossing dirt and spinning recklessly into the road beside the sheriff's department. Tina scooted closer to the car seat on the bench between her and Carl. Her heart ached to burst at the sight of her beautiful sleeping princess. "Be careful," she scolded. "You have an infant in this truck. You have to protect her." She would never let anyone hurt Lily again.

"She's f-fine."

Tina traced the five-point harness with her hands in the dark. It seemed to be correctly buckled, and the seat was secured to the bench.

Cones of light flashed over them as they headed through the center of town, making Lily's sweet face briefly visible in the darkness. An overwhelming sense of joy and relief flooded through Tina with each peek, enough to make her weep if she wasn't so terrified. Carl was right. Lily looked wonderful. Unharmed, clean and content. "Thank you," she whispered. "Thank you for taking good care of her." She stroked her sleeping baby's cheeks and hands, desperate to unhook the safety belt and bring her into her arms. Lily's tiny fist curled instinctively around Tina's finger. "I missed you, too," Tina cooed.

Carl took the next right on two wheels, blowing through a stop sign as if it didn't exist. "I c-can't believe you ca-came," he said with unbridled awe. "I mean, I kn-kn-knew you would, but I was still afraid I—I might be wr-wrong. You know?"

As if he'd left her a choice. Taking a picture of her baby and threatening to never let her see her again. How could she *not* have come to him?

Tina measured her breaths and watched in fear as Carl drove maniacally through the night. Then again, he didn't need to worry about getting pulled over. He'd led the entire sheriff's department to the other side of town. "Carl? Please slow down."

"I know how to dr-drive," he snapped.

"Okay." She quickly agreed. "But you're scaring me. I haven't seen either of you in a while, and I want us to be safe."

"Oh." Carl eased his foot slightly off the gas. "Sorry."

"Thank you." The Thank You for Visiting Shadow Point sign came and went, disappearing behind them in a flash. Tina tallied the turns as they left town, mentally cataloging the convoluted route as long as she could, but she was officially lost. "Where are we going?"

"Home."

She bit her tongue against the obvious. There didn't seem to be any homes where they were going. Just darkness. Forest. And the endless curving road. Soon, a Leaving Cade County sign came and went, as well. Her stomach soured. How far had they gone? Where would they go? "I should stop and get some things," she said. "I didn't have time to pack."

He slowed at a crossroads and turned his face to hers. His expression was shrouded in shadows, much like his intent. "D-don't worry about th-th-that. I'm taking care of you now. Once you get comfortable here, you—you can take care of m-me, too. We're a family now." He reached over Lily's car seat for Tina's cheek, and she jumped.

Her opposite shoulder hit the door. She was out of room in the cab.

Carl replaced his hand on the steering wheel. Rejection colored his cheeks. He twisted his grip on the wheel until his knuckles were bone white. "This isn't h-how I wanted us to start our l-l-life together. I had plans. Better ones. Smoother ones, but—but I think you can still be happy if y-y-you give it a try." He checked his rearview mirror before turning onto an unlit section of a winding mountain road.

They rocked and bumped along a dark gravel lane beside a field of wildflowers for several minutes. Tina recognized the trail as a driveway when a small bungalow came into view, almost completely hidden among the trees.

"Surprise," he said, shifting the truck into Park beside a four-wheeler.

Tina gripped Lily's car seat instinctively. "What is this place?"

The porch light was on and an aged swing hung from the rafters. Nothing and no one else was visible between Tina and the horizon. Just fields and trees and night.

"My old b-babysitter lived here. I spent a lot of time with her when my m-m-mother was gone or had her boyfriends over. If they didn't like me, I—I came here." He opened the driver's-side door.

Tina watched as Carl rounded the truck's hood and headed for her side. He knocked hard on the window with one bent knuckle.

She released the seat belts on the car seat and herself.

"Are you sure we're allowed to be here? Is it yours?" It couldn't be his, legally anyway. West would've checked for properties owned by Carl or his mother as soon as Lily went missing. He opened the door and offered his hand.

Tina climbed out with a shiver. She clutched Lily's carrier to her chest. "What happened to the sitter?"

"She died."

Tina took another look at the home. "When?"

"A few years ago. Before you and I m-met outside the coffee shop." Carl pressed a palm to the small of her back, urging her forward.

That explained a lot. With his mom sick and his preferred mother figure dead, he'd needed to fill that void fast, and Tina was everything he'd hoped for. She'd even showed him kindness when he was still a stranger. She chewed the insides of her cheeks in frustration. Kind deeds were supposed to better the world, not crumble hers.

Tina moved slowly, carefully, toward the building where anything could happen to her or her daughter and no one would ever know. Strips of white paint curled away from the wood. The porch steps were tilted and sunken from age and neglect. "Your babysitter left her home to you?"

"N-no. It belongs to her daughter." He added pressure to her back, forcing her to pick up the pace. "She lives out of state and h-h-hates the thought of the place standing empty like this. It needs a family to care f-for it, to make memories in it like my s-s-sitter and I did."

Tina doubted that her captivity at this place would be the magical experience the woman had in mind. She moved carefully up the crooked steps. "I really wish I had a few of my things," she said in an attempt to stall. "I've never stayed anywhere without taking at least a toothbrush. Maybe there's a little store nearby. We could run in for a few supplies. Is there someplace like that?" A place where she could signal the clerk for help, or make a run for it with Lily? Someplace well lit and public or somewhere they could disappear into the night and wait for dawn. She wasn't picky as long as she and Lily had a fighting chance at freedom.

"No need." Carl turned the doorknob and motioned her inside. "I t-told you. I've taken care of everything."

The home's interior lights flickered on, and Tina blinked to make sense of the scene before her. The sheets covering musty old furniture were topped with afghans and throw pillows like the ones from her home. Even the rug beneath the coffee table and magazines spread on top were all hers. No, not hers exactly, but all replicas, purchased by a man who'd taken great care to re-create a place she loved.

"What do you think?" he asked, flipping a series of shiny new deadbolts on the door behind him.

Tina tried not to wonder if he'd installed bars on the windows, too. "It's lovely," she croaked. Fear and distress tugged at her composure. Her thoughts shredded as she visually toured the room, pretending to appreciate his work.

Reminders of home were everywhere. The lamps and art were so similar to her own that her skin crawled at the sight of them. She'd never seen anything this twisted outside a horror film.

Carl was far more unstable than she'd dared to imagine. Even after the shooting. Even after everything. This creepy house, the time and detail he'd put into it, was evidence of a man beyond her help. Somewhere along the line, Carl had snapped. His reality had skewed. And trying to talk him out of this would only cause her and Lily harm.

Tina needed time to think. The baby carrier was heavy in her arms, and Lily was sure to wake up eventually. Escaping would be much easier with a quiet baby than a crying one. "Would it be rude if I said I was ready for bed?" She forced a smile. "It's been a rough couple of days, and I'm wiped out. I should probably rest now and start getting acclimated to my new home in the morning."

Disappointment clouded Carl's face. "We—we just got here. Maybe a shower will help w-wake you up." He moved to a door in the hallway beyond the kitchen and flipped the light switch. A slow smile replaced his dismay. "Take a look."

Tina inched closer. The outdated bath had pink and black tile, a drippy faucet and loads of fresh hygiene products. Coordinating towels and accessories on the counter matched her shower curtain and bathmat at home.

Tears blurred her eyes, and she disguised them with a yawn, wiping away the drops with the pad of her thumb.

Carl lifted a pink shower caddy. "Toothbrush, paste, floss, s-soap, shampoo." He pointed to all her favorite brands. "I left your f-f-feminine products under the sink. I know you'll need them soon, and you're modest. I d-d-didn't want to make you uncomfortable. Though, the woman at the store thought I was pretty great for b-buying them for you. She said more m-men should do things like that for their wives."

Tina pressed her back against the wall and shifted Lily's carrier in her aching arms. Had Carl's delusion gone so far that he imagined them married? "I just need a minute," she said, shooting a meaningful look at the toilet.

"Oh." He smiled. "Right. Of course." He gripped Lily's carrier.

Tina held tight. "What are you doing?"

"P-putting her in her room. I'll m-make us something in the kitchen while you sh-sh-shower and clean up. I bought you a new n-nightgown. I thought you'd want to start fr-fresh. Wearing something that other men hadn't…" He trailed off. "I l-left it on the bed."

Tina increased her hold on the infant carrier. "Maybe you should show me our rooms first."

Carl's smile returned. He relented his grip, leaving Tina to carry Lily, and moved to the next door in the hallway. He flipped the light switch inside. "Ta-da."

A buzzing overhead light illuminated Lily's nursery. The bedding and mobile, curtains and toys from Lily's room at Mary's home were all present.

Carl knelt before her and reached for Lily.

Tina stepped back, but he caught the carrier's handle in his hands and shot her a warning look. "It's p-past her bedtime," he grumped. "She needs to learn to slee-slee-sleep in her bed."

"I was hoping to sleep with her tonight," Tina said. "I've missed her so much." She fixed him with her most desperate stare. "Please don't take her from me again." A tear slipped over her cheek.

Carl removed Lily from the carrier and put her in the crib. He pointed to the door, indicating Tina should leave.

Tina inched backward. A hole punched through her heart as Carl pulled the nursery door shut behind them.

"Now, ou-our room," he said.

The next door he opened had a tall double bed inside. The room's decor was simple, almost thoughtless in comparison to the others he'd so meticulously staged. In fact, nothing about it reminded her of home.

Carl sat on the bed's edge and patted the space beside him. "I thought you c-could decorate this space. The bedroom at y-your house was designed for y-y-your other marriage. This one should be special. For us." He scooped a length of white fabric into his hand and held it out to her.

She took it up for inspection. "A nightgown." As promised. The delicate fabric was nearly sheer, with a scoop neckline and enough length to cover her thighs. There was no way she was ever going to wear it.

"T-try it on," he said.

"Now?" Absolutely not. She didn't like the implication, or the fact that she couldn't make a midnight escape through fields and trees in a sheer nightgown. She'd die of hypothermia before she found the road.

"Yes, please." Carl smiled. He scooted back on the bed and laced his fingers behind his head. "Sh-show me that you like it."

Tina set the gown at his feet on the bed and crossed her arms over her middle. "Modest. Remember." She backed toward the door. "Maybe we should talk first. Get to know one another better."

Reluctantly, Carl eased off the bed. He joined her at the door and slid his palm against hers, then clamped his fingers down. "I kn-know we're moving a little fast, but y-you like it like this. Y-you only knew Thomas a short while before g-getting married. You were b-barely married for five m-m-minutes before conceiving Lily." He dropped his gaze to leer briefly at her body before returning the heated gaze to her face. "We can m-make babies together, too. Give Lily brothers and sisters. Raise th-them here." He lifted their joined hands and pressed a kiss against her knuckles.

Tina tried not to vomit.

He pulled her toward the kitchen and dragged a chair away from the table. "Sit." He went to the counter to set up the coffee maker.

Tina took a seat. With such attention to detail, she wished he'd included a block of knives like the one on her counter at home. At the moment, what she really wanted was to stab him before he mentioned the nightgown or baby making again. She watched the wall separating her from Lily. She hadn't even gotten to hold her. She'd just gotten her back and he'd taken her again. Slow tears rolled over Tina's cheeks, and she swiped them away.

He smiled at her from his position beside the coffee maker. "Do—do you remember when w-we met? You bought me coffee, then w-waved at me wh-when you pulled away. I didn't know w-why until the lady at the window said you b-b-bought my drink. I followed you home to thank you, but I wasn't br-br-brave enough to do it. It takes me t-t-t-time to warm up to new people." His cheeks flushed, and he turned back to the coffee.

He finished up, and the machine chugged to life. "I tried to talk to you for a c-couple weeks before I m-made up my mind. I was going to d-do it the day you went to the g-garden center for those redbud trees."

"The day I met Thomas," she said. A flood of nostalgia and grief washed over her. Thomas had been so kind. He was there for mulch and saw her struggling with the trees. "He dropped everything to help me." Then he'd followed her home to unload them. A frown tugged her lips. She'd made lemonade and served it on the porch because she knew better than to invite a stranger inside. Thomas was nice, but he wasn't her soul mate, and he was dead now because of her.

Carl selected two mugs from the cupboard with undue roughness, banging them on the counter until Tina was certain he'd wake Lily. "He h-helped himself to my girl is what he—he did. I couldn't f-forgive it. I had to be a man, stake claim to what w-w-was mine."

"You killed him."

"I removed him from our situation." Carl poured the small amount of brewed coffee into a mug and carried it to the table for her. "His loss h-hurt you for a while, I know, b-b-but you're better now. Ready to start again, I think. That was w-why I had to be preemptive with Steven. He'd only been to gr-group a few times and you were sp-sp-spending all your attention on him." He went back for a second mug and drained the pot's contents once again. "You know that old s-saying. Fool me once, shame on you. Fool me twice—" he pointed at his chest "—sh-shame on me. I couldn't watch you m-m-marry someone else again. That would have been my fault."

"I was never interested in Steven romantically," Tina argued. "You know I won't have a personal relationship with anyone in my care. It's unprofessional." She'd told Carl that when he joined the group and asked her if she wanted to join him for a walk.

"Those men were all wr-wrong for you." He sighed dramatically. "Speaking of men who are wr-wrong for you. I don't like the w-w-way you look at the sheriff. I can tell he wants you. Wants this." Carl motioned between them and around the room. "N-not going to happen."

"Is that why you shot him?" she asked, chin quivering. "You didn't need to do that. You shouldn't hurt people."

He lifted and dropped one shoulder. "I saw—saw you with him. You t-touch him when he's near. Lean on him. You've only kn-known him for a few days, but y-you chose to lean on him instead of me." The accusation was thick and strong in his voice and stare.

"I've known Sheriff Garrett all my life," she said, hoping not to set him off. "I grew up in Shadow Point. With him."

Carl seemed to consider the idea. "I didn't know that."

"It's true." She lifted her mug, unable to drink, but unwilling to anger him further by refusing it completely.

"You grew up there, but d-don't have family there?" He cocked his head, maybe wondering if she'd lied.

"I used to." A tight knot formed in her throat, and she set the mug aside.

"Well, I f-forgive you for leaning on the sheriff," he said. "I kn-know what it's like to be l-l-lonely and m-make bad choices. If Sheriff Garrett is familiar to you, it m-makes sense that you'd confide in him, especially once he'd inserted himself into y-your life." Carl leaned across the table and cupped her hands in his. "B-b-but, Tina, neither of us w-will ever have to be alone again."

Her skin crawled and her stomach churned. "I can't be with my patients, unprofessionally. You know that. I could lose my license."

Carl squeezed her hands hard. "Y-you aren't g-going back to work. I'm going to take care of you and L-Lily, and you're g-going to take care of me." He released her hands with an apologetic smile and moved to stand behind her chair. The calloused skin of his palms scraped over the back of her neck and across her shoulders as he kneaded the bunched muscles there. "I only ask-asked to participate in your group to get c-close to you.

I thought you kn-knew that when y-you interviewed me." He gathered the length of her hair in one hand and planted a hot, wet kiss at the nape of her neck. "Mmm."

Tina clamped her teeth together, bucking against the instinct to fight. Lily was in the next room. She had to think of Lily. She had to win Carl's trust and escape with her baby.

He dragged his sticky tongue up her neck until it reached her earlobe.

She dug her nails into her legs as he suckled and winced at the welcomed distraction.

"Gives you a shiver, huh?" he asked. "You l-like that?"

"We weren't finished talking," she said, wiggling away. She needed to busy his mind before he remembered the bed and nightgown that waited in the next room. "Tell me why you went to my place after the shooting. That was you who ran from the house, right? You set the table for two while you were in there."

He tugged sharply on her hair, still wrapped in his fist. "Y-you were supposed to come home alone. I was there to com-comfort you. To listen. I thought we c-could eat, and you could tell me about the tr-trauma. I was going to be your strong shoulder and hero, but y-you brought the sheriff."

He dropped her hair and gripped the back of her chair instead, yanking it roughly away from the table. "Let's dance." He set his phone on the counter and piped a slow country song through the speaker.

Tina needed that phone.

Carl wound one hand over the small of her back and pushed hair off her shoulder with the other. He lowered his mouth to her skin and kissed a disgusting path along her neck. "Y-you taste like honey."

She held her breath, begging her addled mind to create a plan.

"It can be like this for us every night," he said, kissing her jawline and chin, moving steadily toward her mouth.

Tina squirmed harder against his advances. "I still need that shower or maybe a hot bath." A bath would buy her more time to get herself and Lily out the window without him noticing.

Carl's hands slid beneath the hem of her shirt and skimmed her sides. "I could help."

"No!" She lunged backward, instantly horrified by both his touch and her loud reaction. Her gaze jumped to the far wall separating the kitchen from Lily's room. "Sorry," she whispered. "I'm not ready. It's too soon." Suffocating fear silenced her words.

Carl moved slowly in her direction. "I d-didn't mean to scare you. I w-w-would never h-hurt you, Tina. N-not ever. You and Lily, you're my l-l-life now." He pulled her to him again and kissed her roughly. Holding her face between his palms.

Heavy tears rolled down her cheeks as she resigned herself to the worst possible fate. She wouldn't be able to escape with Lily tonight. For Tina, tonight would be about survival.

WEST CREPT ALONG the porch of a dilapidated bungalow in Cress County. It wasn't his jurisdiction, but he didn't care, and he had a team of FBI agents in play to back him up. Tina's text had stopped them before they reached the cabin at the lake and sent them back to the station at full speed. Her camera had caught the top of the blue pickup truck speeding away, but what had saved the day was her phone's presence. A quick search for the number that had sent her the photo of Lily was all tech ops had needed to trace the burner phone all the way to Carl's hideout.

He pressed his back to the wall and peered into the front window. His pounding heart nearly stopped when he saw Tina's tears. Carl Morgan kissed her mouth like the sociopath he was while she cried.

West moved to the slanted porch steps and gave them a kick.

"What was that?" Tina's voice was high and loud inside the home. Desperation had eradicated her cool exterior, leaving sheer panic on her face and tongue.

West moved into the shadows as Carl crept silently toward the window.

Carl glared through the glass. "Go to Lily's room and lock the door," he barked. "Make a single sound, or try anything stupid, and she'll pay for it. Understand?"

West ground his teeth. He hopped over the porch's railing and raced along the side of the house toward the back.

He peeked into each window in search of Tina, but found plywood nailed over the glass every time. Carl had imprisoned her and her baby. West looked behind him, wishing he could be the one to take Carl down, but Tina and Lily were his priorities.

The front door opened and snapped shut. Carl was coming, probably with a rifle.

West hurried silently onto the back porch.

Footfalls pounded over the floorboards on the other side of the rotting wooden barrier. The knob turned and Tina rushed into view, a crying baby clutched to her chest.

She squeaked at the sight of him, dressed head to

toe in black. Recognition dawned slowly as he raised a finger to his lips and reached for her arm.

Lily squirmed and fussed. The sound gonged and echoed like a beacon in the darkness. "Hurry," West whispered. He gripped her elbow and pulled her in a sweeping arch back toward the road, giving the house a wide berth.

Tina shushed her frightened baby as they ran.

The telltale sound of a snapping branch stopped West short. He widened his stance, pushing Tina behind him.

"Nice try, Sheriff," Carl snarled. He stepped into view from the small grove of apple trees beside the home. "I heard you out front, and I followed you around back. Stupid move, leaving your cruiser in the drive." He sent an angry look Tina's way. "Didn't I tell you I wouldn't let him take what's mine?" He raised the barrel of his rifle to West's head.

"No," Tina cried, "please don't. Don't do this."

A thunderous crack interrupted her plea and ignited Lily's screams.

Tina's eyelids fell shut, and she sobbed against her baby's head.

Carl made a strangled sound before dropping his rifle. His expression went blank as he crumbled to the ground.

TINA'S EYES SHOT OPEN.

West wound an arm around Tina as Cole emerged from the darkness.

Cole kicked the rifle away from Carl's body. "I know it's not right to speak ill of the dead, but I hate this guy." He pinched the radio on his shoulder and relayed the news to their waiting teams.

West wrapped his arms around Tina and her baby. "Are you okay? Did he hurt you?"

Tears streamed over her face as she kissed Lily's cheeks a thousand times, sobbing, but not speaking.

"Come on." He led them to his cruiser in the driveway and opened the door so she could sit. "Here." He slid out of his black coat and wrapped it over her shoulders, cocooning her and Lily in his warmth.

A dozen men in black gear streamed from the trees and field, encroaching on the scene around them. SUVs and cruisers crawled over the loose gravel drive, and the low cry of an ambulance rose in the distance. The nightmare had finally ended, and the relief of seeing Tina and Lily safe was enough to knock him down.

West crouched before Tina as she cuddled Lily into contentment. Her smile lit up his world.

"I can't believe you're here," she said.

"Anything and always," he repeated the phrase that had meant so much to them in high school. The words were as true as ever for him, hopefully for her, too.

The pink bundle in her arms had closed her eyes. Her small mouth made quick little moves.

"She dreams of food," Tina said, laughing proudly through a fresh sob. "Just like her mama."

West brushed Lily's soft cheek with his fingertips, then kissed her mother's cheek. "I dream of you."

"I love you," Tina said. "It's okay if you don't feel the same."

West's heart expanded in his chest, stretching a smile across his face and warming him to the core. "I love you, too. I always have. Always will."

"I'm sorry I ran away when we were teens. I should've talked to you. You deserved the whole truth. From me."

"I don't blame you, and I don't care about any of that now."

Tina swiped a tear from her cheek. "I don't want to let my parents' failures affect me anymore. I don't want them to be an excuse I use to avoid finding happiness."

"I can make you happy," he promised.

Epilogue

Bright summer sun beamed down on the oak tree outside West's cabin. Tina adjusted the train of her borrowed gown. Once worn by West's mother and grandmother for the same occasion. The diamond wedding ring on her finger cast rainbows over the delicate material.

"Stop looking at him." Marissa, Blake's wife, laughed from behind the lens of her fancy camera. "He'll be there when we finish—this gorgeous sunlight won't."

Tina forced another smile, but her gaze drifted back to the man of her dreams, *her husband*, West Garrett. She smiled brighter, imagining she gave the sun a run for its money today. West was striking in black tuxedo pants, the sleeves of his dress shirt rolled up to his elbows. A set of identically dressed brothers laughed at his sides, passing Lily from hand to hand around their circle in a goofy version of hot potato. Mary watched with a prideful smile. She'd recovered nicely after Carl's attack, another answer to Tina's prayers.

Tucker Bixby had recovered, too, but he had a long road ahead of him. Tina's testimony had helped Tucker stay out of jail, but he was struggling to deal with the role he'd played in Lily's abduction, and that wasn't something Tina could help him with. She'd recommended a new therapist, but it wouldn't be easy for Tucker's tender heart to get past what he'd done. His silence could have cost Lily and Tina their lives.

Marissa snapped a few more shots, then looked at the little screen. "I'm a nature photographer, and I swear the forest creatures have longer attention spans than you today."

"I'm just really happy," Tina said, admitting the partial truth.

West's dad had walked her down the aisle. His mom had helped her with her hair and dress. His entire family had stepped up at their engagement, as if it was the most normal thing in the world to add another adult and a baby to the Garrett clan.

Tina was the definition of *blissful*, but Marissa was right—she was also distracted.

A loud wolf whistle drew a new smile over Tina's face.

West headed her way with their little girl in tow. Lily clapped her hands and toddled clumsily at his side on chubby fourteen-month-old legs. Her puffy white dress and matching floppy hair bow were the picture of perfection.

West kissed his sister-in-law's cheek. "Finished yet?"

"Never." Marissa scooped Lily into her arms and nuzzled her neck. "Go on," she said to the newlyweds. "I know it kills the two of you to keep your hands off one another for more than five minutes. Your whole wedding album will be kissing photos, you realize that?"

West's lips were already on Tina's. "Hello, Mrs. Garrett," he whispered against her mouth.

"Hello."

West's mom marched into view as he pulled away. "There's my beautiful grandbaby," she squeaked.

Lily struggled free of Marissa's grip, cheerfully reaching for her grandmother's arms.

"Is your daddy hogging all your attention?" West's mother asked.

"Da!" Lily agreed, head nodding. "Da! Da! Da!"

"Well, we can't have that. There's a hundred people here to see you." She turned on her pastel heels and marched back toward the crowd gathered on West's lawn. Lily clapped as they moved away.

"I think they are all here for her," West said. "She stole every heart in this place with her flower girl routine." He pressed a hand to his chest and bowed his head. "Every time she calls me Dad I think I'll die right there of happiness."

The careful rows of white chairs, once hugged in tulle, were scattered over the lawn now. Filled with folks catching up on old times and trading stories. Tina had expected sharing Lily with an entire family would be hard after having her all to herself for the first four months, but the opposite had been true. Each time Lily was doted on by another Garrett, Tina's heart grew impossibly bigger.

She scanned the smiling faces of her new family, then dared a look at her dashing husband. "I love you."

"I love you." He kissed her nose and hugged her tight. "Are you sure you didn't want a big church wedding like Blake and Marissa had?" he asked for the hundredth time.

She laughed. "This was everything I've ever wanted. My personal dream come true. Handsome husband. Supportive friends. Growing family." She pinned him with her most cheeky look.

West smiled. "Now we just need to get Cole and Ryder married off. Get Lily some cousins. Cole will be easier to work with. Let's start with him."

Tina draped her wrists over West's shoulders and tried again. "When I said the family was growing, I wasn't talking about marrying off your brothers or waiting for cousins. Though that will be nice, too."

West wrinkled his nose.

Tina's smile widened. "I meant *our* family is growing." She pulled his palm over her tummy and pressed it tight.

His jaw went slack. "I'm having a baby?" His bright blue eyes went wide with emotion. "You're—I'm gonna be a dad again?" He stared awestruck at their hands on her middle.

"Yes." Tina giggled against her husband's chest, unable to believe her life had become so much more than she'd ever dared to dream. "I love you," she said once more, as West's protective arms banded around her.

He dropped his mouth to hers and planted a kiss to melt the sun. "Always and forever, Mrs. Garrett."

* * * * *

LET'S TALK
Romance

For exclusive extracts, competitions
and special offers, find us online:

[facebook icon] facebook.com/millsandboon

[instagram icon] @millsandboonuk

[twitter icon] @millsandboon

Or get in touch on 0844 844 1351*

For all the latest titles coming soon, visit
millsandboon.co.uk/nextmonth